DARK INDIAN ECLIPSE

Dark Indian Eclipse

Kelvin L. Singleton

Disclaimer

Undoubtedly, Dark Indian Eclipse is a work of fiction. This novel contains the names of actual people in existing and fictitious settings that may even seem real. This novel contains graphically violent scenes conducive to the vivid telling of a story that is not meant to denigrate its readers or the characters portrayed herein. Dark Indian Eclipse is simply a conveyance of past, present, and future possibilities etched upon human hearts. Please remember—it is only fiction.

ISBN Paperback: 978-0-9979041-0-9
ISBN eBook: 978-0-9979041-1-6

Library of Congress Control Number: 2016900563

Printed in the United States of America

Cover and Interior Design: Ghislain Viau

This novel is dedicated to all pioneers of the Civil Rights Movement, both here and abroad...both past and present. I also dedicate Dark Indian Eclipse in honor of President Barack and First Lady Michelle Obama. May the First Family know peace and prosperity in these troubling times.

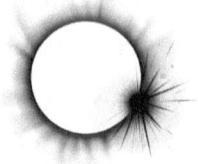

PROLOGUE

Though he is destined to become Mississippi's two-term governor, Judson Martin is quite young when a cocktail of mixed fortunes upsets his life. Unexpected tragedy strikes during a course of days set apart for celebration. The repercussions of these events will germinate seeds of staunch convictions that harbor a deep-seated hatred for African Americans, which already entails multiple murders.

The only son of Abraham and Louise Martin was born on January 13, 1945, in rural Jackson City, Mississippi. Louise Wagner Martin is slowly dying of Leukemia when Jud is eleven-years-old.

She is a gentle woman. Her soul seems as old as Methuselah, taking the brunt of most things in stride during an often-stressful life.

Jud's most profound sentiment of his mother is that she always smiles for her children's sake. Throughout her own suffering, Louise finds kind words to soothe her children's hurt and fears, no matter how gloomy the horizon.

In all of her years of betrothal to a man she hardly knows, as long as she is spared a more intimate exposure to her husband's ugly, nocturnal activities, she lives happily enough. She knows enough to loathe what Abraham and his brethren stand for, but remains silent because he will not tolerate her speaking out.

Because Louise Martin finds a way to live happily enough, however, she only manages to reach a tentatively uneasy peace with God before passing. On this dreadful day, as the tears of her loving children co-mingle with the feverish sweat of her gown, her final prayers express very little concern for the disposition of her own soul. These final prayers are for her family. Mostly, however, she lingers in this Holy place for Judson's sake. Louise Martin asks God to spare her son the life she clearly sees scrawled on the pages of his unwritten future. Even if an early death holds the key to sparing him that life, then so be it…forever and amen.

Many southerners claim that the soul of those who die on his or her birthday is bound for heaven, but the eldest child of the same is doomed to hell. Just an old wives' tale, most certainly.

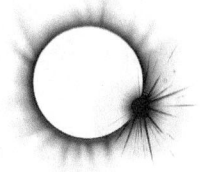

Chapter 1

THE BLACK AVENGERS

Abraham Martin, a die-hard Klansman, goes back a long way with a dogmatic man named Ezra Theodore Krantz. They first met during a nearly disastrous manhunt in the mid-1930s, remaining friends ever since.

Many years later, when Ezra Krantz gains complete control of the beloved organization to which he dedicates his entire life, he decides to move the site of their recreational manhunts to Greene County, located in Southeastern Mississippi. He feels the location far enough away from the big river, hoping to avoid the same scenario that brought him and Abraham Martin together.

In the looming shadow of his mortality, after Louise Martin's demise, Abraham asks Krantz to be the godfather of his two children.

Krantz gladly accepts a responsibility that he considers both an honor and privilege.

At age nineteen, Jud Martin marries his high school sweetheart, Ashley Elaine Clayton, on July 1, 1964. Because Ashley's dream of attending college is not meant to be, they wed a month after their senior year.

The young couple's wedding ceremony is quite a lavish affair for these days. It matters little that the gift-bearing guests are mostly strangers to both bride and groom. After the honeymoon, they plan to work at the Martin Family Plumbing & Supplies, which proves to be a good living for the young couple when the dollar bill is still worth a dollar.

On July 4 of 1964, Ezra Krantz hosts a soiree with honorary Grand Dragons from various regions of the nation. Many gladly arrive for a gathering that will climax with a bold march through downtown Jackson City as a display of their growing support. Meant to serve as a statement of power, Ezra T. Krantz and his followers intend a blatant disregard of federal laws expressly prohibiting masked public gatherings. At this time in Mississippi's history, social unrest peaks on the heels of the infamously hindered, unsolved, racially motivated murders of several African Americans and nigger-loving Caucasians involved in the scurrilous civil rights movement.

After decades of living in fear of the, seemingly, boundless influence of the Ku Klux Klan, the fed-up Blacks of Jackson City take it upon themselves to plot the assassination of the Klan's leaders and followers during a guerrilla blitzkrieg of their own fashion. They are sick and tired of the hollow words of a United States Constitution that does not seem to uphold their civil rights.

These men, incited by the slack applications of Federal laws in a woefully nonchalant justice system where not enough visionaries seem to view African Americans as people deserving of the sainted Bill of Rights, now seek the justice of vigilantism. These bold few no longer pine away in the limbo of promised, but hardly delivered, government intervention. The very heart of this group has been born—forged—within a hatred that only hatred can propagate.

They call themselves Black Avengers. Its leaders are Richard Mack and Timmons Walker. The group numbers at twenty-five men; not much of an army. However, they manage to do some sturdy damage to the businesses and homes of quite a few offending Klansmen.

Under cover of night, the Black Avengers engage in insurrectionary warfare, sabotaging establishments used for housing petroleum products and other raw materials. Their tactics heavily rely on arson as the main tool of destruction, and they wreak havoc while burning lots of good money.

In the meager beginning, they left calling cards to let people know that these disasters are the work of African American dissidents. Eventually, they would decide it is wiser to leave no evidence at all. Even though DNA testing would not be widely used until the late 1900s, fingerprinting in criminal investigations have been used since the late 1800s.

Richard Mack, Timmons Walker, and those bold enough to follow them, hold little regard for the teachings of Martin Luther King. Feeling as though they have already turned every cheek they have to offer, King's pacifistic attitudes in dealing with the likes of the Klan does absolutely nothing for the average Black citizen in this particular corner of hell. These angry men glean no progress in peaceful race relations, seeing no light to mark the end of an endless tunnel of despair. In fact, the Black Avengers feel strongly that just rolling over and playing dead only perpetuates and emboldens the KKK's doctrine of white supremacy. It gives them cause to step on the necks of even more people, and usually for no better reason than the simple fact that they can with impunity.

The Black Avengers believe that a racist man will think twice about grabbing the head of a dog that bears its teeth and offers a threatening growl to boot. They have gotten away with a lot of payback, but the price is escalating. In the end, they only succeed in bringing the wrath of the Klan down upon the very people they seek to protect. They will find this to be true when they finally arrive at the end of the long and vengeful road that they are paving with, somewhat, good intentions.

Washed-up and straggly, Bernie Walker, Timmons Walker's older brother, started out with the dissidents during their humble beginnings. Because he nearly caused the capture of five members during an arson job out at the old Clark farm, they now consider him a great liability. Because he was drinking at the time of the incident, another member caught some buckshot in the hip. The decision to remove Bernie from the inner circle of the small group was swift and unanimous. The measure, however, was not harsh enough for most. Soon thereafter, with little debate, they deemed it prudent to excommunicate Bernie Walker because he is inclined to shoot-off his mouth after getting a bellyful of liquor. In most instances, he will end up beaten to a pulp, puking and puling at the feet of those White men he had somehow offended; a liability.

On June 3, the night before Krantz's grand affair, Bernie Walker creeps about the dark woods hooting back at owls and flinching at shadows while quietly chuckling at his ill fears. As he snoops around, he overhears the plans of the proposed sneak attack on the Ku Klux Klan's march. Every now and then, his drunken feet betray him and someone takes notice. With wide eyes and straining ears, they turn quickly to listen to what could be the movements of woodland creatures or the enemy. When Bernie finally stumbles into the fireside chat from the surrounding darkness, he nearly gets his head blown off. The fact, however, seems lost in his revelry of having fooled them all by sneaking into their midst. Nevertheless, in his own way, Bernie proves a small point.

After bragging of his successful stalking technique, he asks to join the attack. The vicious ridicule that follows should not surprise Bernie because they have very little respect for him. His disgusted brother scoffs at the suggestion and makes scathing remarks about Bernie's drunken tirades, hinting that the smell of him will probably give them all away.

With justification, Richard Mack expresses concerns about Bernie's knowledge of their plans, viewing him as a very real security risk. Timmons Walker steps in and promises to take his brother home, where he will be forced to clean up. He also assures the others that Bernie will stay out of their way once he passes out on a late night, liquid snack. Richard Mack's insistence that they keep Bernie under lock and key seems to lose its fire when they have to load his deadweight into the back of Timmons's beat up old truck.

☙❧

On July 4, 1964, Krantz hosts the barbeque at his stately home, glowing in the presence of senators, congressional representatives, judges, and top lawyers. Such are they who arrive to enjoy generous portions of Ezra Krantz's incomparable southern hospitality.

The bluegrass band plucks and twangs. Pigs roast alongside tender venison and the best beef that money can buy. They swallow oysters and clams from the Gulf. They wash down the potato salads and home-baked goods with spiked punch and ice-cold apple cider. They chug American beer, mint juleps, and prize winning white lightning. Later, while their wives stay behind to help with the cleanup, the men go into town for the rally. At this time in Klan history, women are nearly as segregated as African Americans.

On this day of days, some members of the Black Avengers discretely drift into Jackson City. Those sympathetic employers, who understand their reluctance to hang around, will kindly allow some to leave their jobs in town earlier than usual.

Carrying makeshift hoods and masks fashioned from old rags and itchy burlap bags, they move by way of back streets and alleys that are intimate to them. The Avengers take positions on either side of the street, where the carousing Klan will be shouting their outlandish racial slurs in drunken celebration. The stage is set for a massacre.

These trembling men cradle rusty shotguns and double barrels stoked with buckshot. Some own hunting rifles that still work when called upon to kill some lower form of animal life. Having to hunt for dinner during lean times, most of them are dead shots.

The Avengers do not intend to be captured. However, they never discount the looming possibility of their own casualties of war. Nevertheless, there is no backing out of the opportunity to repay the pain and death inflicted on their people at ruthless hands. Each man is committed to this quest. Their intensely fueled need to exact vengeance becomes motive enough to pledge their very lives.

The older warrior, Richard Mack, fought in World War II from 1940-1945. After serving more than a full tour of duty in the army gained him no honors, no respect on American soil. Although Timmons Walker served Uncle Sam in Korea from 1950-1953, a Purple Heart was worth spit. Though wounded in the act of saving a Caucasian officer's life, he, too, was insulted upon returning home in full-dress uniform.

Because both Richard Mack and Timmons Walker have military experience defending a nation where they are treated with no more worth than dogs before the whip, their tactics have kept their men united and focused. They often cite historical events for inspiration. The Boston Tea Party, for instance. They would also expound on the War of Independence—the American Revolutionary War—to remind these men that theirs is no less noble a cause. This land, once seized by the bloody sword, was wrenched from the grip of tyranny by the same measures and standards of killing or dying for the cause of freedom. Most members of this group knew very little of the blood-soaked history of the land of their birth beyond the scourges of slavery, until Mack and Walker used the very same to beat their plowshares into swords honed for war.

ℰ⁊ℴ

When the jug beckons from the sweaty depths of sleep, Bernie Walker puts on his dusty, worn loafers, and drinks thirstily at his brother's still. Moonshine became both breakfast and lunch for him long ago. He is a sorry sight in his wrinkled Sunday best, reeking of spilled corn liquor and sweat. Coveting the mason jar in the pocket of his suit coat, he takes regular nips and tugs. The opposing pocket harbors the rusty, old gun he found when the Black Avengers broke into the pulp mill they burned to the ground nearly one year gone by.

Somewhere along the way, Bernie urinates in his trousers. It probably happens during an insanely wretched moment of vomiting his

9

guts out. He does not seem to realize that the liquid poison that he adores is coming out at both ends. He is a piss-happy drunk, whose sole contribution to humanity is perfecting the art of swilling, puking, and pissing himself.

On the way to Town Hall, Ezra Krantz will stop at Mitchell's Tavern for a few rounds with the boys, while awaiting the arrival of Abraham Martin and those riding with him. Abraham's car blew a tire, causing it to skid into a shallow ditch. Hardly scathed, they pulled it from the ditch with a pickup truck to change the tire.

The two vehicles are just resuming the trip when Bernie stumbles from Brown's Wood Road, directly into the path of the truck! Simple reflex forces the driver to hit the brakes. He surely would have altered that moment's thinking if given the chance to reconsider running down that ignorant, Black bastard. Sliding to a cloud-raising stop on Bramble Crossing Road, the idling Chevy stands nose to nose with a foolish man who declares himself crossing guard for the day.

Abraham Martin leans on the brakes hard, trying to avoid a rear-end collision. He manages to turn the wheel, but not before tearing away the lowered tailgate of the truck. He is quite incensed after the crash.

Six angry men get out of the two vehicles scowling at the fool in the middle of the road. Bernie is holding a beaker of moonshine, laughing and inviting trouble. When Abraham Martin and Mike Talbot hastily inspect the damage to their respective automobiles, they look to one another before turning toward Bernie with equally hurtful intent.

At Bramble Crossing, one of the six men now stands before the open trunk of Abraham's car to consider their selection of weapons. He reaches inside to drag the coiled length of a leather whip from the corner. It feels good, perfect for the occasion. He joins the others, who stand leering at the subject of their discontent. Each man shares an unspoken thought; this drunken fool is about to experience unknown pain.

Mike Talbot loathes the smirk on Bernie's face. Deciding that he should be the one to wipe it away, he reaches for the whip. With the smoothest flick of a wrist, the braided cowhide snakes along the road to its full-length. Now, he cracks it once for good measure.

Talbot's lips curl as he says, "Nigger, you just fucked your whole world down the crapper, but I'm the one who's gonna flush you like the shit that you are!" He takes two hasty steps forward to close the gap, expecting Bernie to run.

Instinctually, Bernie compensates by moving a couple paces backward. He stops there to display his trusty weapon, which he leisurely waves back and forth as an extension of a scolding finger.

"Uh. Uh. Uh, White boy. Don't any of you crackers even breathe hard, or I'm gonna shoot your dicks off." He hiccups once and blinks his watery, red eyes.

The advancing Talbot stops dead in his tracks. His breath freezes for an instant, as do the others. None of them expected this lush to have a gun. They can clearly see that the gun is loaded through the cylinder portals, and their own weapons are hopelessly out of reach.

Bernie draws a swig from the jar, squinting as the moonshine ignites a new inferno in his throat and belly. Some of the firewater dribbles down his chin as he proclaims, "Well, Gents, it would seem that I have finally found myself in the bird cat seat. I gots you all at a disadvantage, wouldn't you say?"

Abraham Martin calmly states, "Now look here, boy, just put the gun down and we'll try to forget this little incident. Just put it down before you get yourself into trouble and…"

"Shut up before I blow you a new asshole," Bernie shouts, before laughing like a raving lunatic.

There is absolutely nothing the six men can say or do. Much to their disdain, this pitiful looking nigger seems to hold all cards of advantage.

"Maybe you're right, Massa Martin. I suppose I should put this here heater down," the lush mocks. While bending over very unsteadily and nearly losing his balance, Talbot seizes the moment by rushing forward until Bernie levels the gun at his crotch. Bernie places the jar on the road and says, "Back up, lil' boy. Yeah, that's right. You is the *boy* now, motherfucker. Back on up!"

Talbot wisely does as told, but his obedience is spitefully given.

Satisfied with the distance between them, Bernie mutters, "Looks like them Black Avengers are gonna get the chance to do some avengin'. You Klu Klux Klan boys been running roughshod over innocent Black folk for too long, but we gonna get you for it. It be our turn now." He points at the whip and Talbot drops it. When Abraham Martin and the others survey the surrounding woods, expecting to see more people, their ignorance amuses Bernie.

"It's just little ole me out here with you fine, upstandin' gents, but the rest of my gang's in town. You see, they is up there on the rooftops and in the shadows with the sandman, just waiting on that black-hearted leader of yours and the rest of the funky bunch. They gonna get theirs, but it just be too damn bad the rest of you won't make it to the big dance. No, sir, not today you ain't!"

Abraham Martin asks, "What the hell are you talking about? Are y'all plannin' to ambush our peace march?"

Bernie chuckles. "That's right smart of you, Mr. Martin. Somebody, give that smart man a slice of moon pie. Peace march—my black ass!"

Talbot notices the perplexed expression marring the usually sunny face of Abraham Martin. He demands, "You best step aside and let us go, boy. Just let us go before you jigs go and step into a shitload of trouble that hip waders can't see you through. Put it down!"

Looking at his gun, the undeniable power of the moment, Bernie croons, "It seems that we have a little problem here. You see, I have the gun and you has none, so that means I'm givin' all the orders around these here parts. And Simon says, I gots six bullets in this here gun and there's six of you. Now then, who wants to be first? Don't be shy. Come on and belly up to the bar."

They all back away, not wanting to do a serviceman's volunteer. Now Bernie orders them to kneel on the road with their hands behind their heads. At this moment, a flashback causes him to twitch. He takes a good long look at Talbot and says, "Yeah, I remember now. You is that same big fella that beat me up a few times." He points the gun directly at Talbot's broad chest.

Mike Talbot is sweating from more than fear. Like the others, he's enraged at having to kneel before a drunken Black man with a gun. He remembers trouncing Bernie for walking by without excusing himself. On that fateful day, Mike Talbot was just having a bit of fun. He did no real harm. None that the fool should have recalled in his state of inebriation, at least.

"Bye-bye, White man!"

Snap! Bernie pulls the trigger, but nothing happens. His heart sinks. His eyes bulge as he loses control of his bladder. The dark stain in his pants is suddenly alive and spreading to new territories. Having never taken the opportunity to clean or fire the piece of shoddy weaponry, Bernie has no idea that the firing pin is broken and filed down by years of use and neglect.

13

He snaps off a few more muted shots, but wisely decides to run while the Klansmen are still in a state of shock. Before turning to flee, Bernie throws the useless gun at Talbot, striking him in the face.

The strangest thought crosses Bernie's mind when he realizes that he just kicked over his jar of moonshine. He just wasted some prime mash and is, for a split-second, tempted to salvage the last corner still inside the spinning jar.

Bernie wobbles and weaves about fifteen or twenty feet before the whip cracks at his ankles. The hard, dry dirt feels like harsh sandpaper, scraping away the flesh of his palms and chin as he slides to a grinding halt.

As drunk as he is, Bernie knows that he is probably doomed, so he immediately heels like a whipped dog. His only defense is to pretend as if it was all just one big joke; that he meant none of the insane things he has said or done.

Abraham scurries to his car and pulls up next to the five men, who are pummeling Bernie Walker. He orders them to take the drunk to a secluded area of the plantation, but he's to be kept alive. Talbot and two others stop kicking, joining Abraham before he speeds toward town.

Bernie Walker is finally kicked to sleep. After piling his limp form into the bed of the pickup, they dump the broken tailgate on top. Just before completely losing consciousness, Bernie sees his brother's bloody face and hears him say, "You killed us, Bernie. You just up and killed us all with your big mouth."

ⓔⓧⓢ

The youngest member of the Black Avengers watches as Krantz's band of rowdy Klansmen pile into the tavern just three blocks from the ambush site. A nervous smile curls his lips, but he winces when the gravity of the situation returns. It is important that he remain unnoticed so he can fulfill his duty by giving advanced warning of the Klan's approach. He knows that a savage beating or possibly death will be in order if they see him snooping.

Nathan James backs himself further into obscurity, contemplating his reason for joining this group. The seasoned members once listened to Nathan's tearful plea; recounting the rape of his sister and of the police officers, who did nothing to the men she called by name. Though battered...though badly swollen...though torn and bleeding, she described her attackers right down to her teeth marks and ragged scratches. Most of them recalled how his elderly parents wailed when they found her swinging from a beam in a leaky, old barn after, supposedly, hanging herself. Those were terrible times for the boy's family, but these men understood his need for vengeance too well to deny him.

A few moments later, Nathan shakes the memory and moves behind the County Inspector's office. Using the left hand to secure the jostling bulk in his belt, he runs until he reaches the building where some of the others are sweating it out in the late afternoon sun. The young man pants as he climbs the rough, wrought iron ladder to report what he has seen.

The two leaders of the Black Avengers agree that the delay might be beneficial. Originally, they wanted to execute their plans after nightfall, when it would be much safer and easier to escape unseen. It appears that they may get their wish because hearty carousing and the telling of a few fish stories are delaying the Klan. There is nothing left to do but wait.

Huddled against the western wall in what little shadows there are, three of the Black men share a sip of a liquid tranquilizer that solemnly promises to calm their nerves. Meanwhile, others look at cracked, aging photographs of their beloved family members. Those who can read, skim over a few scriptures. One of which begins in Leviticus 24:20. Breach for breach, eye for eye, tooth for tooth: as he hath caused a blemish in a man, so shall it be done to him.

When the old man gets to verse 22, he whispers, "Ye shall have one manner of law, as well for the stranger, as for one of your own country for I am the Lord your God. Amen."

Because white supremacists, brazenly, quote many verses of that very same Bible as a battle cry for evildoing, some of these men are compelled to pray for forgiveness in advance. Others are humming religious hymns and the old slave songs of long-dead ancestors.

After the fish stories are spun, and they have exhausted the wayward direction of this once great nation, Krantz leads his merry procession up the street. Along the way, he stops to ruffle the hair of small children and offer a few sturdy handshakes. Every now and then, he raises his hood to spit at the feet of silent protesters. They are easy to spot; arms folded, with scowls of disapproval etched on their faces. They do not cheer or sing the praises of the Knights of the Ku Klux Klan, who so diligently pursue the God-given rights of all White men and women. None of those people will dare retaliation.

Marching participants pass out racially motivated literature to anyone who accepts it. Most will take what is availed them, whether they agree with it or not. Other members carry tall wooden crosses. Some of them are using bullhorns to shout a few choice words of propaganda. A ragtag marching band follows behind, squawking a motley rendition of the ever-popular "Dixieland".

In direct violation of federal laws prohibiting masked public assemblage, the judges and senators wear their hoods so they won't be recognized or photographed by members of the media that might print such findings. These men are bold, yes. But they are not stupid; even though they know local officials will not enforce the law.

Starry-eyed children in sundresses and sailor suits wave tiny American flags and Old Dixie. They smile up at their parents while licking the cotton candy and candied apples that are sure to stick to their faces and clothing. Most of them are much too young to grasp the gravity of this event. Eventually, the mothers begin rounding up the little ones because the language of such an affair is usually too harsh for tender ears.

Magazines are checked. Bolts are pulled as breeches are shuffled, ramming the shells of destruction into empty chambers. All the while, the Black Avengers sweat profusely, blowing at specks of unsightly dust settling upon their steel weapons of warfare. Candles, anchored by wax, are lighted with matches.

With the time drawing near, they peek over walls at parading Klansmen who have terrified and murdered so many of their people. Right or wrong, they have no care to consider the death of innocent bystanders, since they themselves have lost screaming children in burning homes during the witching hours of the night. At times, they have lost entire generations in the midst of unprovoked KKK attacks. The dirt tracks of poor shanty communities were filled with mischievous laughter on one day, and nothing but smoke and bitter silence where dead children played the next. Many tears spill and the silence is only broken by cries for God's miserly retribution.

Right or wrong, each man chooses a target. Each chosen target holds some special need for a bullet: the rape or murder of a loved one; theft of land or personal property; utter humiliations staged for and witnessed by the loving eyes of innocent children. Those same children never have to be taught hatred by their mothers and fathers when it is driven into them at young ages, breaking the spirits of many and causing others to self-destruct in the throes of self-loathing because they could do nothing. Such images are fevers in each avenger's mind, still churning despite the passage of time or the dying heat of that day. Even though they can't tell who is whom, they see the enemy's face clearly enough. Tears fall, then tears burn away beneath their makeshift masks.

Halfway up the final block, Krantz shakes the hand of a Southern Baptist preacher, and continues briskly toward the podium to make his earthshaking speech. The frantic bleating of a car's horn comes from the rear, but goes unnoticed as a part of the overall pageantry.

Rudely weaving through the crowded street, Abraham Martin nudges people aside with the fender of his car. A plume of steam now blooms from its damaged radiator, but that is negligible.

Mike Talbot and the other passengers shout obscenities from the open windows, urging the parading people to get out of their way. They also take the opportunity to warn some of the late members still making their way down the street amidst the trooping band. Those who are warned, pass the word in disbelief, discretely pointing to the rooftops before rushing to parked vehicles to retrieve weapons.

The music of the ragtag marching band drowns out the warning horn, so Mike Talbot and the others leap from the slow-moving car as it reaches the block where the podium is draped in the red, white, and blue of the Confederate Flag.

Abraham Martin yanks the trunk's key free of the ring so he wouldn't have to shut off the car's engine. When Talbot reaches into the window for the key, noticing a trickle of blood that springs from

Abraham's freshly wounded finger, he thinks of it as an omen of what is to come for some more than others.

Abraham continues to circumvent the crowded street, trying desperately to reach his imperiled brethren. Meanwhile, Talbot and all the support he could muster, rush into the alleyways with their own arsenal of firepower. Even police officers become involved at this point, but they will not hinder civilian participation.

Ezra Krantz arrives at the podium, surrounded by well-wishers that hamper his attempt to gain order and a bit of breathing room. As Ezra reaches for the microphone, someone's clumsy foot tangles with the cord and pulls it from the stand. When Ezra Krantz bends at the waistline to retrieve the squelching mike, he's completely oblivious of the two rifle sights trained on his head and chest by Mack and Walker.

When Krantz tries to rise, Abraham dives into him, driving him to the ground just as the bullets reach their destination! One bullet strikes Abraham Martin at the base of the skull, bursting through his lower jaw. The shrapnel from his exploding teeth blinds the man standing behind Krantz before he's pushed away. The shrapnel sends him screaming into the plate glass door of the building behind him.

The second shot crashes violently through Abraham's back, exiting the soft tissue of his abdomen to claim the life of the man who reflexively reaches for Krantz on the way down. If that person hadn't bent over, the mushroomed bullet wouldn't have ended its journey in the bottom of his skull.

Bottles of gasoline, with tails of fire, explode on the streets, setting white robes ablaze. Terror-stricken people run screaming as gunfire rings out, echoing between the buildings. Police officers assigned to crowd control collapse on the streets and sidewalks. Many of them are targeted for various atrocities committed against the family members of the Black Avengers.

The robes that clad the Knights of the Ku Klux Klan are no longer immaculate, but stained crimson with the blood that is suddenly forced from their bodies. The range of a scattergun is normally poor for distance shooting, especially when the barrel is shaved, but they still maim and kill dozens of people. Lead pellets shred their bodies, even as the result of ricocheting from the pavement. The podium, indiscriminately, ejects shards of wood as it's riddled with bullets. Glass windows shatter, giving up their own unique sounds of death.

As suddenly as it starts, the gunfire from the rooftops take recess, but the screaming chaos below goes on. The Black Avengers are on the move. They scurry down the rusting ladders to the back alleys and streets to disappear.

The fifteen men on the rooftops directly opposite of Mack and Walker all get away and head for the rendezvous point. They exit the city without incident, but that is not so for their counterparts. When the other nine men hit the pavement on the run, they find themselves trapped in a narrow alley by Mike Talbot's gang and the police that joined him before the fracas began. Meanwhile, the young lookout is nowhere in sight.

Since most of the Black Avengers expelled their ammunition, they have not taken time to reload, thinking only of a hasty retreat. The element of surprise is supposed to afford them the luxury, but they are hopelessly boxed-in. Some of them manage to squeeze off a few rounds, but not nearly enough to buy them freedom.

Violent shots are exchanged! Timmons Walker is killed, instantly. His sudden death is an ugly thing to behold as he crashes to the ground a husk of ravaged meat. Richard Mack quickly sees the situation as hopeless. Abandoning their suicidal attitude, he admonishes his men to drop their weapons, which are mostly empty anyway.

The Black Avengers come out from behind the garbage bins and empty crates that tentatively provided them with cover. Gathering with their hands raised, they look into the hateful faces of their nemeses, whispering prayers to God before they are all gunned down. Nine men soon lay dead in a mangled heap when the echoes cease and the stifling smoke clears. A river of blood flows down the crease in the pavement to form a brilliant pool in a nearby gutter.

ℰℭ

Ezra Krantz is rushed to the nearest hospital, where Abraham's tooth is surgically removed from his right lung. He experiences vicious chest pain as his lung threatens to collapse. On this day, Krantz declares to God in heaven that the enemy will not win by such cowardly actions.

Many of the visiting officials suffered serious wounds in the attack. Some of them will die, but the truth of their deaths are covered up, with no mention of white robes and hoods. Some will simply disappear from the public eye, as doctors and surgeons remain silent for fear of their lives.

Satisfied that Krantz is in stable condition, Mike Talbot hurries back to the plantation. There, Bernie Walker is whipped and tortured with a branding iron until he divulges the names of every member of the Black Avengers his foggy mind can recall. Up until this moment, the Avengers have eluded the Klan at every turn.

The fifteen men, who escape, soon learn that their brothers have been captured and killed. The young lookout explains his inability to warn Mack and Walker because of the sudden appearance of Mike

Talbot and those who were intent on ambushing the ambush party. He weeps as he paints a picture of himself buried in a pile of empty produce boxes, forced to watch in silence. When the coast was clear, he crawled from his hiding place on his belly and ran as fast as he could to warn the others. What he tells them is terrifying enough, but he caps his story off by telling them that he overheard Mike Talbot make mention of Bernie Walker. They rush from the secret meeting place in the tall pines and bramble thickets to their homes to collect their families and as much of their possessions as possible.

Three of the sixteen decide to get the hell out of Jackson City without hesitation. Six of the others are apprehended at their homes. These men and their families are caught carrying rickety old furniture, tattered clothing and cracked dishes to their vehicles when they are beset upon.

Soon, they all realize the true worth of the possessions they try to salvage. It costs them, from the youngest to the eldest, their very lives.

The remaining seven members of the Avengers are faster, lighter packers by comparison, but they cannot outrun a police radio or the CB bands of the Klan. They all die along the roadside. Some are lynched; hung by the neck until dead. Some are shot while others burn to death in slow-moving automobiles that promised transport to safety.

Bernie Walker lives in an earthly hell until he is finally, but not mercifully, sent to the real one. He is stretched across a sweltering grill that is still quite hot from the barbeque, and tied down. His screams will do him no good as the iron grating burns waffle-shaped diamonds into his flesh. His oily hair catches on fire as his skin blisters and cracks. The blood boils inside his body until it coagulates and clogs in his blood vessels. He will die with such a powerful thirst.

Bernie's final thought before descending into permanent darkness is of how much worse it will be in hell with the white-hot hatred of the brother he surely sent there. He is quite certain that Timmons will be waiting.

A bitter week of mourning rocks the state of Mississippi, where the only winners in that little war are the undertakers and the hospitals. Federal agents are dispatched to investigate the attack, but their efforts are met with the insurmountable opposition of grief-stricken folks, who take great offense at being questioned. Mourners have very low tolerance for outsiders, especially Feds who treat them as if they are criminals and deserving of what the evil Black men have done. The White folks feel that they are the victims. They feel that they should be exonerated of any wrongdoing that may have possibly led to that bloody conundrum because the attackers have taken the law into their own hands.

Somehow, later on down the line, the incident is all but erased from the annals of American history. The question of why stable family men suddenly went rogue is never really answered, but it is never seen as an absolute necessity to do so.

Wounded political figures, those who could travel, showed up at their hometown hospitals with teeth full of lies to explain their injuries.

⊗

Ezra Krantz lies fuming in his private hospital room for weeks. His anger contributes to his dangerously elevated blood pressure. He is feverish and his white blood cell count is exceedingly high when he suffers a mild stroke. During which, he has his first vision of God's ingenious plan.

Until the terrible news reaches them, the New York honeymoon is a thing of beauty for Jud and Ashley Martin. They return home just in time to lay his father to rest. Inheriting the family business at age nineteen is a burden in itself. He tries to take up where his father left off, being brave for the sake of his family name.

Sabrina Martin is born on November 5, 1965. The girl child brings the gift of happiness in her tiny, magical fingers. She proves to be as smart as a whip with her proud parents watching her grow up. One month prior to Sabrina's third birthday, on a stormy night in early October, there comes a knock at the backdoor as the Martin family sits down to a late supper. A faceless someone passes a sealed envelope to Jud from the gloom. In a whisper, he tells Jud to follow its instructions immediately. Ezra's handwriting is scrawled across the yellowing page. The messenger walks away.

Jud Martin's first reaction pivots between confusion and concern because his godfather has chosen total seclusion until this time. Krantz has spurned Jud's attempt to make contact after Abraham's funeral, which Krantz could not attend.

Under cloaked circumstance, Jud finds out why the man, for whom his father had taken two bullets, suddenly demands to see the godson he ignored for four long years. Jud has been left to wrestle with his demons and hatred for coloreds while struggling to remain in control of his new family and business responsibilities. He's been forced to grow up very quickly.

As instructed, Judson Martin burns the letter and lies to his wife about a broken water main at the supply warehouse. He excuses himself after telling her not to wait up because it could take all night to fix. He drives to the warehouse and parks in the rear, where a waiting car signals with its headlights. The police cruiser leaves the warehouse without lights until well away from the area.

Shadow monsters play along the roadside that eventually ends at the southeast gate of Krantz's plantation. Jud Martin enters the service door where Ezra, a young man named Peter Black, and others greet him.

Jud Martin, Peter Black and the other three men summoned soon find out that they have things in common. None of them have ever been in any real trouble with the law. They are young, married men who lost their fathers in the Black Avenger's raid four years prior.

Each man wants to know why Krantz left him out in the cold. They question his reasons for forbidding their participation in any Klan activities. Ezra explains that it's God's will that they mourned and truly buried the ghosts of their fathers. He claims that it is imperative that they focus and mature beyond impetuous behavior. They have to be above suspicion when they embark on the long trek that lay before them.

Krantz deals with them collectively and individually. Each is sworn to secrecy before Krantz hands them near complete outlines of their future lives, which he has written down like a road map. It is truly the map of their individual journeys, for they are soon to begin swimming up the political stream. Krantz possesses the power and the backing to insure that their secret agendas are not impeded, having lain the foundation of the divine plans during the four years of silence.

The assassination of Martin Luther King just six months prior had been the signal fire to all those of a like mind. Life and lifestyles will soon change for all.

Coming from nowhere, Jud Martin is elected to the school board, serving it vigorously for five years. During his final year on the board, his wife mysteriously disappears. Even so, he continues to be energetic in working to insure the educational future of his daughter and all children, even African Americans.

Jud is twenty-nine years old when elected to City Counsel where he strives for the betterment of his patron city with unmatched zeal until he is thirty-five. The beast is moving steadily, gaining momentum like a runaway train on an icy slope.

In the early 1980s, Jud Martin runs for mayor and wins the office with unprecedented support. After serving this post, he decides to run for the governorship of Mississippi. Again, he takes the polls by storm. His success is due to a number of things. After all, he is the son of a man martyred in this town. Jud Martin is a pillar of his community, especially since he seems to veer away from his father's tendencies toward Blacks by publicly refusing campaign contributions from people of Ezra Krantz's caliber. This is a well-constructed ruse, however.

With the help of his sister, Jud Martin manages to raise his daughter after her no good mother decides she no longer wants a family. Nevertheless, Martin never falters in his duty. He claims that the unconditional love he sees in Sabrina's eyes gives him the strength and motivation to strive onward. Voters are easily swayed by the sentiment of such family oriented political platforms. This is even more evident when one has the likes of Ezra T. Krantz behind the scene, clearing the road of obstacles with payoffs and dirty political tactics.

Jud Martin's popularity continues to grow, so he wins his second term with less opposition than in the early 1990s campaign. With the passage of time, Jud's daughter sprouts wings and is well on her way to becoming a notable doctor in Atlanta, Georgia. All these years, he manages to keep Sabrina in the dark. At the same time, he keeps his hands clean on racial issues to appear the advocate of racial equality. This part is never easy, but biting this bullet is the mother's milk of plans aimed at the White House. Before then, Martin will need another wife, but that is only a minor detail.

During the 1980s and the 1992 Presidential elections, David Duke of Louisiana plays a most critical role in God's plan. There is a powerful current shredding the political stream. Long beforehand, wicked shadows had begun to fall.

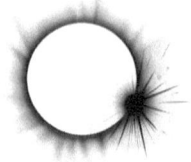

Chapter 2

No Honor Among Thieves

On March 18, 1994, two young men are biding time by telling jokes and little white lies. Standing beneath the fluorescent lights of the East Atlanta basketball court, they wait patiently. The athletic ball players, who ran up and down the cracked concrete, hoping to execute the ultimate slam-dunk, have long abandoned Gresham Park. Only these two remain, knowing that a customer will eventually drive up in need of some recreational substance: Be it cocaine; crack; or marijuana.

Thomas Jefferson Brown and Anthony Jackson, whose street names are TJ and Slim, refer to themselves as the R.E.P. or Representatives of Eastside Pharmaceuticals. The 17-year-old drug dealers from the East Lake Housing projects are about to engage a rather profound conversation regarding the useless course of their lives.

From the depth of the navy blue hoodie, TJ gazes at the eerie mist creeping along the ground around them as the temperature slowly falls.

TJ has finally come to a decision, and he will speak of it for the first time with his best friend. Releasing a sigh that is much too troubled for one so young, TJ Brown whispers, "Man, I've had it with school. This kid is dropping out, and I'm not going back next year."

It is usually in Slim's nature to agree with TJ because they have been inseparable since the age of five. Slim asks, "Are you for real?"

"I'm for real. I'm droppin' out, cuz."

"True. School is whack," Slim complies. "If you go, then so do I."

"Yeah, but my old lady is gonna give me pure hell. I'll probably have to give her some cash or buy her a little somethin' somethin', but she'll get with the program. I mean, what's she going to do, leave her shitty little job to babysit me at school all day? Besides, I can help moms out a little more so she doesn't have to work like a slave all the time."

They chuckle at TJ's assumption because he is probably right. There will be very little Mrs. Brown can do about his decision to quit because there is no father to speak of. Samuel Brown has spent the past twelve years in prison as an accessory to murder simply because an acquaintance came to his home after killing someone.

Because TJ's friend so readily commits to the idea, he begins to feel more confident about his decision.

He says, "To hell with school, man. We don't learn shit from them drunk ass teachers anyway, and there sure ain't no jobs when you do get out. I'll finish the year, but that's it. What good is it?"

"Humph," Slim grunts. "True that. Go to school, graduate. Go to college, graduate with towering debts. Go to work, selling shoes or Avon. Look, mom, I'm a freaking insurance man. Do you wanna buy a car, ma'am? It's a real Georgia peach!"

TJ giggles at Slim's antics and adds, "Besides, we both got fine rides and the honeys love us, so who needs a piece of paper? By the end of the summer, we'll have more than enough cheddar to furnish our own crib outside of the iron gates of hell. Kickin' it on the wild side."

A silky black BMW pulls to the curb.

"Slim, check it out. You know that's the Po-Po. They always think brothers get careless when we see a nasty ride. Supposed to mean that they have a lot of money to spend."

TJ's whisper holds words of wisdom and Slim agrees with his assessment. "The for real fuckers are too scared to come through here in shit like that because they might get jacked this time of night. So how do you want to play it, G?"

"What else? Take your time and go start the getaway car. Call me on the walkie when you get there. It's time to have some fun on a slow night."

They give one another fist bumps and Slim casually walks away. When Slim rounds the corner of the nearest building, he sprints down the alley. He crosses Evergreen Street, continuing down the alley until he reaches the last building. Slim makes a sharp right, racing for the Chapin Avenue crosswalk. As Slim approaches the far side, he takes the walkie-talkie from the large pocket of his sagging jeans and shouts, "All clear on the eastern front!"

Slim disappears behind a garbage bin where he waits in the shadows, priming the quiet engine of the 1993 Sentra.

The horn toots again and the impatient driver threatens to leave, but TJ knows he's faking it. He shuffles over to the car with his left hand raised to obscure his facial features, bending at the waist to look into the passenger's window. The driver looks like a well-groomed police officer. He smells like a cop.

TJ is always sure to take a good look inside of a potential customer's car before doing business. When he sees no salivating dog or anything that could conceal a camera, he lowers his hand and asks, "Yo, blue eyes. You slummin' or what?"

The driver summons a most disarming smile to ask, "What's up, roadie? You workin' it?"

The kid diverts his attention for a split second, smiling to himself when he sees the dark blue van inching along the curb about fifty yards to the rear. When it stops suddenly, he knows it contains the backup unit known as the *Track Team* or the *Jump Out Boys*. Catching the driver's nervous glance at the rearview only confirms TJ's suspicion, but he continues despite the obvious setup.

"I'm always on the clock, man. I can supply whatever you need. Just name your poison."

The driver says, "Well, I want to spend about two-hundred dollars on some rocks and grass. I'll take some good cocaine, if it's clean enough to throw in the water." He flashes four crisp fifties at the young suspect.

There is no desire for tape recordings or cameras because lawyers often use such things to prove theories of entrapment. After this little menace is safely clamped in irons, the usual story about the officer's conduct and arrest protocol during the sting will fall into place. The kid simply made the initial contact in an attempt to distribute controlled substances, and he should be subject to jail and paper trails for the rest of his life because of it.

TJ looks at the money and at the driver's free hand to be certain that he isn't hiding a gun or a shiny pair of handcuffs. He says, "Yo, you never need to chef it up yourself when it's straight drop. I got the hard and the go fast right here. Throw it against the wall across the room and you won't lose a crumb. But the chronic is in the building where my partner in crime just went."

The cop now smiles. "Well, that's okay. Just give me what you got on you for now."

TJ goads Sergeant Pike by insinuation. "Are you sure? We got everything in there. He's weighing up the shit right now. We got enough hydro to fuck up your whole upper-class neighborhood, blue eyes."

The driver's brown eyes light up. "Sounds good. Maybe I'll come back a little later with some bitches. If the shit is as good as advertised, we might get a couple ounces. Just give me that stuff for now, brother man. Half and half." He extends his empty hand and taps the brakes.

"Oh no, Rush Limbaugh. You can see it, but you no touch 'til I get the cash in hand. Kingpin will bury my ass if you drive off with his shit. Know what I mean?" He pulls a sandwich bag from his pocket to prime the narc. This is a brief, but very intense moment for them both, as the adrenaline of the kill rushes their systems.

Sergeant Pike says, "Oh, you don't trust me like that." He hands over the money. "That's all right, blood. I understand bout the kingpin, man."

TJ considers the cop's clumsy use of cool, colloquial language to be hilariously amusing, but he holds his composure.

The cop's empty hand is still suspended in midair when TJ says, "You should know, Joe, when it comes to drugs and money, a cop shouldn't trust his own mama. Or me either, sucker!"

Without warning, he takes off. As the speedy youngster makes his way to the escape route, Pike snatches his radio from the floorboard and shouts for his backup. The van screeches into action as he struggles with the automatic seatbelt.

By the time Pike is free, TJ is already in the alley where he calls Slim to say, "I'm coming in hot!" Slim can hear the twang of the fencing as it sings with the fall of TJ's pounding feet upon the rusted concrete of the overhead crosswalk.

The *Jump Out Boys* get to the abandoned building, convinced they have the boys trapped inside. They kick in doors and cover broken windows with flashlights and weapons drawn. Meanwhile, Slim moves the Sentra to the steps of the crosswalk. Seconds later, TJ jumps in. They flee, but Slim is careful not to burn rubber because the squeal might alert the stupid cops that they just ripped off for two hundred, tax-free dollars. Thanks to the men in blue, it's going to be party time in east Atlanta, Georgia.

Back at the abandoned building, the police spew cuss words into the air, laying blame as they kick empty beer cans and used syringes. They are quite upset at being played for fools by two young thugs, whom they can't even identify. Someone will have to cough up the buy money or explain it to Captain Greer. Over the years, however, they have all pocketed enough money taken from drug dealers to find the loss negligible.

∽

As Slim pockets his half of the cash, he asks, "So do you want to hang out by the Bright Lights?"

TJ smirks at his friend. "Dog, you've been smokin' too much of the chronic. It's Sunday, fool. You know those Methodists are closed tonight. That place is probably a graveyard right about now. Besides, that tweekin' ass manager called the man on us just last Friday because we were making all the paper. Or have you already forgotten that little incident?"

TJ's lips curl and his eyes squint as the dim light of remembrance comes on in Slim's mind.

"Yeah, that's right. I'm brain-dead, man. You know that Blunt makes me flat line," Slims says in reference to smoking grass wrapped in a cigar's outer tobacco leaf. They laugh as usual.

"We better lay low for a minute," TJ suggests. "Let's run by the bootlegger's house for some gin and juice. Then we can scare up a chicken head at the Glass Slipper and take Cinderella to a room. Now that's a plan, son."

Slim smiles at the thought of getting some sex-for-sale. He shouts in his best redneck's voice, "Yee ha! Let's ride 'em cowboy. I sure can use some of that thar sucky-sucky right about now!"

TJ takes a cigar from the glove compartment, using a thumbnail to split it open. He is not to be outdone, however. "Yup, Bubba. That thar little ole frog-sticker of yours ain't seen the insides of anything but your britches in pretty near two moons, pardner. It's probably pretty darn sore from tryin' to make unnatural acquaintances with your zippa."

Slim's retaliation is simply, "Ah, um, fuck you, nigger. You're probably dying from a bad case of poontanglessitis yourself. When you do get some, you better wear your condiments." He puckers, pretending to spit some chew on the floorboard. "Why hell, boy, *the ninja* might be killing you as we speak." The ninja, a silent killer, is simply used in reference to HIV.

After the short visit to Mama Jane's house, where they bought the liquor from the backdoor, they pull up in front of a rickety joint that is almost always occupied by lonely, destitute people. The car is easing to a halt when TJ admits, "I'm gonna miss the Bright Light, but it's just too damn hot for us. That's too bad. Those rich crackers spend that paper, dog. When they party, they buy that shit like they're trying to corner the market. What I like most of all is that they always have cash. No begging, no crying, and no credit."

Slim nods. "Yeah. My uncle told me that people used to just walk around sniffing coke like it was nothing. He said it was something kinda reserved for rich people. After it was outlawed, they still brought that shit over here for us to use, but their own people like it, too. Now they buy it from young, enterprising businessmen like us for even more money. Only in America, dog. Only in America."

Slim gives TJ a fist bump as they walk into the gloomy strip joint called the Glass Slipper. A more commonly used name is *Slippery's*. It has seen better days. The place is smoky and smells of unwashed trash bins filled with rank bottles and cans of long-pissed beer. When they pass the hall to the restrooms, the smell of bad plumbing and unflushed crap makes its presence known with a stifling vengeance. As far as people go, this is little more than a breeding ground for very bad germs.

Thirty-five minutes later, TJ and Slim are partying with two freaks they picked up at the eastside hole in the wall. Slim's older brother works the front desk at a local motel, so they get the vacant room free of charge. As long as no one uses the phone, there will be no record.

All of the necessary party favors are in place. They have condoms, liquor, chaser, and forty-ounce bottles of malt liquor. The smell of marijuana hangs relentlessly in the air. The boys naturally have to have crack for the women, who are somewhat older than their hosts are. They aren't bad looking women, maybe just a bit rundown by their way of life.

The women have coaxed the boys into allowing them to take a few hits of the rock cocaine to put them in the mood, as most crack heads play it. As usual, they go through the paranoia, geeking and peeking out of the windows. Then they beg for more before agreeing to get down to business.

These two drug dealers have already broken the golden rules of trading drugs for flesh: Tease, do not please. Never give the whore anything until her job is done. Work before play, each and every day.

Slim is growing angry and demands satisfaction. TJ is equally frustrated with his trick. He is yet to become so hardened of heart that he'll take some ass without consent, so he curses her out and is about to toss her out when his beeper begins to chatter. He recognizes the number from the payphone near the downtown nightclub. Patrons will use the phone to contact TJ and Slim on Friday and Saturday nights, when they are in dire need of a pick-me-up. There is always the incumbent White boy dealing inside of the club, but he and the manager are dealer/users. They are partying playboys. Therefore, the product is always stepped on too hard, and overpriced for the poor quality.

Customers even used the phone when their outside connections are clearly in sight, laying plans to meet around a corner for privacy. After the payphone's number has been entered, they will use the star key and what they think to be a unique three-digit code so they can feel privileged and special.

This is one instance when TJ ignores his youthful, but very sharp instincts. He allows his curiosity to get the better of him in foregoing the fact that there is no three-digit identity to this caller. He will have to pay for the room, if he uses the phone, but it's probably worth it.

Upon answering the page, he finds the caller to be none other than the owner of Brighter City, the club they hang around. They always stay outside because they are underage and generally unwelcome, but they make the bulk of their weekly take from the party animals that frequent the place. They even manage to polish off what they consider to be a few choice pieces of White ass in trade every now and again. That may be the real reason he answers the page. Their dates are certainly less than compliant.

These two youngsters have just enough balls to take their chances at Brighter City because it is their personal gold mine. The police are never around because they're too busy in minority neighborhoods, unless called for the occasional bar fight. Slim trusts TJ to know when to pull out, if ever the time should come. Being strong and relatively new offspring of the street game, they have been able to avoid or outrun any real trouble. Yet, they also know that the day of reckoning could lay waiting around any given corner. The job is to save their profits, stay undercover, and avoid jail as long as possible.

They could be two of the lucky ones, destined to go far. TJ certainly has developed the instincts for it. Both are unknowns to the legal system at this point in their felonious careers. Therein, anonymity is a true blessing that usually only collapses after greed or an unchecked ego takes possession of the hustler's soul. Being the flash in the foul is sure to get them noticed.

This particular phone call proves to be very intriguing. TJ sees it as an irresistible opportunity to make an inroad with the devil himself. If this is a trap, he accepts that he will just have to eat it and puke later. Even though he's suspicious of how the club's owner got his pager number, the conversation convinces him that they should meet. It could be the beginning of a lucrative and less risky relationship.

TJ Brown will never know if he doesn't take the chance, so he gets dressed and gives Slim the eleven-hundred dollars he has in his pocket. He quietly explains bits and pieces of the deal he has to check out, tempted to take Slim along to watch his back. However, Mr. St. John is adamant about a solo meeting, and there is no need to rock the boat at this point. If this is a setup, one man will be free to get the other out of jail.

Though initially concerned, Slim likes the idea of being alone with their guests. He's never had two women in bed. After all the delays, he feels it time for the freak show to begin. Before actually sticking it in, Slim decides to make them do disgusting things for his perverse pleasure. It won't be as hard as he thought once he dangles a few more pebbles in front of them.

⚭

After circling the block in search of suspect vehicles, TJ arrives at the nightclub and parks around back, as instructed. There is no one around on Sunday night, other than the owner, whose full name is Willard St. John. TJ Brown considers him a rather nerdy looking fellow. He has a strange look in his eyes while allowing TJ to pat him down for a wire. After that, the young man looks around to be sure that they are alone.

Seconds after entering the manager's office, the windows are lit up with the flashes of several gunshots! TJ Brown soon lies dead, with a gun in his hands. Monday morning's headline reads "Youth Dies in Failed Robbery Attempt with Empty Gun".

District Attorney Gavin is an African American with a difficult job. Political, social, and racial implications are developing around this particular shooting because there have been a rash of them lately. The initial investigation into the alleged robbery attempt and subsequent shooting turns up a few disturbing facts. The preliminary evidence indicates that this could be a case of premeditated murder. Only trained eyes see it as someone's attempt to commit the perfect snuff job.

The dead boy's friend and one of the two hookers tells investigators that TJ received a mysterious call on his beeper, which is not recovered at the scene. The weapon TJ, allegedly, used was found empty. His grieving friend and mother swear that TJ Brown never owned a gun. He has never been in trouble for theft or any crimes other than a single traffic ticket for playing his music too loudly within city limits.

In Willard St John's defense, anyone could have answered that payphone when TJ Brown called from room 212. Most likely, as Keith Williams' theory will suggest down the line, it was probably someone who called to report that the owner was alone and vulnerable to robbery.

Upon placing his hand in his right pocket, Willard St. John realized that he still had the clip in his pocket. He pretended to be sick and ran for the bathroom. Once alone, he used his handkerchief to wipe it down, but someone comes in to check on him.

Before running to the bathroom, Willard St. John gave the detectives access to his surveillance equipment, which they had to turn on. It is not until the next day that a homicide detective notices that the surveillance system was deactivated only thirty-minutes before the incident. Looking a bit deeper, a technician discovers that the system is never turned off before, during, or after business hours.

In addition, soon after the homicide detectives at the scene reactivate the surveillance system, Willard St. John's camera captured his very own image as he removes the missing clip from his pocket and kicks it under the desk. Because St. John may have set this up, the kid only has one set of prints on the alleged robbery weapon.

One of the more disturbing facts—something that might go unnoticed by someone other than a homicide detective—is that TJ Brown locked the doors of his car. An armed robber will never lock his automobile when he expects to be making a hasty exit from a place he intends to rob with an empty gun. He probably would not park around back next to the owner's automobile, where security cameras would surely capture his image.

There are no signs of forced entry. The kid was gloveless, but left only one full set of prints on the frame, slide, and front sight of the weapon. TJ Brown's prints were not found on the trigger or pistol grip, where police forensic specialists expect to find them when the user handles the weapon in the attack prone posture. Suppositions all; however, this case has become very interesting.

There is enough pressure and evidence to convince the District Attorney to bring formal charges against Willard St. John, who is arrested on the following afternoon. The incident becomes volatile, instigating civil unrest between the Black and White natives of Atlanta where few people claim to have absolutely no opinion at all.

News polls show a decisive split in the community, giving proof of the growing hostility between those who are taking opposing sides of this tragedy. Some see this as the unnecessary death of a young man, who was set up by an evil man. The recent exoneration of Caucasian police officers in the shooting of an unarmed teenager does not help matters much. That incident is overshadowed by two separate shootings in recent weeks by Caucasian citizens, who swore they feared for their lives. Both men were charged, but the manslaughter charges were dropped in both case. Although the fingerprints of one of the shooters, who swore it was in self-defense was found on the dull knife at the Black man's side, there simply was not enough conclusive evidence to prove he tossed it there after the fact.

During neighborhood sidewalk interviews with those who feel St. John guilty of a crime, a few claim to know TJ Brown or his mother. They refuse to believe TJ had gone that far. Meanwhile, the Caucasian population of Atlanta views this case as further proof of judicial decay because the kid obviously deserved what he got. It is wrong to arrest an honest, hard-working man for defending himself when his own life is clearly in danger.

At best, even if he doesn't get a conviction, the District Attorney believes a trial will go far to prove to the African American community that he isn't just another puppet in the bureaucratic façade. Gavin pursues his instincts, assigning this case to his best prosecutor because the city is a boiling pot of racist emotions. A trial is the only thing that will cool the steaming waters where Black on White crimes are also on the rise.

The only fingerprints on the robber's clip belong, curiously, to the robbery victim. It will be up to the Justice Department to prove wrongdoing. Premeditated murder is a stretch, so they must pursue a vastly unpopular, uphill battle of manslaughter instead.

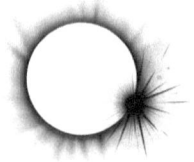

Chapter 3

THE ACQUITTAL

On April 3, 1995, one year and three days later, the Honorable Judge Rupert Asking dismisses the jury upon the delivery of a not guilty verdict. Immediately after, he hastens for the relative insulation of his chambers, hoping to avoid the tongue-lashing that is sure to follow the mother's initial shock. Something about this case disturbs him greatly, but the verdict is in.

There is no backdoor for defense attorney Keith Williams, who will have to wade through a sea of malicious glares and verbal abuse once the judge vacates the courtroom. His client, with closest friends at his side, thanks him for the defense and walks out with two bailiffs. While departing, Willard St. John narrowly escapes having his face ripped to shreds by the slashing fingernails of Thomas Jefferson Brown's distraught mother.

With two African Americans on the jury, at best, the defense hoped for a hung jury. However, he achieved the ultimate courtroom deliberation, and an appeal is highly doubtful.

As Attorney Keith Williams gathers the files and notes that spilled during the sudden skirmish and neatly stacks them in his briefcase, he secretly wishes that the woman and her family would leave before he has to face them. That luxury, however, is not to be his blessing of this day.

A foreboding hush falls across the entire room by the time Keith Williams turns toward the outer doors of the courtroom. The sight of Mrs. Brown slumping in the arms of sympathizers crushes him. Though meaning well, they fail to give her sufficient comfort in this moment of anguish. A so-called jury of peers has set her son's killer free, and she is morose. The attorney, who successfully defended the murderer, is coming her way and she strives to meet him head-on. There is no way to avoid the confrontation, and Williams knows it in the pit of his knotted gut.

Until this moment, the only thing that mattered has been proving his client's innocence; winning the case. For Williams, the rows of occupied seats seem an endless wave of shocked, teary-eyed people, swooning in disbelief. However, disillusion is not the only emotion churning in their hearts. For this grieving mother, Williams feels inexpressible pity, but dark dread overshadows all with their meeting finally at hand.

The 36-year-old woman seems to float in slow motion as she approaches. When Mrs. Brown finally stands toe-to-toe with Williams, she stares up at him with those watery eyes and takes a long-awaited shot. She plants a surprisingly vicious slap across his face that seems to echo forever, and the attorney can do absolutely nothing.

There is a fire in Mrs. Brown's belly. Her saliva is like bitter acid when she sobs, "How could you? How could you even consider defending that evil son-of-a-bitch? What kind of a person are you?" Her heart races, threatening to pound out of her chest. "TJ was my only child, and I'll never have another. Whatever he might have been, he was no armed robber. But you made him sound like a fucking menace!"

Keith Williams feels Mrs. Brown's eyes probing his soul while frozen within a vacuum that only serves to further the divide. The woman, so filled with pain and revulsion, wants him to feel it all as deeply. Nevertheless, he cannot.

"Does it mean absolutely nothing to you? Don't you realize that you're no better than that murderer because you set him free?" Mrs. Brown shakes off her brothers and sisters when they try to calm her. "Let's see how you feel when one of those crackers turns on you, or takes your own child. Will you care then? On the other hand, will you just rush out to cash in the insurance policy? You are a whore, Mr. Williams. You are no better than a fucking whore!"

Reverend Mason Brown, her eldest brother, pats her on the shoulder while looking Williams in the eyes. There is a sad, unspeakable resentment written on his face when he calmly declares, "This is where you've brought us, Mr. Williams. This is what that man's money costs us. This family has suffered the tragic loss of a loved one, and now we have a mother who is even more broken inside because the hope of justice for her son was all she had left. For all the shame that you have brought upon our people, just what will it end up costing you? God has obviously blessed you with an extraordinary gift, but is this truly how you choose to exercise it?" Tears begin to stream down his face. "My God doesn't like ugly, mister, so I'm forced to wonder what it will cost you in the end."

Mrs. Brown clenches her teeth and raises her fists to the ceiling to scream, "As God is my witness, I curse you. Lord Jesus, you will all pay!" She pounds on Williams' chest, but it is not enough. She weeps violently as she falls to her knees, shedding bitter tears that are acid rain upon her newly aged skin.

Friends and family rush to her aid, cursing Keith Williams with their eyes. Someone spits on him. Keith Williams moves away. His voice is barely more than a whisper when he says, "I'm sorry for your loss, Mrs. Brown. Truly, I am. I was just doing my job." His voice chokes off as he begs, "Please excuse me."

He is unable to face the grief-stricken people all round, looking to the floor for comfort. He is no longer oblivious of the purity of loathing that dances across their burning eyes.

The mere slits of Slim's eyes suddenly confront him. Though tears are welling, therein, his message is clear.

With utter contempt, the young man whispers, "Before this week ends, we'll come for you and that cracka. Guard ya grill, mothafucka. Guard ya grill, you bitch made nigga!" Slim's brother pulls him away.

Attorney Keith Williams pushes through the outer doors of the courtroom, filling his lungs with fresher air. The atrium of the Fulton County Courthouse is relatively quiet as he crosses the large room with his eyes averted. He pauses near one of the huge, brooding columns supporting the upper levels of the building, taking a second to regain his composure and fight the lump newly arisen in his throat.

He is using the mini-recorder to annotate the successful results of the trial, its docket number, the date, and the client' name when a familiar, hushed voice suddenly snaps his head about.

Willard St. John is talking to his friends while awaiting the arrival of his limousine out front. He declines an offer to leave by way of the secure exit in the rear because of the angry mass of people who disagree with the verdict. Being the arrogant man that he is, St. John refuses to sneak away because he has just proven his innocence in a court of law.

The proximity of the grieving mother, however, does little to dissuade his fervor in the midst of his friends' admiration of Willard's bold craftiness.

Willard St. John recalls a private instance between himself and Mrs. Brown. There was no one around when he confessed his evil deed to her with his eyes and the sly smile that only she had seen from across the room.

"I want you boys to come over to the house to celebrate properly. Warn your nagging wives because we're gonna play until the sun comes up. I'll have a few women there to keep things lively, if you know what I mean." St. John's smile is perpetual. "And we have my fancy, nigger lawyer to thank for that. Because of him, my corner of the block will be safe from his kind from now on. Please remind me to drink a toast to him, fellas."

As Willard's friends pat him on the back, they share a chuckle at Keith Williams' expense. After looking around, one of the good old boys says, "Willard, I've got to hand it to you. This was truly a thing of beauty. I really didn't think you could pull off whacking that kid like you did. Not to mention getting a spook to defend you. Pretty risky, huh?"

St. John sneaks his own peek around the perimeter to whisper, "Risky? Hell, it was pure genius, if I do say so myself. I knew if I beeped that little spear-chucker and told him I wanted to trade a nine-mill for a couple grams of snuff, he couldn't resist. Hell, he was there almost before I loaded my own gun. It was easy enough. When I handed that fucker the piece—bang—shop was closed." He softly claps his hands together.

One of his pals whispers, "Yeah, but you almost screwed yourself by forgetting to put the clip in the dang gun. It didn't help to leave your prints either."

St. John recalls spreading the cash over the boy's bloody corpse and smiles to himself.

A horrified Keith Williams stands behind the column, listening to this in utter astonishment. He is incapable of moving his feet, or stopping the surging disgust. Nor can he control the anger that now sweeps through him like hurricane winds. His feet are planted in the ancient marble where he is rocked, listing slightly with each nauseating wave of emotion.

The arrogance of this shameless conversation transports Keith Williams back in time.

He is twelve-years-old, living on his parent's farm in Meridian, Mississippi. Standing at the edge of the forest in a cornfield, Keith holds onto his squirming infant brother as he quivers from paralyzing fear. He feels as if the stark images taking place before his young eyes will soon cause his fleeting heart to quit.

Young Williams cannot close his eyes. Just as powerless and impotent as his father, who kneels before those demon men with the ghost-white skin and pointed heads, he watches on. The boy is as helpless as the whimpering child is in his arms, powerless to change the sight of his father cringing and pleading for his life and that of his wife. From different perspectives, both father and eldest son look on while the wife and mother is raped in the firelight of their burning home.

When death finally comes for both parents, it is neither clean nor is it neat. Its clamor is nearly deafening. The gunshots are as loud as the shroud of death is quiet when it blankets a tortured soul. He stands there in the field with his mouth slowly working around a silent scream. Something instinctual causes the young boy to glance at his brother when those evil men begin to look toward the fields. Keith realizes that, in his attempt to keep the child quiet, he has nearly smothered the baby to death!

Placing the swaddled child upon the ground, Keith shakes and massages his chest until the infant shows signs of life. Seconds more, and he would have killed his younger brother. Even though this situation is quite horrific, it is not the worst part of the living nightmare.

St. John looks about again. In a near whisper, he proclaims, "You're right about that, Sully. That slight oversight was a close shave. It certainly was a bit careless, costing me a ton of money and some time behind bars, but Williams sure put his words together nicely on my behalf. He had that poor jury crying in their beers over me instead of that little prick. I'll tell you something else, that kid's coke was excellent. When they came to lock me up, I was high as all outdoors."

They laugh heartily until they begin to move again, rounding the huge column to see defense attorney Keith Williams standing there with fury in his eyes. As if their neckties suddenly constrict like the hangman's noose, the laughter ends with a choke. In the ensuing silence, they all seem to find something to do. St. John has a sudden, profound interest in the subtle paisley pattern of his necktie. He notices that a button has gone missing from his attire.

Collectively, his groupies search deep within the dark recesses of their pockets, where some will find car keys to play with. Those keys very easily could be their balls, which have drawn up as close to their spines as humanly possible.

Keith Williams launches an angry right, making a solid connection with St. John's blushing face. The punishing blow sends him reeling backward to the marbled floor when his best friends part like the Red Sea.

Quite out of reflex, spitting blood to the floor, St. John quickly regains his feet. He charges, or at least pretends to charge, but his friends do not let him down this time. They stop him, knowing that for all his wickedness and mouth, Willard St. John is no brawler.

During his rather nonchalant struggles, he threatens, "Nigger, you just made the biggest mistake of your miserable life." His eyes burn with malicious contempt. "You just wasted all the taxpayers' money that put your Black ass through law school. You are a dead son-of-a-bitch. Dead. You're dead!" His friends drag him away, kicking and screaming creatively combined racial obscenities.

Although she does not know the reason for the fracas, Mrs. Brown watches from across the atrium. Nonetheless, she is not moved by the display because it is not enough. It could never be enough, so she looks to the secret contents of her hands for comfort.

Once Keith Williams regains the ability to move the roots that are his feet, he stumbles into the harsh, spring sunlight into an even harsher group of hungry reporters.

At the feet of the courthouse steps awaits an angry mob of Blacks and some Hispanics, many displaying hand-painted signs of protest and unflattering remarks.

The reporters and camera crews, those not inclined to go chasing after Willard St. John and his groupies, fall on the attorney like urban vultures to carrion.

He immediately assesses that they are, at least for the moment, unaware of what transpired between him and his client. That is evident in the questions they are not asking. Because members of the media were banned from the courthouse at Judge Asking's whim, none of them witnessed Williams decking Willard St. John. Obviously, something juicy happened inside of the building. Their ignorance is a small blessing, but it holds very little consolation in the career-salvaging department.

Williams falls beneath a veil of cameras, a hailstorm of simultaneous questions, and jostling faces that are not completely devoid of the personal opinions of those who ask, "Mr. Williams... Attorney Williams, sir, did Mrs. Brown or members of her family attack your client in the courthouse? If so, will there be assault charges filed against them?"

Keith says nothing. He keeps moving as they shove microphones into his face, cramming more questions into his ear.

"Mr. Williams, can you describe your feelings right now? Do you feel differently now that your client has been acquitted because of your brilliant defense?"

"I do not wish to comment at this time. Excuse me."

"Mr. Williams, how do you feel in the face of this angry mob of people, who now feel that, by taking this particular case, you've betrayed your own race?"

This one stings, cutting to the quick. It is most evident in the contortions of his face as a momentary reflex. Keith Williams looks as if he is ready to lash out, physically or verbally. Either way would be good for a highly emotional ending to TJ Brown's tragic story, but Keith does not give them the satisfaction. He has already lost composure once.

He says, "Still, no comment!" and pushes on toward the parking lot.

The attorney wisely skirts the swelling crowd, merely restrained by wooden sawhorses and a handful of local police officers. Earlier, members of the riot squad were dispatched to the scene at the request of the supervising lieutenant, who has the misfortune of drawing this unenviable assignment.

For a not-so-brief moment, Williams has serious doubts about making it to his car. The unruly mob throws bottles, cans, and curses at him. They look like a giant, rabid amoeba, eager to engulf and devour him body and soul.

Keith Williams hears things like, "Traitor!" and "White man's bitch!" He is called "Sellout!" and the ever-present "Uncle Tom!"

He is thankful that most of the reporters decided to give up for the moment. They are left behind to make their final comments on his lack thereof, so he is able to walk to his car alone. Now, from somewhere deep within the swelling mass, someone launches a softball. Williams goes down as it caroms off his forehead. Luckily, it was only a glancing blow. A sympathetic officer helps him to his feet, but Keith refuses medical attention. The Crowd Suppression Squad is called in.

When Keith gets to his car, he is certain there will be more than a little swelling and a nasty headache to boot. Fortunately, he is getting off easily. Deep down inside, however, Williams feels he deserves their distaste.

The lump rising on his head pales to the aching in his tormented heart. While he speeds away from those who would happily display his innards for the world to see, he replays mental tapes of his most inspired courtroom deliberations and strategies.

He remembers too well the scathing remarks regarding the reputation of the East Lake Housing Projects where TJ Brown and his mother lived. He called it "Little Vietnam." The cop they ripped off on the other side of town was at the scene of the shooting after the fact, but he was unable to give a positive ID. Although the stolen buy money was not found on the boy's body, Sergeant Pike believed that the clothing matched.

Anthony "Slim" Jackson denied being anywhere near the ballpark mentioned during Sergeant Pike's testimony. Slim's testimony on the subject only served as a distraction, taking away a bit of the prosecution's fire in a witness already deemed prejudiced against the defendant. During the time between the shooting and the trial, unfortunately for the prosecution, Slim was arrested on a minor drug possession charge. Slim's testimony was all but ignored when the defense disclosed that fact.

There was one thing Slim blurted out that really should have stuck out of the details. TJ told him that he was going to Brighter City to purchase a gun from the defendant. Keith Williams reduced his words to mere hearsay and had them stricken from the records.

Williams obtained the coroner's toxicology report, listing traces of controlled substances found in TJ Brown's body. There was also evidence of underage drinking. Although Keith Williams did not establish a pattern concerning the boy's possible troubles with the law, he was certainly able to setup associative images of the violent nature of the people living in that housing project and the surroundings of "Little Vietnam."

As expected, the prosecutor offered strong objections to many of the defense's comments, and the judge sustained a great deal of them. Many of Keith's comments were stricken from the record and the jury prompted to disregard. Those were also expected, but the damage had been done. Keith Williams had effectively cast doubt upon the boy's character only to find out that the kid was innocent and undeserving of a vigilante's death sentence. He has defended and set free TJ Brown's murderer.

The subpoenaed phone records of room 212 were eventually thrown out because the financial records showed that the motel room was only paid for after the phone call to the payphone in the parking lot of the defendant's nightclub. It was also proven that TJ Brown was not the registered renter of that particular room, and it was paid for by a close friend with a motive to lie. Slim's brother lost his job when the motel's owner deduced that he had just given his brother the room free of charge on a slow night, and they only payed for it because the phone was used. Room 212 was also cleaned by the house cleaning service, so forensic evidence was invalidated.

This is not what Keith Williams aspires to become. Feeling dirty and abused, Keith resists the depression because he faces the battle of salvaging his career and maybe even pieces of his soul.

He has beaten the odds by rising through the ranks to carve out a sterling career, but the mighty have fallen on this very illuminating day.

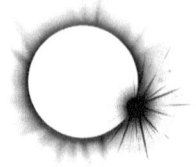

Chapter 4

THE OUTCAST

Back at the law offices of Mitchum, Simms, and Bates, Attorney Keith Williams carefully maneuvers into the underground parking lot. He offers a characteristic wave to the security guard at the entrance. On this particular day, the attorney is glad the guard is there to stave off the reporters, who have taxed his heels since making it known that Willard St. John obtained an African American defense attorney. The well-constructed ruse added one hell of a twist to this story.

News personalities seemed hell-bent on getting the inside story because an intriguing scent trailed Williams, and fresh hounds kept him afoot. During the trial, reporters of either race asked pointed questions that usually raised Keith's anger, but he kept his silence in the face of the media. Following the revelation of Willard St. John's treachery, though, his mind aches with renewed visions of those vicious times when members of the media treated him as if he were the accused. His guilt is now extremely vivid.

Williams takes the elevator to the top floor and goes straight to the senior partner's conference room. Knowing exactly what awaits, he pretends not to notice that people are suspending their conversations as he approaches. He pauses just outside the door to straighten his tie, brushing away imaginary flecks of lint. Finally, Keith inhales an extra breath of air and enters the dimly lit room where Thomas Mitchum is seated in his traditional place at the head of the boardroom table. Elliot Simms and Andrew Bates sit, respectively, to the right and left of him.

They are watching a live interview outside of the courthouse. Apparently, a reporter has found a witness to Keith's seemingly unprovoked attack on his client. The woman has no knowledge of what transpired before the fight, but she is certain of the two combatants. Seconds later, another reporter urges a second witness to come forth.

Mitchum's pencil snaps at the tip, sounding like the crack of a whip in a room where the silence is soon broken. Mitchum rises from his perch, staring. Dark storms are brewing in the shadows of their faces.

Mitchum shouts, "Damn it, Keith, what the fuck is the matter with you?" Until this point, Keith has never heard Mitchum drop the F-bomb. "Would you care to explain just why the hell you'd accept the St. John murder defense, win it hands down, and then risk a damaging lawsuit by beating the crap out of your client? Barring the Trenton scandal, it may have been the most controversial case of the decade for you!"

Mitchum sits down hard, waiting for an answer that he feels will be insufficient no matter what the explanation.

Keith slams his right hand onto the table's surface, leaving something there.

"And what made this case so controversial, so polarizing, was that I—an ignorant Black man—no more than a fucking dupe—defended that disgusting, lying piece of filth. Willard St. John is lower than pond scum!"

His insubordinate attitude tips the scale, bringing down the wrath of the other two. Simms jumps into the fray by saying, "When this escalates, and it will, you are probably finished here and everywhere else. We took you on under the impression that you are a sparkling example of what this law firm is in its very essence. We rave of your successes, and now, because of today's debacle, you have turned out to be our greatest disappointment. How could you be so damned impulsive, Keith?"

Bates slams a liver-spotted fist on the teakwood table with a voice full of wrath when he growls, "Forget impulsive. How could you have been so stupid?" He stands, glaring at Williams. "Not only have you tarnished and decimated your own career, your shit has now become a reflection of us all. I'm just sick over this crap!"

The air is stale. Collectively, their words are full of nasty reprisal. Williams has never seen them so angry. An impending doom looms for him in this room.

Mitchum begins to say, "There is no need to mince words here. You may as well pack your…"

Williams hammers his briefcase onto the surface of the imported wood. He shouts, "He set me up and you damn well know it! I overheard that vile bigot bragging to his friends about how he murdered that kid. He didn't even have the decency or respect for that boy's grieving mother to wait until he'd left the courthouse to start extolling the masterful job he'd done. Oh, yes. I heard him telling them how he had contacted TJ Brown by pager. He did use that payphone to contact the victim. That's why his partial print was really on it. He wiped it down after using it, which is the reason why no others where present. St. John admitted that he lured the boy there by offering to trade a gun for drugs, even though Anthony Jackson lied about it being a cash sale. Immediately after handing the kid the weapon, supposedly, used in the robbery attempt, St. John shot him dead in cold blood. It was a near perfect execution. He had instant fingerprints on the weapon. Nearly open and shut. However, Willard St. John underestimated the homicide detective's power of deductive reasoning in his attempt to commit the perfect crime. He ensnared himself in his own trap when he forgot to put the clip in the gun, but I got him out of it. Like a blind fool, I got him out of it by insisting that the young man's best friend was an unreliable witness. I had a ton of evidence thrown out, tainting the truth with a coat of doubt so thick that the prosecution stood no chance. All that guff my so-called experts spouted about shock and being unaware of certain behavior or acts following a traumatic incident now amounts to nothing more than bullshit. I got him out of it when he clearly tried to plant the weapon's full clip under the desk. My so-called experts helped explain that crap, too!"

The shocked adversary gasps. "What did you just say?" Mitchum asks.

Keith Williams' retort is most venomous. "Are you really as surprised as I was, or are you just well-rehearsed?"

Bates glares at Williams. "How dare you accuse us of participating in such scandal?" His face is quite red by now. He takes the statement to be a personal affront to his character, as intended. Bates' anger prevents the news from really sinking in.

These men bring certain commodities to their law firm: sound and patient judgment; certain degrees of risk-taking; innovative thinking and passion. Such are merely examples of the mixture that plays the greater part in the success of this firm, their lives' work. It represents a balance rarely achieved in any organization, though it places them on opposite sides of an issue now and then. Still, they always find the middle ground to present a united front.

While Williams and Bates sling rebuttals, the wheels of hard logic are at work, grinding away in the minds of both Mitchum and Simms. Something harsh had to have set Williams off, and this seems to be more likely a reason than any other. For all practical purposes, it is the only thing that could have sent him over the edge. After all, Keith pursued the St. John defense with both diligence and conviction. He probably would not have won the case if he felt otherwise. It all seems just crazy enough to be the truth, and Keith has never given them any reason to doubt his honesty before this incident.

Mitchum and Simms arrive at the same conclusion and decide to put a stop to the shouting. They know it's time to sit down and defuse their ticking surprise, which will not be achieved without a calm willingness to hear all of what they both feel must be the truth. Keith Williams deserves no less than the benefit of a doubt, even though it would be much simpler to give him the proverbial shaft. It would seem that they have already been screwed enough for one lifetime in the disturbing situation they are now in.

With most of the electricity discharged into the outer atmosphere, Keith takes the floor. He gives them the story, verbatim, even before playing the recording.

The four, fully rational attorneys, now analyze and attempt to dismantle their bomb. Quite some time later, the dissection of the situation produces an educated guess at the events leading up to this very moment.

Upon request, Keith Williams plays the digital tape recording he was annotating when it inadvertently picked up St. Johns' voice in the courthouse. That shiny object he slammed down and left in the center of the table.

It is clear that Willard St. John is a bigot by his own words. He planned the execution, also by his own admission. There has been friction between TJ Brown and St. John's club manager, which Keith established during trial. There is little reason to doubt the validity of the manager's testimony.

TJ Brown owned a beeper registered to his best friend, who purchased two. Said beeper was never recovered from the scene, so there were no phone records admissible by the prosecution. St. John fired repeatedly when forensic and postmortem evidence suggested that the boy might have died from the first shot to the face. The prosecution upheld this point, but to counteract the facts, Williams brought in a psychologist to explain such things as shock and post traumatic reactions of victims. She gave vivid examples and reasons for the bizarre behavior of people who must repel their attackers with deadly force. Many are found in shock, standing over the body of their dead attacker while still pulling the trigger of an empty gun. This expert testimony was also used to defuse the prosecution's ace card, camera footage of Willard St John leaving prints on the boy's clip as he planted it beneath the desk. There were no bullets in the weapon used in the alleged robbery attempt. The clip, strangely enough, was found under Willard's desk. While in shock, he may have removed the loaded clip from the weapon with no memory of doing so. This explains away the video and the print. No other prints were found on the magazine. However, a captured image of Willard dropping the clip on the floor before he knew that investigating detectives had reengaged the video surveillance, presented quite a problem. Again, Keith Williams debunked the evidence.

Willard St. John expressly sought a Black attorney from the most prominent White-owned law firm for the benefit of the African American community, the media circus, and the jury. The interior security cameras of Brighter City were disabled some time before TJ Brown arrived. The kid's car was found locked with the alarm system engaged, a fact attributed to a rookie's mistake and blamed on TJ Brown's probable state of mind. He was high when he died, and drug use is often a contributing factor in violent crimes.

There was no evidence of forced entry. Willard St. John testified that his manager, after going over the receipts, probably neglected to lock the door on the way out. The loyal manager, though extremely nervous about taking the stand, corroborated the story.

The lawyers' hypotheses now align with those of the defeated prosecution, which implicate that Willard lured TJ Brown to the club and murdered him. However weak or strong the prosecution's theories may have been, Keith Williams raised enough reasonable doubt to secure an acquittal for a guilty client.

Mitchum, Simms, Bates, and Keith Williams have been set up. They now face issues of double jeopardy, attorney-client privilege, and conflicts of interest. Not to mention the possible charge of assault and a lawsuit.

The firm's position is nearly untenable, with their possible courses of action constituting a short list. They could sit back and do nothing, hoping the situation resolves itself, which is highly unlikely now that the media has gotten wind of it.

They could settle the matter out of court, an unsavory solution that will only add insult to injury. Firing Williams for St. John's benefit would be too great a loss. They could assist in Keith's relocation with another firm, also a no win situation. They could help him begin a practice independent of their own, but the stench of this case will still follow him without the firm's backing. The most acceptable thing to do is throw the tape recording in St. John's face, and leave the ball in his court. Blackmail, or simply the suggestion of blackmail, often allays many a scuffle.

After the tedious examination brings the ugly jigsaw puzzle to light, the senior partners fully understand what Keith Williams must have experienced. They allowed the sensationalist aspects of this case to numb their objectivity, causing them to abandon normal scrutiny. All have been suckered into a case that proved to be too juicy and lucrative to pass up.

Mitchum's long sigh reflects grief. "Well, there it is. We've been hoodwinked by a lowly redneck's total fuckery!" He sighs again. "Keith, I'm sorry for doubting you. It is now painfully clear that St. John warranted more scrutiny. Please accept my apology and believe that we had no way of knowing. Looking back, it seems to have been right there all along." He looks away and asks himself aloud, "How did we allow ourselves to get tangled in a mess like this?"

Simms clears his throat, making it known that he will speak next. He shakes his head and says, "I'm afraid we've all behaved impetuously. Very impetuously, indeed, my young friend. I must say that in all the years of this firm, I have never known any of us to be so gullible. I am beginning to feel old, gentlemen. I'd like to offer my sincerest apologies, Keith. We brought you in, and your services have paid dividends unprecedented among most of your peers. The way I see it, we all owe you many debts of gratitude. Furthermore, I will stand beside you in whatever way is necessary. You have my word on that. You have my word."

Keith thanks him for the kind words.

Before anyone has to resist the urge to look the Texan's way, Bates adds, "Well no one's ever accused me of mincing words, so let me begin by saying that I, too, am very sorry. I mean that from the bottom of my cold, black heart." He stands, pacing the length of the table. When his eyes return to meet Keith's, they do not turn away until he says his piece. "I'm asking that you try to forget whatever idiotic things I may have said just a few heated moments ago." Bates smiles, thinking back for a moment. "You really have been a prize and a blessing to us all. Your win-loss ratio is virtually nonexistent because you've only lost once since you've been with us. Even that was not your fault. In your six years here, you've displayed an exemplary work ethic that I must say reminds me of us in our younger years. You have never let us down, Keith. We really should have given you a chance to explain before throwing slaps. I suppose St. John is one hell of an actor, and we assumed that there could have been no viable reason for you hauling off and decking that sick, racist bastard."

"That is true, young man," Simms adds.

"But, as it turns out, there is one reason. It is quite possibly the only acceptable one, as it were. You may have acted hastily in slugging St. John, but he deserves a lot more. We will all stick together, no matter the cost. For the record, we always tape proceedings such as this one started out to be, so everything we've said here has been for the record. Again, I apologize." Bates reaches out and shakes Keith's hand as a gesture of trust.

Williams is touched by their words and deeply appreciative of their respectful attitudes. Still, it only makes him more aware of the position his actions have placed them in.

Instead of exercising righteous indignation, he says, "I suppose the past can really play havoc with the emotions when things like this arise in our well-organized lives. I reacted in anger and lost it. Because of it, I've compromised this firm as well as my career. For a split second of stupidity and my inability to control my temper, we all may face consequences. I am terribly, terribly disappointed in myself, and not at all comfortable with temporary insanity as my only excuse. I am therefore compelled..." He hesitates when his voice rattles. His eyes and right index finger seek the smooth, polished surface of the table. "...compelled to turn in my resignation because I became an attorney to protect the innocent and to destroy people like the men who... the men who..."

Mitchum raises a hand to stop him. He looks at his partners and says, "Just hold on. Let's not be too quick to throw in the towel. We've all been convicted of that crime once today. If I were in your shoes, I probably would have knocked his ass out cold. You've got to work on that jab, son." They share an uneasy chuckle.

A heavy weight lifts from Keith's shoulders, but the burden is far from removed. He asks, "Then what do you suggest?"

Mitchum begins to rock back and forth in his leather chair. His fingers are interlocked and his eyes have focused on some unseen horizon. He remains that way while saying, "This situation may not be entirely out of our hands. For every problem, there is a solution, so let's look at this and see what pluses there may be before giving in because what St. John has done to you, he's done to us all."

"For one thing," Simms interjects, "...those news hounds are still in the dark about what actually happened inside the courthouse. We can count on Willard to say nothing about the true nature of the assault. So let's thank God for small favors."

Bates says, "St. John has never run into the likes of us, and we all know that a stupid animal knows not whom it should fear. Why don't we abandon ethics here and think like that animal. Just forget protocols, ethics, and rules of engagement. Think deviously, gentlemen."

Once they have a tentative plan of action, they are now able to breathe a little easier, but not without concern. After formulating a plan of attack, Keith is happy to see that Mrs. Brown is taken into consideration, which is something almost no one else would have done.

"Take some time off, Keith," Mitchum suggests. "And don't beat yourself up about defending St. John because this is no longer your burden to bear alone. If anything, it's ours to assume for foolishly believing in the honesty of long-standing clients."

Simms agrees. "Yes, you've been working hard. Go off and find a good woman, son. You are too young to go without for so long. Let the old folks get down and dirty for a change. Sneak away and stay out of sight because those eager reporters aren't likely to leave you alone. Take the jet if you like. We're not going anywhere until this thing is wrung out."

Mitchum is on the phone with his secretary.

"I agree," says Bates. "It's been quite some time since we've enjoyed a good game of hard-ball in the rain. I believe I may need some mud on my shoes just to feel young again."

Mitchum hangs up and informs, "Well, they're here in force."

"The media?" Keith asks with dread. He goes to the window, looking down on those he often despises. "Fuck. I'll never get rid of them."

Mitchum smiles at Simms and Bates. "Looks like it's time for the double twenty-four hour shuffle."

"What's that," Keith asks, noting the wicked little smile on their faces.

"That's just our way of dealing with these assholes when they are chomping at the bit. We'll promise them a press conference in twenty-four hours with the express condition that we are left alone until the time of disclosure. Within this period, you will simply disappear without trace, and then we'll do it again just for the hell of it. Two of us will go downstairs to blow smoke up their asses while you make a clean getaway out back. That's the double twenty-four hour shuffle, my boy."

"I volunteer," Simms says with a grin.

Mitchum advises, "Stick with us, kid. Someday, you might be running the joint. God knows our sons aren't any good at it. Now get going, but don't move until we have them all lathered up in one big mud-mongering pile. Get to your car and wait until someone signals the all clear. Try to have some fun while away. You have certainly earned a vacation. I think things will work out just fine. We still have a few tricks stashed here or there. No one messes with us and gets away with it. Being defense lawyers often leads down sullied paths that are mired in half-truths and boldface lies, but premeditated murder is something that all the money in the world will never condone because it undermines the fabric that constitutes the basic canons of this law firm."

With that, they shake hands and Keith goes to his office. His assistant thinks he is coming to clear out his desk. In fact, Barbara is doing it for him with teary eyes. He reassures Barbara Ellis that he is going to be her boss for a while to come. Williams calls his girlfriend only to get her voice mail.

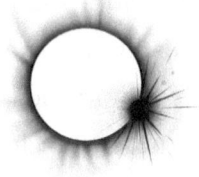

Chapter 5

EVERYTHING BLACK AND WHITE

It is nearly four o'clock when the damage control/war party adjourns to blow smoke up the media's skirt, while telling them that it is only the fog rolling in. When Keith Williams gets the all clear, he sneaks away by taking Northside Drive and hanging a left on Marietta Street.

His cell phone rings twice before snapping him out of his daydream. The hostile voice on the other end says, "Hey, White boy, you ain't shit. We gonna get your bitch ass, you sellout motherfucker!"

Williams takes a deep breath. While slowly exhaling, his head throbs. He makes a mental note to change all existing phone numbers, certain that the new ones will soon fall into the hands of his persistent tormenters. That is not the first death threat, but this one strikes a thrumming cord of serious intents. Knowing that TJ Brown and Anthony Jackson had ties to the drug world forces him to consider it a viable threat of retribution.

He has striven all of his life to be a productive citizen, but his drive to excel now delivers him to the land of the outcast. He is an enemy to his own people, those who clearly saw a killer's guilt when he could not. The revelation of his own blind ambition resounds in his mind, gnawing at him from within. Stifled tears escape his tunnel vision, despite an effort to contain them. These tears are not driven by fear but shame.

Four things will make his gray world a little brighter. He wants aspirin and a stiff drink, whichever comes first. He needs a hot shower to wash some of the stink away. Finally, he wants his woman, which, in itself, is another gut-twisting consideration. This is her day off so he calls again, but there is no answer. Keith is about to hang up when her answering machine comes into play, so he listens to her sultry message.

Some kids are fooling around on the sidewalk. Among them are Tommy Wallace and his eleven-year-old brother, Timothy. Keith often pays ten dollars each to wash his car, before taking it to detailing professionals. When the kids stop to watch him go by, Keith offers them a wave and a smile. What he gets in return is spit on the sidewalk and the middle finger. These mean-spirited little gestures ram home just how severed are the ties. He realizes at this moment that the sky has suddenly turned a morbid bluish-gray.

The distraught attorney parks at the Peachtree Towers Condominiums and goes inside his building. He likes this place because it always smells clean. As he turns the key, the door of the guest bedroom slips shut. An uninvited guest stands silently in the darkened room, waiting for the right moment to appear.

Upon entry, Keith is about to enter the security code, but he seems to have left it disabled. He looks at the bar in the corner with its many elixirs and potions dressed in fancy bottles. They prompt him to think about how much the senior partners drink. Years ago, he figured out that they must all have the same peculiar little scar on the stomach, left there by the surgeon that bi-passed their livers to give them the gift of straight-drive.

He chooses cognac from the array and heads for the aspirin. He walks into the bedroom and tosses his blazer on the bed. Then he stops just inside the bathroom door, stepping back to look down the hallway. He thinks he feels a presence, considers it, and shakes it off.

Keith Williams whispers to himself, "Don't crack up on me now, boy. You just have a little lump on the head." He turns on the shower and downs the pills with a stiff shot.

The hot water quickly fogs the bathroom with steam. He neglects turning on the exhaust fan expressly for that purpose. This way, although he is alone, even the Almighty will not see the tears streaming down his face as he recalls Mrs. Brown's abject expression when she cursed him before God and heaven. He feels so responsible for her pain, knowing an agonizing emptiness in this lonesome moment.

The intruder positions herself beside the bureau at the far and darkest side of the master bedroom. She is holding something in her hands.

Keith finally emerges from the steam with a towel around his waist while using another to dry his hair. He always feels better after a scalding shower and shampoo. On days such as this, he likens washing his hair to scrubbing his brain. It helps to ease the tension, sometimes.

He sits on the edge of his king-size bed and listens to the CD playing. There, with his eyes focused on the floor and the towel draped over his head, he is completely unaware that the shadowy figure is moving closer to him. Deep in thought, he floats away with the smooth rhythm of the music.

The advancing silhouette is much closer when she aims and pushes the button. Suddenly, the selection changes in the middle of the song. Only now, Keith realizes that he did not turn the stereo on. He leaps from the bed and pivots, expecting some sort of projectile. When his feet are caught up, he crashes to the floor. As the woman walks from the shadows, he looks up at her, helplessly.

She is wearing a bronze and black negligee. Her long, dark, auburn hair cascades down the gentle curves of her face like the bubbling currents of a waterfall. Her hazel eyes twinkle in the dim light that escapes the bathroom door.

She says, "Boo!" and falls upon him, laughing at his facial contortions. She descends upon him with kisses.

Finally, he remembers to breathe. Dr. Sabrina Martin is completely unaware of the stresses, and continues to giggle because she had stopped following the news after hearing the verdict.

"You should see your face, Keith," she derides. "You look as if you are ready to fight to the death and make love to me all at once. It is sort of a terror-stricken, come-here-and-give-me-a-kiss kind of look."

After a very meaningful hug, they pick themselves up from the floor. When Sabrina sees the bump on his head, she cries. "Oh, baby, were you in an accident? Does it hurt? Did you get x-rays? What happened to you?" She rains questions on him, not giving sufficient time to answer.

That is okay with Keith, who really does not want to rehash the events of the day, knowing there will be little choice to do otherwise. After Sabrina gets an icepack and makes sure he is not suffering from a concussion, Keith sits her down to explain recent developments.

The lawyer in Keith hates to use euphemisms to substitute distasteful words when discussing events of importance. Although it is difficult to use words like spook, nigger, and spear-chucker when he repeats the day for his Caucasian girlfriend, he manages. The day's explanation ends with an earnest invitation to join him on an abrupt vacation.

"Sweetheart, in the midst of all that's happened, the senior partners feel that I should get away from here for a few days. I would really love to visit my grandfather. Even the kids around here are turning against me, but I can't say I blame them. I really can't." He sighs long and hard.

Lightning suddenly flashes, causing them both to jump. Thunder rolls in the distance. Sabrina snuggles closer to him. "I've got time off coming to me. The administration is bugging me about using it. I would love to join you. Of course, I can't rightly refuse an opportunity to meet the legendary Jeremiah Williams, now can I?" She looks at him coyly. "Besides, it will give a girl a chance to see just what I might have to look forward to in thirty years."

He returns her smile just as lightning whips across the southern sky, again.

Sabrina kisses his lump tenderly. "Poor baby, come to mama, and I'll make it all better. Come on. Let me take all the bad, bad things away."

She crawls onto and over him to perch on her knees in the middle of the bed. When she beckons him to join her, he does so willingly. Sabrina Martin nuzzles him as he gently kisses her neck. Their lovemaking is truly a thing of beauty, as their flesh melds in the midst of a raging thunderstorm. Once sated, they lay nestled in the comfort of one another's arms, where they sleep peacefully. They are safe, and for the moment, tucked away from chaos.

In a world overrun by the pain of bigotry and hatred, these two opposites have been drawn together. The past two years of their semi-private affair have strengthened them to deal with each other's race. The good and the bad. There are always surprises, however. What they feel is much stronger than even they know, but they will soon need every ounce of that strength.

Keith Williams dreams of tom-toms and chanting. He dreams of dancing Africans and Indians around a sacred fire. Sabrina Martin dreams of her childhood secrets. Smiling in her sleep, she moves closer to him.

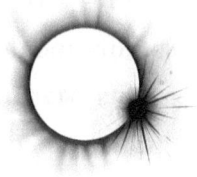

Chapter 6

MIXED CHEMISTRY

Keith Williams and Sabrina Martin first met as attorney and client when he was hired to defend her procedures at the Grady Memorial emergency room. Melbourne Pratt immediately accused Dr. Martin of gross negligence, which resulted in the death of his 20-year-old stepdaughter, Penelope.

Melbourne Pratt, the prominent CEO of a pharmaceutical company he moved to Atlanta only five years prior, found it hard to accept that his daughter died of a massive heart attack after taking an overdose of pure cocaine and OxyContin.

Normally, this should have been an open and shut case of drug use going bad. Pratt, however, was a powerful force in need of someone to blame when the media made a big deal of his daughter's demise. The hospital's covey of attorneys, basically, abandoned Dr. Martin to fend off the sharks on her own. Their scurrilous, hands-off behavior soon took shape. Clearly, there were conflicted interests because Pratt Vista Pharmaceuticals was hip-deep in negotiating long-term medical research grants and joint ventures with the administration.

All they had to do to solidify the deal…leave one of their own swinging in the breeze. Sabrina Martin would be the latest casualty if her malpractice insurance failed to soothe Pratt's righteous indignation. The hospital need not suffer because the deal with Pratt's company could be worth over one-hundred million dollars. That was certainly worth more than Dr. Martin's reputation. The eyes of top executives were swimming in green glory. The hospital board's unstated position that she be sacrificed to the wolves, paled in comparison to the many patients who would benefit from this unholy association. The small people, and their professional integrity, quickly lose value on the market in such treacherous arenas, but Keith Williams did not abandon his responsibilities to this client.

Although this arena rested outside his usual discipline, Keith Williams vowed to rescue her from the savages threatening to ruin her career. The African American attorney retained the services of a reputable medical malpractice lawyer and colleague as part of his strategy to offset his own lack of medical knowledge. Like Keith Williams, Attorney Pamela Leach was a brilliant strategist; more than just a helpful sounding board.

Williams went on the defensive by obtaining expert testimony concerning appropriate procedures from the co-counsel, who also directed him to question uninvolved professionals.

It did not stop there, however. In fact, a great degree of scandal lay wait as this case developed a unique shade of ugliness that was all its own.

Attorney Keith Williams gained valuable insight from former employees of the Pratt household staff, who claimed that Penelope Pratt had been abusing cocaine and a number of other drugs for at least two years prior to her highly publicized death. The testimony of one such person was allowed in this case because the former housekeeper left Pratt's employ of her own volition. Helena Cruz would also attest that Penelope obtained the drugs from the private stash her stepfather kept at his home, not from the party she was attending when she grew ill and collapsed.

Under oath, Pratt's former house cleaner, testified that she had seen Penelope doing lines of the drug from a mirror on the nightstand. Shockingly, she had accidentally walked in on Penelope while in bed with her own stepfather. It was an extremely unpleasant scene.

Pratt fired Helena for the intrusion, but rehired her one week later, with a small addition to her salary. Though warned to keep quiet about the inappropriate relationship and drugs, Helena Cruz did not stay on very long. She testified on behalf of the defense for several reasons. The most prominent of which was that she did not want the suffering of an innocent person on her conscience just so she could keep working for a dishonest tyrant. Helena, a deeply religious woman, viewed their relationship as sinfully unnatural. She believed it to be the overall factor in the deeply troubled girl's drug addiction and manic behaviorism. It all made perfect sense as to why Pratt's ex-wife suddenly left him and, seemingly, abandoned her own biological daughter. Apparently, there was much more to the breakup.

Then there was the fact that Sabrina Martin saved the life of Helena Cruz's only nephew after his appendix ruptured and became septic. Helena Cruz and her sister, Anna Esposito, who was fired from the domestic staff by Pratt for missing days when her child was sick, put it before God. Anna Esposito and her husband used the fortuitous money from a modest lottery winning to start a landscaping and domestic cleaning business. Anna readily secured a place for Helena at her side by the time Sabrina Martin faced Pratt's wrath.

Melbourne Pratt secretly acquired about a half kilo of cocaine from his pharmaceutical company, using an inert filler to doctor the remainder so there would be no discrepancy because the FDA's Office of Pharmaceutical Quality is very strict regarding this controlled substance. With the help of a few faithful employees, he could be very creative when it came to the books and the appearance of strict quality standards.

Things got nasty for Pratt during the hearings. With his indiscretions staring them squarely in the face, the hospital's staff of attorneys rallied behind Dr. Martin, but their traitorous devotion was summarily spurned. With the assistance of an excellent co-counsel, Keith Williams had become the heart and soul of Dr. Sabrina Martin's defense, something they all came to regret.

Pratt's life suddenly went to pot. Grady Memorial Hospital suspended its interests in Pratt Vista Pharmaceuticals. When his home and apartment were searched, he was arrested for embezzlement and the possession of an excessive amount of a controlled substance. In less than a week, the investors of Pratt Vista Pharmaceuticals began to pull out, while the board members scrambled to save the company from the tarnished reputation of its owner. Melbourne Pratt was ruined, but he was granted a substantial bail following the filing of formal charges. He used his time wisely, some would say, taking the easy way out by committing suicide.

Keith and Sabrina had spent countless hours together while working on her defense, a very emotional time for her having been abandoned by all others. Her stifled tears touched him somewhere deeper than he had been touched before. It was at this point that Keith tried to convince himself that theirs was strictly a professional relationship and should remain as such.

Sabrina Martin, no ordinary damsel in distress, was definitely a fighter that vowed to stand on her own through it all. Not even her powerful father was involved in her battle. Keith grew to admire the woman's moments of courage, feeling just as deeply for her in times of overwhelming melancholy and self-doubt.

When they worked together, with co-counsel present, there were no problems to speak of. However, when the threat of them being left alone arose, there grew a quiet, slightly noticeable uneasiness between them. It was not crafted from fear or intimidation, but a sort of unevolved sexual tension. Pamela Leach, the co-counsel of the defense noticed it. When the moment was right, and Pamela just could not seem to help herself, she even hinted as much. It was something they all laughed about, but the not-so-subtle hint helped it to evolve into something a bit more recognizable.

Once Keith Williams had gotten the goods on Melbourne Pratt, he felt free to investigate the hospital's motives, discovering the real reasons behind the administration's uncharacteristic behavior. When all the pieces of the puzzle had come together, Keith Williams made it so that Dr. Martin would be virtually untouchable. She could have sued her hospital and retired if she had so chosen, but being able to continue practicing medicine was enough for her. Keith's strategy in this case was nothing less than genius.

Dr. Sabrina Martin admonished the Pratt Vista board of directors to continue negotiations with Grady Memorial Hospital, transforming the damsel in distress into an instant hero. She was handsomely rewarded for being a virtual saint when she had them all by the tender, swollen plums.

In the end, however, Keith Williams and Dr. Martin took no pleasure in the tragedies of the Pratt family, even though the man had been sludge. The ugly affair was over, and something beautiful had been born within its flames.

Sabrina and her friendly co-workers held a surprise appreciation party for attorneys Keith Williams and Pamela Leach in the ballroom of the Atlanta Hilton. In the stroke of one bold moment, she asked him to dance and they were great together. When the music slowed, they continued to sway through the night with their eyes locked in an unbreakable gaze. The seed of balanced chemistry was sown and watered between their smiles…the blushing…body heat.

They dated secretly for nearly two months before either could admit that they were falling in love. In the beginning, Sabrina was self-conscious and somewhat apprehensive about the direction in which their relationship headed. As circumstance would have it, she made love to him one stormy night in a moment that was too powerful to resist. They stayed together for three days, making love throughout, while constructing an emotional and sexual bond that drove them to the edge of total exhaustion.

Were it not for Pamela Leach's off-cuff and very unprofessional remark, mutual respect and sexual tension may not have evolved into something that could grow to become love.

With the passage of time, Sabrina discarded her inhibitions. She no longer worried about who might notice them holding hands or kissing. Keith, on the other hand, had given great thought to their actions in public. He loved her and enjoyed expressing his affections, no matter where they were. Yet, his logic dulled only temporarily. As professionals living in the mid-90s, he was certain that they were inviting unforeseen problems down the road.

Keith sat Sabrina down one night for a serious talk to examine the possible pitfalls of leaving their relationship open to public scrutiny. He even brought up her father's possible reaction to the love affair, and that of stuffed shirt conservatives in her hospital administration. He mentioned his own law firm. Williams talked about how people always swore that they were not prejudiced or against interracial relationships, until one of their own brought home someone of the opposite race.

Dr. Sabrina Martin—the woman—was confused and upset, but Keith finally convinced her that he was neither unhappy nor ashamed to be with her. She would soon realize that he was just trying to save them both some unnecessary grief by suggesting that they exercise a reasonable measure of discretion.

Exactly one week later, Sabrina Martin got the gist of what her lover was implying when they had a run-in with an ex-boyfriend and his sidekick at a popular nightclub. The couple had a few drinks that night and Sabrina was feeling a bit frisky. They were unaware that her long forgotten ex-boyfriend was watching when she kissed Keith's neck and grabbed his ass as they left the dance floor. This behavior did not sit well with a guy she stopped seeing after only a few months because of his dishonesty and extreme jealousy.

The two comrades approached the couple's table and caused trouble. Words and then blows exchanged.

Keith held his own until two bouncers stepped in to trounce his assailants. After the pounding, Sabrina's ex-boyfriend and his sidekick were expelled into the waiting arms of the police. As it would later turn out, they got their asses kicked again before arriving at the jail. The two officers happened to be African American, and they never pulled their punches when the 'N' word was used in excess.

Before leaving the club, Sabrina was wiping some blood from Keith's mouth and looking at an eye that was sure to shine the next day. Then an attractive African American woman approached. Teesha Mathews dated Keith for nearly six months, ending right around the time he assumed Sabrina's defense.

Teesha walked slowly around Keith, tracing his tender jawbone with a long, manicured fingernail. All the while, this woman stared directly into Sabrina's eyes with a cunning smile etched upon her face.

The curvaceous female cooed, "Poor, poor guy. Is this why you kicked me to the curb? Oh, Keith, I had no idea you liked white meat. Had I known, baby, I would have cooked you a breast...not short thighs." She smiled and walked away. Keith and Sabrina looked at each other, wordlessly.

When they got back to Sabrina's place, she told him that his reason for wanting to exercise caution had suddenly become much clearer to her. Since then, they agreed to restrain themselves, even though there were bound to be times when passion would overwhelm them just enough to dismiss the world. Because neither accepted that they were being forced to live in a vacuum, they went on to be very happy with one another.

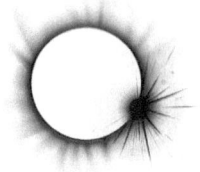

Chapter 7

IN THE HOUSE OF PAIN

The trees and grasslands are ripe, abounding with new life. To the left and right, a multitude of colorful birds go about the business of foraging and nest building, while gray squirrels play swift games of chase. Listening for the sound of dogs packing, a herd of whitetail deer pause their grazing at the woodland's edge to watch the vehicles pass. Ordinarily, they only feed at night and lay during the day. This large herd, however, knows, instinctively, that hunting season is closed. The distant sounds of barking dogs gives cause for no alarm because even the youngest of the herd know them to be stationary.

Throughout the day, with and without police escorts, 33 limousines, limo vans, and private automobiles have been traveling this quiet, winding, country road.

Upon arrival at their destination, the cars park on a vacant lawn or along the lengthy semicircular driveway of a longstanding, southern mansion, which boasts huge pillars and picturesque windows.

This is the majestic home of Ezra Theodore Krantz, the Imperial Wizard of the Ku Klux Klan. His is a grand place, with high ceilings and chandeliers. The ballroom is vast and the billiard tables date back to the mid-1800s. This is a place of very old money, though suffused with an underlying hint of decay.

The passengers and chauffeurs are all Klan. They will not tolerate outsiders here. Well-armed groups of men regularly patrol the grounds of the estate to make sure that no prying eyes intrude upon this meeting.

Nearly 120 men will get out of the seemingly endless wave of automobiles. These people have taken great pains to make this trip without the news hounds trailing, wearing black hoods to protect their identities even though their transports are heavily tinted. The Ku Klux Klan's paranoia even dictates that the mansion is swept for listening devices before and during the gathering. They will find no spy devices, of course. Once inside the mansion, the guests are ushered to the great hall.

At the rear of Krantz's home, a white utility van parks near the service entrance. Inside are two tightly bound, blindfolded, terrified men. Dragged from the bowels of the truck kicking and screaming into gags, their muted pleas for mercy are ignored. Unseen men haul them inside and toss them to the floor of an old food locker.

The air in here is stale, dank. It hints of rust and rotting flesh. The blindfolds remain. From somewhere inside this black prison comes a drip in perfect tempo that will drive them insane with thirst. Because they have been bound on the floor of that van for untold hours without food or water, the drip, drip, drip is maddening.

During the long ride from the West Coast, these wretches urinated on themselves. Somewhere along the way, one of them defecated on himself, mistaking a slamming door for a gunshot to the head.

Exhausted and disheartened, having given up on freeing the bonds, they lay huddled together as that sinking feeling embeds within. Since they have been confined together for nearly forty-eight hours, the fact that they are about to die in what some will see as a fitting end really begins to crown like the blooming sunrise.

Robert James Smith, soon-to-be a former Klan member, slumps by Kenny Andrews—his African American lover.

Robert Smith joined the sacred order at age eighteen. As he now lay on the dark floor, it seems a lifetime ago. Like many of his peers, he was a homophobic gay-basher.

After enjoying ten years of glorious white supremacy, he is arrested for lynching—assaulting gays. An extremely sympathetic, very understanding judge turns Robert Smith loose on society once more. Placed on two years of probation, Judge Mercy stipulates psychotherapy as a nonnegotiable term of his rather lenient sentencing. However, Judge Mercy's leniency has nothing to do with Ku Klux Klan pressure or affiliation. Rather, his leniency in such a serious matter as lynching holds motives that are even more nefarious.

Robert Smith's homosexual therapist convinces the new patient to explore the realms of his obsession with gay men as an integral part of his treatment. Repulsed by the idea, Smith barks like a rabid dog, but his therapist is a calm, soft-spoken man with the authority to have this

Neanderthal tossed back into jail. He is forced to comply, though the choice is his to make since all tough guys claim that they can do two years inside while standing on their head.

Much to his disorienting dismay, Smith comes to realize that he could be bi-sexual. He is convinced, rather, by Cordell Patterson that he is gay and has been fighting his homosexuality by participating in the brutal rituals of the Ku Klux Klan. In many ways, when it comes to treating gay-bashers, the narcissistic therapist is nearly as sociopathic as the Klan. He is convinced that a mind as weak as Smith's is a danger in the hands of evil, white supremacists.

Patterson is simply remolding a pliable bit of wet clay into someone's docile plaything, instead of a hired thug. It is nothing more than a sick, twisted little game to the therapist because a weak mind is a true narcissist's favorite playground. Patterson and Judge Mercy have been friends, among other things, for many years. They absolutely love it when a former knuckle-dragging gay-basher thanks them for turning their lives around before prancing off into the sunset with new friends and attitudes.

Robert Smith meets Kenny Andrews on a fact-finding exploration at a gay establishment in San Francisco, accompanied there by his shrink, of course. Smith makes the astonishing discovery that he really has no reason to hate African Americans when Kenny Andrews turns out to be a very interesting, masculine man—even sexy in a way. With every passing second of their interactions, entire worlds of possibilities open to Robert Smith.

Over a short period, Kenny helps Robert over his fears and shows him the art of their special kind of love.

Once again, the therapist successfully uses his job to take revenge on the type of bully that tormented him throughout life.

For several years, Robert Smith fulfills his duties as a member of the Klan. Eventually, Kenny Andrews decides that he will no longer continue a relationship with a hypocrite, so he lays down ultimatums. If Robert does not cease participation in Ku Klux Klan activity, they are done. No matter what his lifestyle, Kenny Andrews still has his pride. He will turn his back on the things Robert does to other Blacks and gays no longer.

Bordering on panic, an intense fear of losing his first gay lover prompts Robert to drop out of sight, but he is sought out, eventually, because the Klan looks after its own. Because membership is a lifetime commitment, changing names and moving in with Kenny turns out to be a woefully inadequate answer.

Once the Klan tracks Robert Smith down, his immediate superior has him watched, reporting the disturbingly despicable findings to the hive. For days, they both experience an inexplicable feeling of being watched. One night, when masked men break down the doors and smash in windows, Smith formally renounces his status in the organization. There is little choice, after he is caught bare-assed with a Black man. Smith is a top member of the mid-hierarchy of the West Coast division, and this disgraceful behavior cannot go unchecked; he knows things. Robert Smith is tagged and bagged. They kidnap him and his Negro lover to put them down for good.

Smith wakes in a pool of oily sweat after reliving the night before last with vibrant details. His fall from grace will not be an entire waste, however. Their deaths will be tools of initiation for the two new pledges, Coburn Eaton and Gerard Thomas. The former of the two is an attaché to the Vice-President, and the latter is a member of the White House staff. The secret service and the FBI have investigated both intensely before interning, but they came up as clean as the driven snow. Nothing in their past connects them to the Ku Klux Klan. Ezra Krantz and his people are shrewd, if not a bit melodramatic.

ତ୍ୟ

Because he can stand very little light, Krantz's bedroom remains dimly lit. An array of monitoring equipment litters the chamber. Oxygen tanks, medication, and yards of tubing clash with the décor of the room.

With his time near, Ezra feels he must draw the future taut, and deal with it decisively. The doctors' medications and many treatments have failed to arrest the aggressive cancer. Like pure hatred, it eats up this great man from inside out. Even in the feverish latter days of his life, he still radiates with loathing. This will be a suitable end for a man who has engineered the violent deaths of many, those deemed hedonistic and godless. Coloreds, Jews, chinks, wetbacks, and homosexuals are certainly not of Ezra Krantz's God.

His words will reach the gathering in the great hall by way of a video camera positioned at the foot of his urine-stained rice bed. The men who came to hear him speak for the last time will be watching two large television sets at either side of the stage.

Though he will not be convinced of it even to save his mortal soul—ever so close to death's door—Krantz and his kind are an ulcerous blight on humanity. His body and soul—his very life—are a sickness, tempered with the callous convictions of the collectively self-righteous. Whether it is here or in the Middle East, the worst forms of killers are those who do so in the name of God.

Since his induction into the Klan as a mere boy of thirteen, Krantz married death and found many new applications. He grew up willing to spit in the eyes of anyone presuming to judge his brutal methods, so his insatiable zeal for murder catapulted him through the ranks of the secret organization.

Ezra T. Krantz represents the old facet of the Klan. The brutal, cross burning, in your face... murderous type. Back in the good old days, on horseback, and in trucks, he led countless raids on the innocent. They dragged men, pregnant women, babies, and even preachers from their homes during the witching hours to slaughter them. Often, their victims were simply beaten to death; they were considered the luckiest ones. If not whipped into total oblivion, they were raped, hung, crucified, and even burned alive.

Nevertheless, Ezra's personal favorite was the hunt. His kind enjoyed hunting other human beings, and reputed themselves as quite the sportsmen. His kind showed very little regard for the law because, for all practical purposes, they were the law in Mississippi. There was less need to exercise discretion then. Yet, the time came to do so within the accord of God's unchallenged will.

Krantz recruited young, up-and-coming, politically minded family men in the late 1960s. Young men such as Jud Martin and Peter Black, already members of the Klan, were brought into the upper crust as future leaders. They were the boys of new blood, who practically worshiped Krantz for the warped powers they were granted. Great changes were coming. Years later, Jud Martin and Peter Black became the brain trust of the new, upwardly mobile, politically motivated Ku Klux Klan.

Even though representatives of the Klan interests have always been entrenched within American government, the secret society unified under the jurisdiction of Martin and Black. Nevertheless, they are extremely insulated from scrutiny because Krantz remains the standing and absolute figurehead. Behind the scenes, Martin and Black built this organization into one huge shadow monster. Its theme, riddled by secret agendas, bloomed with Krantz's powerful influence backing them.

All of his cruel life, Ezra Krantz has known nothing more sacred on this earth than the preservation of the White man's way of life and purity of his bloodline. Little else matters. The greatest of their tools is sixth of the Ten Commandments, but they consider killing to be a sin only when it is committed by the heathen masses. He wielded death like Moses his staff. His ideal world—the United States of America—is the promised land.

For decades, he watched and nurtured the Klan's budding flowers, as their plans grew closer to fruition. There are few private sector organizations, or government agencies, of import, they have not infiltrated. Having steadfast members holding key positions in the Federal Bureau of Investigation greatly facilitated their goals. Their moles dug in to wreak havoc on lives and mentalities from the shadows, building racism within harmonious establishments throughout the nation by using dirty tactics and deadly subterfuge.

Jud Martin has no close second nipping at his heels for the gubernatorial seat in Jackson City, Mississippi. He is Krantz's personal favorite as successor to the helm of the darker realm. These two men share a special bond; both murdered their own wives in fits of rage.

Peter Black and many more have been groomed for election to the U.S. Senate and the House of Representatives with very little fuss. They are both Democrats and Republicans, buried deep in Washington and getting deeper. Ezra Krantz's political delusion takes the boys of new blood all the way to the White House and the United States presidency.

In the here and now, their political platform is constructed like an inverted funnel. With the power base welded in place, it will be the corridor, through which Judson Martin will travel, virtually, unimpeded. Behind closed doors, his new title will be the Supreme Imperial Wizard of the Ku Klux Klan. All of the steps they have taken and their attention to the smallest details are born of sheer maniacal brilliance.

Such things explain why these men have come to this meeting with the great one under cloak. Secrecy must prevail. In this death machine, a loose tongue, for fear of having it lopped off, betrays no one.

These are powerfully serious men, who are going about God's work in a country overrun with undesirables. Their twisted dream is a country without Blacks, Mexicans, Orientals, Jews, or the sexually deviant. Of course, it is beyond their scope to acknowledge any flaw in the plan. They are quite certain that no one could stop them once the government is theirs to control. Only a few master players are missing from their true position on the board.

A procession of six walks into the great living tomb, the place where Ezra Krantz will draw and expel his final breath. Jud Martin and Peter Black lead the others. The last to enter are Eaton and Thomas, the new inductees. The latter two are filled with awe as each man kneels to kiss Ezra Krantz's ring. They are standing in the presence of unique greatness, even in this advanced state of deterioration

Through Martin and Black, Ezra T. Krantz rebuilt and remodeled the KKK into a thinking man's machine. To great degrees, he curtailed its outwardly brutal nature, but from within, it is still a sadistic killing machine. The Klan is spreading upward and outward in rural and urban society. From Klan love comes unbelievable hatred, and an escalating level of hatred is bred into the masses with each of its offspring being more formidable than the previous.

Six more men enter, wearing the traditional headdress. Likewise, they kneel to kiss the ring. They are figureheads known as Grand Dragons, who supervise the six divisional regions that now dissect the country. The Klan is no longer run on a state-to-state or Klavern-to-Klavern basis.

Benjamin Seals is a respected politician and business executive. He resides over the Pacific Coast region from the state of Washington to southern California, where he lives. Seals has a strong dislike for the wayward lifestyle of homosexuals, vowing to eradicate them from his home state. Why stop there?

Among other things, Seals is directly responsible for the following of those who wish to see Affirmative Action banished from all political agendas. His role is played in covetous secrecy because his feigned open-mindedness toward minorities and immigrants is too well rooted to expose his true intentions. Therefore, from where he stands in the shadows, Seals makes certain that all necessary components for the removal of Affirmative Action are in place. Others will have to brave the racial arena to either become the public enemy of minorities, who would surely fight back, or become the moral heroes of the oppressed White populous of their fair state. Seals never doubted the success of his pet project, content to savor his creation from afar.

Christian Moore reigns over the regions between Arizona, Nevada, Wyoming, and Colorado.

Aldan Banes is the Grand Dragon of the region encompassing Texas and Kansas, all the way to Missouri. He is an oil man.

Joe Mills is ex-army and a paramilitary survivalist, whose heels are dug in from Idaho, Montana, and the Dakotas all the way to Wisconsin.

Michael E. Lee controls the northeast region from Maine to Michigan, New York to Ohio, and Pennsylvania.

Last, but not least, there comes the Grand Dragon of the old South. He is slightly younger than the others, but his reign of terror is never dwarfed by any of them. His domain consists of the region from Arkansas and Louisiana to Florida. He rules from Kentucky to the Virginias, the Carolinas, and his native Georgia. Known in their circles by many as the Patriot of the South, his name is Willard St. John.

There are two classes of Klansmen. One has a lot of blood on his hands. The other is the man who pulls the strings that pulls the fingers on the triggers. Seals, Martin and Black are the latter.

Killing someone is the last rite of passage into the secret organization. One can no longer become a member without the sort of trust such an act instills.

Seals ordered the kidnapping of Smith and Andrews for just such an occasion. Theirs will be a very ceremonious death in the finest of Klan fashion.

Seals, Martin, and Black dreamed up the scenario labeled *Operation Ferret*. Years ago, they groomed and perpetuated an up-and-coming to do great damage to the Justice Department's surveillance of the Klan's political activities and hierarchical arrangements. Most people figure the Ku Klux Klan to be essentially dead in the political world, but some have to be convinced to look elsewhere for skeletons. This is where David Duke, the Klan's lamb for the slaughter, enters the scene. Duke's political career is sacrifice for the greater good of the masses.

The plan seemed simple, but it was very complex. One man and his organization drew all the spies and insubordinates into the great wide open for observation. There was no better candidate for this job than Duke, hot on the political trail, while gaining support outside of all that was going on underneath. His ridiculous pursuit of the presidency served to be the most powerful kind of bait any angler could ever have hoped to invent.

Ezra Krantz had taken a personal liking to David Duke, but insisted that his political demise would be for the greater good of the hive. It would be remiss, however, to imply that Duke took this role willingly and just bent over for the reaming he was about to receive. He did not like the idea at first. He was convinced in due time, seduced, more or less, by the martyrdom of it all.

For a period, Duke had to be excommunicated so others could be insulated from what he was sent out to do. He holds to the promised reactivation, with even greater standing when the presidency is attained. The total pageantry was much too dazzling to resist.

The plan worked even better than expected. So much attention was given to the diversionary Duke campaign that many more operatives than originally planned were elected to respective seats in both houses of Congress. This was achieved by having those politicians join in the frenzied attack on Duke and his kind. In a sense, David Duke became their platform beneath the platform.

Absorbing a wealth of media attention, David Duke was the wounded decoy. He floundered like living chum in the political ocean, making waves and attracting sharks of all manners. The feeding frenzy had begun in very muddy waters.

What some of the sharks did not know was that there were pods of Orca swimming beneath the bloody currents. The inlet to the heart of this country had become the mouth of the Klan's corridor and the killer whales were heading upriver.

By the time the silt settled back on the bottom, even the president's personal physician was in the Klan's back pocket. Men such as the good doctor and many others within and without the realms of government were victims of subtle and diabolical persuasions. If they stood perched atop the racial fence, they were rudely nudged from the comfort zone by the convenient death or immutable damage done to a very close loved one.

Terrible crimes were blamed on unsuspecting African American men, many of whom were imprisoned for rape or murder having never laid eyes on their alleged victims. Sad but true, the Klan often went that far to bring someone over to their way of thinking without them ever knowing that innocent people were the accused.

It was of no consequence to *Operation Ferret* when Bill Clinton ousted the Bush/Quayle duo. It was the same game with different names. In fact, it was much easier to discredit Clinton, who stayed immersed in one controversy after another. The Klan had implemented the White Water investigation and the Flowers sex scandal only months into Bill Clinton's Presidency.

For all his trials and efforts, the Imperial Wizard can finally see daylight at the end of this dark, brooding tunnel. What he sees is a quite beautiful land of freedom.

Fresh off the campaign trail, Ezra's protégé holds steadily increasing numbers as the GOP frontrunner. Governor Martin's numbers are soaring after trouncing his opponents during televised debates where issues of equal rights, foreign policy, job creation, and education, are raised. Like a sinking ship, Kansas Senator Robert Dole, who is not of the hive, is losing ground when he slips below 30%. Governor Judson Martin, arising as the champion of humanity, holds the lion's share in the polls.

Ezra Theodore Krantz will truly let his people go during the upcoming 1996 Presidential Election. As a sign of their exodus, once again, African American churches will burn in the night.

෬෬

Kenneth Andrews lies quivering in the darkness, hating that taunting drip. Kenny could tell by the sound of Robert's breathing that he has fallen asleep. He figures that Robert Smith must have made his peace with God, but there is not enough peace in the world for him. Not even in exhaustion.

He thinks of the things he used to say as a young, San Franciscan street punk, all tough and full of himself. It was during the time before the gay preacher came into his life to save him from the certainty of a violent death on the street scene. Kenneth Andrews recalls regaling the younger boys by saying things like, "I ain't going out like no sucker with my eyes closed. I want to see death coming because I might just get the chance to duck."

Kenny's body is racked by cramps, and his paralyzed mind is stuck on the dripping water. It rings aloud, a mockery of his impending doom. Repeatedly, it echoes that he will get to see death coming, but he will never get the chance to duck.

You will die…drip…because of him…drip…because of what you are!

In the darkness, Kenny Andrews weeps like a scolded child badly in need of a preacher.

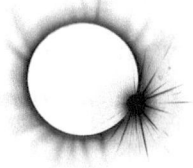

Chapter 8

THE SHAME

In her dead son's car, the distraught woman secretly travels seventy-seven miles southeast of Atlanta to a minuscule, backwater town called Thorny Bend. Mrs. Brown only spends enough time there to ask some very reluctant locals for directions.

One of the country folk, the only one that acknowledges Teresa Brown's presence, is Jasper Downs. The old man's hairy ears twitch when he hears her inquiry over his left shoulder. The silent neighbor shakes her head and hurries off. He nicks an index finger with the gutting knife, before tossing another bloody head to the stray cats. After shooing the flies from his face, he rinses the gutted fish in an old bread pan. As the silvery, scaly water swirls, he considers the woman he is yet to lay eyes on.

Jasper's sight may not be what it once was, but his hearing is just fine. He turns to look at her with his good right eye to warn, "Ain't none them gonna spoke on it, gal. May well turn round. Turn round and leave these ya parts. Never look back!"

"Please, sir, if you know anything…" she begins to plead.

Her sobs and tears threaten to touch the milky, timeworn eyes that still lead to the kindly heart of an old country cuss of a man. When he turns up his last sip and tosses the empty bottle in the trash, they both seem to have something in common; a need for something only the other can provide.

Soon, she pushes the Sentra along a rugged gravel road, ignoring the weeds scraping against the car's undercarriage as she mows them over.

The steering wheel jerks about in her sweaty hands, pitching back and forth because the low profile tires wrap around oversized chrome rims that jut from the wheel wells. The car's belly is low, and TJ Brown would cringe in his grave if he could see what his mother is doing to his dream machine.

With her vision fixed, she pays no heed to the swamp rabbits fleeing a rampaging auto that threatens to mangle them on a road that seems to run on forever.

Mrs. Teresa Brown finally stops when she bursts through a thick stand of shrubbery at the edge of a thriving swampland. The entire world seems darker here. When she gets out of the car, assaulted by the eerie silence that envelops this place, a shiver seizes her aching spine.

She marches toward a short, rickety dock, which stands vigilantly over a somber pool of blackish water. Tiny ripples near the cattails prove that there is life within its murky depth. She does not realize that two sets of eyes are upon her at this very moment.

An old wooden boat, tied to the end of the rickety dock, floats lazily in a warm breeze that whispers things to her mind. The pointed bow is lower from a leak or collected rainwater that now spawns green algae.

Seconds later, someone brushes against the stranger from behind. She cries out, nearly falling into the water as she turns on the stalker. The silhouetted shadow of a huge man blots out the sunlight. When he grabs her by the arm, she struggles fiercely. Teresa Brown screams, flailing with those vengeful fingernails slashing at the assailant's face!

When Teresa Brown gouges a groove into his cheek, he yelps and backs away. His gnarled left hand draws away from his face with a sliver of red upon the palm to prove that she has drawn blood. He whimpers, looking at Mrs. Brown with watery, simple eyes that prove he is unsure of what will happen next.

Mrs. Brown listens to his shy voice, no longer feeling threatened when she looks at the shy face of the simpleton that just saved her life; only, she does not know it yet.

His thick, quivering lips, sloping brow, and those hurtful eyes suggest that he is probably harmless.

She lowers her claws and breathes a sigh of relief when he whimpers, "I mean you no harm." Now he whispers, apologetically, "But you was gettin' too close to the water. There be a big ole gator in yonder. See. He is right down there, just waiting for you to take one or two more steps. And if you stand with your back to it much longer, he's comin' lightnin' quick for you, lady."

She looks back, squinting to see anything in the murky pool. When she sees those lustful, greenish eyes staring up at her, Teresa Brown shrieks, high stepping away.

As her heart pounds in her chest, she says, "Thank you so much, sir."

"Buster."

"What?"

"My name…Buster."

"Thank you, Buster. I'm very sorry for scratching your face, but you really scared the living hell out of me," she says. "Does it…does it hurt?"

He averts those eyes and shakes his head. "No, it's just a scratch."

"God, I'm so sorry," she says as he removes a dingy looking rag to wipe the trickle of blood from his face. She stops him, fearing that he will get an infection from that filthy looking thing. She takes a few clean napkins from her heavy purse, offering them to him.

He smiles, forgiving her quickly. "We should move away from the water just a little more. Old Malice is big, but lightning fast when he is hungry. You come to see her?" He points at a trail along the water's edge that disappears within the trees of the swamp. "You come here to see the witch lady?"

Mrs. Brown nods. "Yes. Can you take me to her, Buster?"

"She sent me here 'cause she knowed somebody was comin' here today. That be you, lady. Follow me."

Teresa Brown places the long straps of the dark blue purse over her right shoulder to keep it secure. He offers her a hand, expecting the usual hesitation in taking it. She does, following him down a trail that winds through wicked brambles and moss-laden trees. They walk in utter silence where only a wailing wind rises to rustle the leaves and vines from time to time.

Buster, hunched over slightly, and dragging a deformed foot, guides her along the path with uncanny grace. His movement is fluent, effortlessly winding with the path. He seems to know where every limb protrudes, barely disturbing the leaves as he goes. She willingly follows, dipping and weaving as he does without hesitancy. Although her pounding heart races at times, Teresa Brown is on a mission of a singular focus, searching for something of vengeance within this stagnant void.

Buster slows to a stop near a very large tree. He peers around the trunk before turning to whisper a warning. "We have to move real slow now. Please don't make no sudden movements, and don't talk. Walk real soft like." Buster places a finger over his cleft lip. "Shh."

She is afraid. In a frantic whisper, Mrs. Brown asks, "What is it, Buster? What's around this tree?"

He whispers, "Bees that make sweet syrup. They are real mean, and don't much like people in their territory. They are always watching, so do not raise your hands at them because at least one or two will come look into your eyes to smell your soul. They know me, but they don't like no strangers. Please remember, when the guardians come, don't move. Do not raise your hands at them. Please don't move, okay? They already know we're here, looking at us right now."

She nods her head and tightens her grip on his large hand. He turns and leads her one cautious step at a time. When she finally clears the tree, she looks to the right. What she sees causes her breath to linger in her lungs.

The nest of Africanized honeybees is massive, exploding from the gutted hollow of an aged tree from the ground to the upper trunk. There are enough limbs with leaves to suggest that the tree is very much alive and thriving. It is now that she feels a subtle tremor through the soft rubber soles as the buzzing vibrates the entire root system below. A relatively small number of drones, thousands of them, hover about the visible part of a honeycomb that continues down into the ground by at least a yard. The old tree stands alone on a piece of raised land. To the far right of the tree, a few yards away, lies the rotting skeletal remains of a black bear cub. It had strayed from its mother's side, and hunger for the sweet honey was its painful undoing.

Buster halts when Teresa Brown squeezes down with both her hands, no longer moving with him. He does not turn to look, listening as their beating wings cause his left ear to contract. As three of the guardian bees hover merely inches before the woman's eyes, he whispers, "Please. Please remember, don't do nothing, lady. No noise. Don't let go of my hand."

Seconds later, the intimidators move aside, hovering in the clearing between her and the nest. She closes her eyes and fights back tears. When Buster hears them move to the side—still very close—her grip begins to loosen just a bit.

"Oh, God," she whimpers.

"Are you ready now?" he asks, still looking forward. "It's almost over, just take one step at a time with me."

She moves, afraid to look at them as they adjust to keep eyes on her. She is sweating profusely by the time she is out of the clearing between the large, mossy trees. Once safe, she nearly drops to her knees, but Buster resumes a quicker pace.

Soon, they arrive at an area where the water has cut a swathe through the raised ditch bank. Buster pauses, breathing harder as his eyes search back and forth. He seems too cautious, looking at the seemingly shallow water to the right. He shakes his head as he searches the swathe from right to left.

"What is it, Buster?" she asks. "It's not that far, I can easily leap across if you're worrying about me."

Buster shakes his head again, backing away from the three-foot wide cut as if to get a running start. He tries to shake her hand off, but she does not release him. When he looks her in the eyes and removes her hand from his, she is confused.

"What is it?" she asks again. Teresa Brown moves back a few steps.

When she starts to leap across, Buster shouts, "No!" His powerful right hand clamps down like a vice on her right bicep. She yelps as her feet suddenly kick out in front of her, and she suddenly crashes on her back. Buster quickly drags her away before helping her up.

He steadies her on her feet and apologizes. "I'm sorry. I'm sorry. Just watch. Watch!"

Buster takes one of three sharpened sapling trunks from the ground on this side. He holds her back as he tips the eight-foot trunk into the trench, steadying its weight with his crippled arm. When he stabs at the dark water to the left, nothing happens. He moves the limb a few yards to the right before driving it into the murky water again. When the water writhes into life, and the gator's jaws clamp down to snap the four-inch wide tree limb like kindling, Teresa Brown shrieks.

Buster continues to jab into the swathe until the twelve-foot predator propels itself forward with a couple violent thrusts of its powerful tail.

The huge man looks at the terrified woman from the city and smiles, triumphantly. He takes the other two sharpened limbs, jamming them into place at either end of the trench. Now he lays claim to a couple vine covered, but sturdy, two-by-eights and lays them across the harmless looking divide as a makeshift plank to cross safely. From the other side, he takes two of the sharpened tree trunks and crisscrosses them with the ones he has already jammed into place.

She is tentative about crossing now that she knows this is an ambush point, but Buster reassures by saying, "I gots you. It be safe now, lady. See, he can't come back in without me seeing him now. Come on cross." He steps hallway and reaches for her hand.

Moments later, they finally come upon an old shack perched at the water's edge where its creaking boards seem to spite gravity by refusing to sag into the black, landlocked sea. A steady pillar of smoke escapes its chimney, and she can tell from where she stands that the windows do not suffer prying eyes.

Near the water's edge, a long fishing cane leans against an ugly oak tree to the right of the shack. The oak's fantastic limbs are thrust to-and-fro, radiating from its ugly trunk like crooked fingers where ancient moss vines flourish. Those gray coils dangle freely, fluttering with the breeze like tinsel on a dead Christmas tree. From one of those limbs hang the half-skinned carcass of a rabbit and an unfortunate opossum. Tufts of fur whisk about the earth in the throes of tiny dust devils, causing the ground to move in her eyes. Strangely, there are no flies hovering about, not even one.

Buster knows this stranger is overwhelmed by fear. The seekers always are. Many will rush upon his heels in search of that evil thing for which they are willing to sacrifice much, but they all recoil when they enter this clearing.

He pauses and looks at TJ Brown's mother with his muddy, brown eyes to say, "Are you sure you want to go in there, lady? She knowed you was comin'. Are you sure all the way to God Almighty?" Discreetly suggesting she leave, pointing at the path from which they emerged, Buster is begging her with his eyes to flee this place.

Teresa Brown shivers when cold, invisible hands caress her body, freezing the thin layer of sweat on her skin for an instant.

"Yes…yes…I'm sure."

After Buster knocks lightly and opens the door, the smell of burnt wood and tobacco fouls the air. Six candles burn, lighting the room with a dim, magical glow.

Breathing as if he has just stopped running, Buster withdraws from the doorway. "What you want is in there, lady. This is your chance to back out now, maybe your last chance."

Still clutching that heavy purse, she enters with caution, politely calling out.

Buster's muddy eyes turn skittish. His lips tremble as he latches the door and returns to the skinning tree to finish his chores.

Mrs. Brown holds herself as her eyes search the twenty-foot room. The open kitchen is to her right, where a dented basin sits beneath an old pitcher hand pump. Nearby, the tin piping of a potbelly stove veers to puncture the wall. Two doors face her across the sparsely decorated room. A shimmering reflection dances upon the stained ceiling above the farthest door, proving that it opens onto a deck that stands over the water. The other door is ajar, but its contents are enveloped by utter darkness. To the far left, the hearth sparks and pops to send tiny chips of red embers flying into the old stone.

In the crimson glow of the fireplace, posted within a six-foot circle of sand poured upon an, otherwise, immaculate wooden floor, she sits with her scrawny legs crossed beneath her. Just rocking back and forth, as if without a care, she watches the wary eyes of her visitor until they finally meet her gaze.

Mrs. Brown flinches, nearly crying out, but her voice jams in her throat. The old woman grins a toothless grin, and her eyes squint to make her cheeks rise. Her leathery, brown skin is smooth and taut, wrinkling only when she grins.

"Hello," Teresa Brown nearly shrieks. "Your son, Buster brought me..."

"Buster ain'ts my youngling. Found him crying in the swamp many a year ago, floatin' gator bait he was. See, wit all the inbreedin' round these parts, they drown the deformed ones as a mercy."

When Mrs. Brown tightens her grip on her heavy purse straps and regains her voice, she says, "My grandmother told me where I could find you. My name..."

"Hush now, lest some uninvited thing follows you home in the dark just cause it knows who you is. Your name ain't that important, child. I know who you is. The spirits already whispered of your comin' here today."

"Yes, ma'am."

The old woman's lips seem to curl into a sneering grimace with the formation of nearly every syllable she speaks, moving the large black mole upon her left cheek. Her gleaming eyes and gray hair are easily pronounced beneath the frail black shawl encompassing her head and shoulders. "You think you're special, girl?" she snarls. "Well, you ain't nothin' when out this a way."

"Please. I was told that you could...do things for a price."

"I know why you came here, child." The old swamp witch laughs. "It's 'cause you want somethin' done. You want to cause a body miserable pain, like what you feel. I know it be vengeful hoodoo that you seek to the root. It's always the same, girl. You got my price?"

Wordlessly, Mrs. Brown draws the long straps across her head, and reaches into her heavy purse to withdraw a purple drawstring bag containing fifty dollars in nickels. No pennies, no dimes, nor quarters—only nickels will do. The old woman groans with approval.

"Well, I'm waitin', child. What else you got for the old witchin' woman of Thorny Bend swamp?"

Mrs. Brown places her purse on the floor next to her feet. With her eyes cast away from that frightful gaze, her anxious fingers fumble with the drawstring until it finally opens. She reaches inside for an embroidered handkerchief, the very same one she ripped from the pocket of Keith Williams' blazer as she cursed him. Nestled within the handkerchief is one of Willard St. John's marbled buttons. She stares down at the cotton swatch in a fleeting moment of uncertainty, but when her burning eyes remind her of her woes—of Willard St. John's sly little smile—she glares at the old woman and spits on it with utter contempt. Now she balls it up within her fist and offers it to the witch.

The old witch of Thorny Bend grins, making a chuckling sound that causes the visitor's hair to bristle. It is so mean, so spiteful a sound. The old woman says, "Your grandmamma taught you well what to do out here. Bring it closer, child." Her withered forefinger beckons Mrs. Brown.

Placing one foot before the other, Teresa Brown slowly closes the gap with her offerings clearly displayed in her outstretched hands.

As she nears the circle of sand, the old woman warns, "Stop right there, child. All that enters this here circle will be mine forever and amen. There will be no Indian givin' here, girl, so you best think long and hard on it first." Without spilling a drop, she spits the brown mush stored between her cheeks and gums into a rusting coffee can.

Mrs. Brown shudders to a halt. She looks down at the circle of sand to utter, "I know, old woman. I will not turn back now. I know."

"Do you now? It be great pain that you seeks here, and if your burning ain't strong enough to die for, you best turn round now, and leave the same way you come. Once the evil lets loose, it will cause your enemy such anguish that even you cannot imagine. However, if your hatred is pure enough, there is the danger that it might just come back to claim you, too. You see, most people don't never know that hatred is a luxury…double-edged at that. It eats us all from within, so careful what you ask for, girl. Careful what you ask."

Mrs. Brown nods, entering the circle. The old woman reaches up and greedily snatches the bag of coins from her hand. She shakes it close to her best ear, testing its weight while listening to that satisfying jingle. She groans with delight as she sets it aside and takes the handkerchief from the patron's trembling hand.

The button falls to the floor, spinning on its edge until it finally comes to rest. It is ignored for the moment. Thoughtfully, she rubs her thumbs across the embroidered lettering of the handkerchief. She brushes it against her cheek to test its softness and sniffs. Her nostrils flare as if this is the very first flower she has ever smelled.

She places the folded cloth in the palm of her right hand and caresses it with her left. It is clear from her groan there is something more. She sniffs it again and looks up at TJ Brown's mother, squinting with those black eyes.

"What is it? What's wrong?" Mrs. Brown asks.

The old woman sneers. "My price is paid, and what's mine is mine. Let that be as clear as the day is long, child, but there is somethin' I feel I should say to you first."

Mrs. Brown crouches and peers directly into her eyes. "What is it, old woman? Tell me, damn it!"

"Mind your tongue!" the witch hisses back. "Mind it before it does you harm."

Mrs. Brown retreats quickly. "Please forgive me for shouting. It was very disrespectful. I'm just very upset because my son is dead and buried. His murderer laughed in my face as if taking my son's life was no worse than squashing a bug. I'm sorry."

The old woman groans. "Yes. I thought so." She looks at the handkerchief. "You might have made the trip way out here for nothing. I say it's so because there is big trouble coming this fancy man's way." She sniffs the handkerchief once more. "I smell innocent blood here."

"What do you mean?"

"I mean just what I said, child. I smell the ugly future coming forth for him. A test will be waged for his soul and much more."

"How can you be sure?" Mrs. Brown questions.

"I knowed you were comin' today, didn't I? You don't have to go no further, but if you want, then so be it. The choice is yours for the makin'." She picks up the button, licks it, and sneezes. Gabnetta Lee, the witchin' woman of Thorny Bend swamp leers at it with scornful disdain. As she considers both items, she says, "Hmm…I sees now. These two are mortal enemies. You hate them both with a burnin' passion, but it be the button man what truly wronged you."

"I didn't come all the way out here to turn around without what I came for. I want you to make those bastards pay, if you really have the power that people claim."

The witch of Thorny Bend licks her lips and narrows her eyes to mere slits. She grimaces a wicked smile, tilting her head slightly to make the aged bones crackle in her neck.

"Almost sounds like you think you're ready to challenge the devil himself on this day. As frozen meat does not quickly spoil, then let it be, child. As dead flesh must return to dust, let it be as you crave it from the pit of the dimming light of your very soul."

As Mrs. Brown sits before the woman, her hand is seized without warning. The old woman slits her palm with the jagged blade of an old, rusted knife!

Teresa Brown shrieks in pain, but the old woman has grabbed her with a firm grip, which pays no heed to her struggle. Holding Mrs. Brown's right hand fast, the old woman drives the knife into the floor and lays claim to three bones. She quickly wraps them in the handkerchief, which she then uses to sop up the blood.

The white cloth is quickly soaked red. The old woman drops it to the floor and jams the bleeding wound between her hungry lips, sucking at the crimson flow as if it is life itself.

Mrs. Brown grows dizzy. Her struggle wanes as her eyes flutter. The stale, smoky air in the shack seems too hot, too thick to breathe. The old woman releases her and spits, spraying the bloody spittle and chewing tobacco at Mrs. Brown's face and sweaty blue blouse. She places her bony fingers to her withered lips, savoring the taste. She snatches Keith Williams' handkerchief from the floor and wipes her chin clean.

Mrs. Brown, though her eyes burn from the stinging tobacco, stares at the witch as she opens the handkerchief on the floor and places the button in the center. With both hands, she shakes it three times. Now she pours the bones upon the floor.

When Mrs. Brown looks down at them, she realizes that these are no ordinary bones; they are the fully intact skeletons of three baby serpents. These are infant snakes from head to tail, stripped bare of the skin and succulent flesh by hungry ants. Each skeleton is held together by thread that has been meticulously sewn through the spinal cavities.

The old woman's eyes are intense as she fingers her talismans of doom, searching their pattern upon the floor in the dying firelight. She cackles again and points to Mrs. Brown with a bony finger.

"As you wish lives for a life, child, then so shall it be as you crave it." Something howls from deep within the heart of the swampland. "Do you hears it, girl? That be the sound of your hatred come to life. It be warning you that your enemies will suffer as greatly as you have, but it ain't over for you, girl. Ain'ts over for you because you'll be leavin' a piece of your soured soul here with it. And if your hatred tastes too good and pure, the evil you unleash here today will surely consume you whole."

Mrs. Brown's eyes dart about, searching every shadow for the thing that made that terrible noise. She is beginning to feel asthmatic, as though the air has lost its ability to carry oxygen. When the sound comes again, she reacts accordingly. Now, every sound that was silent upon her arrival to this place comes to amplified life. Crickets and cicadas chirp. Bullfrogs croak and bellow. Every bird in creation begins to screech.

As Mrs. Brown thrusts her hands to her aching ears, sweat pours from her body. Chaos suddenly fills the entire world.

The old woman is amused. "There ain'ts no creatures out there to bother you, child. The real monsters on this earth are born within the evil hearts of men and women."

TJ Brown's mother faints dead away.

ၷ

Mississippi.

The image of Ezra T. Krantz shocks many in the great hall, but they still regard the screen with reverence. His spotted forehead gleams with sweat as his sunken eyes strain to focus. He has been a proud, dogmatic man most of his life. However, at this miserable moment, Ezra T. Krantz invokes their pity.

The party of twelve in Krantz's bedchamber and the multitude without will make a secret sign with their hands. They form circles with the index fingers and thumbs of both hands. They will interlock the loops like a magician's magic rings and touch the fingertips of the remaining six. It looks like two interlocking rings beneath a pyramid. Better yet, it mimics two eyeholes beneath a pointed hood.

Krantz raises his feeble hands to make the sign. As he does, the others recite their secret prayer. "And God created man to rule upon the earth. We, who are made of the purest fire, He anointed among all others. We have risen to light the tree upon which Our Savior hung crucified by heathen masses that plague this Holy place. They are the unworthy. To damnation, they will return without God's divine forgiveness, for they must atone for a great multitude of sins. Amen, Our Father…and forever…amen."

Against the doctor's wishes, Krantz removes his oxygen mask to speak freely. A microphone transports his raspy words to his avid followers as he croaks, "This may be the last time you see me alive. I only regret that I cannot embrace each and all, but you will hear my call when we meet again. Just keep the faith. During your struggles to complete the mission set before us by God, I ask that you try to remember me as I was in years gone by."

Though Krantz is a miserable sight, most of his men try to visualize his vigor before the sickness took hold. Some of them pray for him aloud, while others fight to hold back tears to no avail.

"See me as I am now, old and withering in human frailty. Nevertheless, remember me as the man I was— strong — vigilant, and true to my calling. My ninety-some years have all been for a moment that I will not witness from this side, but I will be watching from the bosom of our Lord. Remember me as you come into the glory that is to be. Blessed be the true Americans. Blessed be…God's chosen!" When he begins to wheeze, the transmission ends.

Moments later, as the men in the lair of the dying patriarch shuffle out in a single file with teary eyes, Krantz summons Jud Martin for a private conference. As Peter Black moves on for the next stage in the great hall, Krantz dismisses the doctor.

Martin takes the Holy Bible from the dresser and pulls a chair close to the bedside. He carries a heavy heart, for this man has been like a father to him. He owes everything to Krantz, and they share a special rapport.

"What you like me to read for you today, old codger?"

Krantz shakes his head to indicate that he does not wish Jud Martin to read for him.

Martin puts the Holy Bible away, and takes the dying man's frail hand.

"What can I do for you, old codger? Would you like me to call the nurse in?"

Krantz is looking directly into Martin's eyes with a hard, cold stare. He is thinking, wondering if he has made the right choice for his succession. He questions whether Jud Martin truly has the salt to do what is now required of him.

He snaps back to reality and says, "Son, I've known you long before your father passed away while saving my life. As you well know, he asked that I look after you and Janie if something was to happen to him before his time." He wheezes, refusing the oxygen mask. "I did as he asked and it was my pleasure to do so. You've brought me such great joy and pride, son."

Martin smiles at the old man. "Thank you, old codger, but you need to rest easy now. There's no need to get yourself all worked up. Just let me call…"

"I can't rest," Ezra snaps. "Not until things are put right. Now shut up and listen to me." That rattling wheeze rocks him again.

Not wanting to agitate Ezra further, Martin sits quietly.

"I had a vision a while back. Our Heavenly Father was standing behind me and pointing down at you. You were standing on a sheet of white that would blind the eyes of the average man. The Lord's other hand was upon my shoulder to keep me from falling from the cloud we were standing on. He said you are going to take my place at the head of the throne room, and that you will lead his people up the rest of the path in my absence."

Jud Martin nods and smiles with some effort.

"He promised that the angels are going to sing a great chorus at my death, as well as your indoctrination to the White House. But… but there was a problem, son." Martin is looking down with loving, saddened eyes when Ezra says, "You turned around as if somebody called your name, and that was when I saw it for the very first time. A dark, tainted stain was living in your shadow. God revealed to me that you have a blemish that must be erased from the slate of your life, son."

Jud Martin is confused, searching his memory for what this blemish could be, but thinks of nothing. After all, he has done everything required to get where he is now.

The old man catches his breath, and his aging eyes meet with Martin's once more to say. "It's your daughter, Jud. It's the woman you raised as your daughter."

Martin is surprised and fearful of what Ezra is about to say.

"She's not really yourn, boy, and I think you know that." Krantz gasps once before saying, "You killed your wife 'cause she took up with that Black buck. Seems they got to be pretty damn cozy over the years, didn't they? Like a mongrel dog, it comes skulking in with its tail wagging and head laid low until she finally pets it in kindness. Next thing you know, she's feeding it in her lap, licking her face."

Martin releases the liver-spotted hand and stands up. "That's enough, old man. What's the point of rehashing that old mess? That unfaithful bitch and that sticking nigger are long dead, and there's nothing left to do about it!"

Krantz's gaze never leaves Martin. "Sit yourself down, Judson Martin. You just...just sit yourself down and listen because this is God talking to you now. The very salvation of my soul depends on it, and so does your life. Do not make the mistake of offending the Almighty, Jud. You don't want to know what that is like, boy."

Because Krantz is excited, his hands begin to quiver. His rattling cough worsens with each syllable. Martin consents by sitting hard, though fuming still.

After taking a sip of cold water, Ezra proclaims, "Son, I don't want to hurt you, but there's hard work to be done here for both of us. The Lord says that you must oblige, or everything goes to hell in a handbasket. You hear me? Sabrina is not yours. She has the blood of a slave running through her veins, and she just ain't pure. You know blood seeks out its own, boy, and she's taken to her mother's ways."

Governor Martin opens his mouth to protest, but the shock prevents it. "What?"

"The bitch you raised and put through college has finally betrayed her true colors. She done took up with a colored lawyer over there in Atlanta. It's all true. I would never lie to you, son."

113

Krantz points a twitchy finger at the corner of his sweaty pillow, which Martin raises with reluctance. There, he finds a file that fills him with dread. It is a graphically explicit dossier of his daughter, Dr. Sabrina Martin. It seems Jud Martin is to be spared nothing. Somehow, someone has gotten pictures of Sabrina and Keith Williams kissing in a restaurant and holding hands as they stroll through a secluded park. There are even a few photos of them making love, which are the backbreaking deathblows to a proud father.

With vein popping revulsion, Martin throws the file to the floor, stomping it as if it suddenly came to life in his hands. One picture portrays Sabrina as she is about to go down on her lover. It slides out of the folder and underfoot to mock Governor Martin. This is a photo of his baby girl—his only child in life—preparing to perform a most despicable act against nature and God.

Martin's stomach lurches as the shame consumes him. The file goes flying when he kicks it, but not this one special photo, which lies spitefully at his feet. It glares back at him as a mockery of all he has been raised to hold sacred. A wave of vertigo sends Martin to his knees, vomiting and retching violently. His puke splatters the photo, but not that area where Sabrina's head and shoulders are positioned in a kiss. In fact, his rather greasy lunch seems to part like the center of a cloud on the glossy photo where Sabrina's image taunts him. Her dark hair is splashed against the rippled abdominal muscles of her lover.

Once his watering eyes refocus, he rips the photo to shreds. Governor Judson Martin curses unnamable things as he spits on the confetti. He thinks he has finally destroyed the shamefully abominate thing, but the image is etched in his mind. He holds much maligned contempt for the two subjects in the photo. How dare they…?

The Governor of Mississippi now weeps, and woe be unto anyone who brings tears to the eyes of such hard and hateful men. As Martin's head lies upon the bed, Krantz strokes his hair, shedding tears and smiling at the same time. He tries to console his friend, but consolation is not his only goal.

Krantz croaks, "When you are alone at the top, you will understand why God has given you this terrible burden to bear, Judson. The enemy always tries to get at men of power through family, and this is something that can blow up in all our faces. You know what you have to do now, son. This is God's work."

Martin withdraws at these words, moving away from the hand that strokes his hair.

"No. No, Ezra, this cannot be. My God, this can't be."

Krantz twists the knife by saying, "If you don't eliminate them now, the men will find out sooner than later. When they do, they will not follow you, Jud. We must always lead by example. It is our calling, our duty. God demands that you tend it personally because that is the only way to remove this ugly blemish. If you refuse to kill that bitch and her black dog lover, you will never see the White House. Peter Black will take your place, but I will never see those glorious pearly gates for failing the commandments of the Almighty Father."

Krantz coughs up some greenish-brown phlegm, which dribbles down the side of his cheek and drips onto his pillow. It smells like rotting meat and sour molasses.

Governor Martin, done with his puking fit, wipes the filth from that dear old man's cheek and lips. He gathers all the confetti and the rest of the file, which he places in the wastepaper basket next to the bed. He ties the plastic liner before removing it from the container and walks away to dispose of it by fire. As he approaches the door, Krantz warns that the deed needs doing before his death, or their clandestine house of cards is doomed to fall under the heavy toll of God's terrible wrath.

Krantz's final words are, "We are on the threshold of a new era. Nothing and no one must stand in the way of this great movement. Remember your calling, son. Remember your calling."

He wheezes, violently, shuddering as he closes his eyes. A despondent Martin stairs at the floor, not realizing that this is the very spot where Ezra drove a Bowie knife so deeply into his Creole wife's chest that its point protruded through the wooden plank of the floor. That was the last of many stab wounds she endured because he did not have the strength to pull it free.

Had Evalena Krantz not revealed the true nature of her bloodline, she might have lived long enough to learn whom and what she had married on the heels of a whirlwind romance. It may have given her the chance to run, disappear back into the bayous of Louisiana, where she had a better chance with hungry gators and cottonmouths. Even after all the effort placed into reinventing herself to portray an average Southern woman, a simple reference to the life that she finally escaped was what ultimately killed her. For loving this man enough to confess her true heritage—a tainted bloodline that would continue with the child growing inside her belly—she died as the result of Ezra's T. Krantz's righteous indignation.

Governor Judson Martin walks out without another word.

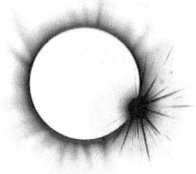

Chapter 9

A PALE HORSE COMETH!

In somber reflection, Peter Black enters the great hall to take his places on the stage at the head of the room. Black stands behind the podium and begins the meeting by introducing the new inductees. Both are greeted with a nonchalant round of applause because they are not yet of the hive.

These are all proud men, honored to be among those chosen to usher in the new way. After taking a moment to gaze over the inductees and the collective, Peter Black begins his speech.

Though Peter Black is in his upper forties, younger than many of the men in the room, he thinks of them as a father will his children because he has played a major part in the KKK's reorganization. He is standing on this stage as a highly trusted, chosen leader.

Mississippi Senator Black begins by saying, "We, of the inner sanctum, have come a very long way to achieve the goals God set before us many years ago. We've been called upon, and sent out to procure the future of this great nation. It has taken decades to achieve. We are the rightful heirs of this land, and there will be little room for other than our own because we must save this great nation from the heathens. We have seen enough of the webacks overrunning our borders to steal good jobs from hard-working Americans. Chinks are stealing our technology… military secrets…selling it back to us. What are we to do, other than what our God decrees? They are all unclean. It is time that the impure are sent back from whence they slither. This is our Holy task, men. You best believe that our children will someday thank us for it."

Willard St. John utters, "Amen to that, Brother Black."

"The Jews denounced Christ, and yet, they live among us in this Christian nation under the pretense of being pious and humble people. Meanwhile, behind the scenes, they are trying to take over. These arrogant sand niggers don't seem to realize that we see them, too. The Negroes have secretly declared war upon the White race. Right now, they are out there killing our children by spreading illegal guns and filthy drugs across this land. Both Negroes and homosexuals wish to use television to brainwash, desensitize, pervert, and subvert our nation as they pass HIV across color lines and sexual orientations. How can anyone justify homosexual relationships while entertaining same-sex marriages when these are clearly contradictions of human nature? Even now, those idiots in Washington are preparing to permit the adoption of innocent children by homosexual couples. Now that is something we never thought we would see in our lifetimes. There is simply a lack of fundamental morality in such people, and the end of their era is coming! This is the calling of every person here. Our God-given responsibility is to rid this nation of all the children of Sodom and Gomorrah. We so clearly see them because our time is truly nigh!"

The crowd rises to its feet, cheering and clapping. Peter Black's heartfelt speech continues as he spews forth his most beautiful poison.

"There is nothing in the foreseeable future that can stop us. The word is out, men. Nineteen-ninety-six will be the year we begin to take it all back. Our campaign funding was secured long ago. The great man, Governor Jud Martin and I have filed Statements of Candidacy Forms with the FEC to run in the GOP Primaries, which we will win by the grace of God. Then, we will go on to enter the GOP Primaries and win the 1996 presidential election because it is the will of God Almighty!"

They cheer the news.

"Some might claim what we've done here to be treasonous. However, when it comes to electing a dope-smoking womanizer as the U.S. President, I say there is your treason. Our so-called leader doesn't have the support of his own damn suspenders, much less the support of the Congress. He just doesn't know it yet. We have quietly gained majority caucuses in both houses. We are soldiers, endowed with intellect, and driven—fueled—by the mighty righteousness of Christianity. We are Senators, House Representatives, Governors, Mayors, attorneys, financiers, business executives, lobbyist, and doctors, in this great organization. Within our hands, we now hold the unblunted sword of God, which tips the balance of power. For all those presuming to stand between us and the destiny of Our Lord and Savior, a pale rider approaches!"

The new inductees clap with the others, never realizing that they have been manipulated into becoming haters of Blacks and gays.

Both experienced tragic losses directly linked to African Americans, who never knew their supposed victims even existed. Prior to sudden arrests, planted evidence, murder indictments, swift convictions, and the harshest sentences imposed by law, they knew nothing. The sky over the future came crashing down for some, while the entire world of hatred opened up for others.

"Members of this brotherhood are sick and tired of what those bleeding hearts in Washington are doing to degrade America. Sure, we had to play along to get where we are, but we are here now. Praise God Almighty, we are here. The rights of criminals now outweigh those of average, hard-working American citizens. The people we call animal rights activists are wasting our national resources on shiftless layabouts, forcing honest taxpayers to support the illegitimate welfare masses. May God have mercy on their souls because we will show them none at all. If those nigger-lovers care so damn much, then they can get the hell out with them!"

Many laugh at the latter statement because they have particular nigger-lovers in mind. The staunch arrogance in this room is well founded, rooted in the fact that they have actually gained the majority of seats in both houses of Congress while biding their time in silence. They owe it all to David Duke, and all those other White supremacists too well known to conceal.

"Many things will change because we have an obligation to God, this nation, and to the great man that just spoke to us all. God called Ezra to this task when he was a mere boy of thirteen and he has dedicated his entire life to this cause. I am here to tell you all that we will not fail him!"

The room extols the master orator. Though dressed in expensive suits, they are a hard driven, bloodthirsty bunch. Because they have behaved for so long, this bone deep desire for blood grows even greater. Something ugly and deeply buried within them now craves the freedom to run amok and bloodlet as they did back in the good old days.

They are certain that by the time Jud Martin's presidential campaign ends, Bill Clinton's stint in the White House will dwindle to a blurb on the pages of presidential history. They have somehow convinced themselves that the nation will concede to their monstrous vision. They strongly believe they will shove generations of entire races out of this nation; uprooting and dispersing them like so much refuse while the rest of the world just stands by and watches.

"If we can't kill 'em, we lock 'em up and throw away the key. The police are here for them, not us. But it is now time for more permanent solutions, my esteemed friends." Peter Black raises his trembling right fist and says, "To the Brotherhood of Light. To the Christian Knights. Our time is near!"

The room shakes, reverberating whistles and applause of a frenzied audience as some dark malevolence fills this place with its power. Even the birds, which are building nests in the eaves of the old mansion, rise and take frightful flight.

It is time for the main event, the moment they have been waiting for. As his home shakes with the sound of rolling thunder, Ezra dreams of his indoctrination many years ago.

᙭

He struggles to find a firm grip on an invisible anvil that rests upon his young chest, feeling each heartbeat in his bulging eyes as he stands alone in the peach orchard. As a sudden bolt of lightning flashes directly overhead, he spins around to face a towering mare rearing to an abrupt stop. He falls backward when nearly run down.

121

The angry lightning flashes again to illuminate the face of the murderous Black rider, who now struggles to control the frightened animal. Tobias Johnson looks at Ezra, terrified that he may cry out. When he finally has the spooked horse under control, he places an index finger over his swollen, bloody lips to quiet the boy. He can see that the kid is frightened of him.

Tobias stutters the words, "N-n-now you be very q-quiet. They is trying to kill Tobias, but I didn't do nothin' wrong." He flinches from the pain in his injured groin.

Ezra's heart is pounding fiercely when he politely moves aside to let Tobias Johnson pass. The scared man is relieved that the boy has not given him cause to do him harm. Accordingly, he thanks the kid for his silence with a simple smile and a nod.

Tobias is home free, so he spurs the horse to spirit him away, while none of the grownup hunters know that he is no longer on foot.

When the angry lightning flashes overhead with a deafening bang, Tobias falls to the ground dead from a fatal volley of buckshot to the back. Like a ghost, steam rises from the mortal wounds.

Young Ezra slowly lowers the smoking barrel and looks at his first kill. The frenzied mare bolts, disappearing into the night. Young Master Krantz is no longer afraid. In fact, he is alive with incomparable exhilaration, riding the rushing wave of his first trophy. He feels strong and grown up. In this profound instant, his soul ages a millennium.

When his father, Elijah Krantz, and the others come back with the limp body of Tobias' victim draped across the flank of one of their horses, they are surprised and exceedingly proud of young Ezra. No one heard the gunshot amid the stormy tumult above. Upon finding their battered brother, they believed that the prey had escaped with the dead man's horse. They are greatly relieved that Sheriff Scrubs need not recapture the simpleton before he tells anyone of the kidnapping and torture he endured before being set free so they could hunt and kill him.

Elijah dips his fingertips into the pool of blood collecting on Tobias' broad back and anoints his son by drawing a cross upon his forehead. Each man follows suit. When the rain finally begins to fall, the blood on the child's head and chest shows great resistance before washing away. He would never forget the metallic taste when he licks his thirsty lips.

The true God of a child's life, his father, reveals young Ezra's true calling. This night, the boy's feverish dreams are of the divine prophecies of future greatness.

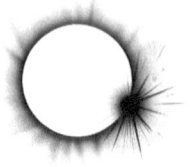

Chapter 10

JUST LIKE HER MOTHER

Governor Martin will not partake in the macabre festivities of the evening. Instead, he returns to his suite and a familiar bottle of bourbon.

With his tie and top buttons loose, he thumps down in an ancient armchair. While swilling, he stares at a picture of Sabrina's graduation on the table directly in front of him. It is a good picture, filled with innocence and the vitality of youth. Sabrina Martin stares back at him with her hazel eyes gleaming. Her heart-melting smile is without falter. He notices the sexy tilt of her head. For the first time he notices her very coy posture.

This father entertains unwanted thoughts concerning the wiles of women. They are also very capable, cunning animals when the time and character calls for it. Martin's mind lurches toward its outer limits, threatening to revive the dark, decomposing bones he buried beneath dirt and gravel. The shallow grave, thought to be deep, begins to reopen, yielding up phantoms he would rather keep buried. By the time Martin finishes his bottle, Sabrina will be laughing at him.

The Governor of Mississippi is bereft. He has not experienced such personal betrayal and anger since he walked in on his wife as she kissed the cheek of her Black friend. Martin never suspected that this man planted the seed that became Sabrina. He thought that he'd done so long before the alleged affair with the Negro had begun. He now drinks to deaden the pain, but continues to reflect despite himself.

Jud Martin remembers his little angel saying her very first words. He recalls her first steps, and the first thing she broke while holding on to the furniture that supported her trembling little legs. It was his mother's antique vase, but it was an ugly thing for which he held no particular regard. Sabrina Martin endured seven stitches back then, crying for days as her swollen little foot healed.

Sabrina played the leading role in Cinderella at age ten, and there was chickenpox during the same year. She grew to love horses, thrown a time or two. She fractured a wrist here or there, but nothing seemed to discourage her young spirit for very long.

At age seventeen, Sabrina graduated as her class valedictorian. Her father was the proudest parent there. By that time, they had become friends again. At least, his moment of temporary insanity was entombed and forgotten.

Sabrina Martin was a stunning young woman on her way to college. She was a cheerleader during her first year, just like her mother had been in high school. Yes, just like her mother.

❧

Jud Martin's words rake across her like steel thorns when he shouts "Shut your lying, nigger-kissing lips!"

The attack is swift and brutal. Thankfully, Sabrina Martin is at elementary school when the Black fixit man runs from the backdoor of their home bleeding from the mouth and nose. After the Negro escapes, Jud slaps his wife silly before kicking her in the face as she lay on the kitchen floor. She still manages to crawl out the backdoor while he goes to the living room closet in a rage. While loading the shotgun, Jud Martin heads for the kitchen.

Ashley Elaine Martin screams for help, but no one hears her cries. There is no 911, and most folks prefer to mind their own business.

Jud Martin nearly kicks the screen door from its new hinges as he comes out back. As he approaches the backyard, brandishing the weapon, she pleads with him to stop.

Mrs. Martin tries to run, but falls down. After all, a White woman's knees are not meant for running; they're made for praying to God to keep their asses out of shit just like this.

The red straps of her apron come undone as she stands on trembling knees that threatened to buckle. She cries, "For God's sake, please don't hurt me anymore. I did nothing wrong. Mr. Willy did not touch me, Jud. He was just here to fix the squeaky hinge on the..."

Her voice chokes off with the sudden and terrifying revelation that, for some strange reason, she is going to die.

Jud Martin's eyes are fearsome jewels set in stone and the harshness of his voice rakes her soul again when he snarls, "Shut your nigger-kissing mouth, bitch, or I'll teach you!" He levels the gun and repeats, "Shut your nigger-kissin' mouth!"

"No, Jud!"

With a memory of his father lying in a coffin, Jud Martin leans forward, slightly, setting his right shoulder for the impact. In a moment of fatal madness, he pulls the triggers, sending buckshot from both barrels at her! Ashley Martin's scream is silenced when her face explodes from the impact. She does not kick, quiver, or jitter upon hitting the ground. Without counsel, judgment is administered swiftly. The punishment…death.

Martin walks back into the house, never noticing that the squeaky, broken hinges have been replaced with a new set from his very own hardware store. He does not notice the wooden toolbox, clearly not his own. At this moment, he couldn't give a damn if he had.

This sort of personal intrusion is unthinkable after all that has happened.

Blacks killed his father, and the thought of one of them violating his bed is intolerable. The episode, however, is far from over so Jud Martin calls on friends. Ezra will know just what to do. While awaiting their arrival, he will not allow himself to think about how easy it had been to murder his wife. Yes, Jud Martin overreacted, but this is no time to psychoanalyze himself. What is done is done. The cleanup crew arrives quickly, and Ashley Elaine Martin simply ceases to exist.

Their fiery eight-year-old daughter never understands why her mother left their happy home. As any child would, Sabrina Martin wonders if she did something to upset her mom. She often asks, but never receives a satisfactory answer when she wants to know just what a Gypsy or a hippie is exactly. She gets little satisfaction when she needs to know why her mother chooses that way of life over them. Five days after her mother disappears, Sabrina runs outdoors amidst a raging thunderstorm and screams for the absent woman who comforted her during such violent torrents. Upon her knees, she looks up at the blurry sky, soaked to the bones, screaming until her father rushes out to scoop her up and take her back inside.

At this age, Sabrina is much too young to comprehend all of the events that are coming into play in her life. As an adult, she searches along false trails, but her mother has gone to great lengths to disappear. For some strange reason, she associates her mother's disappearance with shiny, noiseless hinges. The only viable answer a child's mind could assimilate is that the boogeyman put them on the backdoor so her mother would not hear him coming. Deep down inside, Sabrina feels all her life that her mother would not abandon her this way. Over time, though, the questions only ring aloud occasionally. Although holidays and birthdays are always the worst of times, she never suspects her father of foul play.

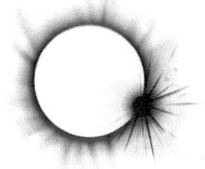

Chapter 11

SACRILEGE

Peter Black is absolutely glowing when he signals the four huge men waiting at the bottom of the steps of the stage. They head for the food locker because time has come to stretch their self-righteous wings.

The door of the food locker offers a wicked protest, sounding as if grave robbers are forcing the rusted entrance of a forgotten crypt. Kenny Andrews and Robert Smith both awake confused and utterly disoriented. Overcome by exhaustion, Andrews managed to fall asleep after all. However, when the lights come on in their brains, they are still bound and gagged.

With a gnawing certainty, it is their time to die.

Groping, gloved hands come out of the darkness, rudely snatching them to their sleeping feet. With razor-sharp hawk billed knives, their filthy, soiled clothing is cut away like false skins.

The captors temporarily loosen and retie their hands in front of their naked bodies. These men are stripping them of humanity, something that goes far beyond simple nudity.

Only the abused captives react when the blades slip to damage flesh.

"Jesus God!" someone scoffs. "That's fucking disgusting. Weren't you potty trained as a child?"

The others laugh. As with the scorned disposition of their lives, the blindfolds leave them with no sense of direction.

Now the captors drag them through a corridor, up eight flights of steps, and through a foyer into a chaotic room where it seems as though the entire world is cracked and crazed. Madness rules here and their respective hearts pound a message dutifully. For Kenny, a single thought resounds throughout his feverish mind; he wants to die quickly.

Kenny Andrews and his Caucasian lover are both stark naked, completely undone. The rhythm of their quivering hearts are a rapid stammer.

The room goes quiet just before they snatch away the blindfolds. Their tongues, swollen from thirst, offer a relentless throbbing in their mouths and throats. While they squint against the harsh lights, Robert Smith's hands are finally freed. Those of the Black man are left bound before him.

Someone ties a rope between Kenny's wrists. From the shadows, another man will soon appear to hoist his muscular arms into the air before tying the rope to a brass cleat anchored to the wall.

Now the spectacles to behold, they are viewed as things. Not people. The Christian God does not create fags, so their type is most certainly of the devil. Completely stripped of clothing, the captives stare in disbelief at the scowling mass of hatred that pauses ominously before them.

Robert Smith's knees buckle as if the collective stare holds actual weight. His hollow stomach is queasy gelatin, threatening to swallow him whole. Both men begin to weep.

Kenny Andrews is blabbering a prayer to God, who probably would not lift a finger to save him from his fate. Out of shameful reflex, they both put their hands down to cover their penises.

Seals steps from the shadows, allowing Robert Smith to see him before shouting, "Don't cover those up, boys and girls. After all, this is the reason you're both here. Hey, fellas, can you tell us one thing first? Which one of you is the bitch?"

The man at the other end of the rope yanks it taut, wrenching Kenny's arms into the air. The rope whines, crackling a straining protest as he secures it to the brass cleat.

People laugh when someone in the audience yells, "Must be the White girl because that nigger's pecker looks too damn big to be hangin' from any bitch I've ever seen!"

Robert Smith crumples to his knees, clutching Seals' robe as he begs for his life.

Disgusted by his touch, Seals asks, "What the hell are you doing down there, young lady? You want to suck my cock now, do ya?" He gives Smith an obligatory knee to the face to send him sprawling across the waxed floor. "You're just not my type...hair ain't long enough!"

The entire room roars with laughter among a slew of nasty insults.

Seals reaches down to snatch Smith by the sweaty hair, moving in close to growl, "It seems like I've got to deal with queers every fucking day, and then you turn out to be one, too. You've become human refuse, boy." He spits on Smith's unguarded face, shoving him away to stand erect. "Now get your sorry ass up. Look at yourself—down there—kneeling at the feet of a colored dog. You make me sick!"

As Robert Smith attempts to wipe the spittle from his face, one of the others shouts, "Don't you dare wipe that shit off your face. Don't it feel just like warm cum running down your cheek? Good for the complexion, I hear!"

Meanwhile, Kenny Andrews feels as if he's about to go mad. He is sweating bullets, shaking as if holding on to a runaway jackhammer. Having given up on the possibility of life after this veiled affair, he wants to die quickly.

Mr. Seals now directs attention to Kenneth Andrews by asking, "You wish you were already dead by now, don't you, sissy? Right about now, I bet you even wish you liked pussy, too. Don't you, boy?" When Andrews fails to reply, Seals demands, "Look at me and answer the question, nigger!"

The Black man whimpers, "Yes. Yes, sir."

"What did you say? We can't hear you!"

When Kenny Andrews shouts, "Yes, sir. I wish that I liked…" he is slapped for simply raising his voice.

Seals' eyes narrow as he ramps up the ridicule by asking, "Did you take this here fine, red-blooded, American White boy in the ass, nigger? Did he suck your hard black pole? Did he drink your jizzum, son?"

Willard St. John bellows, "Answer him, or I swear I'll kill you right where you stand. I'll do you right now!" When Andrews fails to answer, Willard punches him, ejecting a bloody stream from his busted mouth.

Andrews looks sheepishly at his lover and stutters, "Y-yes, sir. I'm so sorry."

Immediately, men in the crowd shout things such as, "String him up. Hang that nasty fucker!"

Peter Black turns to the new initiates, Eaten and Thomas, whispering instructions while handing a gun to one and a knife to the other. Now he winks at Seals.

Seals turns to Smith, saying, "You know it's a crying shame you allowed yourself to be seduced by Satan. At least you know it now, and knowledge is power. I bet you would do absolutely anything to go free. Am I right, son?"

Robert Smith looks up at the sincere smile of a chameleon and allows himself to cling to a ray of hope. He nods his head and says, "Yes…anything."

The two pledges move closer. With a honed knife hidden behind his back, Thomas positions himself slightly behind Kenny Andrews.

Seals says, "Well, you have to get down on your knees. Show everyone here how you sucked that Black man's cock, so you can feel the utter shame of this entire procession as it cleanses your wretched, lost soul. That's the only sure way you'll never be inclined to disgrace yourself and your race in the future."

Robert Smith pleads with his eyes, but they are met with granite. He looks to the floor.

Kenny Andrews tries to back away as Smith slowly turns toward him. He says, "For the love of God, please don't make him do it. Please."

"Shut the fuck up, boy. This is God's work, so do not bother calling his name because we are working for the man upstairs. It wasn't enough that you were raping our women, but you had to start in on the unnatural raping of White men, too!"

Left no alternative, Robert Smith kneels down. Sniveling, he looks up at the man he thought he loved; the man he suddenly grows to hate. He reaches up, taking Kenny's penis in his trembling hands.

When he turns to plead with Seals once more, he is greeted with a smile and a reassuring nod to proceed. Robert reluctantly turns back to the work at hand. When he opens his mouth, closes his eyes and takes the soft penis into his mouth, gasps of utter revulsion escape the collective audience.

On this day, Kenny's penis smells of old urine, sour sweat, and bacteria. It is not quite its supple self, tasting very dry on Robert's swollen tongue.

Someone yells, "Do it like you mean it, boy. You had better give it some real feeling. Make it hard like you used to. Some of us want to measure that puppy!" It would have taken St. John to make such vile statements.

Kenny Andrews knows that his penis will never stand erect again.

Fearing their wrath, a sniveling Robert Smith increases his suction. He pulls back to stretch the soft member to its boneless length and tickles the head with his tongue. At this very moment, Thomas steps forward with his right hand raised. To Kenny Andrews, it all happens in slow motion, yet he finds himself paralyzed as the knife makes its downward arch. In an instant, his penis severs from his body!

Kenny Andrews screams, ripping the cleat from the wall as he grabs his bleeding stump on the way to the floor. His head fills with starbursts. The world grays from the clouds swiftly cluttering his mind. Smith rocks backward with the severed penis still in his hands and mouth. He opens his eyes and throws the bloody appendage away in utter disgust. When it stops rolling, it squirms. Smith falls back on his elbows, retching and heaving vomit over his own chest. They are both screaming.

The crowd shouts and claps, but not in celebration of Robert Smith's redemption. Their cheers are only partially motivated by seeing the Negro suffer. It would seem that Mr. Thomas has passed the test. He is now one of them because a man would surely kill if willing to hack off the sexual member of another.

Someone tosses Smith a piece of twine. He points at Andrews' groin area and says, "Now you tie that up, boy. We don't want him bleeding to death just yet."

With all that blood, no one realizes that the tip if the knife has gashed the Black man's thigh.

Robert Smith scurries on hands and knees to do as told, fearing he will be next if he fails to comply immediately. When he is done, they throw a bucket of ice-cold water on Kenny Andrews to rouse him from his stupor. He is issued a crisp, lip-splitting slap to force him back to full attention. He continues to whimper on the stage floor.

Seals grins as he approaches Robert Smith, helping him to his feet. Smith babbles, incoherently, just like his mutilated lover.

Seals looks into his eyes and asks, "Are you alright, son? Do you want a glass of water to wash the taste away? I bet you're powerful thirsty right now." He gives Smith a cold glass of water, which he gulps before choking.

As water sputters out of his mouth and nostrils, he catches a glimpse of his blood spattered face in the glass before it falls to the floor and shatters totally wasted. As Robert Smith stares at his feet, Seals puts both hands on his shoulders and says, "You have to kill him to be reclaimed by us, Robby. You know that, don't you? You have to know that that is the price of reclamation to the fold, son."

Robert Smith looks back at Kenny. His lover is being helped to his feet as he clutches his bloody wound. Those helping him are careful not to get his germ-infested blood on them. There is a look of scorn on their faces, as if somehow defiled by touching this bleeding homosexual.

Seals gives Smith a pistol before turning him to face his lover for the last time. Coburn Eaton, thinking of his murdered loved one, moves behind Smith when Seals says, "If he doesn't do as I say, kill him." Coburn puts the gun to the back of Smith's head, his mind flashing homicide photos from the scene of the crime. Hatred rules his heart.

Now Seals asks, "Do you hate the devil for seducing you, son? Tell Satan that you hate his Black ass. Tell him!"

Smith's hands shake violently as he raises the gun to his lover's unguarded chest. Kenny Andrews is fully awake and his bleeding lips are quivering, as he pleads, "Robert, please don't. For the love of God…please…don't."

Robert Smith's heart is no longer confused by choices of love or self-preservation. His vision now locks on to the growing point of light coming from what surely must be the end of his plight. He shouts, "I hate you!" as he aims the weapon at Kenny's face.

"Louder!" Seals demands.

"I hate you fucking niggers," screams Smith, who pulls the trigger repeatedly.

The deafening roar of a single gunshot blares like a thunderclap in the room. There is a brilliant flash as a bullet passes through the back of his head, exiting through skull above his left eye socket. Staring straight ahead, he is invited to kiss death full on its cold lips. His brain, purged through the mammoth hole in his face, deposits on his lover's chest.

It is a cruel joke of sorts, a permanent reminder of all those wonderful head jobs given and received. Quite symbolic.

The crowd regales Coburn Eaton for his passing into the realm of the Ku Klux Klan. He is overwhelmed by shock and regret, which soon passes like evaporating sweat. The dead man laying before them never knew what hit him.

Mercifully, Kenny Andrews passes out. He has finally died, never again to worry about the problems of life. So he thinks. Yes, this has been a very cruel joke indeed.

ତ୨୦

Kenny Andrews comes to with his groin on fire. The pain quickly clears the fog from his brain. However, when he regains a semblance of focus, he looks up into the face of infinite grief and terror.

He thought he died when the gun discharged. He was sure of that, even welcomed it. Once again, he wishes for the grim reaper's sweet embrace. A bullet to the brain, what envy. Why had the White boy gotten off so easily?

Kenny Andrews is laying spread eagle on the grass at the edge of a field in the southern part of the plantation. His skin is searing fire as hundreds of nerve endings relay the message that he is lying upon an angry red ant hill that someone stirred up just for him. His weak hands lazily swipe at the tiny assailants, but that is the extent of effort. The fight has drained away during endless hours of captivity and humiliation.

Directly above, a burning cross looms. Its heat causes his wounds to ache even more, while its flame illuminates the cloudy sky beyond. He knows that God has forsaken him.

When his trembling hands reach for his ravaged penis, he looks up into the faces of rigid angels adorned in white gowns. He realizes that he has died after all, but these angels are the ones from hell and they've brought a cross to burn at his indoctrination. When Kenny's ears begin to work again, he wishes he were deaf.

"Get up, jig. Get your lazy ass up. You must think you're at work after lunch, nigger!" One of them kicks Kenny in the ribs.

"Yeah. Get up and see what we got for ya," says another.

Vicious kicks rain down on Kenny Andrews as he tries to oblige the command to stand. Despite the infinite pain, he has a funny thought about how hell is supposed to be hotter than this. His scrambled mind is certain that grass should not grow in an inferno.

"We're going huntin', boy. We're going coon huntin', and guess who the coon is. Tag. You're it, nigga."

Andrews rises to his feet on the cool grass, aching from every nerve ending in his sweating body as the ants continue the assault. As reality sets in, bringing with it a renewed fear of what is to come, a raven calls out in the night air.

"You better run, boy!"

When someone kicks him in the balls, Andrews drops. White-hot agony sears his brain as he convulses on the ground.

It is truly amazing how men of such public grace and eloquence so easily revert to unrefined dialect and staggering brutality. Finally, after a long stasis, the animal in them is set free.

"I'm gonna kill you, nigga. I'm gonna kill you like you did my little brother when you hijacked his car and raped his woman. You hear me, boy?" says the man who lifts his veil of cowardice to spit in Andrews' face. This man is Coburn Eaten, who will never know that those Black men living on death row are innocent of the crimes of which he speaks.

"I'm gonna gut you just like a fish. Then we gonna feed you and your white piece of pussy to the gators in this here swamp, but you'll still be alive, boy. They're gonna crunch your bones like toothpicks, and when they shit you out, there won't be no evidence that you ever existed," another says.

Andrews' mind snapped after his penis was hacked from his body. He manages to get to his knees. Looking from hood to hood, he begins to laugh with them. The demon men suddenly stop threatening, as they look at each other completely dumbfounded.

None of them knows what is so funny about dying in the terrible manners they have described to this fool. Some of them look down at themselves when Andrews points as if they are covered in vomit or dog shit.

Kenny Andrews is going to win this round. He is actually going to beat them by laughing himself to death, but it is more likely from blood loss and shock. Andrews falls forward dead, staring at the blades of green grass that now caress his oblivious eyeballs. It almost seems fitting that he has fallen forward on his knees with his bare ass pointing at the sky. He enjoys a final moment of silent laughter as he enters the light.

The circling demons are incensed. One man turns Andrews over with a boot, ordering him to get up. When no response is given, he kicks Andrews for good measure.

Willard St. John rips away his hood to get a better look. "You better get. Shit…say it isn't so!" He is actually pleading with God to raise this man from the dead so they can hunt him down and give him a proper sendoff. "Christ Almighty, I don't believe this crap!"

St. John lays a well-placed boot to the dead man, soon joined by the others. They are fuming because Andrews has cheated them out of their grand finale. Beating them all to the punch, he just up and quits the game. He leaves them no joy after all the trouble they went through.

"Well, that's just like a fucking spook for ya!" a demon declares.

Kenny Andrews takes no exception to the name-calling. He is gone from this place. They stomp his corpse, breaking his jawbone until his teeth sound like wet ball bearings in a baby's rattle. Under boot, Kenny's skull is partially crushed to let the grey matter flow from his deaf ears. His rib cage is smashed until pieces of bone are coming out the other side.

The Klansmen are bloody when they finish defiling this man's body, but they remain disgusted and mad with the killing fever.

Finally, they haul Kenny and Robert's broken bodies to a deck that juts out over the pond where they use long fishing canes to agitate the water's surface. They wish to simulate a large animal, either trapped or foolishly swimming across the pond. When they turn the lights on, they see their first customer for the night. It is old Abaddon himself, a fourteen-foot alligator. They toss the two corpses into the drink.

They are about to leave when another fellow reaches into his pocket. Pinching the lifeless flesh between a gloved thumb and fore-finger, he says, "Oh yeah, almost forgot. For your appetizer, we have black pipe soup." He tosses Andrews' severed penis into the water right in front of the alligator's snout. The beast snaps it up before it can sink. Abaddon has acquired quite an appetite for human flesh over the years. As they walk away, the great reptile thrashes about. Of course, there is the crunching of bones.

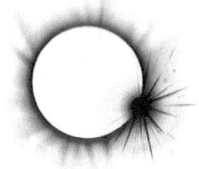

Chapter 12

CAPITULATION

By 5a.m., Jud Martin sloughs off the night's inebriation. Although those red eyes serve as reminders when Jud finally confronts the image in the mirror, he woke with a clarity of mind and thought. There are things to do. The first of which is to clean up the mess he has made with Sabrina's smashed picture and the broken bottle of bourbon.

This morning, he embarks upon a journey that leads him closer to the White House. It is what he is called upon to do by God. There is a peculiar irony in all that has transpired up to this moment. His purpose, and that of the Ku Klux Klan, is to eliminate this sort of thing from happening in this great nation. Bloodlines must be purified. At the forefront of monumental undertakings, Jud Martin must clean up the very mess in his own backyard. For who among them can truly lead without having sacrificed?

Although he showers and shampoos to shake off the lingering sickness befallen the night before, the nasty infection Ezra Krantz implanted is much too deep to wash away with water or booze.

Jud Martin goes to Ezra Krantz, who is barely awake. Not taking into account all the meds pumping into the old man through those ugly tubes, Jud Martin enters quietly and considers leaving.

Krantz stirs, noticing Jud Martin standing there with his long shadow stretching across the floor in the light of the hallway. Krantz has been having somewhat of a waking dream, and until he is fully able to focus those milky eyes, Martin looks like the grim reaper coming to fall harvest.

Martin waves a reassuring hand. "It's just me, old codger. How are you feeling this morning?"

Because this is the first time he will speak since the nurse left his bedside, Krantz sputters a short burst of words between his coughing fit. "Son, you scared me. I thought you was the man with the big scythe come to get me."

Martin chuckles while Krantz's attempt to do the same fails miserably. Bouts of coughing and wheezing replace his attempt at cajolery. Krantz points a bony finger at a small tray on his bedside table, which Martin places to his chin so the miserable old man can unburden himself of a wad of phlegm that he will have to swallow, otherwise.

"You ain't going anywhere, old fella. You're too damn mean to die," says Martin as he takes a seat. He can almost smell the old vomit...see the burnt photos.

Krantz follows Martin's movement with his puffy eyes.

"Oh, yeah? You wanna switch places?" he wheezes. "You know, it's funny. Ever since I was a child, I never used to dream so much. My mother told me it was because angels have everything they want, so they never need to dream. Others might say it's because the devil has no conscience."

Martin takes Krantz's withered hand. "Ezra, I've decided I must do what's required of me. It broke my heart to hear what you said last night, but it was nothing that a little bourbon could not fix. I know that nothing can be allowed to stand in our way, even if it is a zebra child I thought to be my own. Her blood isn't clean, and she could ruin everything if it ever gets out."

The old man pats Martin's shoulder. "I knew you would come around. It just had to soak in is all. You will need help, and I fear that the best man for the job is Willard St. John. Your…" Krantz strategically clears his clogged throat with a raspy gurgle. "…the woman and the lawyer are in Willard's territory, so he can help you with the proper disposal of both. There it begins and there it ends. As I am sure you already know, I had the photographer permanently relocated. He was just a local nobody, one more pea for the soup. I know what you're going to say, son. In the end, you will have to clean house right away." There is more wheezing.

Martin frowns. "Yeah, but Willard is a hothead and he's ambitious. He could get messy on me."

"You have no choice in this matter but to tell him everything. If he rides you for it, slap him down, son. You had better slap him down hard. For all practical purposes, you are the Supreme Imperial Wizard, the greatest and most powerful. No one questions that authority, or he will find it pretty damned dark inside a gator's belly. Do you hear me? Handle him because everything that's his is yours, and don't you let him forget it." Krantz finishes with another wrenching cough that seems to rattle on for an eternity.

Strangely, there is no will to stand without. There is no resistance to sway Jud Martin from his appointed duty because there is no love left in his heart for Sabrina Martin. No love at all. He chooses this path without so much as a whispering doubt because Krantz has powered the center of his entire world for far too long now, and all outsiders are in peril's way. Dr. Sabrina Martin simply has to die.

"I know it hurt you, Jud. I know. You must trust in the Lord when I say that this is the greatest test God has placed before you to date. You must keep your heart open to my words, Jud. He has placed a sign right before your eyes and you did not see it because you were caught up in the emotion of the moment. You must learn to see farther than most, through both fire and rain, even unto the bitter end."

"What sign? What do you mean?" Martin asks.

"You never looked at the rest of those photos or the newspaper clippings. You must be the one who knows all now. It is no mere coincidence that the Williams boy represented both Sabrina and Willard St. John in court. This is why I say you must see farther than the rest. God has raised the stakes, so you must prove that you are worthy. Nothing can stand against you when you see farther than the rest. If that means peering into the depths of darkness, then so be it, for God's divinity will always be your guiding light."

Martin nods in agreement. "You're right, and it shall be done. It shall be done." His eyes are strangely glazed over, reflections of a dark and decisive commitment.

When Governor Martin rises to leave for his appointed task, Ezra Krantz says, "Remember, Jud, God is doing this for his own reasons.

This is nothing to play with, son. You must destroy her with your own hands before I die. It will make you pure like the flame that lights the cross. Please believe that this is the final cross to bear. At the end of your appointment, you will gain total power. Think of total and complete power, Jud. This is most likely the last time that we will talk face-to-face from this side of the great divide, but my heart will be with you all of your days. I will miss you, Jud."

Krantz is fading into the sunset, but before losing consciousness, he sees and feels Jud Martin's final embrace. Martin kisses the clammy skin of Krantz's withered forehead before he leaves to face an annoying ass of a man. First, he returns to his own room to arrange his thoughts.

The shadow of Jud Martin's true father has made its presence known. It is powerful voodoo, this guilt, because his adoptive parent now clings desperately to life. All things owed to Ezra Krantz may become total power. God's power.

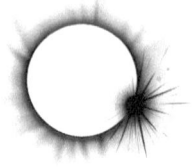

Chapter 13

TO SHARE
THE DARKNESS

During the course of the night, the couple packs Keith's things and relocates to Sabrina's place, where they make love once more before settling in for a hard sleep.

They awake around 7:00 a.m.

While he showers, Sabrina makes a light breakfast. She has never been married, and of all the men she has dated, Keith is one of the few who actually sits down at the table in the morning.

Though Sabrina Martin has dated men of refinement, the type many women consider the right sort, the relationships always fell apart. She has never been the overly subservient type, and most men of refinement—most men in general—seem to have problems with independent women.

Over the years, she has even dated the roughnecks, crossing tracks in search of excitement. However, the blossoming intrigue of novelty was usually just that.

With Keith Williams, things are different. He clearly loves her, a feeling that is wonderfully mutual.

Her career as a surgeon is fulfilling, deriving great satisfaction in making a difference in the lives of patients with physical ailments. She saves lives, losing a few along the way every now and then. The losses are always hard to take, so Sabrina purges her heartfelt sorrows with a good cry now and then. Deep down inside, after much self-examination, she recognizes that the little girl in her wants to save her patients from whatever had gotten her mother. In this respect alone, patients are more than just paychecks. They are much more.

Having Keith Williams, a kind and supportive friend whenever she has a heavy heart, makes quite a difference. He is an intricate man, but not too complicated. Like most women, she wants a man with whom she can speak on subjects that range from the negative ecological effects of burning the rainforests to kidney stones. Keith not only listens, he actually participates, and engages conversation. Often, he offers perspectives that open up entirely new ways of thinking or coping.

Sabrina feels cowardly about never introducing her significant other to her father. She has no knowledge of Governor Jud Martin's activities in the Ku Klux Klan, but she knows her father's political aspiration forces him to conceal his underlying racist attitude. After all that preaching about racial tolerance, she once overheard her father's utterances of unflattering Black remarks at a dinner party several years ago. It was more than a "two Black guys walked into the store one day" type of joke, but something mean-spirited and even a bit insidious. This is something they never discussed, but his appalling words were sufficient evidence of a veiled fundamental truth.

Sabrina Martin always feels a twinge of guilt whenever the two men intersect her thoughts because a small part of her wishes that Keith was White. It certainly would make things less complicated, but she loves him no less for it. It is only natural for a woman to want the two most important men in her life to like and respect one another, if ever comes the day.

The couple experienced at least one narrow escape at a chance meeting, but her quick thinking averted what surely would have been a disaster. While her father was on the campaign trail, he popped in on Sabrina, who practically shoved her lover into a closet where he sat for half an hour to avoid a potentially volatile situation. She apologized later, of course. In fact, she did so several times because that is what it took to keep from losing him.

Eventually, Keith forgave the trespass. A woman's tears seem to have that affect, but, still, it was not granted easily. If her quick solution to avoid a bad scene had been a simple matter of modesty, and a daughter's respect for her father, Keith could have laughed about it. However, he knew that it was something more. It was something anyone else would have seen as shame, and it stung him. It hurt.

After breakfast, she takes her turn in the shower while Keith calls his brother, Kevin, to inform him of his plans to visit their grandfather on the off chance he might want to come along.

The drowsy youngster quickly declines the invitation by claiming, "Not possible. I have a game tomorrow. Thanks anyway, bro."

Keith laughs. "You've obviously forgotten it's spring and tomorrow is Saturday. There is no practice or game this time of year. You must try to remember that I'm the lawyer in the family. You are the person who has obviously taken one blow too many to the helmet. You got me once—okay twice—with that bogus excuse, but I'm on to you. If you don't want to go, just say you respectfully decline the invitation. It's okay if you're still afraid of wolves, owls, and bears."

"Oh my," Kevin says in a high-pitched voice. They both laugh for a little while. "Seriously, it's our spring scrimmage. I'm not shitting you this time. For real, bro."

"Oh, right. My bad, man. I completely forgot about that. I planned to come and watch. I can delay my trip if you like."

"Nah. Don't sweat it. We won't be hitting hard anyway. It's just a glorified practice to see if we are in shape."

"Well, did they fix the air conditioning at your place?"

Kevin says, "No. They say the entire unit has to be replaced, and it may take up to a week. Man, its sweltering."

"How's Jasmine?"

"Shorty's fine. Just fine."

"Yes. She sure is," Keith says with a chuckle.

"How's the mystery woman?" Kevin asks.

"Sabrina's doing okay. She'll be joining me on this trip."

"Oh shit! She won't be a mystery much longer. This relationship must be serious. Tell Sabrina I said hello."

"Will do. Since I won't be here, you can stay at my place. Use the pool if you like. Do some laps."

"Really, you mean it?"

"It's all yours. I'll leave the passkey on the kitchen counter. Just don't break anything, and stay out of my liquor."

"Thanks, Keith. You da man, bro. I swear to God."

"No problem. One more thing before I go. The St. John case is over, but there have been extenuating developments that must be resolved. I need you to do a few things to keep my mind at ease."

Kevin says, "Damn. Sounds serious. What's up?"

"While you guys are here, especially at night, set the alarm. The code is still your birthday."

"I always do. Are you expecting trouble, Keith?"

"It's probably going to be okay, but just in case. I'll explain it all later."

"What's up?" Kevin asks. "Oh, that's right. I saw something on the news yesterday about you going straight ham on dude in the courthouse."

Keith considers his brother's safety. It is distressing. "Maybe I should just put you up in a hotel for a week."

"Nah, big bro, don't worry about that. I'll be careful."

"You sure?"

"Yeah. Yeah, don't give yourself a heart attack. I'll be fine."

"Okay then. Please don't talk to any reporters. They will be looking for me, so it's important that you avoid them at all cost."

"Did you really just raw smack that guy? What happened?"

Keith sighs, not wanting to say anything more. "I'll explain it all when I get back. Just remember what I said, and change the damn sheets when you're done. I love you, kid."

"The same, big bubba." They laugh and Keith hangs up.

After Sabrina finishes some last minute packing, they take that dreadful ride to the airport.

༄

Keith is glad that he decided to drive his car and sleep at her place because some reporter is probably lurking in the shrubs, waiting to pounce the moment he appears.

Upon arrival, they drive to the hanger that houses the firm's Gulfstream jet. The pilot's name is Wallace James, the first and only Black pilot Keith has ever known. The two men shake hands and share a brief, brotherly embrace before the attorney introduces Sabrina. Twenty minutes later, they are soaring toward Great Falls, Montana.

When the firm's private jet levels off at its designated altitude, the attendant pours two glasses of wine for the passengers before disappearing. She is determined to finish a great read during the flight.

Keith and Sabrina sip their after breakfast drinks and settle in. Neither person usually drinks this early in the day, but they both hate flying. Snuggling together, they giggle as the plane rises through a bit of turbulence. Sabrina Martin experiences a brief bit of nausea that passes quickly.

After the turbulence, though, Keith Williams becomes distant and solemn, staring silently through the portside window at the terrain moving in reverse far below. The attorney thinks about his younger brother's reaction when he learned that Sabrina is joining him.

She endures the silence for five or ten minutes, trying to fathom Keith's thoughts. Very softly, she whispers, "Tell me." She says nothing more, patiently awaiting his response.

When he snaps out of the trance, he says, "I'm sorry, honey, what did you say?"

Sabrina places her head upon his shoulder and smiles, thinking about how cute her man is when he is out there in la-la land.

"Can you tell me what you were thinking about just then, counselor?" she answers. "I've taken inflation into account, so I'm fully prepared to offer you a buck-fifty for your thoughts."

"I want cash. No checks, I've seen the way you balance your checkbook." They share a kiss and she returns her head to its familiar perch. "Is it the St. John matter?"

Keith shakes his head to the contrary and begins with, "I was thinking about gramps and you. God knows I hope I'm wrong, but there's more than a slight chance that he won't like you because of your race." He draws in a deep breath, for this is not an easy admission.

Sabrina gazes at Keith for an instant. She stretches out to nestle her head in his lap, looking up at him almost apologetically. He returns the gaze, but his sad thoughts seek the window and the world passing beyond.

She asks, "Do you really think it will be a problem? If it is, I can stay at a hotel. I can go back, if you like. I really don't want to be the cause of ruining the reunion." She is earnest, though saddened by the prospect.

Keith does not look at her. He stares out at the clouds and landscape while gently caressing her silky hair. "No. That isn't necessary. I invited you along so we can spend some time together. Our busy schedules separate us as it is. I've missed you, baby. You're good for me."

She smiles. "What a sweet thing to say. I've missed you, too."

"I want you there. My grandfather is a tough old bird, but if he does not like it, he'll have to get over it as best he can. We'll be staying in the cabin just up the trail from his."

"Why would he dislike me? I've done nothing to you or him, and he doesn't even know me. I'll charm the pants off of him, you'll see."

Sabrina is overconfident, without fully appreciating the situation on its true merits. His sigh causes her concern.

"Sabrina, do you remember a conversation we had when you were feeling guilty about certain things? I told you that I did not want or need to meet your father. Well, that's because he's from the old school, just like my grandfather. No matter what they say, this just isn't kosher. And it will probably never be right to them. To them, a Black man should be with a Black woman, and vice versa. We both know from experience that prejudice and racism know no color barriers. Black people are just as capable of racist attitudes as the next group. Some people, though, feel they have more reasons or rights to it than others do. At least, they believe they do. I don't think my grandfather has ever forgiven Whites for what they've done to him, his friends, and our family. That's why he chooses to live and die on that mountain."

"Does this have anything to do with the death of your parents? I know the scene at the courthouse must have brought a lot of old feelings to the forefront." Immediately, she decides to retreat, having witnessed the transformation of a thought into a twinge of pain. "Oh God. I'm sorry, sweetheart. It is really none of my business. Forgive me."

Keith furrows his brow. "The nasty scene at the courthouse...my grandfather's possible angst concerning your race...it all seems to tie in more than you may realize."

For a moment, his countenance is a dark cloud that looks hauntingly morbid. Then it is gone, soon to be joined by his very last secret.

Finally, he looks down at her and asks, "Do you know how much I love you, Sabrina? Do you really have any idea?"

She nods. "Of course I do."

Keith sighs before beginning a difficult journey into the past. Until now, he has avoided discussing the details surrounding the death of his parents with her. They have been dating for a little over two years, but certain truths of his past remain discretely sketchy.

"They came in the night when I was only twelve. Kevin was just an infant." He falters in the throes of suppressed anguish, prying open the gates that have long held back the chaos of distant days. "Those men were just like Willard St. John—worse—they had absolutely no humanity, Sabrina. I had to watch the Ku Klux Klan murder my parents and my world. We used to live in the Mississippi Valley on my father's farm. Things were so good until that night, but I could do nothing to stop them." Keith fights the tears welling in his eyes.

Feeling great empathy, Sabrina tries to stop him, but Keith Williams needs to do this painfully therapeutic thing. The only other people with whom he has ever spoken these words are his grandfather, a man named John Greycloud, and a child psychologist. He has never mentioned, in truth, any of what he knows to his younger brother because of the violent nature of the angry younger generation of the day. The availability of handguns on street corners or back alleys of Atlanta is another powerful deterrent of the truth.

Keith Williams visualizes his brother having mental flashes of the death of their parents after some drunken redneck makes the mistake of calling him out of name. He envisions the gun coming out of the jacket or belted waistline. He sees his brother saying, "Fuck you!" as he pulls the trigger. Being an officer of the court, having knowledge of such things, he envisioned his brother raped behind prison walls or dying as a death row inmate. He tells Sabrina these things; the real reasons for telling his younger brother that their parents died in a house fire.

Sabrina is moved to tears, and her tears summon his. She hugs her lover, wanting desperately to absorb the pain. She would do anything for Keith Williams in this moment, if only she could.

Somehow, he continues through the tattered tapestry of his parent's graveyard, dredging up soured emotions that sting his eyes and grate against his heart.

"I felt so small…so impotent…useless. Just useless. My father begged on his bleeding hands and knees for their lives, forced to watch as those vile men raped my mom. They violated her right there on the front lawn for god sake. I was standing at the edge of the woods in our cornfield with Kevin in my arms when they shot our parents. I thought I'd go blind and deaf from the sight and sound of it all. I may have done just that were it not for that squirming, hungry kid in my arms. God, it was horrible."

Sabrina tries to hush him, but Keith trudges on to the bitter end because this journey is not complete. "Shh. Baby, you don't have to…"

"The worst part of it was that my mother, after all of that, didn't die from the gunshot wounds. She was screaming my name through a wall of flames, telling me to run if I was still around. You see, instead of putting my mother out of her misery, those sons of bitches picked her up by her hands and feet like a sack of flour and tossed her through the window into our burning home. As I listened to her screams, I wished with all my might—God Almighty God—I wished with all my might that she would just hurry up and die. I felt so guilty for that thought…as if I had killed her myself. As if…as if…oh God. Oh my God." He bows his head with his eyes tightly clenched.

Keith's passion is enormous, overwrought with sorrow. He weeps in his lover's arms like the child that he becomes in the memory of this dark moment. Meanwhile, Sabrina holds on as if afraid he will take flight.

"So all of this time, you have carried this burdensome knowledge alone because you're being strong for Kevin's sake. I am so sorry, honey. It's a wonder that you can even stand to be around people like me. God, just let it out, sweetheart. I love you, Keith. I love you so much."

They hold one another as he lets these bitter tears flow to cleanse his soul. After carrying this burden for so long, Keith is thankful that he survived it emotionally.

Sabrina Martin is more appreciative of the depth of his commitment to her. His very painful confession is proof positive of it. She gains a better understanding of his anger when she forced him to hide in a closet on the day her father showed up for a surprise visit. The revitalized shame of it washes over her, again. However, her concern quickly returns to his emotional state of mind, his need for comforting.

Moments later, the flight attendant, who inadvertently overheard the entire conversation, forces a smile as she checks on the passengers. She sniffles and wipes a tear away when she looks into Keith's eyes. After overhearing the saddest story she has ever heard, she quickly excuses herself to regain her composure. Losing her job for eavesdropping just will not do.

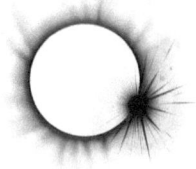

Chapter 14

SLAP HIM DOWN

W illard St. John is in his east wing bedroom observing the coming sunrise when Jud Martin knocks. Willard has been up all night, drinking and getting high. The fact that the Andrews hunt was a total fiasco depresses him, and he just cannot seem to let it go.

It is actually his attorney whom he envisions hunting down like an animal. Mr. Andrews was merely a convenient substitute, a living effigy of sorts. Mostly, they all look alike to St. John anyway. He is a psychopath, and at this moment, not unlike a cannibal long starved of meat.

Willard wonders how his lawyer feels standing in the unemployment line. He broods after plotting all night long, putting together the perfect scenario for counselor Williams' death. Parts of it came to him like a dream on the previous night. He would send his men to get Williams and any bitch with the unfortunate luck of being present. His minions will take them deep into the woods where even witches dare not go. There, he will defile and strangle the woman while Williams watches.

While Williams still breathes, St. John plans to cut off both his ears for the mantle place of his secret trophy room. Then he will de-dick him, just like Kenny Andrews, but he will stuff the severed penis in the lawyer's mouth before chaining him to a four-wheeler for a great American swamp drag. He will shackle the chain about the lawyer's neck. So Keith Williams does not strangle to death, they will shackle both wrists to the chain high above his head to prolong the agony of having his flesh stripped as his bones break. For all his planning, there is still the question of just how he will finish Williams off. Should he put a bullet in Keith's brain, or gut-shoot him and watch him die slowly? Willard also considers slitting Keith's throat. Decisions, decisions.

One thing is for sure, Keith Williams will be gator bait! There will be no grave for that nigger. St. John is quite inventive when it comes to the administration of death. Clearly, he believes death the only suitable punishment for those who offend. Moreover, he is offended quite easily and all too often.

Controlling the largest region of the new Klan only boosts Willard's arrogance. He has never been above terrorizing or murdering his Grand Dragon counterparts to get what he covets. When the new order reined in under Krantz, Martin, and Black, he seized every opportunity. Their plan eliminated the state-to-state, Klavern-to-Klavern networks, which were too loosely affiliated and often rival.

There were many Indians, but far too many chiefs, which left more than enough room for dissension. Each boss had his own personal interests to guard. One Klavern would not agree with this or that, while other Klaverns did not like that or this. Eventually, such tendencies for bickering was eliminated by simply showing them that they either joined the collective or died trying to be a big fish in a personal pool of standing water. The many, those who did not suffer suspicious deaths, found great merit in what the boys of new blood had in mind.

The hierarchy of the Klan became more defined and refined. Jud Martin and Peter Black are Supreme Grand Dragons, which are the equivalent of generals. Grand Dragons or full bird colonels follow them. Of which, there are only six; one per region designate. They control the majors down to the privates, the street-level, working-class stiffs. For them all, murder had to be the rite of initiation.

The new Klan is a very neat, very concise arrangement. The dispersal of power is designed to keep blood from staining the hands of the key and elect of the hive. It insulates them and their covert activities in government. Overall, the lowly grunts knew nothing of the inner circle's infiltration of the government, which keeps the loop airtight. Thusly, Robert James Smith, who took a Black, gay lover, had to die. He simply knew too much.

St. John is a colonel and he rides shotgun, literally. Some men are thinkers and others killers. He is a little of both, but a killer mostly.

Willard acquired a string of businesses along the Southeastern Seaboard from Virginia to the Florida Keys when called upon to sweep clean the dissident Klaverns. His holdings stretch into

Mississippi and Louisiana, where the, presumably, defunct David Duke resides in a state of semi-retirement. Willard takes what he wants to get where he is going, which even includes stealing from his own beloved organization. With the money he ferrets away for himself, the South could rise again.

Eventually, someone will have to knock him down a few pegs, if not completely off the board. His deeds are not unnoticed, but for the time being, he is a powerful go-getter whose assets still out-weigh the liabilities. In silent contempt, the upper crust is planting infiltrators throughout Willard's holdings so that they can usurp them covertly. To that end, those well-placed moles will use every legal and illegal means possible, including embezzling from Willard's resources; even to the point of bankruptcy.

Ezra Krantz knows that a direct confrontation in the latter days of their plans will not be conducive to their cause, so he cautions both Martin and Black to avoid an intramural dispute at all cost. The time will come to confront Willard St. John.

Before recent developments, they planned to give Willard St. John a chance to come clean. They will order him to divest, giving up what was wrongfully obtained from the organization he swore an oath to uphold. If Willard denies the truth or blatantly refuses to do what is demanded of him, those who have infiltrated his network will decimate his finances within the span of a year.

For the time being, they still need the most powerful Grand Dragon of them all. When a job does not require an excessive amount of tact, but more force than finesse, he is the man to call. Willard St. John understands that judges are as culpable as his executioner, which is the position he prefers to hold. He simply loves to get his hands dirty.

Jud Martin knows he will have to keep Willard St. John on a tight leash, less he will blow tires the good governor needs to navigate in bad weather.

The very last thing Ezra said about St. John was malicious and spiteful. All of their previous plans for dealing with him are off. Krantz had said, "Of course, it's up to you to decide how to deal with Willard through this mess, but it was up to God to decide who would deal with him. Make his men yours, those who would bleed for your sake. I will notify the moles we have planted throughout his organizations. They will rape his assets into oblivion, like twisters ripping through a shantytown. We will even pillage his stash of gold bricks. Willard is not to return from this assignment. Let him take the rap for their deaths as a dead man. You must promise that he will never stand over my funeral and smile. Do this for me, son. Pretend that his actions have gone unnoticed. Act as if you have not made the connection with the lawyer. When he serves God's purpose—whatever that may be—you rain down on him with a quickness and totality. Willard St. John has been much too defiant, a roaring jackass that has overestimated his place among us. To me, he ain't no better than a biggity nigger, cock-strutting' in a high-yellow pimp suit. Destroy him, Jud. Utterly and completely destroy him."

When Martin knocks at Willard's door, he emerges from a daydream in time to stash the nose candy, and meets Martin as he opens the door.

Martin enters saying, "Good, you're awake."

"I've always been an early riser. Can't sleep the world away you know. What can I do for you, oh great one?" St. John sniffles.

"We must talk. I have a dilemma which falls under your jurisdiction." Martin studies St. John's behavior and his mood. "Ezra assures me that you're the man for the job."

"High praise indeed. It must be messy work if you are personally involved. If that's the case, then I'm your man."

These two men are not far apart in age, but they are as different as is day from night. Martin, by comparison, a man of great intellect and tact. Willard is more the intelligent, but ruthless barbarian. They sit facing one another.

"Ezra wants me to take you along when I go to Atlanta to eliminate a male and female target. Your end will be garbage disposal. The primary target's name is Sabrina Martin."

Willard's head snaps back and he becomes wary of the man he faces. "Your daughter? Isn't she your daughter?"

Martin is exasperated only seconds into the conversation. "She's no longer to be considered my daughter. Ezra has given me proof of that. She is a threat to our work, so she's got to go." He is looking at his hands.

"But why, and what evidence could prove that she isn't yours? Did she find out something and turn against you, what?"

"I really don't want to get into the details with you, Willard."

"Well, I don't care what you want. If you expect me to help you snuff your own kid, you better give me a damn good reason."

Governor Martin recalls Ezra saying, "Show reluctance to share the details, but give him the bone of boldness. When that disrespectful dog chews on your gristle, it will give you every reason to slap him down!"

Jud Martin is forced to come clean about the shameful thing in his closet.

"She's not pure. Her actual father was really an African American, and now she's taken up with Blacks." He grows angry just hearing the words come from his own mouth. "Get the fucking picture?"

St. John's smile is a grimace. He leans back in his chair and derides Martin with no caution for the man's mood. "Say what? So let me get this straight. You're missing wife gave a nigger some ass and you raised his pup, thinking that it was your own?" He chuckles, and then he laughs so loudly that some men hear him down the hall. Willard points at Governor Martin and says, "And now she's fucking a Black man. Oh, this is rich. This is just too much, oh Imperial Sage of the Realm!"

Until this statement, Governor Jud Martin remains humbled, but he is quickly reminded of what Krantz said. His blazing anger displaces the embarrassment. Before St. John knows the governor has left his seat, Martin pounces. He snatches St. John from the chair, slaps him, and rams him into the wall. He moves in close to the astonished adversary, staring into Willard's eyes with deadly intent.

"Listen to me, you ignorant son-of-a-bitch," Martin says with his hot breath surging into St. John's face. "You had better remember who I am. Fuck with me on this and you won't live to regret it." Martin slams him into the wall again. "Everything that is yours is mine, and I'll see you set out in a field and hunted like a rabid dog. If you keep shoving that shit up your nose, you are bound to make mistakes. Your first was messing with me. You have no future unless I allow you one, so you had better remember your place, boy! You're dicking around in the water with the Orca now, Mr. Great White. And this latest embarrassment to my person whets my appetite for blood. Don't make me chew you up and shit you out. Got it?"

The big man, Mr. St. John, is nothing without a gun in hand or a pack of wolves to do his bidding so he backs down posthaste.

"Alright, I got it. I'm sorry, boss. Really."

Martin releases him, backing away to straighten his cuff. He is still enraged, but rapidly regaining his composure. He turns away so St. John cannot see the evil little smile of satisfaction that threatens to crack his rigid posture. He suddenly understands exactly what Ezra meant by 'high-yellow pimp suit' because this man is a coward with a yellow streak a mile wide. What he gleaned from Willard's eyes was not respectful acquiescence, but full-throttle fear.

"Now then, she's working at the Grady Memorial teaching hospital. I will need your help with disposal. She has been spending time with a Black lawyer named, ah, Williams. He works for some big firm in Atlanta."

Willard is hurled back into life. Quite out of reflex, he grabs Martin by the arm and spins him around. "Williams? Keith Williams of Mitchum, Simms and Bates?"

Martin relaxes the hands he raised to a fighting position when he thought Willard had gotten foolish enough to retaliate. He says, "Yes. That's him alright. Know 'em?"

St. John runs his fingers through his hair. "Well I'll be fucked up the ass like a fag in heat. Why didn't you just say so? Yeah, I know him. He is the spook, who got me out of that murder charge when I erased that punk kid. He is a hell of a lawyer, and he has a nasty right when he gets riled up. Bastard nearly took my head off." Willard is salivating and Martin watches as he goes into a momentary trance. "Dreams do come true sooner than later. I owe him. Boy, do I owe him big." He rubs his jaw with his left hand.

Martin watches him intently. "That's why his name sounds so familiar to me. He defended Sabrina in a malpractice suit with a pharmaceutical mogul. That's probably when the affair started."

"Now that you mention it."

"So you did set up that shooting. And then, you used a Black lawyer to have you exonerated. Need I ask why he attacked you?"

Despite himself, Martin finds new respect for a man he just slapped down hard. Maybe St. John is not as stupid or as careless as he appears to be. Maybe he is just a glutton for the kill adrenaline.

St. John beams with pride. "Damn right I did. That fucker deserved to die." After a brief pause, he adds, "Don't worry, I'll do them both. I would consider it an…"

"No. The girl is mine. It's got to be done by me. I've got plans for her before I do her!"

Two powerful men, who never liked one another, temporarily unite in light of a slightly more than common enemy. The irony is that a Black man bears the cure for their rift. That common enemy is someone else to despise, and his name is Keith Williams.

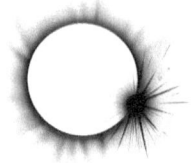

Chapter 15

AN ALLIANCE
WITH LIGHTNING

After three o'clock, Keith and Sabrina's flight touches down at Windfall Airfield, just outside of Great Falls, Montana. Keith looks at her as the plane comes to a halt. "Are you absolutely sure, Sabrina? Do you really want to do this?"

She smiles and says, "Without question."

He smiles and jokes, "You do realize that this is the plot of every crappy, cut-rate horror movie we've ever seen together." She smiles when he raises an eyebrow to begin a truly bad impression of Rod Serling of the original Twilight Zone.

Sabrina laughs before he even begins.

"In a world where we open doors that promise freedom, we find ourselves staring right back at our own image, trapped in a room somewhere in a hellish corner of undiscovered territory. Two lovers, desperately in need of a fresh start, venture into the deep woods to get away from hustle and bustle of big city life when they encounter a hungry ancient evil just yawning awake after a long sleep in the mountains of Montana. There is no rhyme nor reason for what happens next, just the wrong place at the wrong time in The Twilight Zone. Woo!"

His woman chuckles, wildly. "God you really stink at that, but it was your best one yet."

They power down their cell phones and pagers before placing them inside a storage bag, asking the attendant and pilot to look after them. Moments later, they wave goodbye to Wallace and go to their rental car, the Hummer all-terrain vehicle Keith always wanted to test drive. He tells Sabrina it must be the redneck soldier in him.

Jeremiah Williams could have greeted them at the airfield with the rugged Ford Bronco Keith bought for his birthday two years ago, but this is a surprise trip. He often wonders if the old man even bothers to drive the truck, other than coming down the mountain to pick up his mail, monthly staples, or horse feed. Thinking ahead, Keith suggests they load up on supplies and extra gasoline. He doubts his grandfather buys anything other than canned and dried goods, which are the bulk of those staple items.

The couple, ignoring a few glaring looks, get everything they will need at the local store and set out on the four hour trip. Keith drives onto Route 91, heading up the northwestern valley just below Window Lake.

They see elk, wary black tail deer near the forest's edge, and quite a few vultures feeding on roadkill. Much to his surprise, Sabrina is not repulsed by the sight of the winged scavengers, which only stop picking at some dead roadside animal to take flight as the SUV approaches.

"This is a really beautiful place. It's like something out of time with the rest of the world," she declares, taking in the sweeping green slopes of the landscape. "Maybe I'll retire here when I'm old and gray. What do you think?"

Keith, who's feeling much better after purging his soul, smiles and says, "I can see you and them old bones of yours mullin' around in a Rocky Mountain blizzard with the hungry wolves, Ms. Brina."

They laugh at what he calls his Mudbush slave's voice.

Moments later, she snugs the warm Afghan turtleneck sweater up and asks, "Tell me a little more about what your grandfather. Besides not being too keen on White women dating his handsome grandson, that is."

Keith grunts. "Humph. Jeremiah Williams, also known as Geronimo. Age sixty, and as sound in mind and health as that old bear he chases up and down that mountain. My grandfather is a good man. He really is, Sabrina. He may be a little rough around the edges, but he's a good man, nonetheless. Also fancies himself quite the tinkerer actually. In ironic contrast, he spurns most modern day gadgets, but he is an astute problem solver, with an inventive mind. My grandfather is not to be underestimated."

"Tell me more." Sabrina smiles at him.

"At age seventeen, Jeremiah married my grandmother, now deceased. Her name was Liza Whitefeather, a Mymawgua Indian. Their son, Keifer Williams, my father, married Kalla Greycloud at the tender age of eighteen. She was the niece of John Greycloud, who lives with my grandfather. Now you know where all the Ks came from in my family. As luck would have it, all the people with Ks in my family were born in the first week of November. All Scorpios, if you're into horoscopes and such."

"No kidding?" she interjects. "I can't believe you never told me that."

"Jeremiah moved north from Mississippi when he was still a boy. Being an only child, my granddad inherited a great deal of prime property in the Mississippi Valley territory, but with all the racial stuff going on down south, you know. My father, on the other hand, wanted to start a family. He wanted to work that land, his inheritance bequeathed by Jerimiah Williams, so he took my mother and moved south years later."

Sabrina leans over and kisses his cheek. "I never would have guessed that you are partly Native American. Never in a million years."

"Oh? Is that what they're calling us these days?" Keith asks with a smile. "You would not believe how the scorn of racism plays out in the Native American community in this country. In many ways, they are just as hateful toward anyone of mixed African American decent."

Shocked, Sabrina asks, "Are you serious? You would think that two people, with such similar histories of enslavement and genocide, would bond together. Wow."

Keith says with a smile. "Well, that is another story. After my folks died, there was no one left but my granddad. He took us in and sold thousands of acres of farmland to a big corporation, and to some of the farmers that held leases. He made a tidy sum, I might add. He used some of the money to fix up the cabin and the barn. Much to the surprise of many, me included, he moved down the mountain so my brother and I could get an education and proper medical attention whenever needed. There was…there was a period of time when I had a few problems that required professional help. I suppose you might say I had to be shrunk."

"You did? Get out of here, Keith. You're the most stable man I know."

"Well, we all have our secrets, dear. Besides, I was a kid then and still traumatized by my parents' death."

"Apparently so. Please go on."

"Jeremiah really hated the city, but sacrificed his personal desires so we could have some kind of future. When I finished high school, as you already know, I went to Notre Dame. I passed the bar exam on the first try, and I was recertified to practice law by the Georgia Bar Association. When I finally got myself established at Mitchum, Simms, and Bates, there was no looking back. I am truly blessed to be a part of such a well-respected firm. Just when I thought it was safe to go back into the water, Kevin joined me. That damn boy was a real handful, I'm telling you. Man, we went through some changes. Jeremiah and Greycloud often called him Chief Little Mischief, but I suppose he turned out okay. If Kevin hadn't grown up to be such a responsible and mature young man, he wouldn't be living in his own apartment. He would still be living with me, and we'd still be getting on each other's nerves. I love him, though. He's a good kid."

The radio crackles and sputters bits and pieces of the news when the signal could penetrate the surrounding mountain range. The top story is the upcoming lunar eclipse, which brings fond memories to Keith's mind.

"As kids, we spent weekends and entire summers on the mountain where my grandfather and Greycloud used to tell us old Native American folklore and legends. We had such great times, just listening, sitting around the fire and drinking cider made from the apples of a wild orchard. They never realized how strong it was or just how tipsy that shit got us. When they said something funny, it was just a little too funny. We'd laugh way too much. It's a wonder we aren't both alcoholics right now."

Sabrina sees a light dancing in his eyes, which primes her womanly curiosity. Her voice is that of a child eager to learn when she says, "Wow, sounds priceless. Tell me one of those stories, Keith. Please."

Keith continues to maneuver up and down the winding country road, digging through old layers of fabled memories in search of details from the best story.

After the brief pause, he says, "Now, let's see. My favorite story is fitting to the occasion, since there's supposed to be a lunar eclipse coming soon."

Sabrina curls up in the seat. "Well, counselor, I'm all ears. Tell me a story."

Keith looks at her. "Are you sure you wouldn't like to wait for a campfire or a blazing fireplace and a glass of wine? A little ambience, perhaps?"

She shakes her head. "No way. I am fascinated by your stories. Each one seems like a part of you that I'm yet to fully discover. I think this beautiful countryside will provide all the ambience I'll ever need, just as long as you're here with me." She hugs him and settles back for story time in the Rocky Mountains of Montana.

Such moments are truly what makes dreams, and great relationships. Sharing the darkness, as they had during the flight, was the best assurance of appreciating the light of a new dawn on the horizon.

ഐ

When Martin and St. John land in Atlanta, two of Willard's top cronies meet them. He counts on these men when there is delicate work to do. That is delicate work of the killing kind. The hulking brothers, Billy Joe and George Fellows, both have seen action in Grenada and the Gulf War before retiring from the Marine Corp. Their father is a retired Marine, who was twice passed over for promotions he felt were given to less qualified Black men in his unit. The Fellows brothers joined the corps with his bitter poison already pulsing in their veins. They were brave men, patriots to the death for the red, white, and blue. However, their nasty, insubordinate behavior toward any non-White soldier kept them from gaining the rank they deserved. Their father had done things the same way.

Although they are not twins, the resemblance is astonishing. Billy Joe is ten months older than George, whose mother practically cloned the younger brother. They are huge men, with penetrating blue eyes and blonde hair.

Willard finds uses for them in several capacities. For instance, whenever he needs information on a person, they will simply charm the pants off anyone that knows him or her. When push needs shoving, they simply kill it out of him or her. It is always better for a person to volunteer the information, even if he or she realizes that they are being picked for it. In most cases, they leave no dangling ends.

The four men get into the limousine and hit the highway. The younger of the two hands a folder to St. John. "We have the photos, sir."

Martin's stomach rolls for a second, until St. John opens the folder to produce a picture of Keith William's alone and fully clothed.

After a wave of relief sweeps the nausea away, Jud Martin takes the newspaper photo from St. John. "So, that's the great man in all his splendor. The previous photo of him was a bit marred, so I never really saw his face clearly."

"Yeah. That's the champ, but what he doesn't know is that we are about to have a no-holds-barred rematch. This time, all the rules are going right out of the window. Hell, maybe he will, too."

Billy Joe continues the briefing. "We attempted to place the subjects this morning just so we'll know exactly where to get a hold of them, but neither is at home. George called the hospital, not there. At that time, I called the law firm for an appointment with Williams. I insisted on having him work on my case, but I was informed that he left town on an extended vacation. His destination is unknown. It is reasonable to assume that they are together."

"Fuck!" says St. John.

"Damn it," comes from Martin after dialing her cell only to get the voicemail.

George says, "Don't worry, sir. If anyone can locate them, we can. It's just a matter of time." The brothers are not visibly disheartened.

As St. John picks up the phone, he says, "That may not be necessary. They probably fired the bastard. They just said he was on extended vacation because it sounds better. You know how those fucking lawyer types are." He, sheepishly, looks at Martin. "Just give me a minute."

◈

Exactly twenty-eight senior partners representing top law firms across Georgia and bordering states listen with intent as Mitchum, Simms, and Bates reiterate the latest developments surrounding a complete debacle. Because voracious lawyers are notorious for going after other lawyers, this voluntary disclosure is not without risks. Without ever mentioning the subjects name, as the front page of the newspaper sits before them, an unmistakable conclusion is drawn by them all. However, this exclusive invitation actually places them all in a class reserved for the respected elite. The invite was very short notice, with first class transportation and five-star amenities thrown in at the expense of MSB. It was an offer not refused or easily shrugged off because in one way or other, they all owed the law firm of Mitchum, Simms, and Bates. This polite gathering is more of a warning to everyone present; you know who the enemy is so tread lightly.

Mitchum stares them down, his smile fading into a dour glare before saying, "Take on hostile opponents of Mitchum, Simms, and Bates at your own risk, and we will call in all favors before crushing you. All past favors and collaborations will be off the table. All agreements not written in stone between attorneys and firms will become warrior pawns against anyone who foolishly represents that particular enemy combatant claiming to have a grievance against the most powerful firm in the South and it means war. Hold true to our alliances while discretely poisoning the waters. Warn affiliates, who may be tempted to step across the line drawn in the sand. It is simple really. We offer no concessions here, but that doesn't mean this cannot be a win/win situation."

At the conclusion of the meeting, Simms holds up a min-recorder and states, "Of course, distinguished colleagues, you are free to vote your own conscience. Criminals use lawyers to defend their wrongdoing all the time. However, the buck stops when predators brag about blatantly seeking us out to free him of the responsibility of murdering another. This kind of thing gives us all black eyes and bad names on the tongues of the public—without which—we cannot function. Without their confidence, we are worthless to innocent victims and priceless to the whims of evil.

The audacity…the utter hubris of this man is an insult to us all. We will not condone, by action or words, the murder of an innocent person for a client's perverse pleasure. It does not matter how deep his pockets are because we all have a God to answer to some black day. I would like to meet my maker with a clear conscience. We, at Mitchum, Simms, and Bates, look forward to future collaborations with you all as wards of the court and comrades in arms. Keep the mesh tight on this conspiracy. We've all made deals with the devil and come to regret them when it's time to smile at our children or grandchildren…when it's time to enjoy our simple pleasures in life…when it's time to sleep in peace. Let us stand united against this one, and maybe, just maybe, a multitude of past sins will be forgiven. Now then. We have set up a sumptuous buffet in the fourth floor banquet hall. Enjoy and imbibe to your individual contentment. Thank you all for coming in person, and to all in attendance via videoconference. This particular recording is a reproduction of the original, edited to remove the name mentioned by a compatriot of a villainous killer to avoid any incongruities of an ethical nature. Good day."

Hours after the early meeting with the elite, whose influences spread throughout the southern regions of the United States, the polite receptionist answers, "You have reached the law offices of Mitchum, Simms, and Bates. How may I direct your call?"

"Let me speak to Mitchum. This is Willard St. John."

"Right away, Mr. St. John. It seems Mr. Mitchum has been attempting to contact you, also. One moment, please."

"Good to hear from you, Mr. St John. Listen, you should come into the office. I believe we have things to discuss. Problems, to be exact."

Mitchum is smiling as he begins to spin his own web of lies. The other senior partners are now huddled at his sides. Though this is a conference call, they are to remain silent.

"Problems. What problems?" Willard's voice fills with anxious curiosity. "We have no problems as long as that fucker is history."

Mitchum pauses to assume the mind-set of his role before blasting St. John. "That ungrateful, bastard is blackmailing us all. If we even hint at firing him, Williams threatens to go straight to the press with information about your very unwise confession to murdering that Brown kid. The press has already found out about what happened inside of the courthouse, but they don't know the why of it yet. Still, your face is on page one of the Atlanta Journal-Constitution. Williams portends to tell the world that you mentioned getting away with this sort of crap in the past! It seems he did a little digging into your hotly disputable past. It appears you were implicated in a double homicide four years ago in South Carolina. Dropped due to lack of evidence. You were also a person of interest in another double homicide investigation in Alabama about ten years ago."

St. John's mouth falls open as his eyes dance back and forth. He has not considered Keith Williams playing dirty pool. Perhaps his arrogance is getting the best of him because destroying Williams' career is the only thing he considered, other than a horrid death. The news of Krantz's flagging health had come and there was the meeting, so he left town abruptly. Willard soon finds that he may have seriously underestimated this particular adversary. "Say what?"

"Yes. That is not the worst of it. He also threatens to conduct this big press conference in the heart of the blackest community. I know that he spoke to the U.S. Attorney General in Washington. He would not divulge the reason or substance of the call. However, I know he is seriously contemplates telling the fucking world that you shot the kid in the face before shooting him an additional fourteen more times, but he had the evidence suppressed. This firm will be implicated in the cover-up as well. He will tell the press that we knowingly entered into contract with you and set him up as a courtroom tactic…a sacrificial pawn. Do you hear what the hell I'm saying, you fucking prick?" Mitchum's words seem very venomous, while he reels St. John in like a trophy largemouth bass.

Willard ignores the insult in light of greater issues. "He can't do that. I was already acquitted. They can't do anything if they wanted to. Where is he? I'll blow his freaking head off!"

"Now, now, Mr. St. John. That is exactly the kind of loose talk that places both our asses in this predicament. If you had just kept your yap shut about what you did, we would not be sharing this mess with you. Mens rea…actus reus, Willard. The terms are Latin for—you premeditatedly executed an innocent kid with malice aforethought. All this shit, and for what? Christ almighty. I bet I know what your feeble little mind is thinking right now, but you dealt a severe blow to his pride and heritage. Keith Williams is so angry right now, he no longer cares about his job because his entire race has turned on him. Therefore, he is not going to allow questions of ethics or confidentiality to have any bearing in this matter. I am sure that is what you're counting on. Can you say civil lawsuit, Willard? The boy's mother can sue us both if he takes it public. If you want to risk it, please get it through your thick skull that this is no longer just your problem. You used Williams and bruised his ego, turned his own fucking people against him in the process. He is so pissed right now that the certainty of disbarment holds no consequence. I just spoke to two federal judges about getting a gag order to keep him quiet. Both judges agree. We can do nothing until Williams makes a definitive move. We will not know where or who he contacts, and we will always be one step behind. In the end, he may get an insignificant punishment for inciting a riot. No matter what, you nor this firm is fast enough to catch that cat once it's finally let out of a stinking bag full of fleas." Mitchum eases up, but he is not finished because he is waiting for St. John to say something in particular.

"As I've already stated, I've been acquitted by a jury of my peers. What can he do, honestly?"

Mitchum gets technically superior now by saying, "Just how much do you know of the law, Willard? Just how ignorant are you pretending to be? I only ask because even back alley lawyers, like yourself, should know that any case can be retried and the verdict overturned with the introduction of viable new evidence from credible sources. Didn't know that, did you?"

"He can't prove anything, even if he tries," shouts Willard, forgetting the company he keeps. He does not appreciate being spoken to in this manner.

"Willard, you're a bigger fool than I thought…a freaking mental midget. What do you think we do here, sit around twittering our thumbs all day? Don't you know that all lawyers walk around with those godforsaken mini-recorders? It just so happens that Williams was making a personal notation on the damn thing when he strolled up just before you talked about how good the kid's cocaine was. I especially like the part about handing the kid the empty gun. Pow! Would you like to hear my copy of it? Why don't I play it over the loud speaker for everyone to hear? I hope the Feds are listening. Would you like that?" He pretends to speak to his assistant. "Pamela…Pam, get Williams' recent recording from the safe please.

Never mind that, just drop whatever the fuck you are doing right now. Get it, or you're fired. And bring me some antacid."

"No don't. That won't be necessary," Willard says quickly. Obviously, this killer recognized specific words uttered by his very lips. "No. Really, I'm sure. I believe you."

"Are you prepared for an all-out riot, Mr. St. John? I can assure you that once that man makes it known that you have been preying on minorities and gays, those bloodthirsty gangsters will come down on this place like a ton of bricks."

"You listen..."

"No, you listen to me, Mr. St. John. You will become public enemy number one in a town where we—we—just happen to be the fucking minority. This will become scorched earth all over again. They will burn this city down, as if Major General William Tecumseh Sherman never existed, and all because of you. By the time those hoodlums are through, there won't be anything left standing. The real tragedy is that human life was destroyed, even if it was only a young thug. The unsavory fact of the matter is that we will go down in flames with you because Williams is willing to incinerate us all. You have jeopardized our life's work with this clever ploy, and I'll be damned if we'll sit back and let that happen. My senior partners are incensed over this, and they both want a pound of flesh for what you've done."

"But...but..." is all St. John can say. He is trying not to look at Martin or allow him to hear the loud, looming words that are coming over the line.

It is time to land this fish. "You have really put your foot in all of our mouths, Willard. How could you stand in the very same courthouse, where you were just acquitted, and confess to murdering that kid? What were you thinking, man? All Williams has to do is lose that tape recording in a very public place, like the lobby of the Atlanta Journal-Constitution Newspaper and you are through. Remember, your voice can be digitally verified, and one of your sycophant bunkmates actually called you by name. Anyone can turn it in to the DA. If that happens, we will lose our copy of it and deny any knowledge of its existence. That means you will be on your own. Fuck me stupid!"

Sweat is forming on his forehead. "What now? What do we do now?" asks Willard with amazing meekness.

"We're going to play ball with that man, whether we like it or not. That means Williams will retain a position here at this firm. Not as a fucking janitor, but as a full partner. That is the non-negotiable price Mitchum, Simms, and Bates has to pay for your indiscretions. Of you, he requires that the boy's mother is compensated with a sum of no less than one-million dollars. Payable anonymously through this law firm, and I mean ASAP. Otherwise, this very cunning young man takes you to task. Remember, Willard, District Attorney Gavin is also African American. Do not forget that little fact. After they get through reaming your ass, which should make it just about primed enough to accommodate all the Black prison cock that awaits you, it's off to civil court, mister. But you will probably be wearing an orange jumpsuit, ankle shackles, a bulletproof vest, and a nice shiny pair of handcuffs!"

"Hell no! You must be insane if you think..."

"Shut up, Mr. St. John. Please, just shut your mouth. I suggest you pay the cost of undeserved freedom and cut your losses. Otherwise, you might not live long enough to see the death chamber after the new evidence sends you there. If need be, I will be there to throw the switch myself. Just count your blessings and cut your losses because a man of your standing can surely afford such a negligible loss. If you end up in civil court, this will easily soar into the tens of millions. The criteria for establishing liability in a civil suit is less stringent than criminal trials, so you can count on getting both barrels. Keith Williams has already decided that it is worth risking his disbarment to see you twisting in the wind. When he gets with that kid's mom and expresses how horrible he feels, how dejected he feels since discovering the truth, they will both take you to task. Push this thing and you're done, Willard. The bar's new rules of ethics state that we can also sue you for deliberately misrepresenting the truth, thereby making us unwilling accomplices in the murder of a minor, which completely tarnishes this law firm's reputation in this entire state. Push us there and the price tag rises into the hundreds of millions. Right now, I want you to hear me loud and clear, Willard. If this firm is forced to join in the fray because of your little bout with diarrhea of the mouth, you will lose it all. Everything. I will personally make sure that you won't have toilet paper to wipe your ass with when the dust settles, motherfucker. Do you understand me, Willard? You picked the wrong attorney to involve in this twisted game. If you don't agree to these terms before tomorrow night, the price doubles for both of us."

Of course, only some of what Mitchum so passionately declares is truth, but it will take Willard divulging too many details of this conundrum to get an accurate assessment from another attorney. A rational person would not dare risk that, but Mitchum suspects that he will probably try.

Willard decides on a strategic retreat. "Well, where is he? It sounds like he has us all by the balls. I suppose I owe him an apology."

If he kills Williams first, this unfortunate turn of events will never become subject to public recrimination. He can also keep his money, trusting that Mitchum would keep quiet. Although he dares not state it, Willard feels that another murder is the answer to their problems.

Bates and Simms are now patting Mitchum on the back. Ordinarily, they would be on the verge of wild laughter, but TJ Brown's murder is a sobering thought. By giving Willard an out with a mere million-dollar price tag attached to it, makes them all feel just a bit cowardly. Yes, they are trying to save Keith Williams' career. Yes, they are trying to save face, but a murderer is still getting away with murder.

If Willard is allowed to even think about seeking counsel on this matter, he could find that he is being sold a bill of soured goods. Now comes the second act.

Bates gets up with a heavy law book, and slams it on the opposite end of the table as if it is the office door. He shouts, "Damn it all to hell. Where is that bastard of a man? Have you heard from that murderous fuck yet? I am telling you right here and now, we are not going down for St. John. I will see him burn in hell first. I listened to that tape recording, repeatedly, and now I wanna kill him myself!"

A young woman's voice says, "Here you go, sir. Will that be all?"

Mitchum says, "Thank you, Pamela. That'll be all."

Bates says, "For God sake, please don't play that debacle again. I never want to hear it again."

Simms picks up the book and slams it on the table. At the same time, Simms and Bates' assistants are calling Willard's cell phones and offices, leaving urgent, ominous messages.

There is a moment of silence, before Mitchum sighs long and hard. "Did you hear that? This is some serious shit, Willard. Williams went away on an extended vacation, from which he will return at his own discretion. This vacation is all at our expense, I might add. We don't know where he went, nor do we want to." Mitchum grunts with disgust. "I know what you're thinking, but you better not do anything rash. We are in enough trouble as it is. You had better stick to the terms laid down before you like the Ten Commandments. I assure you, we have given this a great deal of thought and we see it as the most amicable of alternatives in an otherwise untenable situation. Williams has leverage over us all, and he's willing to use it to whatever end. That said, I trust we will receive the money for the boy's mother within twenty-four hours so we can all try to put this travesty behind us. It is only costing you money, but my partners and I must pay a much higher price. One more thing. Don't even think about getting another lawyer involved because Mitchum, Simms, and Bates is the biggest, baddest wolf of them all. There isn't a firm in the South that doesn't owe us several favors. Not one. It'll cost you a whole lot more than a million dollars to go against us with a novice because only a novice doesn't know whom to fear amongst rival lawyers."

Bates says, "Is that him on the phone? You should let that idiot know that my friend, who is a judge by the way, advises that the DA is already bucking for a hearing that may introduce new evidence. He will not divulge the source or content because he is yet to confirm it. I suppose Williams has already found a way to hang us all if we even think about refusing his every demand."

"You hear that? Just count your blessings. After all, you're not going back to prison where you will probably become some big Black man's bitch! Let that visual sink in whenever another brainless thought enters your head. Goodbye, Mr. St. John. I trust we won't be doing business, other than this, in the future. You've got exactly twenty-four hours to deliver the money Willard. After that, the price only rises, and all bets are off." Mitchum hangs up.

Willard repeatedly slams the phone into the cradle, reducing it to a useless mass of loose wires and broken plastic. A runnel of blood drips from his palm at the end of the childish display, but he ignores the pain. Now, his cell phone rings so he turns it off.

Martin watches his comrade's actions and knows instinctively that there is trouble. "Just what the hell was that all about?"

St. John turns away. "Nothing I can't handle. Don't worry."

He decides it best not to mention the guts of the distasteful conversation. If he does that, Jud Martin may enlighten him on the finer points of swallowing a barrel of bullshit.

"That sounds like a very expensive load of crap to me."

Willard is afraid to tell Martin the true nature of the phone call because his actions have seriously compromised him. The entire Klan, for that matter. No one is supposed to make waves while the Klan embeds deeper into the system. No one is above reproach when the plans of this secret organization are so close to actuation. Willard has broken many rules.

Martin overheard enough of the heated conversation; he is not convinced. However, before he can grill Willard, Billy Joe Fellows intervenes by saying, "There's a kid brother, sir. In fact, he's staying in the lawyer's condo. We saw him moving some of his things in around noon. We can extract the information from him."

The Fellows brothers are very thorough, which makes them Willard's favorite operatives. Surely, they will get the job done. They have to because these are now desperate times.

184

"Good work," says Willard with relief. "He would definitely tell his brother where he's going, but the kid won't just give up that sort of information."

"Leave it to us, sir. He also lives or dies at your discretion. Judging by the urgency that this matter seems to hold for both of you, I suggest he die. He'll definitely remember us if he's allowed to live."

Martin says, "If you kill him to make Williams return, we can't take the chance that he might not get the news for days. Extract the information, but leave no evidence. I want this done quietly. We don't want to raise suspicions. By the time the dust has settled, the cops will have to invent a killer." Martin resists the urge to look Willard in the eyes as he remembers Krantz's decrees. This, too, will lie at Willard's door in the end.

"Leave it up to us, Governor Martin. We will take care of it after dark. Such moves must always be made at night," says Billy Joe. There is no quarrel.

The limo pulls into Willard's parking space at his swank uptown restaurant, the White Room. The brothers leave without hesitation. The others go inside for dinner. Afterward, Willard will see that the governor is taken care of at one of his private properties. He makes two appointments and insists on the first one being an immediate meeting.

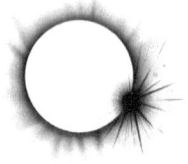

Chapter 16

DECEPTION

When the elevator opens on the tenth floor of Atlanta's pristine Queen Tower, the lobby of this law firm is bustling with well-dressed women going busily about their work. As they examine briefs with studious intent, Willard feels a little ignored. The only men present all seem to be clients.

The receptionist approaches from his blind side to ask, "Hello, sir. Welcome to Dahlman Law Offices. Do you have an appointment?"

He turns, adjusting his glasses. "Yes. I'm here to see Attorney Alice Dahlman."

The receptionist says with a cordial smile, "Oh yes. I was told to expect your arrival, Mr. St. John. Right this way please."

He follows her to the classy, glass enclosed office at the opposite end of the floor where she politely knocks before entering.

She directs him to have a seat before saying to an attractive young woman with black hair, "Kerry, this is Alice Dahlman's late evening consultation."

The young woman smiles at him and asks if he would like anything to drink. Willard St. John declines the offer. She picks up the receiver and presses line one.

"Hello, Alice. Your late arrival is here. Shall I see him in? Oh. Okay, I understand. Yes of course." She addresses St. John by saying, "It will be just a moment, sir."

Alone behind the partitioned glass wall of her office, Alice Dahlman twists a gold pen between her fingers as she leisurely swivels her chair back and forth. She rotates to the left for a quick glimpse at King Tower and smiles. The King and Queen towers are beautiful, blue glass enclosed buildings. Each building boasts white, uniquely shaped crowns to set them apart.

Alice Dahlman continues to smile, thinking of prophetic words recently spoken to her by a very wise man. While making St. John wait, she places a quick call to leave a brief message.

A few moments later, she comes out to greet Willard St. John, personally.

Wearing a stylish business suit and stilettos, the beautiful redhead smiles as she offers her hand.

"Mr. St. John, so very nice to meet you."

"Likewise," he says as he shakes her hand.

She directs him into her office where he sits before her desk. "Kerry, can I get a cappuccino? Thanks so much." She asks from the doorway, "Mr. St. John, would you like a cup?"

This time, Willard accepts. "Coffee. Two sugars and cream, please."

"Okay. Kerry, did you get that?"

"Yes. No problem," Kerry answers.

Willard looks at his watch, catching a glimpse of Alice Dahlman's ass in the Houndstooth skirt as she returns to her seat.

Very nice, he thinks to himself.

Behind closed doors, the attorney offers a disarming smile after catching him ogling her rear end. "Now then, welcome to the Dahlman Law Firm, Mr. St. John. I intuited a sense of urgency when we spoke earlier, so how exactly may I be of service?"

Willard, who has already rehearsed a carefully arranged dialogue, clears his throat. "Well, quite frankly, Mrs. Dahlman, I'm considering bringing a lawsuit against an attorney and, possibly, his entire law firm."

For his benefit, he smiles, wryly. "Hmm, my favorite kind of lawsuit. Go on."

There is a polite knock before the secretary comes in with two steaming cups.

Kerry closes the door as she exits. Alice uses the gold pen, a gift from her father commemorating graduating law school at the top of her class, to notate on a legal pad. His name is clearly the first thing written down before she places the pen to the side and picks up a pencil.

When the pencil pauses, Willard looks into the anticipatory gaze of the attorney. Since he says nothing more, she asks, "The attorney's name and that of his firm, please."

"Attorney Keith Williams and the law firm of Mitchum, Simms, and Bates…possibly."

With great deliberation, she applies enough pressure to snap the tip. The broken pencil pauses at the end of a graphite skid mark on the page. Taking a moment to look up at Willard, she grabs another pencil and writes down the names.

"I see. And what, may I ask, is the exact nature of your grievance against the persons named here, Mr. St. John?"

The hush of a sudden vacuum threatens to suffocate them both now that they have finally come to it—the threshold of peace—the doorway to all the potentials of hell.

In the absence of his voice, she looks up and asks, "Mr. St. John...?"

He clears his throat, again. "I have reason to believe..."

Alice Dahlman recognizes his hesitation so she sits back in her seat to take a sip. She places the cup and saucer on left side of her desk. Now, Alice picks up a copy of the newspaper, which clearly displays a photo of Willard being dragged away from the courthouse. She places it to the right of her desk for his reading pleasure.

"Obviously, this is a stressfully uncomfortable subject for you, Mr. St. John. So why don't we start over? Mr. Keith Williams is a extremely respected gunslinger at Mitchum, Simms, and Bates. Williams is highly sought after because his knowledge and prowess within the bounds of different edicts makes him a formidable counselor that successfully practices in multiple legal disciplines. A rarity, for the most part. Mr. St. John, not only is Williams very good at what he does, he is backed by what many people consider the most powerful law firm in the state of Georgia...if not the entire South." His expression sours. She rocks back and forth in her chair with a wry smile, adding, "But they don't scare me, so please...continue."

"Really?"

"Not in the least," she says, confidently. "Isn't that why you sought me out? So why don't we get to the meat of it?"

"Well, I have reason to believe that Keith Williams…Keith Williams is going to…"

Willard's well-rehearsed intro now seems inadequate, and his reluctance is beginning to try her patience. She looks to her right and lays claim to the newspaper. She glances at it and then at Willard for a second.

Alice sighs. "Mr. St. John, I can assure you that I will not divulge the reason for this meeting, whether I decide to take you on as a client or not. However, even though initial consults are free of charge, my time is valuable. You cannot expect me to go up against Williams or the entire MSB firm without knowing what I'm getting myself into. Maybe you just need more time to consider your options. Figure out if this tasty little can of worms is worth looking for a can opener."

Willard says, "No. That won't be necessary. May I ask you a question?"

"Certainly."

"Well, I didn't notice any male lawyers in the lobby or offices. Do you have no male attorneys?"

Without diplomacy, Alice Dahlman says, "I find your sexist question a bit offensive, Mr. St. John, if not a little misogynistic in nature. Are you implying that men are better attorneys?"

Willard retreats when her cross expression and burning eyes zoom in on him.

"Oh no," he lies. "I was just curious. No offense intended."

"Well…in that case, none is taken. You are somewhat of a curiosity yourself, Mr. St. John. For instance, Keith Williams just represented you in a haphazard manslaughter trial pushed forward by the District Attorney. I haven't the slightest clue as to what they discovered during the investigation into the shooting that could motivate them to move forward with a trial. I am very surprised that the prosecution didn't just scurry away with their tails tucked between their legs when you, a supposed racist and alleged murderer, walked in with an African American defense attorney. That was a brilliant move by the way. Williams won your case hands down, and, today, you are here to explore bringing a lawsuit against him. How did you get from there to here? I know that you two had a physical altercation inside the courthouse not ten minutes after your acquittal because it is plastered all over the news with lots of wild speculations flying about. Sources claim that Williams attacked you without provocation. However, that's just what the naked eye sees. Is it only punitive damages you seek for the assault or are there much more juicy details to come?" With girlish enthusiasm, she adds, "Oh, please say there is more. I simply love it when the plot thickens."

"Yes," Willard states. "There is, possibly."

Alice Dahlman's smiling eyes twinkle with intrigue. "Well now, that's a start. At the urging of Mitchum, Simms, and Bates, Williams will most likely settle out of court. If your proposed litigation extends to the firm itself, they will probably follow suit. I'm certain that I can get you satisfactory monetary compensation. However, I will need to know much more to judge whether this is personal and heading for a nasty, public court battle. Now, I will need the names of any witnesses, anyone who was close enough to testify as to what exacerbated the attack. I believe supportive friends of yours were present for the reading of the verdict. Yes? Great. They're your friends, therefore anything they say will be deemed prejudicial and virtually meaningless, but that won't stop me from using them like blunt swords. Tracking down the first eyewitness interviewed by the press concerning the attack should be easy enough. I'm certain I can file and get an evidentiary subpoena for the courthouse security film footage. I will need to know the content of any verbal exchange just before he struck you. Of course, if you haven't already done so, I must insist that you to file an assault charge with the local police ASAP." She pauses, tapping a manicured nail against her pearly whites and says, "I wonder…hmm."

"What's that?" Willard asks.

"It's probably nothing, but some courthouses are upgrading their surveillance equipment. It may not be necessary to have eyewitnesses if the cameras are the new ones with the audio feedback. For various civil right reasons, audio feeds are a bit more difficult to attain, but you will find that I am very capable in such areas."

At this point, Willard St. John begins to sweat, loosening his tie.

"Is all of that really necessary?" Willard interrupts.

The attorney looks at him with concern. "I assure you it is, Mr. St. John. Are you feeling okay? You look a bit flush. Would you like some water?"

"No. I'm fine," he says. "What about client/attorney confidentiality?"

"What would you like to know? As I already stated, I won't divulge what we discuss…"

"I meant Williams. I…ah…I have reason to believe that he intends to spread confidential information and outright lies about me to the press."

With another wry, wicked little smile that Willard interprets as greed, Alice Dahlman says, "In that case, he will be disbarred. We can allow him to speak—sue both Williams and his firm—for really, really big bucks. On the other hand, I can petition a judge for an injunction that will place a chokehold on him. Without proof, however, this action will only garner a stern warning to remind Williams of his legally binding obligations to the client. Most attorneys do not physically assault their clients, no matter how angry they may become. Although, I must warn you that, from time to time, depending on the circumstances, attorneys have been known to throw away their lifelong pursuit when something is very personal. Do you have any credible witnesses willing to attest that they heard Williams making these threats? Whatever catalyzed Keith Williams' willingness to recklessly pursue such a vendetta…I sincerely hope it isn't incriminating. He will be held liable either way, but once a bullet is shot from the barrel, no one can put it back. What do you believe he plans to disseminate to the public?"

"I'd really rather not say at this moment," he quickly replies.

"Not even if I tell you that I will take you on as my client because it looks like I can't lose?"

"No. I just don't feel comfortable with that at this time," Willard says.

She considers this man. His unraveling demeanor pleases her.

"In that case, Mr. St. John, I must tell you that you have very little, unless he actually talks to the press. I must warn you that no one else will proceed against any of them without you answering these very same uncomfortable questions, including the police. If you file assault charges, and even an attorney fresh out of law school will insist on it, you will be questioned by police as to the context of the unprovoked attack to determine whether your accusation warrants further action. Keith Williams' impeccable repute will precede him so they will eventually press you both for answers. If you lie to them and the answer adds up to be a very different truth, you are once again in front of the cue ball. I, on the other hand, can hit them hard and fast.

However, you can't expect me to go up against this formidable group of people unless I'm loaded for bear. No one will give you different answers, but you are free to shop around and prove me wrong. Just what are you afraid of, Mr. St. John? Why does a cool, calm, and seemingly very collected man like Attorney Keith Williams wish to launch such a hate campaign against you?"

Willard St. John considers her words and retreats. "Mrs. Dahlman, I believe I should take your earlier advice to consider my options. I'm very sorry for taking up your valuable time."

As he stands to leave, she rises to shake his hand. "That's perfectly fine, Mr. St. John. If you should decide to move forward, the Dahlman Law Firm is at your disposal. Please enjoy your day."

He leaves without another word. Willard's angry frustration is evident in his fretting blush.

After calling the front desk to ask if he has left the floor, Alice makes another call.

When Mitchum answers the phone, she says, "I have gotta hand it to ya. You were right, of course. That evil, sexist bastard tried to worm his way in without putting out. How did you know he would come to me first?"

Mitchum chuckles and replies, "Bergman-Klein and Associates has shown a string of defeats lately. We nailed them to the wall three times this year alone. You beat them recently, and quite handily. Straus, Straus, and Eckhart have had similar issues of late. Then there is the ongoing Eckhart sexual harassment lawsuit. It had to be you because you have what they call juice, Alice. Young lady, you are one of the best. I really wish you had stayed with us."

"You know I love being on my own. This is my dream come true. Besides, I kinda like being the queen bee of Queen Tower, with all of my busy little female worker bees buzzing about. I love putting on my crown every morning, dad."

They share a chuckle together. "I understand, and I'm very proud of you, sweetheart. I wish I could have been a bee on the wall during that consultation."

She smiles, turning toward the window. Now she bursts into laughter.

"I gave him the full court press. When I pushed for definitive answers, Mr. St John broke out in a cold sweat. He was squirming in his seat like a five-year-old who really needs to pee. I gave St. John a disturbing glimpse of the very big picture, what any lawyer will require to proceed against Keith and your firm. And just like that…poof! He was gone like a shot from a cannon. I doubt you have to worry about St. John seeking counsel elsewhere. Not after the number I did on him. However, a man capable of the premeditated murder of a teenager may consider doing it again. Please make sure that Keith is safe."

Mitchum says, "We are considering the very distasteful thought as a very real possibility. That's one of the reasons we thought it best to send him away for a while. This entire thing has taken a toll on us all. Thanks, baby. I love you. Please tell your mother I said hello."

"Okay, dad. I will. I love you, too. Bye."

They hang up and go about their business, respectively.

ⱷ

Kevin Williams is a strapping eighteen-year-old rising senior at Woodward Academy. Heavily sought after by Georgia, Georgia Tech, Florida State University, and Alabama, the War Eagles' athletic starting quarterback has a laundry list of schools panting for him. If he stays healthy, this youngster has a promising future in college football. At six-foot-six on a 275 lbs. frame, Kevin Williams is a man standing among boys on the gridiron.

Kevin and his girlfriend, Jasmine, have smoked a joint he lifted from his brother's limited stash. Feeling full of giggling fun, they have sex on Keith's bed just for the hell of it. Afterward, they take a shower together. Things are heating up again for the teenagers, who seem to have unlimited energy for one another.

The Fellows brothers are watching with their night scopes from across the street. While the kids are in the shower, they cross the street and enter the Peach Tree Towers complex unnoticed. Once inside the building and certain that the area is clear of people, they make it a point to avoid the security cameras. By keeping their faces pointed down, the worn baseball caps and false beards affectively conceal their identities.

Billy Joe removes an E-Z Lock Pick Gun from the toolbox, going to work on the lock. In the meantime, George removes a flask of whiskey from his breast pocket to douse both their faces and clothing because they are about to get stinking drunk. They swish the booze around in their mouths and swallow, knowing that spitting could leave traces of their DNA for authorities to find.

A moment before, they only looked like toolbox-toting workers on their way to fix an appliance at the request of the absent occupant of unit 2315 Peachtree. They remove the nametags as they slip into the dim lighting. A strap of Billy's coverall goes slack, hanging at his side when he places the toolbox at his feet. They are inside in just under ten seconds. Billy Joe puts his nametag and the lock pick under a cloth at the bottom of the toolbox. George keeps the flask in hand for authenticity. Both are relieved that the alarm is not engaged.

They could easily snatch the kid, forcing him to talk with intense torture, but they choose to play the game. It will be less messy and less risky to gain the information this way. In addition, they can have a bit of fun.

They slide the tool boxes forward with their feet and walk a bit further into the room. Now that they are standing arm-in-arm, listing as if inebriated, they call out in their simulated drunken voices. "Keith Williams. Hey, Keith, old buddy. We're here, bubba!"

While her boyfriend stands with his strong hands spread on the shower wall to support his weight beneath the warm stream of water, Jasmine looks at Kevin with enchanted eyes. She slowly scrubs his back with a large sponge, following each soapy stroke with the admiration of a painter with a brush in hand.

Kevin and Jasmine are startled when they hear the voices of intruders. They turn off the water and grab towels before running into the hallway. Kevin kicks himself for forgetting to turn on the alarm system.

There are two swaying men holding on to one another in symbiotic support, looking like they came straight from the swine farm. One of them seems to have a bad case of gas. He burps or farts. Difficult to tell by the facial expression.

Kevin Williams knots the towel quickly and snatches a hefty statuette from the table. Brandishing it as a weapon, he demands, "Who the hell are you? How did you get in here?" The veins of his right hand bulge as his grip tightens around the black marble.

The brothers pretend to be confused as they look at each other, swaying and holding on. One of them says, "Hey, you're not Keith. What are you doing in our buddy's home?" His voice is slurred. Both are blinking, incessantly, but they are extremely focused.

The other says, "Please don't tell me he moved."

"Who the hell are you people?" Kevin repeats, as Jasmine cowers behind him.

Billy Joe says, "We're the Switzler brothers, Billy and Bob!" He allows some spittle to dribble down his newly bearded chin to his chest.

Now George asks, "Who are you, and what are y'all doing in our pal's towels?"

"I'm his brother. Tell me how you got in here. What do you want? You better answer me right now, or I'm calling the cops and security." Kevin also tells his girlfriend to grab the phone.

"Wait, just hold on there," Billy says. "There's no real need for that, young fella. We have a key. See. Keith gave it to us and told us to stop by any old time we come to town." Billy singles out the keys for Kevin's closer inspection.

"Well, he never mentioned you to me. How do you know my brother?"

The pair looks at each other again, trying to focus their eyes. George smiles and says, "Oh, that's right. I do recall him making mention of a kid brother way back. Keith and your name...your name also starts with a K. Don't tell me. Don't tell me. Let's see, Calvin. No, that's not it. Oh, Kevin right?"

"Yeah, that's my name, but how do you know my brother?" Kevin asks, suspiciously.

George smiles and snaps his fingers three times. "Keith is a real good guy. We had big fun together."

Billy lies, "He's a real dandy lawyerer. He defended us when we tore hell out of that gay bar. The... ah...the Blue Oyster Cult, or somethin' like it. I still don't remember how we ended up at that kinda place."

"Yeah, that's right. You see, we are professional wrestlers and we just don't cotton with them pansy types. It just ain't natural, if you know what I mean," George points out. He cranes his neck to the side to get a peek at the girl behind Keith Williams. He clears his raspy throat and says, "Well now, I see that you do. Howdy, young lady."

"We're the Switzler brothers, hailing from Tennessee. Rocky Mountain wrestling is our name, and the Switzler brothers is our game. Yes sir, indeed!" proclaims Billy. They face each other for a high five, but miss so badly they end up trading places.

Kevin says with a grin, "Wait a minute. You guys are really reporters, right?"

Billy and George laugh at the idea. Billy slaps his knees and says, "Hell no. We're here cause we're trying to get away from them vultures. They'd pick the meat from the bones of our long dead pet cat just to get the stink on us."

George says, "That's a good one Billy Joe." He throws his hand in the air for another high five, but Billy burps instead.

"Excuse me," Billy says.

Jasmine giggles, but Kevin's alert eyes seek the curious boxes at the feet of his uninvited guests.

Billy follows his gaze and says, "There now. You have keen eyes, young fella. You want to know what's in the poke." They both kneel and reach into their toolboxes.

Kevin Williams is not sure if he should retreat or close the gap between them. This is an anxious moment of suspicion as the two intruders fiddle around in the dimness.

George's eyes darken, and then he smiles up at the teenagers. As his right hand glides across the surface of his firearm, he says, "This here is the killer!"

"This here will kick holes in your bare ass, young fella. Oh, shoot. Please pardon my language, young lady," Billy adds as they slowly raise the quart jars of liquid from the depths.

Jasmine laughs, which causes Kevin to laugh, also. He cannot help being amused. These drunken fools are just too comical. The Fellows brothers are thinking the same thing; Kevin Williams is finally beginning to relax.

Swollen raisins swirl at the bottom of the jars as George proclaims, "Now here's a thing of infinite beauty, made it for Keith myself from our pappy's secret recipe." He kisses the jar and falters slightly before putting it back.

Kevin places the statuette down and says, "Look, my brother went out of town on vacation. I don't know when he plans to return. In fact, you just missed him. If you want, you can leave whatever that stuff is."

George says, "Dang it. We missed our friend because you just had to keep playin' around with Ms. Lola Bell. This is all your fault, Billy. First, you went and lost his phone number. And we won't be back this way for the better part of a year." He starts to blubber, whining like a baby.

It is quite annoying to watch a grown drunk cry, and Kevin Williams wants to be rid of them. He says, "Look, guys, please don't tell anyone else. No one. Keith went up to my granddad's place on Big Bear Mountain. That's all the way up in northwestern Montana, about a hundred miles from the Canadian border. I can't seem to reach him right now. I've been trying all day. He probably hasn't gotten there yet because it's really out there. Too bad you came all this way for nothing. You really should call first next time. Now I'm sorry, but I'm gonna have to ask you to leave. I don't mean to be rude, but you know." He hikes his left shoulder, glancing at his girlfriend.

Billy takes the hint. "Oh, I see. We understand." He feigns preparing to walk away before saying, "Hey, uh, we've been drinkin' up somethin' awful tonight. Do you think I can use your facilities real quick? I gotta go somethin' fierce." He shifts from foot to foot, with the pleading eyes of a miserable grownup who is destined to answer the call of nature, whether he wants to or not.

Kevin sighs, openly annoyed. Jasmine's whimper causes him to act against better judgment.

"Sure, second door on the left. Please hurry. I have a big game tomorrow." Kevin moves aside so the drunk could pass.

As Billy approaches, he whispers, "Thanks, little buddy. Look after him, will ya? He really had his heart set on seeing our good friend tonight. My brother tends to be a might emotional. He gets it from our mammy on account of our pappy being gone all the time. You know how it is."

Kevin's nose wrinkles, thinking they are stinking up the place with every passing second.

"Aww," Jasmine whimpers for their plight before stepping out from behind Kevin to go to George. She pats him on the back and says, "It'll be alright, Bob, you'll see. Maybe Kevin will be able to contact his brother for you in the morning. Please don't be upset." She is such a gentle creature, out of the bedroom.

Billy Joe takes a leak and flushes the toilet. Careful not to leave any prints, he wipes the inner doorknob clean and turns the light off. At the same time, he reaches back to turn on the tap so it appears he was raised to wash his hands after handling his winky.

Ever so quietly, Billy eases out of the bathroom. He is about a yard away from Kevin when Jasmine sees the hulking man stalking her boyfriend from behind. Before the breath catches in her throat,

Billy grabs Kevin Williams sternly by the back of the head and front of the jaw a flash before giving a quick shove to the left and a harsh jerk to the right. Kevin's neck snaps with a vicious crunch.

Jasmine never gets to scream because her sad little puppy suddenly turns rabid. George drives the ball of his fist into her nose, shoving bone and cartilage fragments upward. With lightning quick agility, he snatches her hair with the left hand and drives the right knuckles into her esophagus. He snaps her neck for good measure. The teenagers die without as much as a whimper.

With gloved hands, they use common cleaning rags, hydrogen peroxide, and a strong ammonia solution to rid both bodies of fingerprints and DNA. Billy uses thick Q-tips, often used by boxing trainers, soaked in both solutions to sanitize inside Jasmine's nostrils. Now, they deposit the bodies on the floor of a closet in the guest bedroom.

Choice items, including Kevin's wallet and Jasmine's purse, are bagged. They quietly trash the place to make it look like a robbery. They open cabinets and drawers, tossing the contents to the floor. George Fellows pours hydrogen peroxide and then ammonia into and around the toilet bowl, using rags to soak up the liquid.

Meanwhile, Billy scatters more than an ounce of marijuana about, with a small amount of cocaine leading from an empty shoebox toward the door. The stolen items must be burned. They will never see the inside of a pawnshop's display case because such things invite trouble.

No one saw them enter. No one sees them leave. The brothers move like lightning, and lightning is most difficult to catch in its darkest element.

With the deed done, the objective achieved, they are unable to reach St. John because he could not resist the need to see his favorite whore.

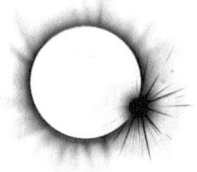

Chapter 17

DIVA JONES

W illard St. John is not a person overly given to sexual inti-
macy. In most cases, he is simply a get-grab-go kind of
person. However, for every misogynistic man on earth, there is one
woman in particular that gets to him severely. What he feels for Diva
Jones should not be confused with love, not even in the most twisted
capacity of the word. In the mind of the depraved, however, sexual
attraction, love, and loathing, are often separated by too thin of a
line to truly differentiate.

Denied the hunt when Kenny Andrews slipped fatally into shock,
and narrowly missing Keith Williams the next day, Willard St. John
needs someone to absorb his frustrations. It has to be someone who
understands Willard's particular compulsions in stressful times such as
these; someone who concurs with the occasional domination therapy.

Diva Jones is such a woman. This tall, beautiful, sassy female, stops the clock when she walks her walk into any roomful of men or women. This woman is not just an average prostitute. She is a professional escort, if there is any real distinction between the two.

Ms. Jones is very sensual, and as intelligent as one needs to be in her choice of careers. She always comprehends Willard's special needs, supplying them most willingly. However, this Black woman is just fare enough of skin to cross the barrier of contempt in Willard's warped mind.

Enduring a number of humiliations, Diva Jones allows spankings with a riding crop. Being tied up, sodomized, smacked around, and even spat on, are not new or unexpected. If it is a special night, she may even get laid for a good two or three minutes.

For the base price of one thousand dollars per session, Diva Jones is most willing to call Willard St. John 'Massa' or 'Master Will'. She is always battered, and bruised the next day. It is nothing two kinds of alcohol will not remedy. The worse it gets, the bigger her tip.

The intuitive woman feels that, whether he chooses to admit it or not, Willard St. John may be addicted to her in his own very perverted sort of way. Like a junky hooked on the needle, he is taking his doses in increase. Nevertheless, Diva Jones realizes that this opinion could be a product of her own distorted vanity.

This beautiful, fair-skinned Black woman is making a fortune in Atlanta, getting rich by specializing in the stranger sexual propensities of the wealthy. Her pride and honor are small sacrifices. The money will buy her a real life someday, as long as she finds the will to break the cycle when she has banked enough to never look back. The money is, however, just as addictive as the pure womanpower she holds over her exclusive clientele.

ॐ

Because Willard falls asleep at her place, he will leave an additional two-thousand dollars on the dresser. He does not say goodbye to the woman, who snoozes in a steaming alcohol bath. He does not return to Martin until around 4:00 a.m.

Every muscle in his body seems to ache when he shows up to find a very angry dragon lurking behind Martin's cold, ardent stare.

The first thing Martin says to a very hung-over St. John, before battering him to the floor is, "Maybe you don't fully understand that I have to do this before the old man dies!" Then, from nowhere, a lip-splitting slap sends Willard reeling to the floor. Only for an instant does he think of retaliation for a blow that he thinks is wholly uncalled for.

Governor Martin is confident that he will have no more problems with Willard St. John.

Martin sees it in those eyes as he stands over the coward, showing Willard the peace sign to indicate two strikes. St. John fully understands the meaning of three strikes, having been a man not prone to giving that many chances.

Since Ezra Krantz's stark disclosure, Governor Jud Martin quietly reconnects with the meanness within; reacquainting with his dormant evil side. The sterility of his official status seldom affords the opportunity to ride roughshod over anyone. He has become a thinking man over the years, a diplomat wrapped in the insulation provided by the outer arms of the killing machine he is soon to fully control. However, this…this feels good!

For Jud Martin, the raw physical domination over the cringing man at his feet is rejuvenating the madness for blood, which he has not drawn with his own hands for far too long. Seeing the crimson trickle running from St. John's mouth holds powerful connotations that begin to eat away the thinning layers of restraint and the cleanliness of diplomacy.

There is a macabre satisfaction in still knowing how to teach a stern lesson when one needs teaching. He relishes the sight of St. John's bloody nose and he wants more. Drawn by the bloodlust, he needs more. As he stares into Willard's eyes, he is certain that killing this man will be an enjoyable experience.

Martin and St. John finally connect with Billy and George. After the debriefing, they make plans to leave for Montana.

Much to Willard St. John's disdain, Jud Martin is beginning to warm up to Billy and George Fellows. Jud Martin knows they have great loyalty for Willard, but he plans to change that by offering them his position in the South. It would be the ultimate promotion, but first things first.

St. John has been adding to his own secret list of agendas since his conversation with Mitchum, and the female lawyer, who is actually Mitchum's daughter out of wedlock. After the second assault, he needs someone else to take it out on. Jud Martin may catch a stray bullet in the back soon enough.

After the governor calls Ezra Krantz's home, and the doctor tells him that the old man is holding his own, he asks to speak to Joe Mills.

Joe Mills is ex-military, a retired general of the United States Army. He retired an honored man, despite the fact that he openly worked a young Black corporal to death in the sweltering August heat or the numerous, unexplained, disappearances of Black soldiers under his command when he held ranks of captain and major. They were usually tagged AWOL, but it was in life that they were truly Absent Without Official Leave. The shameful status of *deserter* marred the name of the missing men and their families.

Mills, known as a paramilitary crackpot, in some circles, runs survivalist-training camps in the northwestern regions of the country. They are used, mainly, in the winter. Many Klan members have trained there over the years during the summer months. He keeps these places occupied year round. Mills plans many exercises for those who enter these camps in the depths of winter cold. His soldiers can never become fully trained without this sort of exercise. There are things to learn about surviving in the bone-chilling frosts of winter.

One of the camps is located in North Dakota, and the other in northwestern Montana. The men and women who visit these camps often engage in competitive war games. The age of participants rarely matters to Mills, who is the type of man that loves the phrases: "If they're old enough to hold it steady, they're old enough to pull the trigger. If they're old enough to pull the trigger, they're old enough to kill a nigger."

Mills integrates every military and counter-military tactic he knows into training programs.

He is really training people for the day when the Brotherhood of Light is in charge. Then it will be time to rid this country of Blacks and other minorities, hunting them down from the valley floors to the mountaintops. Discipline is the key to every successful terrorist, and terror is a Ku Klux Klan specialty.

When Joe Mills finally answers the phone, Martin gives him an abridged appraisal of the situation.

Mills says, "If the targets are actually located on Big Bear Mountain, it's only a matter of time before they're pinpointed. We happen to have a camp in the valley just a few miles south of there. I know a few local boys, loyal and trustworthy men, who have hunted the surrounding terrain. It's rough territory."

Martin feels hopeful. "That's great. Because of the delicate nature of this mission, I do not want a bunch of wild hog hunters with itchy trigger fingers turning this into a media event. It has to be neat, clean, and quiet."

In the back of Martin's mind, he now knows, without doubt, that this cannot be coincidence. He considers this providence because all the pieces are falling into place like an architect's building blocks.

"Not to worry," Mills assures. "Most of the men are away or preparing for the funeral. I mainly use the camps now for hard-core winter training. Will you be bringing Billy and George? If you do, I won't have to wait for you at the airfield. I can go and get things lined up. They know the way to the camp. However, I feel it best to add a few loyal and trusted men to make sure the targets are properly caged it."

Martin says, "Yes, they will be coming. I trust your judgment on this, General Mills. If you vouch for their loyalty, your word is good enough for me."

They hang up.

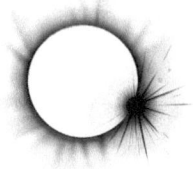

Chapter 18

THE LEGEND

Many, many years ago, long before the pale skins came with shooting sticks, iron horses, and firewater, there lived a majestic tribe of people on the Mountain of the Moon. Because of tragic events centeries ago, this sacred place is now known as Big Bear Mountain.

The people living upon the great mount are the Mymawgua Indians, known by many as the Children of the Moon because they worship the Moon God Shashana.

Whenever the shaman predicts a lunar eclipse, the tribe is overwhelmed. On any given night of a lunar eclipse, they fear Shashana might not return from the darkness. They are terrified that he might someday choose to go elsewhere, blessing others with his powers because he no longer deems the Mymawgua worthy. To prove their merits to Shashana, they perform a strangely dangerous ritual.

The women of the tribe will sew together long strips of deerskin, beaver pelts, and vines to make very strong ropes nearly two-hundred-feet in length. High up on the mountain lies an area the Mymawgua call Totem Rock, a mystical and powerful place. From up there, one can see far over the surrounding range of mountains, and deep into the lush eastern and southern valleys below.

On Totem Rock, two trees stand near the edge of the cliff. They have become more like stone pillars that had been trees long ago. The Mymawgua carefully carve the faces and symbols of their chiefs and wisest elders into the unusual pillars. Many believe they contain an essence of the spirits of all fallen Mymawguans. They are nearly seven-feet apart. While one of them stands in sand and earth, like a regular tree, the other is anchored in solid granite.

Either side of this sacred place is earthen and grows shrubs, grass, and trees. Yet in the center, lies a smooth slate of granite that runs on and on up the mountainside. No one knows how far because the Mymawguans fear that their God will be offended. Though forbidden to venture to the summit, they believe it the place where the hard and soft of a person's soul meet.

From where the slate of sacred rock originates, there also comes a slim stream. This water is cool and refreshing. It has never dried up, freezing only in the depths of winter cold. The sacred water runs the entire length of the granite to its very end, where it flies into the air with a breeze that usually blows at the cliff's edge.

The strongest young men are led to Totem Rock on the day of the predicted eclipse. The elder women will sing beautiful, sad songs to the beat of drums, while the younger women of the tribe paint the faces of the men or dance to the music.

The fearless warriors draw lots to see which of them will be first and last to perform a ritual known as *wingless flight*. The elders attach one end of each rope to the bottom of each totem tree. They are stretched as far up the slope as they will go, kept separated to avoid tangling. The elder men fasten the ends to each ankle of a young warrior before saying a brief prayer. Following the prayer, they will say to each one, "Be brave, my son. For within the true strength of your heart lies the future of our people, the Children of the Moon."

The young warrior gives his greatest war cry before leaping into the stream on his stomach. They have to do it this way because the steep granite slate is too slick, so anyone attempting to stand on such a sacred place will slip and slide to their death. It is nearly impossible to stand where water meets stone.

The brave will slide faster and faster toward the end of the world. Faster he would go until he jettisons between the two totem pillars and flies into the sky with his arms stretched wide like the great eagle.

Before plummeting straight down, he must conquer his fear and shout, "For you, I die!" Then the ropes will grow tight, saving him from certain death.

He will have to climb back up on his own, if it is possible. Abreast the face of the cliff lays a great pillow of leaves and grass to cushion the recoil. Sometimes they are injured or knocked unconscious, but Shashana always spares their lives because they have proven their love for him.

The shaman is always the last to fly, no matter what his age is. His turn comes much later, during the exact moment of the total eclipse.

During this particular time in Mymawguan history, the shaman is called Dingahay, which means Mighty Bear. In few native cultures, it is rumored that the medicine man is not allowed to marry. Not so for the Mymawguans because his power of healing and intuition is believed to pass through bloodlines.

Trained by his father, Dingahay has lived for nearly thirty-three cycles of the moon, soon to marry the chief's daughter, Nomanni. They love each other very much, and her father thinks it is a good match.

This year of the moon brings strange visitors to the territory from the northeastern region beyond what is known as the Endless Valleys of Water. The visiting tribe are the Crow. At first glance, they look to be a somewhat warlike people.

The Crow leader humbly asks the chief of the Mymawguans for permission to move his people into to the valley below because his tribe has suffered greatly during the last season of winter blizzards in the unforgiving north. Many of them died from the coughing sickness and starvation. Radical, unforeseen changes in the travel routes of migrating game, like the Canadian caribou, left the Crow winter stores of food severely depleted, despite strict rationing. The tribe was forced to move southwest and has traveled far to get here.

Chief Makona is filled with compassion for the plight of these destitute people, so he welcomes them. Chief Makona allows the Crow to settle the western valley of Big Bear mountain to replenish themselves before moving on to find their own territorial lands. For several months, the tribes will trade secrets, and the Crow are taught about planting and irrigation. Things are good between the two people, but it is not to last for days of great sadness are soon to come.

Two days before Shashana closes his eye, Chief Nooksa of the Crow comes to the Mymawgua encampment with his daughter, Crazy Bird, in tow. He is very angry because Crazy Bird is growing heavy with child, and she blames her condition on Dingahay.

Crazy Bird's tongue is false because her father must never know that his own brother shames her, even if it means war. To avoid trouble, Chief Makona orders the shaman to honor the girl and her father by marriage. Although Chief Makona does not believe Dingahay has betrayed Nomanni's love, honor compels him to do this terrible thing. However, he agrees to do so with a very heavy heart.

Much sadness fills the hearts of Dingahay and Nomanni. This night, as they weep in one another's arms for the very last time, they swear their undying love. On the next day, the wedding is to take place.

A distraught Nomanni cannot bear the painful shame of watching the man she loves married to a woman from another tribe, and forced to raise the bastard whelp of an unknown coward. On her way to Totem Rock, she says goodbye to her father, who chose not to attend the ceremony in the valley below. Sadly, when Nomanni hears the wedding drums pounding in the wind, she kisses the small, wooden carving of a bear that Dingahay has given her as a gift before throwing herself from the cliff at Totem Rock.

Dingahay is at the marrying stick with Crazy Bird when he decides that he must disobey his chief. When he flees, Crazy Bird's furious father declares war in the face of yet another insult.

The shaman reaches his tribe just ahead of the attacking Crow, so they have little chance to prepare. Many of Dingahay's people die before they are finally able to fend off the Crow's vicious onslaught.

Chief Makona is badly injured and he is taken to Totem Rock for safety when nightfall has long since come. The moon is high and nearly fully eclipsed when Makona tells the shaman that their beloved Nomanni has flown to her death in grief and shame. Makona also tells him that he is very sorry that he sacrificed the happiness of two people for a peace that is not to be. He asks the forgiveness of his people, but there is nothing to forgive. They know that he had made the right choice at the time, no matter how wrong it seemed…no matter how much pain it would bring.

Dingahay weeps at learning that his sweet flower has been plucked from the earth far before her time. It is as if the heart has been torn from him. He feels the need for guidance so he prays to Shashana, both for his beloved and for the safety of his people.

After having a vision, Dingahay stands tall and proud, gazing up at the moon and then at his huddled tribe. He says to them, "Fear not your lives against this night, my proud people. I shall fly into the heavens, for Shashana has promised to give me the heart of the Great Bear. Fight on until my return!" Without warning, he runs for the cliff's edge. As he takes wingless flight, Dingahay screams, "It is for you that I die!"

The moon is fully eclipsed at this moment, and there comes a mighty shaking of our mother earth. The quaking of the ground breaks the totem tree that grows from the granite of Totem Rock.

The Crow are closing in on the Mymawguans, but they begin to retreat when the earth moves beneath their feet. They run screaming into the night, howling like wolves. Surely, they have angered the god of the Mymawguan people. Shashana seems to be much stronger than their many gods, who fail to make their presence known.

Dingahay does not die on the rocks below the sacred cliff because he suddenly transforms into a grizzly bear cub in midair. Now, a great eagle of fire forms in the sky. It plummets from the heavens to snatch the bear cub from the hungry jaws of death lying in wait below in the screaming darkness.

The fire eagle lifts Dingahay high into the air where it hovers for all the tribe to see. Its great flaming wings beat against the night air, forcing the hair away from the frightened eyes of the Children of the Moon. There comes a mighty rumble like thunder and then a voice says, "My children are worthy. Great Bear shall protect you and lead you to my side when your time upon this fertile land is done. This, I promise. So shall it be until the moon goes forever dim in the night sky!"

The bear cub lets loose a mighty bellow, a roar that sounds as if it is coming from a fully-grown grizzly. The fire eagle screams, flying over the mountain to swoop down into the western valley where it sets Dingahay upon the ground.

The Crow are never again seen in these parts. Dingahay slays them all, growing fatter with every enemy he devours.

Nomanni still waits at the edge of the eternal bridge so she may wave at Great Bear when he escorts another Mymawguan soul to Rashndana…or heaven. There, she faithfully holds vigil until Dingahay is released of his charge because she took her own life before knowing that he was still hers. She waits for her one true love, vowing to remain even until the end of time.

☯

When Keith Williams finishes his favorite childhood story, he looks at his audience of one and sees a single, glistening, teardrop cascading down the gentle curve of Sabrina's cheek. She is still captivated, entranced.

She finally realizes that he has gone silent and says, "Wow. That was so sad…so powerful. It was beautiful." She wipes the tear away.

"God, look at me. I must look pretty silly right about now, but I just couldn't seem to help it."

Keith smiles at her, lovingly.

"Not at all. I'm sure that I was sniffling when John Greycloud told that story to me many years ago."

"I can't wait to meet them. That part about the place, Totem Rock, does it really exist or was it just part of the legend?"

"Yes. It is as real as we are. I'll show you tomorrow. We're almost there."

Night has fallen. To gaze up at the skyline so beautifully draped across the tall treetops is to experience the true meaning of awe. The constellations wink down on them like brilliant uncut diamonds parading before an unseen firelight. Ever-present is the full moon, as if greeting a long lost child on his journey home.

"Didn't you mention something about your granddad chasing a bear up and down the mountain? You were just pulling my leg on that one, right?"

Keith grins. "Old Dingahay, himself. That is what they actually call him. Dingahay, the Mighty Bear, shaman of the Mymawgua. There is big medicine there, baby."

They are both filled with growing anticipation.

Keith adds, "The last time I visited, I saw him. I even took a picture."

"What? You actually took a picture of it?"

"Yes. I was clumsy one day and rolled my left ankle. After I healed, I needed to stretch my legs so I decided to take a walk to Totem Rock. The wind suddenly shifted and I smelled something unfamiliar to me. It was a pungent, musky odor with a hint of sweetness. As I rounded some shrubbery and trees, there it was. I had stumbled face-to-face with the grizzly. I had nothing to protect myself. No rifle, nothing but my camera. I felt like such and idiot, and I was probably about to die for it!"

She gasps. "Oh my God. What happened?"

"My heart was pounding like a rivet gun. I was taught at a very young age that a bear is most dangerous when a female has cubs or when they are surprised while feeding. This one was gorging himself on wild blueberries. That's why I didn't recognize the scent. I froze, like I was told, but I couldn't move backward even though I wanted to. The animal lowers its head, ears pinned back. Its lips curl outwardly. These are definite signs of aggression. It looks me in the eyes and stands on its hind legs...just a...just a massive beast. It twists it neck, baring its teeth and growls so loudly that I break and run. I didn't crouch to show it respect, I just hauled ass. Those blueberries were at the height of ripeness, so it didn't bother giving chase."

Sabrina Martin is awestricken, hanging on his every word. In the absence of her inquisitive tongue, Keith continues.

"When I realized that I wasn't being pursued, I stopped to catch my breath. As I bent over with my hands on my shaking knees, the camera was swinging from the strap around my neck. I couldn't resist sneaking back up the trail. I was downwind, and I didn't have to get too close because I had a 250 millimeter zoom lens. Sabrina, I was only able to capture its image safely from two angles...two angles. Yet, when I took it to a photo shop to have the film developed, there were three images on the roll. Somehow, out of sheer terror, I guess, I had squeezed one off as it stood on its hind legs."

"I just can't imagine," she says.

"The guy who developed the film once lived in Alaska. He told me that I couldn't have taken that photo around here because it was from a subspecies only found on Kodiak Island. He used a device to calculate its size and weight, determining that it stood over ten feet tall. He even compared it to photos he had taken while living in Alaska. After a few moments of discussion, I convinced him that I had no reason to lie. I got the distinct feeling that he wanted to hunt it down and kill it as a trophy, so I didn't tell him anything else. Even though that may have been a safe thing to do, I couldn't. If anyone is going to get that bear, it will be my grandfather and Greycloud."

"That's some story. What did you do with the photo?"

He smiles and says, "You will see, sweetheart. You will see."

She settles in for the rest of the ride.

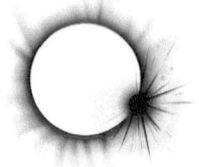

Chapter 19

GRIZZLY

At 4:30 on the morning of Keith's departure from Atlanta, Jeremiah Williams and his blood brother, John Greycloud, are sleeping peacefully. In an hour, the two will wake like clockwork to greet the morning sun and give God thanks for allowing them another day upon the earth, as they always do.

Even though it is spring, they still burn a small fire at night to keep the chill out of their aging bones. By now, the firewood has reduced to mere embers.

Either man is the picture of health. Clean living and pure mountain air makes them what would be the envy of all elderly people in the smog and fumes of big cities.

John Greycloud is the very last Mymawguan living on Big Bear Mountain. The younger generations have long since spread themselves throughout the greater northwestern states.

As he would say, "The young people have grown tired of tradition. They discovered television to be the bait that drew them from this majestic place to find themselves or their misfortunes in life." The rest have died and gone on to the other side with Shashana.

Greycloud is a strong, old man with copper skin and long grey hair, which he keeps in a ponytail that ends in the center of his back.

Jeremiah Williams is a tall man, who shaves his head bald from stem to stern. He is in exceptional health, knowing beyond a shadow of a doubt that living here plays a great role in that. He prefers the quiet solitude he finds here, except for a few friends and visits from grandsons that never visit often nor long enough. Jeremiah and Greycloud have made a good life in their twilight years, sharing many happy and a few sad memories.

They built a corral several years ago, which separates into three sizable paddocks that share a common lead into the barn. One compartment of the corral is reserved for four horses and a mule. The second is where they keep three black-tailed yearlings. The deer, captured very young, are fattened up for winter when hunting for fresh game is hardest. The two men only see these animals as food, never allowing themselves to become attached because that makes them hard to eat. It is not to say that, from time to time, someone will not let one of them go.

The final section of the corral is where they keep the pigs, which forage freely in the woods during the day. They always return, unless a hungry bear or wolves get them first. If the pigs ever suspect that they will sizzle in a hot frying pan someday, they may choose to take their chances with the bear and wolves.

Further up the hill to the northwest is a flat area, cordoned off by sturdy posts, treated lumber, and barbwire. This large expanse allows the horses and the mule room to run and graze in relative safety from predators.

Inside the barn, two dozen fussy hens are roosting along with a single speckled rooster. They would not have eggs for breakfast without old Frisky. When there are chicks running about, Jeremiah and Greycloud enjoy the occasional batch of fried chicken because fresh replacements are handy. That's if the weasels or the hawks don't eat them.

The old-timers also hunt snowshoe rabbits, geese, grouse, and mule deer, which they cure in the smokehouse. Nothing goes to waste. Unlike some city dwellers, they will never starve. What these two men have is a small paradise on earth, the kind of life some folks will kill and die for.

With the help of the few friends they have, and Keith Williams, they built a second cabin for the grandsons' visits. Someday, hopefully soon, one or both of the grandsons will surprise Jeremiah with a wife and a peck of kids underfoot. They sorely miss the laughter and mischief of children at play, hoping to experience it again before passing on.

Electricity, supplied by underground cables that connect with overhead powerlines many miles away, was added to the cabin when Keith was around sixteen. Having survived a few Christmas vacations with power failures in his youth, Keith furnished both cabins with state of the art power plants, refrigerators, televisions, and an accursed microwave that sees even less use than the Ford Bronco.

Keith, a good grandson, wants them to live out their fine old years with all the comforts he can provide—not that Jeremiah Williams skirts the poverty line. The very successful attorney is forever grateful for all the sacrifices made on his and Kevin's behalf when orphaned.

In his stubbornness, Jeremiah balked at the second remodeling of their cabin and all the fancy gadgetry a few years ago, but the voice of reason, which is Greycloud's, convinced him that it would be an insult to reject the gifts. Besides, he rather enjoys seeing the news programs in color and cartoons that come through when bad weather is not a hindrance.

Inside the old folks home, as they lovingly refer to it, they keep two rattlesnakes in a huge fish tank. The snakes feed on live wood mice taken from benign traps near the feed bins in the barn.

Posing motionless along the walls overhead are stuffed deer heads, Canadian geese, and a wolf baring its fangs. After many years of practice, John and Jeremiah are quite accomplished taxidermists. They are even better hunters, except when it comes to a certain ghost they can never seem to bag.

They spent countless summer hours in the big bush with Keith and then Kevin, when they were old enough to hunt. The boys learned how to track and ambush animals by using wind directions to mask their scent. They were also trained to shoot in a strong breeze. Keith excelled at this sort of training more easily than his younger brother. Most importantly, they were schooled in the proper use and handling of handguns, rifles, shotguns, crossbows, and compound bows.

Such training is never excessive in the wilderness. "After all," Greycloud would say, "what will a Mymawguan brave do if he could not catch his own meal? He will probably have to steal someone else's dinner and eat it on the run." These are some of the things their dreams are made of.

At 5:05 a.m., a great black muzzle sniffs the early morning air for the familiar scent of man. It only discerns the scent of the horses, deer, and those fat, juicy pigs, that sleep with no hint of the danger lurking just inside a nearby stand of trees. There is still the smell of smoke in the air, but it tells him that the spirit of the fire is nearly gone.

Eyes of brown coal survey the barn door, searching that of the cabin for the men who might be lying upwind in wait to spring a lethal trap. Unsatisfied with its findings, it circles the encampment to be sure that the two old ones are not hiding. Only when it hears snoring sounds coming from the cabin is it reassured. The dark hulk patiently circles back to the southwest to attack from a better vantage point that counters the breeze.

The beast now turns, circling back toward the corral area. Smelling it first, the horses and deer spook fully awake. The whites of their eyes reflect the fear and panic brewing inside them. Animals rely heavily on instincts; senses of smell and hearing are life-saving attributes. Unlike man, it is more difficult to sneak up on them while sleeping.

The horses and deer know its scent…the danger it represents. Complimented by a surety of foot, it hardly cracks a twig while in stealth mode. Despite its size, the dark, shadowy creature moves swiftly. When it does step on an unseen alarm, the huge paws and thick fur muffle most sounds quite effectively.

It is coming and they know it; except for the lazy, dreaming pigs. No longer trying to counter the betraying breeze, its pungent, musky odor increases in strength. Now, there is a telltale tremor, which means it is running!

The deer bleat. The mule brays. And the snorting horses begin to whinny as they paw at the earth. The pigs wake up, standing in a circle with their hindquarters touching. They snort and grunt in equal alarm as their foggy eyes squint to adjust to the darkness. Suddenly, there it is, a massive grizzly bear standing more than nine feet tall. This is a beast made for killing.

It rises on its haunches and batters the corral, breaking the pen where the pigs abandon their defensive stance. The deer attempt to leap the fence, but only manage to capture the grizzly's attention. It walks to that part of the corral and smashes the rails to the ground.

Two of the black-tailed deer manage to escape when the bear's attention focuses on the third yearling, which has slipped its head between the inner slats separating the compartments. The trapped animal sees the bear coming, struggling furiously to free itself. In doing so, the animal breaks its own neck!

The horses and mule are bucking wildly. They whinny and bray while standing on their hind legs, kicking and boxing at the air. They are panic-stricken, knowing they are next. After all, they do have the most meat.

The uproar is finally enough to wake the dead inside the cabin. Jeremiah and Greycloud would have been up with only a fraction of the disturbance, had they not overindulged the fruit of the still before bedtime. They have been celebrating something that neither would remember the next day.

The two old men are forced from the thick, cloudy layers of sleep much too quickly. Just as a frightened diver suffers the bends from swimming too rapidly to the surface, they will surely have skull-splitting headaches. For right now, the pain and nausea go ignored as luxuries.

Wearing the moth-eaten thermal underwear they customarily sleep in, they tumble out of bed grabbing at their boots. With his foul morning breath blazing to bring tears to his eyes, Jeremiah only locates one boot and decides to let the other go to the devil.

"Damn it all to hell," he curses. "That bear is going to get it this time!"

Jeremiah hobbles to the gun rack where he meets Greycloud and his booted feet.

Greycloud says, "We better hurry. It sounds like a massacre out there. Wait, here's some ammo. You can't kill that big grizzly by beating him over the head with your empty gun, Geronimo."

Their hunting rifles are usually loaded, but they spent the early part of last evening cleaning all their guns. They hastily load the rifles as they reach the door, not noticing the abrupt silence.

As Jeremiah grabs the doorknob, he says, "Old Dingahay, we got your ass now."

He yanks the door open to find death standing there on hind legs, brandishing its glistening teeth!

The bear bellows a deafening growl with its hot breath no more than two feet from the faces of its would-be-killers, who fall to the floor on their backsides screaming like frightened women. The bear takes a swipe with its left forepaw, narrowly missing them as they go down. The paw smashes into the inner doorframe, its four-inch claws carving deep grooves into the wood where shrapnel and kindling fly. Its deafening roar fills the morning air.

Realizing they only have seconds to live, both men instinctively grab at the guns that have fallen from their fear-frozen hands. They fire the four or five rounds they managed to load in their rifles, and they continue to pull the triggers on empty chambers.

When they finally open their eyes to the expended gunpowder that clouds the doorway like a ghost, they have managed to kill all the air they could hit. They have murdered a whole flock of oxygen, but no more than that. The accomplished hunters didn't even cut a hair. Now, from the distance, comes a bellow that makes them flinch, shamefully.

With a sigh of relief, they look at one another and lay back on the floor. They soon begin to giggle and laugh wildly as their pounding hearts finally start to slow down.

Geronimo, which is what Greycloud calls Jeremiah Williams when the grizzly is involved, looks at his best friend to say, "That old bear scared you shitless!" He begins to flap his wings, screaming as if he is being mugged.

Greycloud fires back by saying, "Oh yeah? You're the one who jumped out of his boots!"

"Hell! Maybe that's where your shit landed. Got so greasy, it just slipped right off my foot. I'll never wear 'em again!"

The statement sends them both over the edge with weeping laughter that eventually ends with each of them coughing up a lung. Greycloud gags a little leftover moonshine and raw stomach acid. It is good to laugh this hard, considering what could be the case right now.

After the laughing conniption runs its course, and their belly muscles loosen enough to operate, they get up and dress. It is time to survey the damage, and they know from experience that there will be plenty.

As they walk into the early morning light, Jeremiah says, "Better take your rifle. He might double back on us."

Greycloud grunts. "Yeah, I'll take it, but we both know that old devil is headed down toward the valley. He won't be back, not now anyway."

What they see at the corral is amazing destruction. The 4x6-inch wooden beams of the outer fencing are splintered, lying askew the yard like discarded toothpicks. The pigs and surviving yearlings have taken off for parts unknown. The other deer hangs untouched. Its head is stuck between the inner fencing with its tongue sticking out. Its eyes, soon to haze over, have already fixed on some faraway place.

The horses have run off, scattered like the four witches of the wind. They must be tracked down. The mule is still there because it is always tied inside the corral to prevent it from kicking the horses with its hind legs at feeding time. Old Gideon is a nasty tempered thing and a greedy one at that.

Jeremiah says, "Heads, you take Gideon and track down the horses. Tails, you mend the corral, and skin and butcher the deer." Greycloud nods in agreement and Jeremiah flips the coin, which lands heads up.

Greycloud reaches down for the coin. "Now you wouldn't be using my own two-headed coin would you, brother?"

Jerimiah replies, "Hell, I wish I were, but you never call heads."

Moments later, Greycloud saddles Gideon and heads out while Jeremiah goes about his substantial tasks. By far, Greycloud has drawn the easier job.

About two hours after the incident with the grizzly, Greycloud returns, riding a horse with the rest of them in tow. He guides them into the repaired corral just as Jeremiah emerges from the smoke-house. Still wearing a timeworn apron, he has butchered, salted, and hung the deer carcass. While wiping the excess salt from his hands, he says, "That was fast."

"Even without tracks to follow, they wouldn't be hard to find. They always run in the opposite direction of the bear. Now you know why I've always called heads when you thought I didn't realize that you were using my two-headed coin." He smiles.

Jeremiah looks over the horses to be sure that none of them are injured. "That's what I get for trying to cheat a man with his own coin. I see that you left Lightning saddled. Are you thinking about going after that ornery cuss of a critter and putting him out of our misery once and for all?"

The grey one looks up and replies, "Don't we always, Geronimo? He has been playing this game with us for years now."

Jeremiah Williams says, "You know he set us up this morning. Dingahay got a real good laugh on you and me, old friend."

"The shaman wants us to play tag one more time before Shashana blinks his eye to darken the moon in the night sky. By the way, I see that you have already gathered our weapons, bedrolls, ammo, and camping supplies for the hunt."

"Well, you didn't name me Geronimo for nothing," Jeremiah says with a wry little smile.

They eat some grub and pack the mule with overnight gear and provisions for a few days. This time, they are determined to return with the fixings for bear claw soup and a new bearskin rug to lie before the fireplace.

For years, this hunt has become a much expected, even celebrated event. It would seem that for both men and bear, this has really become a sort of game, not unlike tag or hide and seek. Sometimes, those two brave and vengeful men, depending on what sets them off, will just up and chase after the bear. Only twice have they encountered it by surprise, nearly trapping and killing the resourceful creature. Yet somehow, it always seems to have a trick up its sleeve. Often times, the hunters became the hunted.

Every now and then, Dingahay will sneak up on them and terrorize their animals. He almost never kills the livestock, except for the dog and a few of those juicy pigs. The squealing excites it. They assume that the dog was killed while they were away because the bear could not have it chasing after him or constantly announcing his presence in the compound when he comes to raid. He kills the pigs because they simply taste good. Curiously, though, they never got another dog.

A few years back, the bear sneaked onto the homestead when Jeremiah and Greycloud had gone hunting for elk in the western valley. Dingahay knocked the cabin door off its hinges and tore up the doorframe getting in. Once inside, he proceeded in the very passionate destruction of the man den. Shortly after eating all of the sweet things to be found, it took a long awaited dump in the middle of the floor. It then proceeded in tearing the cabin a brand new door and disappeared. His only trace was the roar that echoed over the valley and bounced from mountain to mountain to cling to the minds of all animals within earshot. It leaves precious few tracks to follow because it always heads for a hard rock slope, giving the illusion that it just flies away.

The mountain men transform into Geronimo and Chief Greycloud at the first sight of tracks they know will lead into the eastern valley. The horses are led down the rugged incline of the rock face until it eases into a less treacherous downward slope where the tracks always disappear into thin air. They know that once the rock meets again with earth, they will have to resume a wide sweep in opposite directions along the leading edge to find Dingahay's tracks.

They pick up the trail again in late afternoon, deciding to make camp and rest up for the rigorous exercise they will undergo the next morning. It is no easy decision to let things lie until dawn, but they know there will be dangerous consequences if they camp too near the animal at night. A fresh start will be much better for their old bones and the horses. They hope against the odds for a different ending to this story.

Neither could figure out how the bear manages to escape them each time, and they are obsessed with breaking the code. The wheels are turning, pitting their decades of hunting experience against the unsolved equation that is the animal's unfailing means of escape. However, this time—this time—Dingahay has made a huge mistake.

Thirty minutes after making camp, the answer comes to Jeremiah like a bolt of lightning. He leaps to his feet and cries, "Hot damn, I got you now, you son-of-a-bitch!"

Greycloud looks up from the firewood he's about to ignite, laughing without a clue. "Hey, Geronimo, are you having some kind of flashback or a conniption fit? If it's the conniptions, I'll tie you down and put a root in your mouth to keep you from biting off your tongue. But if it's…"

"Dingahay! I done figured out how that critter has been foolin' us all this time," Jeremiah shouts. "Old tracks, he's been leading us to his old tracks. Don't you see? That's why we always seem to be tracking a ghost. He walks up the slope onto the rocks from the north on the night before he visits. Then he turns around and walks off the rocky slope a little to the south. Those are the tracks we follow into the valley at the foot of the mountain. "

"What are you talking about?" Greycloud asks, looking at his friend as if he's crazy.

"Come on, I'll show you what I'm talking about." Jeremiah takes Greycloud by the arm, quickly leading through pine saplings and underbrush to a place where they picked up the trail. He explains what he feels in his gut to be the only thing that makes sense. Dingahay's tracks are always easy to identify, but nearly impossible to follow.

"All these years we've been hunting this critter, but we could never catch him. It's so simple, I feel like a fool. Look at these tracks, Greycloud. They're fresh alright, but not as fresh as the ones at the cabin. We always catch the fever, never considering that the tracks could be from the night before he comes calling. Look here. These tracks are from another bear, probably a female. She is following his trail because she might be in heat, but I doubt if she did it in between the time he raided and the time it took us to find them. No, sir. See here, her tracks seem slightly fresher than these do. What do you think?"

Greycloud looks up the mountain. He removes his hat and scratches his tingling, damp scalp. He looks down at the tracks once more before looking back up the mountain.

"I'd say Dingahay takes the stone face down the mountain a ways before crossing that ridge into the southern valley in an area where we wouldn't see his tracks. Maybe he makes a point not to step in the stream that comes down from Totem Rock on this side of that ridge yonder to keep us heading straight down into this eastern valley. Makes too much sense to me, Geronimo." John Greycloud takes off his hat to scratch his scalp, again. "How the hell is it that we never even considered the possibility before now?"

Jeremiah smiles before saying, "Because where that ornery cuss is involved, we always catch the fever."

There is still daylight left so they break camp and head back up the rock face, moving in a southwesterly direction this time.

Dingahay, the bear, is a truly magnificent creature. Its cunning would frighten most hunters back into the safety of their homes, having discovered this large animal capable of such intelligent schemes. The fact, however, only gives Jeremiah and Greycloud a greater sense of respect and determination to outsmart him.

Old Dingahay knows something else about these two old fools: they never search for where he makes his grand entrance, only where he exits. The false trail begins the moment he leaves the homestead on a suicide run down the steep slope of solid rock. It begins before he makes a drastic right, going over a ridge into the south valley.

None of this is typical bear behavior, but it is the pure animal genius of an aberration. His would-be-killers head straight down into the east valley every time, never suspecting that the bear has not gotten that far because he's laid a false trail on the night before.

Jeremiah and the grey one reach the top of the ridge, rooting out a theory. After finding the real trail of their quarry, they descend into the valley. They are sure beyond all doubt that the bear is smarter than any man could have guessed it to be.

They decide on a cold camp, which means canned beans and deer jerky for dinner. A fire would be very foolish, giving the animal more than a hint that they are in this valley. Greycloud suggests they find one of the many dandelion fields he knows from his childhood. That will be the best place to hunker down and wait.

Once camp is set up, they place makeshift dust masks over their animals' snouts to keep down the snorting and sneezing. Bear will eat them, but they hate dandelions for this very reason. If Dingahay detects their scents in the downward sweep of the wind on the valley floor, he could come looking for them, but the sneezing will warn them of his approach.

From here, they will strike out deeper and deeper into the basin until they find the bear or its den.

The two hunters feel that, with a little patience and a lot of luck, they will finally have him. After years of having their traps busted up, their animals terrorized, and their own near heart attacks, they will finally have him.

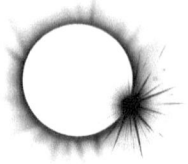

Chapter 20

A PLACE OF POWER

O n the first trip up the short path from the truck, Keith opens the windows to release the stale accumulation of air. After several trips, he starts a cozy little fire as the cooling night air circulates throughout. While he does so, Sabrina Martin inhales the environment, noting definite signs of his influence in the decor of the modern day cabin. This is a nice place, very soothing.

While the warm glow of the fireplace dances along the soft shadows, Keith's lover blesses him with an embrace before a painting of Harriet Tubman's Underground Railroad. Yet to adjust to the higher altitude, they put away the rest of the groceries and sit for a moment to catch their breath. During this short expanse, Keith catches Sabrina's glance at the telephone, and she knows she is busted.

"Ah huh. I saw that. You are thinking about the job. You can't fool me, Sabrina."

"Now that you mention it, you're right. I was thinking about checking my messages."

"There's no need to feel guilty, Dr. Martin. You did dump your caseload in someone's lap with very little notice. I understand completely."

"It was really good of Dr. Gaines and Dr. Wright to split my caseload, but there are a few patients I'd like to check on."

"By all means, Dr. Martin, and let it never be said that Keith Williams is not an altruist at heart. Besides, I was thinking of the same thing. You go first." He gives her the phone.

She smiles and takes it from his hand. "Really, you have landline service up here."

"It's an old, glitch-riddled system from many years ago. I was fortunate enough to find a way to get a tie-in up here. I'm considering having things upgraded and bundled into the satellite service, but since I hardly have time to get away, it always slips my mind."

"It's okay with you? I mean, we did promise to leave everything behind."

Keith nods his head. "I don't mind at all. I think we both knew that our pact to sever all ties to our careers was wishful thinking. Besides, we have total control because they can't reach us without leaving messages."

She gives him a peck on the cheek. "You're absolutely right. I really like the way you think, counselor."

Sabrina calls her answering service, finding nothing of great significance. She also calls the hospital to speak to one of her colleagues, who reports no unanticipated events. Dr. Rita Gaines advises Sabrina to forget about work so she can enjoy a much-needed vacation, indicating some immediate sexual contact as the answer to all her woes. The call finally eases her mind.

"By the look on your face," Keith observes, "I'd say there are no problems to speak of."

"That's very astute of you, counselor. Now, I'm all yours." Sabrina is about to place the receiver on the cradle when she discerns that Keith is actually experiencing his own separation anxieties. "Fair is fair. It's your turn, so go on and get it off your chest. I did, and it feels wonderfully guilt free. You know you want to." She passes the telephone back and forth before his eyes like bait.

He reaches for it, admitting, "Guilty as charged, doc." He takes the phone but pauses.

"What's the matter?" she asks.

He smiles and shakes his head. "I was trying to remember. Have you ever noticed how cellphones are actually replacing our brain's ability to recall the most used numbers in our lives?"

She bursts into laughter. "You know, you're right. God, I have the hardest time remembering my own phone numbers. I've even reverted to looking at my own business cards when I have to give it out."

"Use it or lose it, they say."

Surprisingly, there are only five messages for Keith. The first states, "Mr. Williams, this is Sylvia. Mr. Mitchum asked me to let you know that he hasn't been able to contact Mr. St. John as of yet, but he does expect to hear from him today. He also advises that you enjoy your vacation. That's all for now."

There is a pause, and then his brother's voice comes across the line. "Yo, Keith, I figured a workaholic like you couldn't resist checking your messages, so I just wanted to let you know that I'll be taking you up on your offer to stay at your crib while you're away. I'm gonna hit the pool and do some laps. Tell grandpa and Greycloud that I said hello. That's it, see ya. Oh…yeah…I almost forgot. Ah, I thought I should tell you before you hear it from someone else. Mrs. Brown, that kid's mother, they found her in her son's car in a ditch outside of town. She wrecked the car, but she's alive. The news report said that she might have had some kind of mental breakdown or something. When they found her, she was screaming like crazy. I just figured you'd want know. Love ya, man. Please try to remember it's not your fault. Bye."

With a momentary return of vivid guilt, Keith's mind reels, spinning out of its peaceful orbit. He does not notice the pause before Mitchum says, "Keith, Mr. St. John and I had a very intense conversation. Nearly messed his pants when I told him you had him on tape. Willard did not want to hear it after I repeated a few of his more damning statements. I upped the ante to a million dollars because he pissed me off. Son, we realize that no amount of money can take the place of a child, but it will help Mrs. Brown a little."

The message ends, and another takes its place. It seems that Mitchum has much to report.

"Stop beating yourself up because I'm sure he's going to play ball after trying to pull the old end-around. That slimy chiseler met with Alice about suing us all, but she worked him over like the heavyweight champion of the world. She countered every slithery move he tried to make, sticking him with her stiff jabs and wicked uppercuts until he tossed in the towel. Please avoid Willard St. John at all cost. We cannot afford to trust him. He is a snake, that guy. And there is the very real possibility that he will try to buck." Again, the message ends to be replaced by the third and final one from Mitchum.

"One more thing, Keith. Those news hounds are probably camped on your doorstep by now. As you already know, those media vultures are tricky bastards when they smell rotting flesh. If you haven't taken your kid brother along, warn him to watch his back because Willard tried to get me to disclose your whereabouts with false contrition dripping from his lying lips like bile. All for now. Good-bye."

The automated instruction to repeat the messages plays, but Keith does not press one. He hangs up and quickly dials his home phone number, pacing back and forth, but there is no answer. Kevin's cell is the same, but he leaves messages asking his brother to call so he can arrange for a hotel suite. He realizes that he may have placed his brother in harm's way by inviting him to stay at the condominium.

His sigh prompts Sabrina to approach and say, "Judging by the look on your face, we may regret the decision to backslide on our oath to leave the world behind." She smiles, but it is not returned until she takes his hand. "Please try to let it go, Keith. Whatever's happening back there is not your doing."

"I'm not so sure," he utters. He decides to force Kevin's voice as far back in his mind as possible, knowing that it's bound to intrude upon his peace of mind if he doesn't.

He looks up at the framed photo on the wall, pointing it out to her.

"What...is that the...?" Sabrina pauses with her hand on her chest as she stares at the grizzly. "Are you shitting me?"

"Yup, that's old Dingahay in all his majesty. One hell of a specimen, wouldn't you say?"

"You actually stood still long enough to photograph this beast?" she asks in amazement.

"Good camera. A very good camera. My hands were shaking like I had the DTs."

"Wow. My god," she says as she touches the glass shield.

"Well, there's no time like the present. Are you ready to face the music, babe?"

She is, so they walk arm in arm down the trail toward the barnyard. They had taken the other trail from where the trucks are parked about thirty yards away, so Sabrina is yet to see this area.

A sudden spark leaps into Sabrina Martin's eyes, and her voice fills with girlish enthusiasm when she says, "Horses! I love horseback riding. My aunt had dozens on her farm when I was a kid. After she taught me how to ride like a proper Southern lady, I spent hours on end out in the fields with Plunkett. That's what I called him. I really loved that horse."

Keith smiles. "Then I'll give you the grand tour on horseback. Wait a minute. I only see two horses in the corral. My grandfather must be out hunting. Let's see."

They walk across the yard and he knocks. After getting no answer, Keith uses his key to let himself inside. He turns on the inner and outer lights, but no one is at home.

Sabrina admires the trophies as she walks around the cabin. Her admiration of the artistry causes her to venture too near the fish tank, and both rattlers take a stab at the glass. She screams as they recoil and rattle their tails.

Keith rushes to her aid and apologizes. "I'm sorry. I forgot to tell you about Yin and Yang. Are you okay?"

Shaken, Sabrina holds onto him until led away. At a safe distance, she says, "I've never seen a live rattlesnake, much less two. I was thrown once, and broke my arm when a cottonmouth sprung and spooked my horse. God, they just scared the hell out of me."

He takes her hand to walk outside where the cooling air is brisk and refreshing. This is when Keith notices the jagged claw marks on the doorframe.

"Well, I'll be damned. Look at this!"

"What is it?" she asks as Keith examines the grooves. He bends at the knees to place his hand in the bear's paw print. It swallows his hand.

After placing his right index finger at the tip of one of the animal's digits to the claw mark, he says with surety, "Dingahay must have paid them a visit this morning. I guess that explains why they left with the other horses and that crazy mule."

"Are you telling me that this thing just waltzed in here, big and bold...just like that? Christ, it must be huge. Aren't you worried?" She brushes a lock of hair from her eyes and places her size six in the paw print.

Keith shows her an empty shell casing from ground level and says, "Not really. It looks like they were waiting for him this time. The bear could be wounded, so they probably struck out after it. They should be back by tomorrow, most likely. I've never known my granddad or Greycloud to waste meat or opportunities. If the animal was wounded, they had no choice but to follow. It may sound gruesome, but that is the law of the hunt and the land. *Ahyake lokliot kalelea ota leokna.* No man eats well if he does not eat what he kills. Killing for sport or trophies is only honorable when the substance of that which we kill goes not to waste. Throughout human history, that is something often forgotten."

She is stroking Keith's hairline, witnessing a subtle change in him. Even in the dim light, Sabrina sees and feels something that leaves her in simple awe. As she looks down upon her man, she pictures Keith Williams when such profoundly meaningful words were spoken to him as a child on this mountain. A new smile is born upon her lips.

When Keith's mini-trance breaks, he rises and asks if she is tired. She feels fine, exhilarated in fact, so he goes back inside for a rifle. They go to the corral to saddle the horses.

Both animals took the sweet granola treats from Keith's hand. It has been a while, but they still remember his voice and scent. "Ms. Sabrina Martin, this is Zeus, and this one is Apollo. Take your pick."

Sabrina chooses the Appaloosa so he takes Zeus, the black stallion. Both are powerful and spirited animals, but well behaved. They head up a trail for a place that overlooks the eastern and southern valleys of Big Bear Mountain.

Wherever they encounter a downslope, they sidestep the horses for safety of both rider and animal. Sabrina is impressed.

As they talk during the leisurely ride beneath the night sky, Sabrina Martin keeps her eyes open. Her caution, however, does not prevent her from enjoying clean air filled with the scent of spring flowers, night noises, and the smell of fresh pine. This world is infinitely different from the crowded streets and sirens she has grown accustomed to seeing and hearing. The air up here is charged with a new, different kind of life.

In dashes of spectacular moonlight reaching through the treetops, he watches Sabrina as she soaks in the radiance. She is truly a beauty in nature, rising and falling with Apollo's steps. If there was no sound, she could have floated in slow motion to the stars on her ghost white horse.

They dismount to tie off the reins. Sabrina takes Keith by the hand and follows him to the place of power. The couple stops at the granite slate where Keith is immersed in his childhood memories. Nothing ever seems to change here.

Sabrina is wowed, charged with a strange energy she can only attribute to her surroundings. They both lose sight of where they are for a moment, even though it is the very focus of their thoughts. She steps away from him without warning and slips when she steps in a sliver of water!

Keith grabs Sabrina, pulling her close. "You really don't want to do that. Not until you grow wings, anyway." He tries not to let on as to how close she had actually come to a very thrilling death.

Sabrina is startled, breathless. She says, "You mean this is where…?"

"Yes. This is the place where my ancestors invented the American version of bungee jumping. Come, follow me." Keith lets go of her and backs away from the stream. He takes a couple strides and hops to the other side where he waits for her to do the same. "Always remember to leap across the water because this slate is too slick to stand on. The depth, speed, and force of the water are very deceptive. Especially in the worn center."

He puts an arm around her midriff as they move closer to the standing totem where he points out the stump of the other one a few feet away.

Sabrina touches the totem tree, which vibrates with an unknown power source buried deep inside. Her skin tingles and she instinctively caresses her stomach as some small, baseless fear washes over her. Thankfully, the feeling is only momentary.

When Keith takes her into his arms, they gaze into one another's eyes before a long kiss. When their lips part, she places her head upon his chest and they begin to sway. Their eyes wonder to the serene skyline, falling to the silhouetted valley floor.

He whispers, "When I was very young, and still could not open up to my grandfather about my parents' death, Greycloud brought me here to camp out for the very first time during a full moon just like this. I believe, in a way, the experience sparked my healing process. If you can still your beating heart with your eyes closed, you can almost hear chanting and the sacred drums of this place. I have always gotten that sensation. It feels the same, even now. It is as if some amazing force is dancing all around us, just above or outside of our abilities of perception. Just staying slightly out of reach. Sometimes, especially at night, I feel as if I've gotten a little too close to the moon. So close…so very close that I can just reach out and touch it…be touched by it." He smiles at having said these words to someone special.

The moon is high and the night sky is bright with its fullness. A blanket of stars twinkles down on the two lovers, who are listening to the sad lament of a lonesome whippoorwill. Soon, they return to the cabin where they make love throughout the night.

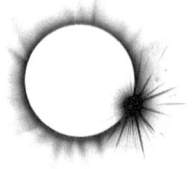

Chapter 21

QUESTIONS

Jeremiah and Greycloud are sipping coffee with their eggs, bacon, and beans before sunrise. They no longer care if the bear gets wind of the food because there's a slight chance it might bring him to them.

They are sopping up the last of the bean gravy with homemade bread when something moves in the dandelions. The rustling weeds give it away and then it sneezes. Moving with quiet swiftness on their hands and knees, both men grab their rifles and take positions on opposite sides of the camp. They wait, pensively, aiming at the area where they think the animal will come into view. It is big!

Frozen on one knee, they squint down the rifle sights with their hands trembling slightly. Each passing second seems like hours, and their rifles are getting heavier.

It sneezes, again. The movement is much closer, so is the sweat on each man's brow to falling. They hold their breaths when the bear walks into the clearing with its upturned muzzle sniffing heavily at the air. It looks from man to man and suddenly comes out of its bacon-induced haze.

It reverses polarity, bolting through dandelions that go flying into the air to mark its path. The black bear's amplified growl rings out as it carves a three-foot wide path through the field in its headlong retreat.

Each man nearly pulls the trigger twice, at least. The second time is due to anger. Something in them just wanted to shoot it anyway. The animal's life is spared, however, because it isn't the one they are after.

Jeremiah and Greycloud allow the stale air to exit their aching lungs until their pounding hearts subside and, eventually, resume normalcy. They broke camp and head deeper into the ravine, moving further south after regaining the clever tracks that had not initially led them into this valley. This day would be quite a day indeed.

ॐ

Keith Williams is a brilliant attorney and a grateful grandson. He is also a very tolerant adoptive parent to his brother, to whom he has a hard time saying, "No."

Then there is the other Keith Williams, who is quite the romantic at heart. He sits in the recliner, slowly rocking back and forth as the sun rises on the horizon to creep over the bedroom windowsill. Across the room, Sabrina and the sun-brightened window lay directly in his path. The scenery is looking better and better, as precious moments pass. The yellow orb in the sky illuminates her skin with an almost saintly glow.

Sabrina is smiling in her sleep, clearly dreaming of something pleasant. He cannot help wondering about the private contents of her dreams. With the pad and pen from the bedside table, Keith Williams has written a few lines inspired by Sabrina's image.

The woman is truly a bright spot in his life. Wise fate has made a masterful match, he thinks. His love for her seems bottomless, prompting him to contemplate marriage. However, something profoundly important has kept him from popping the big question up until this point. Of course, there are the usual doubts. He knows she loves him, but he is uncertain if she's willing to go that far, given all the age old taboos. Then, there is her father; a public figure. The cat will certainly be out of the bag then.

What if Sabrina Martin can go that far? Say yes. He wonders what their lives will be like out there in the great wide-open. No more clandestine meetings. Never the need to pacify passionate gestures in public, even in the state of Georgia.

What if she agrees to be his wife and they have children? Just what will their world be like? Will their kids have to grow up in a vacuum? Will they grow up resenting one parent or the other, and maybe even both?

Could he make and keep this woman happy and content, or is it best to leave things as they are?

Questions, questions, and more of the same are swimming around in Keith's head.

When a random thought enters his mind, he actually laughs aloud. The thought of a previous conversation they had about never seeing a White man on television with a larger, maybe even less attractive Black woman causes him to continue chuckling under his breath. The conversation was truly comical, but his thoughts soon resume a more serious tract.

Engrossed in deep thought, Keith Williams is completely unaware that his lover is awake and looking directly at him. Her smile is ever-present.

Sabrina sits upright in the bed for a good stretch before reaching for him. A little voice in the back of his mind assures that, if their love is as true and as strong as it seems, they will survive all opposing obstacles.

When she questions him about the sudden burst of laughter after such deep thought, he answers truthfully, which causes them both to laugh at that ridiculous conversation.

Keith is quite unaware that he has been writing down bits and pieces of his thoughts. At the bottom of the page are scrawled the words: *could she, marriage, what if, yes,* and *children.*

He puts the pad down and joins Sabrina for the morning kiss and hug that is yet to feel like a routine duty. Holding her close, he is assured that it could never feel that way.

Keith and Sabrina share a cheerful breakfast. Afterwards, he offers to do the dishes, but she takes care of them because she knows he is anxious to check in on his grandfather.

Keith leaves the cabin at about 10:30 a.m. While walking down the winding trail, he suddenly experiences an extremely uncomfortable sensation. While looking over his shoulders, as he turns a small bend in the trail, he trips over something that moves!

Keith scoots backwards on his hands with his ass end dragging on the ground, stopping abruptly when he realizes he has come face-to-face with a snorting, frightened pig. The animal regards Keith with caution, trying to decide if he is friend or foe.

When Keith remembers to breathe, he laughs at himself for having nearly panicked. He gets up thanking God he hadn't released the scream that threatened to part his lips. That really would go over big with Sabrina, who would probably say, "The mighty attorney and brawny hunter, Keith Williams, was mauled by Porky the killer pig."

He chuckles at the thought and says to his four-legged companion, "You know, Porky, you really are lucky I didn't have my gun just then because you would be bacon before your time." Grunting is the animal's only reply. "Come on. Let's get you back where you belong."

Sabrina reads what Keith has written and floats into outer space. The poem entitled *Her Awakening* leaves her blushing as she holds the pad close to her chest. When she looks down with the intention of reading the poem again, she notices the words at the bottom of the page.

She has seen this sort of writing before. In fact, she named it *writing aloud* when she first called it to Keith's attention. She has mentioned it on a few occasions, realizing that he usually only writes aloud while working out a particularly perplexing problem. In this case, her immediate interpretation of the keywords suggest that he is thinking about marriage. Sabrina's answer is no mystery to herself, but she decides not to bring it up.

Keith walks Porky back to the pen where the other three pigs are sunning themselves outside of the corral. They happily follow him inside the pen, thinking that he might have some good slop in his pockets. He locks them in and goes over to the cabin.

Greycloud and Jeremiah are still out, so he goes inside for his crossbow and some targets. He also retrieves his compound bow and arrow set. Before leaving, Keith goes to the cellar in search of something from his childhood.

ℭ℧

Martin's party lands in Great Falls and takes a chartered flight to Windfall Airfield, where they meet Joe Mills. Apparently, Williams has taken the last of only three rental vehicles, so Mills and his driver waited because Martin would be along soon enough.

Bo Tuttle, the driver, informs former General Mills that there is only the usual dozen at the camp and most of them have gone on an all-day hunt in the northern end of the valley. They are after a bear, whose tracks someone stumbled upon. Tuttle also tells Mills that they will probably shoot at whatever they jumped first—be it deer or bear—and to hell with closed hunting seasons. The six men cram into the big camouflage-green truck and head for Camp Righteous K.

Camp Righteous K, the K standing for Kill, of course, is located at the southeastern end of Big Bear's southern valley.

A ten-foot fence surrounds the entire compound. It is topped with razor wire, like those used at maximum-security prisons. These are very paranoid people indeed.

At either side of the main gate, there are lookout towers, which stand approximately ten-feet higher than the fence itself. With only the skeleton crew, and because of a lack of maneuver activities, they brood abandoned by the men that roost there when the camp is alive or receiving very important guests.

On the eastern or left side, the central command building is reserved for the chief righteous brother, Joe Mills, the so-called officers, and VIPs. The primary munitions cache is housed here in a fireproof vault. There is also a bomb shelter in the basement.

The compound boasts two barracks that could house a couple platoons. The mess hall, which also serves as a secondary command post and auditorium, accommodates about 100 people at a single sitting. Attached is a dry supply building.

The infirmary is of a modest design. This is a place where many wayward asses have had buckshot removed or worse.

The camp also sports both public and private showers, latrines, and indoor plumbing.

Further down, on the same side, a stern wall stands between these buildings and a fuel dump, where barrels of gasoline, diesel fuel, and kerosene are sorted in their own respective categories.

The largest buildings on the opposite side from the fuel dump are the maintenance garage and a machine shop with various types of heavy-duty equipment.

Along that fence on the western side of the compound are a few smaller shacks that are mainly tool sheds for things like trimmers and lawn mowing equipment.

Before reaching the maintenance garage and machine shop, the last shack is empty, except for a motley cot and chair that looks to offer little comfort. It is a place of punishment, their Hotel Misery.

☙❧

Sabrina is daydreaming with the new issue of a popular women's magazine lying virtually unread in her lap. She is lightly caressing her stomach. Drifting far away in her private theater, she watches a little girl with curly black hair playing with familiar dolls. When mommy walks in, the child gives her a great big hug and a smile that can melt mountains.

Dr. Sabrina Martin is pregnant. She loves the life growing inside of her, and the man who helped in its wondrous conception; the man she is yet to inform.

Something rushes past the window, and the sudden blur brings her back to reality. Sabrina approaches the window where she tentatively looks out, but sees nothing. A scratching sound comes from the door. She is apprehensive about opening it with marauding bears and the like in the area.

When she calls out, no one answers. The scratching continues, so Sabrina grabs a heavy frying pan from the kitchen and eases over to a door she just has to open. She takes a deep breath, raises the pan overhead and snatches the door ajar. Sabrina eyes bulge and she squeals, dropping the pan on her foot! She feels nothing, backing away from the door with her hands clasped over her mouth. She screams!

Keith is standing there with a kiddy tomahawk, wearing an Indian headband with a sorry looking feather in it. He is bare-chested with war paint smeared on his face. Certain that he has her undivided attention, Keith Williams performs an Indian war dance around an imaginary fire, whooping and patting his lips with his free hand.

He is the picture of a true warrior. Chief Little Idiot, to be exact. In the throes of fearless laughter, this unexpected performance is truly ludicrous. The sight of him has weakened her knees so that they will not support her modest weight. With his girlfriend snickering on the floor, Keith feels his mission accomplished.

He walks in and stands over her with a big grin curling his lips. Her presence always helps him to wash away the grime of dealing with legalities and the debris of his clients' lives. He is secure in his manhood, so he does not mind bearing the brunt of a practical joke or two. However, he always enjoys playing them on other people even more.

When he can finally peel Sabrina off the floor, he leads her down a short foot trail where he has already set up the targets in the much larger horse corral. There, he shows Sabrina how to shoot the bow and the crossbow. To his pleasant surprise, she seems to be a natural.

Sabrina Martin, however, neglects to mention that she was on the archery squad in high school and in college, or that she was considered to be a bit of a tomboy as a kid. Slingshot Annie rather enjoys having him so close behind her while he instructs on the finer points of looking down an arrow's shaft.

They take a nature walk, during which, they see a doe with her yearling still trying to nurse. There are squirrels foraging and chasing each other up and down trees. From a hilltop, they watch as a red-tailed hawk swoops down to catch a large rodent, and take it to the nest for her young.

This is nature at its best. In the face of all this wild beauty, they cannot help making a little nature of their own. When they get back to the young folks home, Sabrina is tired and wants to take a nap before starting dinner.

Keith goes back to the barn to feed the animals. He gives water and oats to the horses. Now he mixes a batch of mush for the pigs, which are eager to plow their snouts in the trough for the goodies that float there.

After everyone in the barnyard is happy, Keith takes Zeus for a ride back to Totem Rock. He looks over the valleys with a pair of binoculars, trying to speculate his grandfather's location in the foliage far below. For all he knows, they can be on the western side of Big Bear.

He sits up there for quite some time, thinking about serious issues. What to do about the St. John mess, for example. There may be no easy solutions to dealing with that evil man, and it could be far from over. Keith has come to this place to get away from the subject, so he decides to drop it and head back, hoping Sabrina is done with dinner.

During the return trip, he finally decides to propose over a bottle of wine, allowing those all-knowing chips to fall where they may. Upon his return to the corral, Keith gives Zeus and Apollo a rubdown. He takes the saddles inside the barn where he cleans and polishes the leather. Earlier in the day, he had forgotten to feed the chickens, so he takes care of them and collects the eggs in a small basket. All the while, he is thinking about retiring here with Sabrina. Eventually, Keith comes to the conclusion that he's merely stalling. The saddles had no real need for polish, and he feels silly for the delays.

Keith walks out of the barn and closes the doors behind him. When he turns around, there is a gun pointed at his face! He is startled, dropping the basket of eggs. In the fading twilight, he can see that the hands holding the gun are shaking and anxious to pull the trigger.

"So this is how it ends," runs through his mind. He thought he had left the big city crime behind in Atlanta.

A voice, as shaky as the hands on the gun, comes from the darkened figure. "Boy? Is that you, Keith?"

As the barrel of the gun slowly comes down, Keith realizes that Jeremiah Williams had nearly blown his face off. A feeling of relief washes over him, flowing out of his mouth with the air he had trapped in his lungs. Keith says, "Grandpa?"

Jeremiah drops Greycloud's Winchester on the ground and hugs his grandson. Keith knows it has been a while since they have seen one another, but for some reason he feels his grandfather is just a little too happy to see him. It is evident in how tightly he is being hugged, and Jeremiah would never drop a rifle in the dirt.

There is a whinny and Keith looks over Jeremiah's shoulder to see Lightning with Greycloud slumped in the saddle. He waves, unknowingly, at a badly hurt man.

The horse whinnies again and falls forward to the ground with the grey one still in the saddle. Jeremiah and Keith rush to take hold of Greycloud, managing to pull him free of the saddle before the horse rolls over on him. It is a very close call.

Keith can see that the sweaty horse is wounded as it writhes, laboring to breathe. The animal will eventually recover from the exhaustion of hauling two men up the mountain. It would seem, however, that Greycloud has been shot.

"Help me get him in the house, son. Hurry!" Jeremiah pleads.

As they carry the wounded man, Keith asks, "What happened, was it an accidental shooting? Did that grizzly turn on you?"

They are moving Greycloud with his arms draped over their shoulders while his feet drag behind them.

Greycloud's head is sagging toward the ground, but he manages to say, "Now, Little Bear, you know Geronimo would not shoot me without good reason." He falls silent. Unconscious, again, he will be out for a while this time.

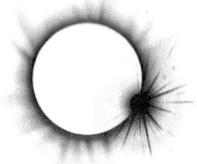

Chapter 22

ORPHANS OF
RIGHTEOUS KILL

Hot beads of sweat run freely from his drenched hairline, sliding between his blue eyes to fall from the tip of his pointed nose. He is panting from the climb to the top of the southwestern ridge.

Eleven young men and a boy left Camp Righteous Kill at dawn to hunt a large bear. Jim Morton leads this trip into the bush, which is merely the latest distraction from the infinite boredom of camp life. Eric and Derrick Glover, Tommy Swinton, Perdie Jake, and others of his faithful following have dispersed throughout the valley floor.

These young men are considered the orphans of Joe Mills' Klavern of the Klan because none has seen a family member for years.

Jim Morton is eldest at twenty-seven, while Tommy Swinton is the youngest at age fourteen. Not one of these young men has seen the inside of a classroom beyond the ninth grade. Some were abandoned as children. A few were adopted and ran away, as the Glover brothers had done.

Miraculously, Tommy Swinton survived the crash of his parent's small, private airplane in a neighboring range of mountains. The crash that killed his mother and father spared his life. A hunter found the starving, wounded boy wondering in the wilderness. He took Tommy to a country doctor, who set his broken arm and mended his minor wounds. The camp has been his home ever since.

Jim Morton, however, is guilty of murdering his parents following an intense argument when he was eighteen. He is the undisputed leader of the Orphan Squad, having the nastiest disposition of them all. They do everything he tells them. Some simply obey out of fear of bodily harm. Others obey without question because of nothing less than admiration.

Perdell Jakes, who is called Perdie Jake as a cruel joke, is an overweight pimple-puss. From ages eight to sixteen, his drug-addled parents sexually abused this stuttering child. When Perdell's parents were finally jailed for manufacturing methamphetamine, child endangerment, and the sexual abuse of a minor, he was passed from one foster home to another. To his woe, the last foster dad turned out to be just like the boys sick biological father.

When Mr. Waller finally fell to his disgusting temptations, paying a visit to the teenager's bedroom late one night, Perdell stabbed him twenty-six times with the filet knife he kept under his pillow. He left it broken, but buried to the hilt in the old man's gut. After killing Waller, Perdell wandered aimlessly, turning tricks for food from Polson to Columbia Falls, Montana until he finally ended up at the camp. As if the things he experienced over two years of vagrancy were not enough, Perdie was then forced to take it in the ass from the Glover boys. They smelled something weak in him, homing in on the soft boy with a warped, sadistic aggression.

The Glover boys keep their little secret as the price of his initiation, but the other orphans know. They just don't talk about it because Eric and Derrick aren't the only ones guilty of fucking Perdie Jake in the ass. In fact, Tommy Swinton is the only innocent in this regard, but the kid has heard or seen them on occasion. Although the young man is still a virgin, he feels that something about this is not quite the norm as normal goes in his distorted world.

Tommy used to like Perdie and felt sorry for him. In truth, Perdie was no more than a fifth ward bitch on any D-block of a maximum-security prison. Tommy had a great deal of empathy for the older boy until Perdie mistook the youngster's friendship for something more. When Perdie offered Tommy *"the favor"*, he was appalled to discover that Perdie has actually come to like it. With the passage of time, Tommy Swinton's disgust has silently grown into loathing for Perdie being so weak and spineless.

One so young and essentially innocent could not begin to fathom the terrible things that have scarred Perdell Jakes' life. Those things have long since ravaged his self-esteem, such that he now accepts, without any real will of his own, that he enjoys being the bitch of the pack.

Yet Tommy understands far more than accounts by age warrant. He understands the concept of freedom because he has very little. He also understands the concept of personal choice. The young man sees in Perdie that which he loathes in himself; the powerless futility of the man he is becoming. In a sense, Tommy has no more individuality than a slave would have here.

Somewhere along the line, Perdie girly Jake grew to like the poking and prodding. Somehow, his twisted mind is convinced that he is fulfilling a purpose. Loved, he is needed.

Although Joe Mills' stern restriction on access to the whores in town may be the catalyst of what he considers deviant sexual behavior, he will put them all before a firing squad if he ever finds out.

The rest of the Orphan Squad is more of the same gutter wash, white trash fugitives that this cruel and unforgiving world has ravaged at very early ages. Fleeing dysfunction, they found sanctuary within the loving arms of the Klan in the mountains of Montana, baptized in the healing concept of their white supremacy.

Just after dawn, the orphans of Camp Righteous Kill set out, heading north on either side of a ravine that runs alongside the camp. If they do not flush anything into the open, they are to rendezvous at the north end of the valley where it flattens out at the foot of a ridge. There, it widens and continues in a more westerly direction along the base of Big Bear Mountain.

Everyone carries MREs and water. They are also equipped with radios and M-16 rifles; except, for Jim Morton. He shoulders something more of a traditional hunting rifle, although, in any other case, it's more of a weapon suited to hunting men. The Savage 30.06 caliber rifle, with a thirty-millimeter Redfield scope, is a lethal combination that gives Morton an excellent range of 400 yards.

During the past night, Dingahay pursued a female in heat. She actually sought him out, but chose to play hard to get when he showed interest. The female made him work for her affections by following her throughout the valley and back toward the northern end. The musk of bear is strong.

The animals normally found in this valley have skulked away, fearing the rulers of the range are on the hunt. Otherwise, there would be ample targets to spook these trigger-happy hunters into expelling a few hundred rounds of ammunition into the brush. Despite their training, none of these orphans are real hunters, so they will not hesitate to shoot at a noise rather than waiting to see what's actually making it. This group is an accident-in-waiting.

As the hunt progresses, they begin to bore with the endless walking. Incessant mosquitoes nail them in places they missed with repellant.

Jim Morton is about to call it quits, so he wipes the sweat from his face and makes a final sweep of the terrain with his binoculars atop the western ridge. This is when he sees Jeremiah and Greycloud on horseback just north of the rest of them. Much to his perverted delight, the unsuspecting riders are heading in the direction of his squad of orphans.

Jim calls the others, telling them to be quiet and stay out of sight. They are instructed to converge on an area with thick underbrush, where the ravine bottlenecks in a level area. He tells them that he sees game that is much better than a bear. They are to wait until he arrives.

Greycloud's horse hesitates for a few steps before reluctantly resuming its slow pace beside Dingahay's tracks. The wise old native of this land suggests to Jeremiah, "Hey, Geronimo, take a whiff. Dingahay's musk is very strong and the horses are getting nervous. We should leave them over there and walk through that thick brush because Dingahay and his woman may still be in there."

"I agree, let's leave the horses. They will remember that animal's scent a hundred years from now. If we ride them through that, they might throw us on our backsides. I don't rightly know about you, but mine is already sore as hell."

Greycloud chuckles, trying not to burst out laughing when he recalls the very close call in the doorway of the cabin.

After maneuvering the horses into a nearby stand of trees at the base of the southeastern ridge, they check their firearms. Greycloud draws his crossbow and makes sure the safety is latched before strapping it to his back. Meanwhile, Jeremiah cinches the loosened lace of his left boot before doing the same with his crossbow. Guns are subject to jamming at times, but crossbows do not. It is always better to be safe than sorry.

Because he will be flushing or driving the bear, Jeremiah Williams arms his crossbow with a razor-sharp arrow rather than a bolt. The crossbow's overall construction keeps the bolt or arrow from falling out even when pointing downward. A small, steel spline holds the projectile to a magnetic slot until the pull drives it out of the shaft.

Keith's grandfather looks at his friend to say, "It's my turn to walk the brush while you flank. If he's in there and detects me, he'll surely bolt."

Greycloud agrees. "I'll go to the far side. If he runs, he will probably head for the southwest side of the ravine instead of the bottleneck on the other side of the brush. That'll leave him in the open and we know he's too wily for that."

Because he needs to be in position before Jeremiah moves in, Greycloud heads for the far side. The wind is favorable. Once there, he gives a unique birdcall and Jeremiah starts in. They both have the distinct feeling of being observed. It has to be the grizzly.

Jeremiah is tracking on foot, alone for the moment. Excited by the hope of catching the grizzly with its proverbial pants down, their ears are sensitive to every sound. Their eyes are wary of all movement around them.

Greycloud imagines how good Dingahay's liver will taste with wild onions, wild garlic, and wild mushrooms. His mouth waters at the prospect.

Jeremiah quietly weaves back and forth in a zigzagging pattern. By the time Jeremiah gets halfway through, he concludes that the bear is no longer in the area. Although the intense feeling of being watched forces him onward, he is greatly disappointed, emerging on the opposite side of the bottleneck without even flushing a rabbit.

Jeremiah kneels next to some tracks, touching the soggy indentations in the mud. Suddenly, something moves, shifting positions to his left on a hill above. Bringing his gun up, he freezes when a stranger's harsh voice threatens, "Drop that gun, or we'll shoot you on your knees. Do it now!"

Jeremiah Williams is now looking down the barrels of at least five guns, so he wisely complies. He sets the rifle down and raises his hands.

Eric Glover's half of the hunting party, includes: his brother Derrick, Tommy Swinton, Boy Simmons, Perdie Jake, and Peter Mueller.

"Hey, Jimmy, you read?" Eric shouts into his radio with excitement. "We got 'em. We got the nigger. He came right to us, just like you said."

The panting Jim Morton stops running to say, "Where's the injun? I told your dumb ass that there are two of them!"

Eric looks around and says, "We ain't seen hide nor hair of any injuns. Blackie's all alone."

Jim Morton sweeps the terrain with his binoculars and sees no sign of movement. He tells Eric that he is going to initiate Tommy by giving him his first kill in the field. He demands that they wait for him and the rest of the gang. Afterwards, they will hunt the other one down.

The hunters all move in on Jeremiah. This is the very first time Tommy Swinton actually sees a Black man in person, but it does not look nearly as ferocious as the other boys have described. He is not allowed to watch television programs with Black stars, but he sees them in magazines and television advertisements.

The person kneeling before them in the soggy mud has only two eyes. His hands are without claws. He seems to have normal feet and ears, and has no fangs. Nor does froth come from his rabid mouth. Such are just a few of the things used to describe what normally happens to Black people after sundown in the scary tales that are told by torturous, older minds.

Eric and Derrick escort Tommy right up to Jeremiah, pointing at him as if he is the premier exhibit in a zoo for strange and exotic animals. Eric puts his boot under Jeremiah's rifle and kicks it away.

When Jeremiah notices the insignia of Camp Righteous Kill, he knows that he has stumbled into a hornet's nest. He sums them up as being more than potentially dangerous. These young men also seem a bit simple-minded. On the other hand, they were smart enough to ambush him.

Although Jeremiah is a bundle of nerves, he remains calmer than most because he knows Greycloud is somewhere, watching.

"Now, boys, what's this all about? I'm certain that I'm not trespassing, am I?" asks Jeremiah in an attempt to reason with them.

Eric laughs when Tommy flinches. He says, "You scared of him, Tommy? He's just one of them spooks that done been trained to talk. Did you see how he was tracking that bear? He's just like a dog with two feet that can talk, but you're gonna take care of that by shuttin' him up real good."

Tommy glances over his shoulder at Eric and Derrick to ask, "What do you mean?"

The brothers are grinning their ugly grins. Their tobacco-stained smiles are flush with that nasty brown shit they love to chew. Tommy detests that grin because he learned to associate it with trouble long ago. Being the youngest orphan of all, he is always at the mercy and whim of his miscreant elders.

Although the youngster hates the Glover brothers most of all, he is powerless around them and will usually do as told for fear of punishment. However, Tommy is yet to be so fully trained of mind as the others are. He will not act without hesitation, simply dismissing his own thoughts like a puppet on a string because it is easier to comply. His struggle is fierce against succumbing completely. He doesn't want to become something that need not think for itself. He is locked in a battle of wills, but his is waning against those of the older boys, who constantly bombard him with torturous cruelties.

Tommy Swinton is truly alone at the bottom of the totem pole. He dislikes them all, but he is afraid. The kid is fighting to become an individual, which is no small task at his age. It would be so easy to let go and become the thing he secretly loathes.

"Jimmy said you can kill this spy, and then we're gonna hunt down the injun that was with 'em, too," says Eric.

The brothers begin to snicker that irritating noise they make when mischief is afoot. For an added attraction, they do it while nodding their heads up and down. To him, they look like two people having simultaneous seizures. It is sheer lunacy.

Tommy's eyes grow wide as he looks at Jeremiah, and then over his troubled shoulders. He asks, "Why me? I ain't never kilt nobody before. Why it got to be me?"

Eric is displeased by Tommy's attitude, so he takes it upon himself to force the issue right here and now.

Eric growls, "Now, you listen to me, boy. You gotta do it. He is yours. Killin' your first nigger is how you get to be a full member in the Klan. That is the only way. Hell, he ain't nothing but stinking animal no how!"

"Just wait one minute here. Can't we talk about this," Jeremiah protests while looking directly into Tommy's eyes. "Why don't you fellas just let me go before this has to involve the law? Son, you don't really want to kill me because I've never done a thing to hurt any of you."

"Shut up, old-timer. You shut up, or I'll plug your stinking, filthy pie hole full of lead!" Eric Glover's stare is ice cold.

Derrick and Eric interpret Jeremiah's appeal as begging. They all do, which only increases their appetite for bloody violence.

Eric gives Tommy a harsh nudge. "Go ahead, shoot him. Shoot him dead right between them squint eyes of his."

When Jeremiah hears a whippoorwill's call, he knows Greycloud is about to make a move. He is saddened a great deal at the prospect, but they are outmanned and outgunned so the element of surprise is the only recourse. His old knees are beginning to ache and he prays that they do not seize up when he needs them.

Eric and his brother push Tommy until he is about a yard away from the man. Peter Mueller closes ranks with the rest of them. Meanwhile, Boy Simmons stays at least five-yards away. He is looking out for the Native American and Jimmy, who should be here soon. Peter thinks they should wait as they were told, but he is not about to rebuke Eric's decision. He is certain that this will become a cause of disagreement between Eric and Jimmy Morton soon enough, and he will have a ringside seat.

Derrick Glover shoves the kid again. Eric slaps him on the back of the head. "Do it, Tommy, before I whip your ass like a sorry dog. Shoot him!"

Drained of fight, the boy slowly raises the gun while Jeremiah looks from one face to another. They are chewing tobacco and spitting aimlessly with their eyes glued on him and the youngest boy.

Jeremiah Williams wonders which will die first. Sweat floods his pores, coming down hard.

Eric and Derrick begin to chant, "Kill him. Kill him. Kill him!" while pumping their fists, as if banging gavels on an imaginary pulpit.

Tommy's arms and hands tremble with reluctance, feeling as if they are tied to rubber bands anchored to the ground. His eyes apologize to Jeremiah as the weapon creeps higher and higher.

Now a bobwhite calls from the brush. Everyone notices his own raging heartbeat in the ensuing silence because this is the kind of quiet that one not only hears but also feels. Just as the boy's first teardrops fall from his eyes and the gun is about where it needs to be to kill Jeremiah, there comes a buzzing noise that discretely pierces the soundless vacuum. It ends with a rude thud when the arrow from Greycloud's crossbow hits Boy Simmons in the chest. Boy is snatched from his feet before crashing to the ground on his back, gasping while grabbing at the projectile that has already pierced his lung and heart before exiting his back.

The others look around, including Tommy, whose gun is pointing at Jeremiah's face. Like a cat, the old man grabs the barrel of Tommy's M-16 and shoves it in the direction of one of the other boys. When he gives it a stiff yank, pulling the trigger toward Tommy's finger, it fires twice. The gun recoils and the kid falls backward with it in his hands, but not before dropping Peter Mueller with bullets burning in his chest and stomach.

They all turn, looking to the right at Peter, who is screaming from the hot lead in his body. Now, Jeremiah reaches over his left shoulder and lays claim to the handle of the crossbow, which comes easily from the Velcro securing it to the strap. He rolls left toward his rifle and fires the arrow that obliterates Perdie Jakes' right eyeball, piercing his brain and killing him instantly! He is not Perdie anymore.

Greycloud fires his rifle at the feet of the three remaining orphans. As they scrambled for cover, Jeremiah drops the crossbow and quickly retreats into the bushes from which he emerged just moments and a world ago.

Jim Morton and the others are running. He curses when he hears the gunshots.

"Damn idiots. I told them to wait until we get there. I'm gonna kick Eric's ass!"

Jeremiah and Greycloud meet on the other side of the under-brush in the middle of the ravine. While huffing and puffing, they hobble against the cramps in both their sides. They have to get to the horses because more of the murderous youngsters are surely on the way.

Jim and the others careen down a small outcropping of boulders into the ravine where the shocked survivors are standing over their dying friend. Upon reaching the scene, which none of them expects, Jim places his hands on his knees and bends over to catch his breath.

Eric and Derrick are babbling. Of course, they are laying blame on one another, before placing it all squarely on Tommy Swinton.

Jim Morton is angry enough to wallop them both while shouting "Shut the fuck up! Where did they go?"

Derrick points north into the underbrush and says, "There was two of them just like you said, Jimmy. The injun ambushed us by shooting Boy. And then that no good nigger, got Perdie and Pete while we was all looking to see what was ailing Boy. It happened so fast, we couldn't do nothin', Jimmy. Honest."

Tommy is shaking like a jackrabbit when Jim looks down at him and asks if that is the way it actually happened. Tommy only nods his head to affirm.

Jim kneels beside Pete Mueller, just as his screams stop. The writhing young man is lying on his back with his legs curled to his chest. Blood begins to seep from his lips as his eyes beg Jim to save him. He reaches for Jim's arm, clamping down like a vice. Pete Mueller convulses three times before fading away. His Adam's apple contracts twice, his eyes grow dim.

Jim Morton squints to hold back his tears. He yanks his arm free of Pete's grip and takes off on the run, again. "Let's get 'em before they reach their horses. The hunt is on!"

The rest of them follow suit. They are certainly faster runners than two old men. Tommy also runs, but only because he does not relish being in the company of corpses. He runs out of sheer terror.

When Jeremiah and Greycloud finally reach the horses, they double-over, panting like dogs to the chase. They are in excellent shape for their ages, but sixty and sixty-one are far from young.

Gideon's reigns are a tangled mess and completely wrapped around the tree only inches from the bridle. There is simply no time to undo it all so Greycloud slips his knife between the mule's ears and cuts the bridle loose. Meanwhile, Jeremiah snatches at the off and near billets on Gideon's underbelly, dumping their supply rack to the ground to relieve the animal of any burden. At least the animal will have a fighting chance at survival. Beyond that, old Gideon is on his own.

After nearly catching their breath, they mount the horses and move out at a tear. Gideon, sensing their urgency, tries to follow, but the horses are much too fast.

Greycloud is a wise man. He has seen many things since childhood in these mountain ranges, but nothing like this. The incident prompts him to say, "Got to get out of this valley. They may have horses of their own. I think we should do it the way Dingahay did so they cannot easily follow us back up the mountain. When we get home, we'll have to call that racist sheriff to report this mess."

"No way. Much better chance explaining this to the state police. Those are some sick sons of bitches down there. I thought I left the Klan back in Mississippi. Thanks for saving my hide, partner. I owe you one."

Greycloud nods. "You would have done the same for me, old friend. I'm afraid it had to be. If I had let them kill you, who would cook for me?"

Although he seems to make light of it, Greycloud is beginning to wonder if he could have achieved the same result by simply wounding someone in the leg or firing benign shots into the air. Nevertheless, that was nothing less than a life or death situation. Life or death.

They are heading up the ridge at 200-yards when the Orphan Squad reaches the opening at the north end of the brush. Gideon hears them coming, instinctively moving back into the trees for cover.

Jim sweeps the terrain for the two men, continuing to run when he fails to locate them. They run at a suicide pace for another one-hundred yards or so before stopping to take a breather.

Tommy flops to the ground; he is dead tired. Most of the others will do likewise.

Eric gives the youngest kid a harsh stare. Between his laboring breaths, he yells, "This is… your…fault. If you had done what you were told, we would just…be…huntin' the injun!"

Derrick adds, "Yeah, you little…sissy!"

Jim says, "Shut up. Don't try to blame a kid for your screw-ups." He scans the terrain with his binoculars. "Where did they go?" He turns completely around, searching both sides of the ravine for naught. He faces north again, searching high up on the ridge. This time he sees them. He says, "Got ya. They made it to the horses alright."

One of the others whines, "We ain't never gonna catch them now."

Jim raises his rifle and says, "We won't have to, not with old Widow Maker here." He pats the rifle and raps the strap around his left arm before getting down on one knee behind Derrick.

"Hurry up. I need a brace, so get down here."

Derrick assumes the same posture. When the rifle is placed on his right shoulder, he bends his right arm to plug his ears with a thumb.

Jeremiah and Greycloud are pushing the horses hard, but they have to slow down when they come to a dangerous area of loose earth on a steep incline.

Jeremiah says, "That was close, too damn close. I knew you wouldn't shoot that boy first. He really didn't want to do it. I saw it in his eyes, heard it in his voice."

Derrick's lungs are screaming for air so he takes a few quick breaths while Jim adjusts the scope. He estimates the riders to be about three-hundred and fifty yards away, but that steep incline nearly places them out of range.

He puts the rifle back on his human cradle. Derrick's heart is pounding from the run and anticipation of the shot.

Greycloud's reply is, "I would have, if he was more willing to shoot you, but..." Blood spurts from his right upper chest and splatters the face of Jeremiah, who was looking down at his friend at the time. When Greycloud inadvertently jerks the reign to the right, the horse obeys and turns slightly. Now echoes the shot as sound catches up with the bullet.

Greycloud is shocked, staring straight ahead with his mouth agape. Everything grows silent, as if he is enveloped within a silent void. A second shot hits his horse in the soft tissue of its neck and exits, grazing Jeremiah's horse where its neck becomes its broad chest. Both horses and riders tumble backwards, sliding down the incline of loose shale. Greycloud falls awkwardly, breaking his left leg in two places. His horse flails while sliding further down the incline. It soon dies, thrashing in a pool of blood.

Jeremiah leaps clear of his animal, but he is able to hold on to the reins. Greycloud is screaming as the last echo flows up the ridge where they have come to rest.

Jim Morton is jumping up and down, shouting, "I got 'em. I got 'em both. Yeah!" He takes high fives and pats of the back.

Tommy Swinton is speechless, and his eyes have grown large in disbelief. From the moment of the first shot, he transports back in time. He is suddenly five-years-old, again, singing happily with his mother while flying through the air on the day of the crash. Suddenly, they are plummeting to the earth when the second shot is fired. Now comes the crashing of trees and an enormous explosion as the airplane barrels into the unmovable ground. He wants to scream.

Jeremiah moves quickly when he and his horse stop sliding. He ties the frightened animal securely to a well-rooted shrub and rushes to Greycloud. He readily takes the glove from his left hand and stuffs it into the grey one's mouth so he can bite down against the bright, crimson pain.

Neither of them wants the Orphan Squad to know that they are still alive. Thankfully, they slid down to the tree line where they are no longer visible. Jeremiah knows that the shooting would not have stopped if they were still visible to the young men in the valley.

He takes Greycloud's left index finger and shoves it through the hole in his shirt, directly into the chest wound. He knows that the bullet must have come through cleanly; otherwise, the nickel-sized hole would be a crater. He turns Greycloud slightly to get at his back. Taking his knife, he cuts away the buckskin jacket and shirt.

The bullet entered just below the right shoulder blade and slid neatly between the bones of the rib cage, then continued in an upward climb to exit from the front. Greycloud is lucky that the bullet did not mushroom to explode through his chest because it had not hit any of the bones squarely. As the pain blooms, Greycloud draws closer to passing out, but he continues to scream his muffled complaints into the glove. There is blood everywhere.

Through quivering lips, Jeremiah says, "Hold on, my friend, just hold on. I'm sorry for the things I'm about to do to you, but I have no choice."

He cuts a long, four-inch wide strip of cloth from his own shirt and cuts it again at about six inches in length. Now, he rolls it into a tight cylinder and stuffs it into the entrance wound, getting about three inches of cloth inside. Greycloud balks at the intrusion, holding on to consciousness by a silken strand.

The world threatens to abandon him when his friend lays him back against a rock. Jeremiah pulls Greycloud's finger out of the exit wound and proceeds to stuff it as he had the other.

Greycloud hears nothing at this point, but he sees a beautiful meadow of swaying grass. He blinks against the hallucination.

Jeremiah uses the knife to split Greycloud's pant leg, trying to put his companion through as little pain as possible. He splits the blue jeans up the middle to the hip and opens it to survey the extent of damage. It is bad, and he curses because Greycloud has sustained compound fractures of both the thigh and calf.

Through the blood, he sees the splintered white bones protruding the flesh, which jerks against itself. He looks at his friend, apologetically, as he grabs the ankle and the upper calf just below the knee. He whispers, "Please forgive me, Greycloud. Forgive me."

Greycloud peers through the haze of the other world to which he has been transported. When he finally sees Jeremiah's face, he nods his head. Jeremiah maneuvers the femur back into the spastic flesh, which he knows will be easier than the calf because the bone is much larger. He binds the wound and proceeds to the next.

Jeremiah raises the leg, twisting and pulling the lower half away until the bone disappears into the flesh from which it has come. Now he pushes the lower half until he feels the sections of bone scrape against one another. They finally fall back into place or as closely as he can get them.

While the bones grate, mercilessly, it is a sickening sensation for them both.

Greycloud shakes as if he has trapped an earthquake in his body. Both worlds quickly swim away. His head wilts backward while his eyes flutter and roll upward until only the whites are left of them. The glove falls from his grimace to his chest before rolling to the ground.

Jeremiah looks back, knowing that this is what he will see. He uses both sleeves and strips of his shirt to bind the flesh wounds, making sure to tie the knots on top. Now he rips the sleeves from his light jacket, thanking God that the bones are not fragmented, breaking into pieces he couldn't reset.

Now Jeremiah Williams takes the rifle, hatchet, and canteen from the saddle of Greycloud's dead horse before cutting splints for the leg. With the bloody pant leg closed around the flesh for extra support, he secures the splints inside, outside, and behind the leg with wider slivers cut from his bedroll. He takes off his belt and loops it, making a half-hitch knot when he put it around Greycloud's thigh right up to the crotch. He puts a stick in the belt and twists it to cutoff the circulation for a little while.

Jeremiah touches his friend's hot face and shakes him gently. He pours water on Greycloud's face and into his mouth. He does not expect to get a response, but the old man is tough and he comes around. Jeremiah is relieved when Greycloud finally opens his eyes.

"Hold on while I rig you a litter." He has already cut down two sturdy saplings for just that purpose.

Greycloud touches Jeremiah's hand and says, "No, Geronimo. No time for that. They will leave tract marks. And the others, they may be coming for…for trophies."

"But you can't ride like this. If they come, I'll just have to kill them all. God help me, but I will."

Greycloud insists, "Just get me up. I'll hold on. I have to."

When Jeremiah gets him up, it is another painful experience for both. Jeremiah hands Greycloud the pole.

After a quick inspection of its wound, Jeremiah unties his horse. "You'll live, but the climb might kill you. We need you, boy!" The horse whinnies as it is led to the grizzled looking Greycloud, who is standing on one leg atop the large rock.

Jeremiah says, "Here comes the hard part. You ready?" Jeremiah Williams positions the horse beside the grey one so that the good leg can swing across the saddle as he takes the weight off the broken limb.

Greycloud puts the glove back into his own mouth and bites down as he is hoisted onto the saddle. The pain springs into life with vivid, new colors, and he wavers badly in the saddle before Jeremiah could grab hold. Huffing and puffing, Jeremiah climbs up behind Greycloud and takes the rope tethered to the saddle. He wraps it around them both and the saddle horn, allowing a little play when he needs to shift their weight backward as a counterbalance.

The horse protests the extra weight, but gets used to the idea. The wounded man holds on to the saddle horn desperately. When he finally passes out, Jeremiah sits taller in the saddle and pulls Greycloud's wagging head back so it rests upon his left shoulder. He takes the reins and spurs the horse with the heels of his boots.

Jeremiah is thankful that Greycloud has passed into total oblivion. It allows him to push faster.

He says, "Come on, War Paint. We really need you now, brother. It's up to you to get us home alive, boy." He looks back for the orphans, but sees none. He wonders what will become of old Gideon, but that mule is an ornery cuss.

He wants to take a more direct route, but he remembers why he should not. It is a gamble with Greycloud's life, but if those bastards are allowed to track them too easily, they both may end up dead.

Therefore, he pushes for the top of the ridge and then he will push the eastern valley to the rock face for that dreaded skyward climb.

Far below, the Orphan Squad begins the long walk home. They started in the direction of the fallen riders, but Jim suddenly changed his mind. He has in his possession a new Winchester rifle and a classic Browning crossbow to show as trophies.

However, he also has three dead friends as proof of their misadventure. Truthfully, Jim senses that he had not killed the second man. That very fellow killed two of Jim's flunkies by himself, and at close range. He could prove to be most formidable with the advantage of higher ground. Therefore, Jim Morton decides not to corner the wounded animal, leaving well-enough alone. He is tired and leaving a potential witness alive is a product of his fear and irrationality. Because they are old and the fall was hard, it is possible that there are no survivors.

They collect the bodies of their fallen comrades on the way back. The mid-afternoon heat will make them fester and bloat. Jim, being the privileged leader, feels no special need to assist in carrying the dead. He does not lift a finger in that regard. It will be nightfall before they get back, and he sees no need to burden himself with stiffs. This way he could get back ahead of the flies and yellow jackets that will follow them all the way to Camp Righteous Kill.

Even Tommy Swinton has to carry his share of death when he is not shackled to an armful of guns. They are thankful when the heat of the sun gives way to dusk, but Tommy's reason is augmented by the fact that he will no longer be able to see dead eyes staring up at him from their bobbing heads. To his dismay, there are times when the glow of the rising moon reflects tiny shimmers of light that can only be described in his mind as the night vision of the dead.

In all of the murder and war movies he has seen in his lifetime, someone always closes the eyes of the deceased or covers their faces at the very least. Tommy could not grasp why their eyes won't just shut on their own. However, he most certainly understands the concept of moral bankruptcy when it concerns his peers. He senses that this is not the end, and there are much worse things to come.

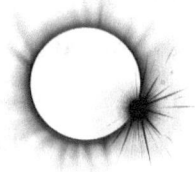

Chapter 23

INTO THE BUSH

Martin's crew stops in the small of town of Caribou Lake, which is about fifty miles northeast of Big Bear and about seventy-eight miles from Camp Righteous Kill. While there, Mills places a call to Jeremiah's cabin from the rudimentary switchboard operation yet to be completely phased out in this part of the country. When someone answers the phone babbling about an emergency, he hangs up. The call serves its purpose, assuring that someone is there.

The wife of one of the local Klansmen works the phone relays in this backward part of the world. She found Jerimiah's old phone number, which has never changed, and shuts down all lines of communication to the cabin and the surrounding area.

Because of the extremely inconvenient fire that took out the County Tax Office one week prior, it is impossible to get a fix on the cabin's exact location. The monthly electrical bill is automatically extracted from a bank account, and those records are not given to third parties without proper authorization. Other monthly expenditures, such as phone and satellite bills are sent to Keith Williams in Atlanta or auto drafted from checking accounts. They soon discover that the lawyer's grandfather has had a post office box for decades, so no one, not even the mail carriers know where Jeremiah Williams lives.

Joe Mills contacts Sheriff Milton Percy to enlighten him on the situation before asking for his cooperation. Milt is also a man of light, and most willing to do his bit for the cause. He is asked to send a patrol car to block the road leading to Big Bear, but he decides he can go one better by cutting down some trees with chainsaws. Never having cause to go to the mountain, he has no idea where to locate Jeremiah's homestead. He knows that somewhere along the route, the power lines have been placed underground because of the monstrous snowstorms in this part of the country. Therefore, they cannot follow them to the cabin. Even so, the sheriff thinks it best to disable the power lines at the foot of the mountain, which will, undoubtedly, affect others. However, this is not the depth of winter cold, so these mountain folk will make out just fine.

Governor Martin has the power to make inquiries concerning Jeremiah Williams, but doing so will expose him once the deed is done. The frustrating challenge only makes them more determined. They are confident that they will think of something.

With such frenetic anticipation, Willard St. John can hardly keep from bouncing off the walls.

Martin's gang leaves for the camp to await sunrise. With a little luck, they will have a better fix on the homestead. That is the plan.

An hour later, they pull up to the main gate of a camp where there is no one to greet them. It makes Mills angry enough to cuss his driver, who can offer no explanation. The Orphan Squad was supposed to leave a man at the post, and they should be back by now.

The camp is completely vacant when the big Chevy stops in front of the command post. Bo climbs out with his hand-held radio and tries to make contact with Jim Morton's band of flunkies. Unsure of their designated frequency, he is forced to switch channels until he receives a response.

Jim Morton's voice finally comes back to him on channel twenty-seven. "Bo, I'm here. You back?"

Bo answers, "Yeah. Where in hell are you? There's supposed to be someone here at all times."

"Well, we're about fifty-yards from the back gate. We ran into some trouble."

"What kind of trouble? Okay, who got shot?" Bo looks at the others, anxiously awaiting an answer.

"We sustained three casualties, sir. Perdie, Pete, and Boy. They're...they're all dead, Bo," Jim informs, not wanting to say anything more.

Bo Tuttle almost drops the radio. There is great concern on Joe Mills' face.

"Dead. Did you say they are dead? What the hell happened, you corner that grizzly?" The group of men starts running toward the back gate, but they stop to hop into an old army surplus jeep that will get them there much faster.

They are just starting out when Jim's voice comes back saying, "We're almost there, sir. Can you come and give us a hand?"

"We're coming."

They reach the gate just as the ragtag hunting party comes into the compound with three bodies.

Joe Mills says, "Shit on toast. This better be good. That bear must have torn them new assholes out there."

Once they are inside the gate, the orphans of Righteous Kill relieve themselves of their heavy burdens. They all sit on the ground, excluding Jim, who stands and salutes his superior officers, as a good soldier should.

Mills and Tuttle quickly inspect the bodies. Joe Mills swats Jim Morton with his hat and demands an explanation because these dead boys were not attacked by a grizzly.

The Orphan Squad looks like whipped dogs, and they have the scared, averted eyes to match. The ground suddenly become interesting. Even a beetle crawling along becomes fascinating at this time.

Jim flinches and declares, "It ain't our fault. We was huntin' that old grizzly when we spotted some spies. It was a nigger and an injun what killed them."

Martin suddenly looks up, as does Willard. They ignore the local hunters, who followed them from Caribou Lake, quickly approaching Joe Mills.

Joe Mills grabs Jim by the shoulders, pulling him close. He asks, "A Black man? Was he a young, tall, kind of a spry looking fella?"

Jim's shaky reply is, "No, sir. They were much older. I'd guess about late fifties to mid-sixties for sure." His voice assumes an air of redemption when he says, "They killed them boys for no good reason, but I got 'em both with my rifle."

Eric Glover adds, "Yeah, that's right. We saw them go down. Didn't we Derrick?"

Derrick Glover only nods because his throat is too dry to talk.

Governor Jud Martin steps forward, asking, "Are you sure? Did you inspect the bodies?"

Jim says, "Yes," but at the same time, Eric says just the opposite.

Martin looks at Mills, who backhands Jim Morton and shakes him hard. "Somebody is lying here and I think it's you. Now tell the truth because it holds consequences that your prepubescent mind cannot possibly begin to understand. Out with it, or I'll put you in front of a firing squad right here and now, soldier!" Mills is yelling and spraying spittle in the head orphan's red face. His breath is hot and his eyes serious.

The other orphans, like Tommy, are just too worn out to fully enjoy this rare moment in which the almighty one is being treated no better than he usually treats them.

Jim relents. "No, sir, we didn't. I didn't think we needed to. They're dead, I'm tellin' you. I put the Widow Maker on them at three-hundred and fifty yards. They both fell down the side of the steep ridge they was on."

Jud Martin and Joe Mills quickly glance at Eric, who confirms. Then Mills turns Jim loose and rubs his raspy chin. He turns around and says, "This is a class-A cluster fuck. They are normally good boys, but today they may have fucked up a shit sandwich. What if…what if that was the grandfather he came up here to visit?"

Bo Tuttle adds an unwelcome twist by saying, "What if he isn't dead and makes it back home to warn the lawyer and the bitch?" He knows little of Sabrina's relationship with Jud Martin, who glances at him out of simple, lingering paternal reflex.

Martin is thinking hard on the *what ifs*.

They move away from the boys to talk.

George Fellows speaks up. "If I may add, sir, this is a bad situation. If the old man reaches the targets, it may just make our job harder than it has to be." He faces Jim. "Is there another road to this ridge you spoke of?"

"No road, but the ridge is near the end of this valley," Derrick offers in the absence of Jim's tongue.

Mills says to Martin, "Well, that's it then. Billy and George will have to take some volunteers to check." Without looking back, he asks, "Do I have any volunteers, gentlemen?" When Mills receives no answer, he turns and locks his narrowing eyes on Jim Morton and crew.

Jim finally says, "I'll go back, sir. Can I get something to eat first?"

Bo Tuttle and Squeaky Smith also volunteer.

Mills is appeased. "Good. Now, show these two men to the primary weapons locker and get some chow. While they're doing that, two of you go and saddle five horses." He turns to Martin and St. John to say, "Come with me, gentlemen. Let's get you settled in."

Billy Fellows interrupts by saying, "May I suggest a contingency plan?"

"Sure. What's on your mind, Marine?"

Billy checks his watch and then he looks to his brother before continuing. "If we don't find the bodies of both men, I would strongly suggest that we go after any survivor. We have no problem tracking at night. If one or the other is wounded, we may be able to intercept. I would not suggest we wait until morning to execute our plans. If they survived, they will try to leave the mountain to seek medical attention. In which case, finding the phone dead and roads blocked, undoubtedly, puts them on high alert."

George Fellows says, "We'll track them back to the lodging, if necessary, and then we'll retrieve the woman. We'll keep in touch by radio if the terrain permits."

Mills and Martin agree to this course of action while St. John protests. He says, "But what about the lawyer? I want him. Martin, you promised him to me!"

George says, "If we run into the lawyer and he's been alerted, he will put up a fight. We may have to take him out, but don't worry, sir, we'll bring you his ears."

That is as good as it will get, short of Willard going along for a long, tedious trek so he agrees. Willard says, "Don't you dare hurt him more than necessary. I want him alive, if possible!"

They disperse. Jim and Squeaky go to the mess hall to wolf down some sandwiches. Meanwhile, the rest of the orphans store the bodies until morning, when they will be buried a few miles away in a one deep grave.

Bo Tuttle takes the Fellows brothers to the weapons locker where they collect a few goodies. Twenty-minutes later, they are heading out the back gate with sufficient firepower, field rations, and large flashlights with long lasting batteries.

The Fellows brothers are dressed in camouflage, wearing shoe polish on their faces to keep down the glare of the moon. They love the bush and all of its primitive elements. It is commando time.

Inside the H.Q. building, Mills is pouring drinks for three when a disturbing thought occurs to him. He looks at his esteemed guests and says, "My God…!"

"What is it?" Martin asks.

"Now that I've had some time to think about it, it's beginning to make sense."

"Spit it out, already," Willard snaps.

"When I called the old man's place, someone blurted out that there was some kind of emergency. He told me to call back, later."

"You don't suppose ..." Martin's voice trails off.

"What else could it mean? The old man or the Indian must have survived and made it home. If not both of them," Mills observes. "They were probably about to contact the Medivac unit when I called, if they hadn't already."

Willard says nothing, but his behavior indicates that he grasps the seriousness of the implication.

Martin begins to pace. "Let's pray that the lines were disconnected before they made that call."

"I better get on the horn to let Billy and George know about our suspicions. That kid has really mucked this up!"

Moment later, the Sheriff is contacted and asked to check on the status of Medivac activities in the area.

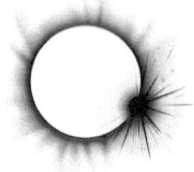

Chapter 24

BROKEN VESSEL

K eith and Jeremiah take Greycloud inside, laying him down in his bedroom at the north end of the cabin. Once he is as comfortable as possible, Keith tries to think clearly about first course action. He does not waste any more time on the details of the shooting, which they will discuss, eventually.

"I'll call for an emergency evacuation chopper at Window Lake. Get Greycloud some water. He looks parched."

Just as Keith reaches for the phone, it rings. He answers saying, "Whoever you are, we have an emergency up here. Please call back!"

The caller hangs up on the other end, so Keith hits the reset button and dials 911, wondering if such an animal even exists in these parts. After a painfully long pause, it rings once before going completely dead.

He franticly pushes the buttons to no avail.

"Hello, hello! Is anyone there?"

There is nothing, not even that annoying buzz.

His grandfather emerges from the room to ask, "Did you get them? Are they on the way?"

Keith places the receiver back on its cradle. "No. I don't know what happened. It just went dead." His voice is a mere whisper, with greater emphasis on dead.

"But I just heard it ring, and we rarely get calls. It can't be dead!" Jeremiah rushes across the room and checks for himself.

"I know. The person hung up without saying anything because I told them to, I guess. But when I dialed 911, it rang once and then…nothing."

Jeremiah slams the phone down. "Damn it all to hell, it's them. I know it's them. They cut the phone lines!" He is utterly perplexed, knowing that they are all in danger.

"Who are you talking about?" Jeremiah Williams just stares, wordlessly, at the telephone until Keith says, "Go down in the cellar and get the first aid kit. I'll get my girlfriend. Sabrina's a doctor."

With that, Jeremiah snaps out of it. "What? Your woman is a doctor? Well, go get her. Hurry up, son." They both turn and race to their respective tasks.

☙❧

Sabrina is humming as she removes the roast from the oven. She always hums a tune when she cooks, especially when she is nervous. Her mother used to hum the same soothing melody while stirring a simmering pot of stew. As Sabrina played where she could keep an eye on her, she would smile lovingly at her beautiful child.

Keith is late in getting back, and Sabrina has no idea where he is. She hopes that his absence means he has found his granddad and is soon to appear. She has worked furiously in preparing this meal, hoping her cooking is to the old man's liking in the event her skin tone is not.

The table is set for four people, complete with candles and an open bottle of wine breathing.

Sabrina will welcome any pluses, so she has stirred, kneaded, seasoned, and taste tested her feast. Meanwhile, she watches a newscast about an observatory's proposed activities during the lunar eclipse. There is a real geek on the screen, wearing a lab coat and ugly nerd glasses. He tells a rather dry joke about mythical correlations of lunar eclipses with sexual perversion and madness.

When Keith bursts through the door, Sabrina nearly drops a hot pan of biscuits, which slides across her forearm before landing upright on the stovetop. The hot pan sears her arm, but she shrieks more from surprise than pain.

"Sabrina, come quick. Greycloud needs your help. He's been shot and his leg is busted!"

Sabrina immediately drops the potholder and rushes around the kitchen counter. "Is he conscious? Where is the bullet wound located?" Keith takes her by the hand and starts for the door when she says, "Wait. I brought my bag just in case."

When Sabrina runs into the bedroom to get her medical bag from a suitcase in the closet, Keith checks his own phone. It is also afflicted with dead silence. Sabrina rejoins him and they run headlong into the flames.

They may both regret agreeing to this non-cellular vacation. They left ties to the outside world in the outside world so they could forget its painful miseries for a moment. With the madness of the moon in a place that is too close to the heavens, there is always something to try a person's soul. They are concerned, running into the vibrant moonlight.

Jeremiah is in the cellar, tossing a lifetime of accumulated junk to-and-fro as he hunts for the first-class first aid kit. He has never really found such dire use for it, until now.

"Where in tarnation is that infernal thing when you need it?" He slaps the palm of his left hand against his sweaty forehead, as if trying to will it to appear. When he hears Keith and his friend go rushing to Greycloud's room, the old man calls for help.

Sabrina is at Greycloud's bedside checking his pulse and then the dilation of his pupils, since he seems to be unconscious. His blood pressure is next.

Keith goes to his grandfather's aid.

When Keith's eyes adjust to the dim lighting, Jeremiah is clearly winded. Wearing that tattered, blood-splattered shirt, the old man is a sorry sight. Realizing that Jeremiah must be dead tired, he assumes the frantic search.

Keith is certain that the contents of the first aid kit will be useful before the end. After trashing the already trashed cellar to no avail, he quits.

"Can't you remember where you used it last? Try to calm down and think a moment."

Jeremiah's haggard face suddenly brightens. "Greycloud patched up Lightning when that infernal bear slashed her across the shoulder. It's still in the pantry by the barn door...to the right side as you walk in."

Keith pivots for the steps. "I'll get it. You catch your breath."

Jeremiah goes upstairs, trying to ignore his aching back. When he sees the white woman messing around with Greycloud, he tears across the room shouting at her. He snatches Sabrina Martin by the hair and yanks her backward. She crashes into the small card table, upon which Greycloud spends countless hours playing solitaire when the spirit of sleep abandons him.

She screams as she spills over the table to the floor. In a flash, Jeremiah is upon her. He seizes her by the throat, choking off her screams.

"How many of you followed us?"

The old man's mind interprets Sabrina's shaking of her head as proof of her loyalty to the others, and that she will never tell. She needs to die quickly so he can hunt down the others.

With madness in his eyes, Jeremiah draws the knife from its sheath, raising it overhead to strike!

When Sabrina looks into his stormy face, her attempt to scream becomes a gurgle. Jeremiah drives the seven-inch blade toward her defenseless chest!

His mind has flipped a switch to the off position, disregarding something that exists even in dogs. This instinct usually prevents a marauder from killing the females of the species.

Some animals are rabid in times such as these, and like them, Jeremiah Williams is consumed with the killing fever. At this moment, Sabrina is just pale enough to be neither man nor woman. He can only see in her the enemy.

Something crashes to the floor just before Keith charges the hand wielding the knife!

Its blade now glistens, coming to pause merely three inches from Sabrina's chest. Keith barely stops Jeremiah from plunging the knife into her heart, but the old man will not relent his force on the blade even after its interception.

Jeremiah has the look of madness about him. Never in his wildest imaginings has Keith figured on such a violent reaction as he wrenches the glistening weapon from his grandfather's hand.

When Keith drags Jeremiah off her, Sabrina hugs him as if her life depends on it. Though gasping for air, her watery eyes return to Greycloud.

Jeremiah stands back and says, "What the hell?"

Once Keith helps Sabrina to her feet, she returns to the bedside of her flagging patient.

Jeremiah rushes her again, shouting, "Keep your filthy hands off him, bitch!"

When Keith curtails his pursuit, Jeremiah backhands his grandson squarely on the jaw, sending him down quite easily.

From the floor, Keith shouts, "Don't, Jeremiah, she's a doctor. He will die without her. Is that what you want? Are you crazy?" When he gets up, his sparring partner takes another swing at him with wild eyes blazing. Keith avoids the blow and launches himself at the old man's midsection. When he catches hold of Jeremiah, they both go spinning through the bedroom door. They spill to the floor of the den where they knock over the table, upon which, a stuffed badger is baring its teeth and claws. It and the table go flying.

Sabrina is worried, taking nervous glances over her shoulder. Her immediate concern is for her new patient, who has been awakened by the disturbance. While wetting his lips with the water from the nightstand, she tries to talk him through the fog into the world of conscious focus. Greycloud is badly in need of fluids.

Sabrina, though focused on Greycloud's condition, knows that Keith is pulling his punches with his grandfather. She has seen him in the fray against two men, and this is not his best performance. She hopes he is not hurt too badly before taking control of the situation.

Jeremiah attacks his grandson, growling, "That's a white woman in there. They're the ones who did this!" Then he clips Keith across the jaw, trying to get back to the bedroom.

Keith partially blocks the punch, but not before losing a tooth and his balance. He manages to trip Jeremiah as he tries to pass, then leaps on top of the old man, who raised him from a cub; the man who does not seem so old at this moment.

While holding Jeremiah down with his weight, he wipes his left palm across his bleeding mouth. He shows it to the struggling old man, who he has finally pinned to the floor. "Is this what you want, my blood for theirs? Is it? Are you fucking crazy?"

Jeremiah stops struggling at the sight of blood he has drawn. He finally gives up. Pinned down on a stomach full of bitter emotions, he begins to weep like a spoiled child.

"Say it ain't so, Keith. Say you didn't go and fall for a White woman. Please tell me she ain't the woman you mentioned before. For God's sake, say it ain't so." His plea is pitiful…painful.

The very depth of the scars left on his grandfather's heart by his Southern ties vexes Keith Williams. The minimal exposure to Caucasians in this part of the country is evidently a good thing for Jeremiah. Only now does Keith truly realize how much of a sacrifice it must have been to move to the big city when they were kids.

Jeremiah had instilled in them the need to be polite and courteous to teachers and all elders, no matter what their race. Nevertheless, Keith had no idea that the old and new circumstances, separated only by time and nature, could bring out such irrational hostility in Jeremiah. He seems to be so unreasonable that Greycloud's health has taken a backseat, even though Sabrina is clearly his only hope. It is a scary thing—this much hatred—this much animosity.

Keith lets go and sits next to his grandfather while trying to seize some oxygen from the thin mountain air. He spits blood on the floor and retrieves his canine from the carpet with his own tears streaming. He says, "I'm sorry. I should have told you sooner."

Jeremiah feels as though his heart has shattered into a million pieces and he will die from it.

"We really don't have time for this right now, grandfather." For some strange reason, the word *grandfather* rolls off his tongue as if glued to sandpaper. It feels as if he has become unworthy by having betrayed Jeremiah in some dark, unseemly way. Once more, his is the kind of guilt that is born in the purest state of self-persecution, for it is to question the betraying of one's entire race.

Still, Keith says, "Greycloud is in really bad shape, but Sabrina may be able to save him. Accept it or not, she is his only hope right now. If he has any chance, it would be better with her than without. Please don't interfere with that. I'm sorry that this is hurting you, but I love her, Jeremiah, and she loves me. So if you don't agree with our relationship, then that's just the way it will have to be. You'll either get used to the idea, or you won't."

It is good that Keith is sticking to his guns because, before very long, Sabrina might have to do the very same with her own father. Nevertheless, such things are second place and bridges not yet in sight.

Jeremiah sits up, disgruntled still. "But why her, Keith? White folks killed your parents—my son—your father and mother. How could you ever forget that? How can you do this to me?"

Keith looks away. After several deep breaths and a few wordless beginnings, Keith confesses, "That's just it, Jeremiah. To me, she is not White, yellow, brown, or green. Sabrina Martin is the woman I fell in love with, a woman who just happens to be Caucasian. I can't be expected to apologize for that because she's been good for me, Jeremiah. You know I used to be a tramp in high school and in college. That continued when I moved to Atlanta, but we've been together for nearly three years now. I have never cheated on her. Not even once. Nor do I have any desire to. That is my gauge. That's how I know it's real."

His grandfather looks at him with an expression Keith cannot fathom. Keith is not sure if it is surprise or utter revulsion. Perhaps it is some mixture in between, but he decides not to address it.

"Believe me, I fought it. I debated and rationalized every possible angle of argument and still I fell. All of the old issues were there, yet something about her just ate away at them until the excuses were all used up. Even if I could turn back the clock, the path of life would still arrive at same destination. You see, it's all in there…everything that makes me happy. Everything that I need in a companion is all inside of that woman, and the color of her skin just happens to be a paler shade than my own. She really makes me happy. When I smile, it's on the inside, too. I love her with all of my heart, but that will never diminish my love for you or the memory of my parents. In fact, it is a testament of both, and of how far I've actually come from being a traumatized little kid who wouldn't talk for months. We love each other."

Having said these things, Keith is silent. He contemplates his dislodged tooth, knowing that he should try to replace it.

Sabrina's voice cracks the quiet fallen between them. "If you two are finished making fools of yourselves out there, I can really use a hand!"

Keith helps the old man from the floor and hugs him. Though he is reluctant, Jeremiah returns the gesture. He says, "I still don't have to like her." When they walk back into the room, the power suddenly goes out.

Sabrina shrieks, surprised by the touch of the unexpected hand coming out of the darkness.

"Shh. It's just me," Keith says.

Sabrina takes his hand. "What happened to the lights, Keith? We need lights!" She is very uncomfortable in the eerie gloom, where only the moonlight intrudes upon the darkness.

Calmly, her lover says, "Don't worry. I installed backup generators in both cabins, so we'll have lights soon." He turns away, bumping into his grandfather in the nightshade. He quickly reaches out to grab Jeremiah, knowing that he must be off balance. Keith catches the old man by what is left of a tattered shirt. The sound of ripping cloth fills the air just as the old man stumbles over the broken card table.

After recovering his balance, Jeremiah declares, "I'll do it. You're so damn clumsy you might kill yourself trying to find the door."

Heading for the kitchen, he feels his way to the rechargeable flashlight. Five minutes later, there is gentle hum and the lights come on.

"This man is badly injured. We have to stop the bleeding." Jeremiah walks in just as Sabrina is saying, "It's a wonder he's made it this far. Your grandfather did a very good job under the circumstances. I'm not at all sure I could have done the same. He...could have been a doctor."

If she was a Black female, Jeremiah might have thanked her for the compliment. Instead, he says, "Never mind all of that, young lady. Can you save him?" Jeremiah Williams is still being a little rude, but he seems calmer.

She turns to Keith. "I can call for a Medical Rescue chopper. With all the climbing accidents that are bound to happen in a region like this, there's got to be one in range of here."

Keith shakes his head. "The phone lines just went dead when I tried that earlier. We're going to have to drive him."

Sabrina looks back at Greycloud with Jeremiah at his side. She is worried.

"He won't survive that. The bumpy road down the mountain will kill him, never mind the extra fifty or sixty miles to the next town." She is feeling desperate, and tears are welling in her eyes. "The power is out, the phone lines are dead, and someone tried to murder him. Keith, what the hell is going on here?"

Keith holds her tight and whispers, "I need you to hold it together now."

Sobbing is the first sign of her coming apart. "Are we in some kind of trouble? That man is dying and there's not much I can do about it without proper medical equipment."

The floodgates open wide and she washes Keith's shirt in her tears.

Barely a whisper, Greycloud's raspy, labored words come to her. "Little sister, don't be so discouraged. It is not your fault. If I should die, I will join my ancestors and we will have big fun around the eternal fire." His voice sounds like that of a drowning man.

"Sabrina, you must try. Are you certain that there's nothing you can do? Please don't fall apart on me, girl. We need you—he needs you—so show these old-timers your stuff. Please try."

Greycloud looks at Jeremiah, who is giving him a drink of water to battle an insatiable thirst. The wounded man takes his lifelong friend's hand and scolds, "And to you, my brother, you are wrong to hate this person because she is White. Please allow me to speak,

Geronimo. You must look beyond her pale skin. Only then will you see the goodness in her that my aged eyes have already seen. If you do not trust your grandson to know whom he loves or who loves him, then you cannot trust yourself because you raised him to be the good, strong man that stands before us. If she was not filled with goodness, she could never weep for me...a man she does not even know."

"You need water, drink," replies Jeremiah, feeling a bit of shame.

Greycloud takes another sip of water before continuing. "You should not hate her for the things her forefathers have done. She is no more responsible for their actions than she is for the color of her own flesh. You dislike her because, in your eyes, she is not right for Little Bear. This is for little reason more than her differences. Have we not seen enough of this in our lifetimes?"

John Greycloud winces because the emphasis he is placing on these important words are causing his lungs to burn.

Jeremiah wishes him to be quiet.

"We are not of the same color, but that does not change the fact that we are family, my friend. If I should die, you will not be losing a Native American, you will be losing a brother. You are living in the past where the pain is strong, but your grandson chooses to live for the present and for the future where his joy is strongest." When he coughs, his eyes squint from the anguish. "I must rest now and prepare for my journey. Great Shashana has long since reserved a place for me at his side where I will see many old friends again."

When Greycloud fades away, Jeremiah Williams searches Sabrina's face with pleading eyes that are no longer dry to the touch from burning rage. As Jeremiah sheds those bitter, morbid tears, he need not speak.

Sabrina rushes to the bedside and feels for a pulse. It is weak, but he is alive. She turns to Keith, barking instructions. He promptly goes to the kitchen and turns on the burners of the stove, which uses bottled propane. He takes the poker and the spade from the fireplace, which he washes after breaking the shovel end of the spade from its shaft. He places the tips of them in the flames. Keith also boils water and collects clean towels from the linen closet for whatever purposes they may serve.

While tying up her hair, Sabrina asks Jeremiah to start a fire because there is now a chill in the air. Greycloud is dangerously close to going into shock.

When she is alone with John Greycloud, she whispers, "Thank you, old man. Now let's see if we can't save Keith's other grandfather. You lost a hell of a lot of blood, but I know you're tough. I won't give up on you because you didn't give up on me, a woman you don't even know."

Greycloud clenches her hand and grunts to her.

"He will come around, you will see," Greycloud whispers. He also displays a smile that lasts only for a second or two before fading. She is worried, but hopeful. It is time to show Jeremiah Williams what she is made of. She secretly scolds herself for showing yellow when so badly needed.

Sabrina takes a pulse and blood pressure reading. At least Greycloud seems to be stable, something that is bound to change by the time she finishes with him.

Sabrina takes a bottle of Demerol and a syringe from her bag and injects it into Greycloud's hip. He is reacting to pain and by injecting the painkiller into the fleshy muscles of the hip, she could insure a slower dispersal of medication into the bloodstream. She doesn't want the narcotic to drastically affect his respiration. Nor does she does want him to wake when it is time to do the hard part.

She listens to Greycloud's chest to determine the extent of damage. Her findings are encouraging. Sabina cleans the shoulder wound after removing the piece of cloth Jeremiah used as a makeshift plug. She spreads the wound to test for bleeders, but finds no gushing fountain. It appears that the bullet only grazed the lung, which is a miracle in itself. His breathing is not too bad, and she suspects that the lung would have long since filled with blood if the bullet had done any real damage.

She quickly washes and disinfects the exit wound. When Keith comes at her request, she takes the cool end of the red-hot poker and spreads the wound before sliding the tip into the hole in the man's chest. She feels the poker vibrating as it sears the flesh deep inside.

Dr. Sabrina Martin squints against the steam, the stench of burning flesh and boiling blood, which immediately fills the room. She is careful not to singe the outer flesh, which she would stitch closed after she does the entrance wound. Jeremiah and Keith help to roll Greycloud over, so she can do the same with the entrance wound. When she is done with the tentative stitching, it's time to turn her attention to the leg.

If by some small miracle she is able to save this man, in all likelihood, he is going to lose the leg without proper medical care. It looks like there could be arterial damage or ruptured ligaments. Her worst fears are blood loss and infection. She takes a bottle of Lidocaine, a local anesthetic, and injects huge doses of the stuff directly into the wounds themselves.

Sabrina assess the disposition of the broken calf, amazed at how well Jeremiah set it without tearing up any major arteries. He even used a belt as a makeshift tourniquet. She finds hope in that she only needs to slightly adjustm the bones, but there is no sure way of knowing without an x-ray. There is so much swelling.

Keith brings more towels and hot water, so she can clean Greycloud's leg of the dried and clotted blood in order to get a better idea of the tissue damage. She needs to know where the worst of the bleeding is coming from.

After a thorough inspection, Sabrina tells Keith that she has to cauterize specific wounds to stop the blood loss, hoping against all hope that it doesn't push Greycloud over the rim into shock or cardiac arrest.

When Keith returns with her red-hot tools, Jeremiah is standing in the corner of the room in silent, unfathomable awe. The old man has been running on automatic pilot from the moment Greycloud's blood spurted into his face. He is slowly winding down, but his adrenalin level is still extremely high.

Dr. Sabrina Martin proceeds to burn the leg wounds, concentrating on the areas where the blood collects in small pools. She thanks God that the bone has been driven forward instead of through the calf muscles. The smell is sickening, and they all dry heave a time or two during the operation.

With the dressings in place, Sabrina removes her bloody gloves to check Greycloud's pupils, pulse, and pressure. She stands there and says, "Now, we have a lot of praying to do."

Keith holds her tight. As he kisses her on the forehead, Jeremiah bites down on his lower lip in silence. He sits at his friend's bedside at midnight.

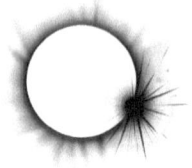

Chapter 25

INTERSECTION
OF DREAMS

A cool breeze fouls with the scent of ravaged flesh, as they stand under the full moon gazing down at the dead horse. This is a morbid sight; good horseflesh gone bad. The animal lays motionless with its bloody mouth agape, and its gnawed, purple tongue glued to the side of its face. The moonlight plays trickster with its opaque eyes.

Lightning's belly is laid open. Her liver and pancreas are gone. The rest of her innards splay out along the slope. The hindquarters have been partially eaten away by nocturnal scavengers. A pack of timber wolves heard her call in the westerly wind, taking without hesitation the invitation to feast. They did not leave willingly, however, but the sound of gunfire prompted them to seek refuge within the trees. The thriving pack will soon return, but only after the men have eaten their share. The following day will surely offer the vultures an invitation to dine at Club Lightning.

Bo Tuttle glares at Jim Morton, who avoids making eye contact. Using an annoying whine to deride Jim, Bo mocks, "I thought you put the Widow Maker on 'em at three-hundred and fifty yards." He throws his hands up in disgust. "It just looks like a fucking dead horse to me. Do you realize that you've compromised us all?"

George Fellows sneers, "Amateurs. You assholes couldn't stack a shit sandwich if you were squatin' over the fucking bread."

"But they went down hard. Those two old geezers should be right here," is all Jim Morton can muster as a defense.

"King of the damned orphans...good for nothing on the shit market," Bo Tuttle says with spite.

Meanwhile, Billy Fellows kneels to shine his light on a piece of cloth and a split sapling just a few yards away from the carcass. He touches a spot of dried blood, which he sniffs with an educated nose. He touches one of the saplings Jeremiah had cut down and spits.

Billy says, "That's enough. We are just wasting time. By the amount of blood, at least one of them is badly wounded. The other field dressed the wounds right here. He wanted to make a litter to transport the wounded man, but he must have reconsidered the danger because there are no drag marks. If you had just kept coming, you could have caught them. Let's move out."

George tries to make radio contact with the camp, but they are too deep in the mountainous terrain. He tries his cell phone, but the battery charge is weak. His spare is in his bag back at the camp. He is not pleased.

They mount their horses and follow the tracks over the ridge into the east valley. The trail is soon lost at the foot of the stone face, so they spread out in futility.

Hours later, the five men rendezvous at the original point where the scent grew cold, knowing only that the lone horse has gone upward.

In frustration, George Fellows looks skyward as a small airplane passes over the mountain.

He nudges Billy and asks, "Do you see it?"

A wry smile curls Billy's lips. "Well, I'll be damned. We got 'em now."

They watch as the flare falls slowly back to earth, with its light dwindling. Soon, thereafter, another lights up the sky.

"Mark that spot. Mount up, guys," George orders. "Looks like we've got a long ride ahead of us."

"They were trying to get the pilot's attention, but he didn't circle," Billy observes. "He may not have noticed the flares."

George adds, "Some dumb hick in a crop-duster probably thinks it's just a fireworks display." He and his brother laugh, which is a rarity for them these days.

ᘯᘓ

Keith collects the bottle of wine and the food, which is cold, and takes it back to Jeremiah's cabin in a heavy picnic basket. No matter how bad things are, they still have to eat.

He is near the barnyard when he hears an approaching airplane and bolts for the cabin to plunder the first aid kit for the emergency flares. When he runs back outside, the plane has already passed overhead in a southerly direction, but he fires anyway. He quickly reloads and fires again because he's not willing to wait until another comes along. They're all discouraged when the plane fails to circle.

Sabrina and Jeremiah are watching from the doorway when she asks, "Do you think they saw it?"

Keith's dour expression is all she needs.

Sabrina goes inside to warm the food as best she can without drying it out. While it warms, she checks on Greycloud, who seems to be gaining ground. As she watches the shallow rise and fall of his chest, she thinks the clouds are truly gray in his face. Even with such a great loss of blood, his chances are no longer slim or none. There is still hope for him.

Although God did not answer her prayers when her mother failed to return, Sabrina wants so much for him to answer her on Big Bear Mountain. Sabrina gazes into her inner thoughts for an instant, recalling the moment she touched the totem pole. Something must have happened during that brief contact. It seems as if she has, somehow, upset the balance and harmony of this place simply by her presence. She shivers.

After Sabrina Martin does what she can for Greycloud, she convinces Keith to sit still long enough to deaden the nerve in his gum. She cleans the vacant spot with her personal water pick to reseat his tooth, and applies a few drops of super glue to hold it in place. She holds his bottom lip away until the glue sets between his teeth.

They finally sit together to eat Sabrina's meal, which is surprisingly good after being uncovered for hours. Jeremiah feeds as if he has not eaten in a week, shoveling down wads of meat and biscuits with absolutely no thought of his detestable table manners. He has always disliked the taste of dry wine, but this merlot is quite good. Meanwhile, Keith is forced to chew with great care.

As far as Jeremiah goes, the lovers understand. Although Sabrina is especially pleased, she can only wonder if Jeremiah's enthusiastic consumption of her food is a testament of its taste or of his starvation. Eventually, she decides that it really doesn't matter.

Keith asks Sabrina if she thinks Greycloud will be okay. It is a definite maybe.

With a gaping yawn, he says, "I think I'll start down the mountain in a few minutes. I'll try to get to town and call Window Lake. I may be able to find a doctor to give us a hand. Can you make a list of any items you might need in case the chopper is unavailable?" He yawns, again, and rubs his red eyes.

Sabrina touches his arm out of concern. "You're worn out, Keith. We all are, for that matter. What good would it do to leave us here just to end up falling asleep and flying off this mountain? Please wait until you've had some rest. I don't know what's keeping Mr. Greycloud as strong as he is, but I believe he'll be okay until morning."

"I suppose those are doctor's orders. I am tired, but I doubt I'm as bad as you, old man," he says.

His grandfather grunts. "Never mind me, I'll be okay. She is right, son. It's best that you wait out the rest of the dark with us. In the morning, I'll go to Totem Rock and keep lookout over the valley. I just don't trust those Klansmen because the ones we encountered were a might young to be in total control of who does what round here. Whoever they answer to probably decided it best to check for our bodies. Most likely, they are hell-bent on locating us because they can't afford to trust us to keep quiet about what they done. I don't rightly figure them to be smart enough to track us, but you never know. Somebody trained the evil bastard that took those long-range shots at us. Either way, we never should have exposed ourselves, broadside like that. We underestimated them." He seems very depressed.

Sabrina asks, "Can you tell us what makes you think they were members of the Ku Klux Klan, Mr. Williams?" This is the second time Sabrina addresses Jeremiah directly, but by some distinction, it is the first time she actually engages him personally.

Jeremiah looks at Sabrina Martin, thinking that it's good that she has respect for her elders. He is stuffing his pipe when he answers her question.

"Well, when I was on my knees in the mud with my hands in the air, I saw some kind of patch on their clothes. Then one of them said that the little one had to kill me to be a full member of the Klan. That poor kid couldn't have been more than fifteen or sixteen-years-old. I saw his tears as the older ones forced his hand."

Sabrina is truly repulsed. "My God that must have been awful for you. I think it is sick and repugnant to twist young, impressionable minds with prejudice and hatred. It's just not right."

Jeremiah considers her words because the window of admiration, which has already opened, now threatens to bloom despite him. He experiences a powerful twinge of shame when he meets Keith's gaze. He knows exactly what that stare means, so it is time to relent. Jeremiah raised his grandsons to respect all life, and Keith has clearly learned the lesson beyond his teachings.

Jeremiah Williams inhales and expels a deep breath before saying, "That's how they have to start 'em out—young—so they can continue hating for the rest of their lives. Back when I was a boy in Mississippi, my father and all the older folks used to tell us horror stories about the Klan." He grunts with distaste. "But their stories never compared to the real life experiences that we had to endure. Some were lucky and others were not. You see, my father was a wise man. He saw that there was a change coming in how they did things, so he sent me away because he figured to be safe." Jeremiah looks at his hands and shakes his head as he skims the surface of bitter memories he had long buried beneath a mound of graveyard dirt and shattered dreams.

"I can't imagine what it must have been like to live with such tyranny that your own father thought it best you leave home." Sabrina makes a tentative attempt to reach out. She is still very wary of Jeremiah's mood because the subject matter is obviously upsetting to him.

He nods. "You see, the younger folks, especially the young men, were less likely to shy away from transgressions as we were always told to do. My pappy was right because we were seen, somehow, as threats to those perverted people. We were subject to even greater persecution…the deadly kind of persecution. Therefore, he sent me away. Lord knows I hated him for making me look and feel like a coward. I left our cousin's farm in Idaho after a year because they were having hard times. Because they were Black, the market, which was owned by the deed holder of his property, would never pay them fair market prices for his superior produce. I was just an extra burden no matter how hard I worked from sunup to sundown. I took off with less than twenty dollars to my name, and I ended up here half-starved to death. This is where I've been ever since, but I'll be damned if they're going to move me again!"

"I can certainly understand your anger, Mr. Williams," Sabrina says. She is being sincere, hoping that she doesn't seem patronizing. That just isn't her style.

Suddenly, for an instant, Jeremiah's eyes burn with contempt. How dare she claim to truly understand?

"I left Mississippi before they killed me or turned me into a killer, but the ghosts of the past never seem to go easily. It really broke my heart when those evil bastards murdered Keith's father and mother.

When Keifer took his wife home, we all thought they would be safe. Maybe things had changed some. But I reckon Keith hasn't told you that part of it."

"Don't get yourself all worked up, Jeremiah," Keith intervenes. "That won't do any good right now. Sabrina may understand more than you give her credit for."

Jeremiah Williams waves the hand of dismissal, plowing onward to bitter truths. "No offense to you, but White people came to this fertile land and stole it from the Native American Indians through all manners of horrible, insidious initiatives. They reaped great wealth and prominence through direct and indirect commerce with African slavers. All the while, even to this very day, using rival African slave owners selling captives to rationalize what they did to absolve themselves of using human beings like soulless pack animals to build this stolen nation for them. After the Civil War, which was greatly about continuing and expanding slavery into the new territories, Black and free still wasn't really Black and free. The South lost, sure, but free wasn't free. After building it up, they didn't think we belonged here, so they started killing us off. It's strange how we were considered to be no better than animals, but our women weren't so much the animal that they couldn't be raped and defiled." Jeremiah Williams sighs, deeply. "However, the vice versa brings the chokepoint. The Klan, I believe, exists for three reasons. To keep Black men away from their money, property, and their women. None of which is mutually exclusive, mind you."

"That's enough, Jeremiah. Grandfather, please…that is enough." Keith's annoyance is clear, but he is dismissed yet, again.

Jeremiah lights his pipe, taking another deep breath before saying, "You see, young lady, I learned to hate hard because it kept me going.

I suppose, after such a long while, that is all I know how to feel when it comes to White folks. It's funny, hate is. Double-edged, too." He looks down at his pipe, whose flavor goes bittersweet during his pause. Jeremiah says, "So…I guess I've become just as bad as them. I suppose you can say that I've become that which I loathe most. I am so sorry that I repaid your kindness with such bad behavior. I can't say that I'm all together pleased about you two. But, if Keith is as happy as he says he is…well…I suppose I'll just have to get used to the idea, now won't I?" He looks to his grandson. "Keith, I'm sorry that I hit you. Can either of you find it in your hearts to forgive an old man's foolishness?"

Jeremiah sees tears when he finds the will to look at Sabrina Martin. Keith comes over and places his hand on the old man's shoulder and she joins them. They both give Jeremiah a brief hug and total absolution.

Jeremiah adds, "Besides, she's pretty enough, and not a bad cook all together. Maybe a little thin for my taste, but you're not so big yourself. I guess she'll do in a pinch."

They share a tension-releasing chuckle. Keith and Sabrina are grateful that the thunder in the air has eased in intensity. This is a time for healing, not only for Greycloud, but also for them all.

Sabrina checks on her patient once more. After waking him with smelling salt, Sabrina sees to it that he drinks as much water as possible. She is pleased that he takes the antibiotics and iron pills to assist in thickening his blood just enough to catalyze its coagulation without drastically changing his blood pressure. Iron in his blood will also assist in the red blood cell's ability to transport oxygen to his tissues. She also wanted to jumpstart the marrow of those old bones to produce blood by stimulating the Hematopoietic stem cells. Her greatest triumph is getting Greycloud to suck down some soup.

After Greycloud takes sustenance, Sabrina dabs blood from his wounds and disinfects them with alcohol and peroxide, again. She uses iodine on the wounds to draw the excess drainage. He would not feel it so much as the burning sting of the alcohol.

Once done, Sabrina finally joins Keith on the couch in the den. Awash the moonlight, Jeremiah clenches the barrel of a rifle while sitting by the open kitchen door. He's obviously worried about unwanted visitors, and Keith is flanked by a weapon himself. The last item mentioned on the newscast is tomorrow night's eclipse. They all finally go to sleep.

Keith is naked but for a loincloth. High upon a hilltop, a wolf casts an upturned gaze to the moon. Its howl resonates as an eerie lament throughout the night air; a sound that would haunt any dreaming mind.

The full moon is so close, he can almost reach out and touch it with his fingertips. Its radiance causes his skin to tingle with sensation. From the distance comes the beat of drums pounding him a summons. As the drumbeats grow faster, the intensity swelling in his ears, he runs barefooted to the call.

Keith hears the quiet padding of feet. When he looks down to his left, he sees the yellow-rimmed eyes of a black panther keeping in stride. To his right, a bear cub plods in the darkness of the forest.

He stops at the edge of a clearing and moves the limb of a small spruce blocking his view. A mass of people are dancing and chanting around a fire. In the background, Native American tepees and African kraals are dark monoliths of awe. The people are red and black, Indians and Africans, dancing around a great bonfire that glows with a strange aura about it.

They dance to an Indian drumbeat, which would go faster until coming to a sudden stop. Now, they begin to dance to an African beat, going faster until it is again time to shift. As he approaches the eternal fire, the changes in the music and dance increase in frequency and vibrancy. It is harmonious and strangely intoxicating.

There are nearly naked women, black and red, shaking hollow gourds with dried seeds rattling inside them. The women part when Keith finally walks into the circle of chiefs, who are sitting with the full moon illuminating their backs at the cliff's edge.

As he stands before these men of power, the music and dancing cease without warning. When he looks down, his woman is sitting at his feet. Her skin is tan. She wears a feminine headdress and a string of beads about her neck. Her hair is braided into a long ponytail. With her eyes smiling up at him, Sabrina offers Keith a drink from an open gourd that has been fashioned into a ceremonial cup.

Keith takes it and drinks deeply before offering it to the chief sitting the highest amongst the others because it feels like the thing to do. That man takes the cup and drinks from its content before throwing it into the flames, causing the fire to blaze into the night sky. There comes a great whooping and screeching lament from the women, and then the drums resume their tumult.

Keith feels strange as the dancing starts up, again. When he turns around, a huge grizzly bear stands fearlessly before him on its hind legs. It towers above Keith Williams, pawing at the air. Suddenly, it bellows a roaring growl that shakes both earth and sky.

Keith stares at the full moon, which is in the first stages of eclipse, and then he spreads his arms wide as if to fly.

ഗ∞

Sabrina is eight-years-old. She is playing tea party in her bedroom with her dolls, Mr. Boo Bear, and some of her imaginary friends. They are sipping from the tiny, white, plastic teacups Sabrina refills constantly for her very thirsty guests.

They're talking about the weather and how badly Mr. Boo Bear wants to be president of the world. A momentary hush falls across the room as the guest of honor makes her way into their presence. She is graced with an inspired round of applause by an adoring public.

It is mommy, the Queen of America. She is tall and quite beautiful in her white dress and pearls. Her movement is so graceful; she seems to float as she approaches the little table. The queen leans over and kisses Sabrina on the cheek. She shakes Mr. Boo Bear's hand and greets the other guests before squeezing into the tiny seat to sip her tea.

She comments on Ms. Sabrina's decor. She says she especially likes the totem pole that stands in the corner overlooking the table, and wonders where she might get one. Unfortunately, this is the only one of its kind in the world.

They are having a grand time until it suddenly grows dark. The ground begins to shake when an evil ogre comes into their house and disrupts the happy party. His face is scruffy and his breath smells foul. He shouts at the Queen of America and pulls her into the hall where he slaps her face and makes her cry bitter tears.

There is a sudden flash of light and Sabrina is fifteen-years-old. She and a young Black friend named Keith Williams are talking about home-work, while running sticks along a white picket fence in the backyard. Again, the evil ogre appears without warning. This time, he bares his terrible fangs and roars to frighten her friend away.

The monster digs his tarnished fingernails into Sabrina's arm and drags her into the dark storage shed. Mercilessly, the beast slaps her several times before trying to touch her where her mother and Aunt Jane told her she should never be touched by any boys at that age.

Sabrina runs away, crying from the utter shame of the experience, but she somehow knows that the evil ogre will never come near her again. She stops running when she finally accepts that she can never leave the yard, no matter how far she goes. Out of breath and panting, she stares up at the moon, half of which has grown dark. It is all there, but she just can't see parts of it.

Suddenly, the man in the moon speaks. His rattling voice causes her tummy to ache, so she slumps to the ground and curls up to cry herself to sleep next to a tall post with faces and glowing symbols carved into it.

♲

Jeremiah Williams wheezes and flinches in his sleep as he enters REM state. He whimpers something incoherent.

In a meadow, high up on an unfamiliar plateau, tall grass sways with a lazy summer breeze as if all of nature is in a slow dance. The warmth of the sun caresses his skin like the brush of a feather. Jeremiah is standing just inside the shade of the forest at the edge of a surging sea of green when Greycloud speaks in his slow, soothing voice.

"Hey, Geronimo, are you still asleep?" Greycloud chuckles. "You never did get used to Native American hours."

A question is asked.

"This place?" Greycloud replies, "We are but a whisper on the other side of Totem Rock. Beautiful, isn't it? Here, the sun is gentle on my old hide. Listen, my friend, the birds are now singing to us. It would seem that in all the years I have walked the earth, I do not recall ever really noticing how lovely they sound. They are telling us stories about our past and future. I am not yet certain that it's all real or just a beautiful dream, but if this is a part of heaven, then it is a very nice place to be."

A fearless sparrow perches on Jeremiah's left shoulder, tugging at a loose thread on his shirt.

"*I am accompanied by someone you should meet sooner than later. I know you cannot see him yet, but he is here. If you allow the anger in your heart to quiet and listen very closely, you will hear his laughter. He is always laughing. Can you hear?*"

Jeremiah smiles in his sleep.

"*He is very happy and maybe just a little sad, as I am. He is your great grandson, Geronimo. Forgive me for giving him a name, but you may change it if you wish. I call him Laughing Spring Chicken. He runs like a chicken and cackles like one, too. And his hair flaps like a chicken's wings when he is riding horsy on old Dingahay's broad back at a full gallop.*"

Jeremiah squints.

"*No, old man, your ears do not deceive you. The shaman is here with us, as he has always been. He walks the plane in between, for he is to be our guide through the land of tomorrow where the sun and the moon share the sky in perfect harmony. Here, we are not enemies. Nor have we ever really been it would seem.*"

Jeremiah smiles again.

"*He told me that he is looking forward to playing tag with you again. He also wants you to know that it was never his intention to do us harm, and that he only wants to have some fun with us in his old age. We are just two old men he can still outrun. We are all waiting for you. Dingahay says we will make our greatest journey together when the Crow warriors return to the mountain. Until then, be strong, my brother. And remember…*"

Distant drums began to beat, and within them, Greycloud chants, "*Ny-y-y na-na hayyy-ya na-na hayyy-naa-yaaa hayyy…*"

Day becomes night as the full moon replaces the sun. Greycloud's chanting fades and finally goes silent, but the breeze continues to whisper through the tall grass. It carries, like a precious gift, the fading laughter of a happy child at play.

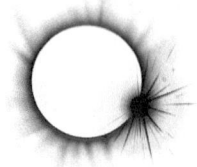

Chapter 26

LIGHTNING STRIKES

The assault team rides throughout the night, constantly climbing. The lower case rednecks are catching pure hell keeping up with the city boys. There have been far too many near mishaps. Yet, they continue to strive onward and upward through the dense moonlight, faltering through bramble thickets and rock-sliding sand on skittish animals.

The smell of bear is strong, keeping the horses on constant alert. Their eyes are wide as they waltz through splashes of lunar light seeping through the spruce saplings. There is a look of lunacy about both horses and riders. They are dead out and pushing for the top, etched against darkness, shimmering politely.

There is not enough caution, though. The horses know this, for every limb could be the swiping paw of a hungry grizzly. The animals' breaths are catching in their lungs until each brush passes without the razor's edge trailing to lay them open to the bone.

Each slide could render broken bones while scurrying up narrow ravines where loose trenches of runoff often give way to gravity.

While startled birds complain unseen in the night, the curled fist of Billy Fellows hauls Jim Morton in by the collar for closer inspection. His eyes are afire in a splash of lunar glory. His breath is hot and angry when he threatens, "You listen to me, boy. If you give our position away just one more fucking time, I'll silence your sniveling forever. Hear me loud and clear, little tough guy. I will, without even blinking, open you up like the Grand Canyon and leave you for the vultures, so you better get focused on what we're doing out here."

Jim Morton looks up into his face, sweating and trembling. He believes Billy means every word.

Billy points up the mountain and zooms in even closer to say, "You see—that's where we're going—moving onward throughout the night because they're up there. They are highly valued targets, who need to die, people for the up-close kill. It could be you, who will get the thrill of it, or you can die right here on this mountainside. Makes no matter to me because, one way or another, I will still get a thrill. You'd better focus on that. They are up there, and they are waiting for us." He shoves Jimmy to the ground and says, "So get your sorry ass down this slope and catch your horse. And stay the fuck out of my way!"

They stop briefly for a drink and some field rations. This is as good a time as any, since Jim Morton had made a foolish maneuver to beat Billy to the last narrow stretch in a trench, causing an ungracious spill.

The plan is simple enough. Once they reach the approximate area where they sighted the flares, they will fan out until someone locates the lodging. That person is to do nothing more than make radio contact with the others, so they can all converge on it together.

The Fellows brothers are very impressed with the way the old mountain men handled their desperate escape, admitting to themselves that the false trail would have had them guessing in the wrong direction all night long, were it not for the fires in the sky over the big mountain. They will be there soon. Their estimated time of arrival is sunrise.

ⱭⱰ

At five o'clock in the morning, Keith and Jeremiah wake to the smell of sizzling bacon, ham, toast, scrambling eggs, and brewing coffee. Sabrina Martin never expected to find such things in the house, but contrary to what Keith described, things are well stocked. She just doesn't realize that most of this stuff is not store-bought.

She has been up for more than an hour. After getting another dose of germ killers and a full glass of water into Greycloud, she decided that she does not want Keith going down the mountain on an empty stomach. This is also another opportunity to see if Jeremiah Williams really likes her cooking. Any new inroad is a plus after their horrid introduction. Ultimately, these are small distractions to keep a worried mind busy.

Jeremiah enjoys the food, showing true appreciation after years of eating his own cooking or that of his friend. To her delight, both men ate as if last night's meal is a mere dream.

She is a doctor, a professional woman, but her Aunt Jane instilled cooking for one's mate and oneself into her roots. Sabrina feels no guilt for getting at Jeremiah through his stomach. She believes it is

317

important to gain his complete confidence before the baby comes. The importance of this child is growing with each passing second.

Sabrina is two months pregnant, having given no hint to the child's father because she does not wish to pressure him. She is doing something that most men truly despise, and rightfully so for many reasons. Although she is taking a chance on raising that male righteous indignation, termination of the pregnancy is not an option she is willing to consider. Being witness to so much death at work, a son or daughter could be very good for her. Even though it is not a planned pregnancy, it is a pregnancy nevertheless. All life is sacred to her.

Doctor Sabrina Martin has spent her time in the kitchen obsessing over her decision to delay telling Keith until this nightmare is over, or at least until they are sliding into home base. Her fear of a negative reaction is quite normal, but she is almost sure that Keith will take the news well.

This had not been some well-laid trap, but just a matter of nature taking its course. Sabrina's birth control prescription, which she has taken religiously, simply failed her. Unfortunately, for some people, it happens. She was pulling her hair out by the roots just one month ago, but she is ready for it now, come what may.

When Keith enters Greycloud's bedroom, he's stunned. He looks over his shoulder and says, "You've been very busy. Did you get any sleep?"

Jeremiah joins him in the doorway and marvels. During the night, Sabrina found a sterile, hollow rubber tourniquet in the first aid kit. She sterilized some old bottles she found under the sink. After forcing one end of the tubing over the end of a small syringe, she drove a pen through the cork before removing the ink cylinder.

She cut off both ends of the ballpoint's plastic shaft and forced the other end of the tourniquet onto it. Then she mixed a solution of distilled water and salt, which was allowed to cool before she could use it as an IV for Greycloud. The bottle itself hangs from the sturdy hat rack taken from a corner in the den. There is a clothespin midway the tubing to regulate the flow. The primitive contraption seems to be working perfectly.

Before either man walks outdoors, Jeremiah loads Greycloud's crossbow with a razor-sharp shredder and lays it beneath a beach towel at his side. The safety catch is on, so Sabrina agrees with it. For her, Keith loads a Taurus 380 pistol, placing it on the kitchen countertop only after familiarizing her with it.

Moments later, Keith carries a thermos of hot coffee into the crisp, early morning air. It is still dark, but he can see the faint aura of the reddish and dark purple that heralds each spectacular sunrise on Big Bear.

When he kisses Sabrina good-bye, Jeremiah is at the corral where he saddles Zeus. The old man pats War Paint, his favorite horse. As he does so, he whispers, "That's a good boy. You deserve a break after that hard climb last night. It's time for you to rest and heal, so don't get jealous on me."

When the horse whinnies softly, Jeremiah smiles and turns to the end of Keith and Sabina's embrace. Surprisingly, seeing their display of affection no longer bites.

He says, "Son, it would make me feel better if you take your shotgun. Hell, take the handgun, too. It will put my mind at rest. When you get down the mountain, stay away from that ornery sheriff because he's not to be trusted. Let's get Greycloud into a hospital before alerting the authorities. It has to be State Police at the very least."

Keith looks into Sabrina's worried eyes and says, "I guess it couldn't hurt to take some protection. I'd probably feel a lot safer myself. State Police only, got it."

Sabrina agrees wholeheartedly. They both wish that she could accompany him on the long trip, but the reality of the situation requires that she stay with the patient until a Medivac arrives.

"You never liked that sheriff, Jeremiah. I remember as much, but I never knew why."

"That's a story for another day's telling, but, suffice it to say, over the years, we have seen and heard some disturbing things. Just stay clear of him. Try to get to Doc Crenshaw, but go about this business quietly. He's still in the same place. Remember?"

"Yes sir. I remember."

Keith goes inside and comes out with a Browning nine-millimeter pistol with two full clips. He shuffles it, admiring the flawless action of the well-kept pistol. He also shoulders a 12-gauge Browning three-inch magnum, which is a five shot semi-automatic shotgun with a thirty-two inch barrel. Keith is most familiar with these firearms. He starts down the trail to the vehicles.

Jeremiah turns Zeus away from the corral with Greycloud's Winchester rifle, a handgun, binoculars, and his own thermos of steaming coffee.

He pauses to tip his hat at Sabrina, who stands in the doorway of the cabin. Jeremiah pauses to say, "Make sure you don't stoke that fireplace. Too much smoke rising from chimney can mark this position and make you both vulnerable. And don't worry, Keith will be fine. He'll make it alright. Just make sure your patient lives long enough for the chopper to get here. Those people will charge us double for the fuel they burn if there's no one here to rescue." He smiles at Keith's girlfriend, genuinely.

Grandpa Williams is trying to reassure her when he is just as concerned for Keith. It is too soon to tell, but Sabrina Martin believes she and Jeremiah are going to get along just fine. It is not only because he is trying for his grandson's sake, nor because he would be beholding to her for saving Greycloud's life. She believes he might actually grow to like her. Something definitely changed over a matter of hours. It is a dramatic change, according to her mind's interpretation.

Sabrina says, "I've got it. Please be careful, Mr. Williams." She returns the smile as he heads for Totem Rock.

From the distance, she hears him say, "You can call me Jeremiah from now on, but I'm Geronimo today, Sabrina." She smiles to herself as a tear falls from her eye.

When Jeremiah reaches Totem Rock, he sits on his horse for a moment, facing the orange sun on the distant horizon. The melody of morning birds prompts him to reflect on his dream as the cool, still morning air makes a steamy mist of his and the horse's warm breath. He spurs the horse with his heels and they get a running start to leap to the other side.

Keith drives down the mountain as fast as he dares. The empty seat to his right will not allow him to stop thinking of Sabrina. He decides to propose upon his return. No matter her answer, he will accept it.

Jeremiah settles down on a blanket in a spot where he can get a good look into the valleys below. He scans the east valley first, and then the ridge in between. Finally, he searches the southern valley, where they ran into the devils of Camp Righteous Kill. He nurses a cup of coffee, enjoying the warmth of the morning sun.

ℭ℘

Sabrina awakens Greycloud and helps the old man relieve himself in an old pickle jar. After washing her hands, she gets another dose of medication into him, along with another tall glass of water.

Greycloud is ravenous, so he doesn't object to being fed lukewarm food. This is a good sign because dying people seldom have healthy appetites. Unless, it is the food that ultimately does them in. He is in good spirits, considering the low-grade fever that sprang up in recent hours. It seems, however, that he is going to make it after all.

She washes the dishes, trying to keep busy. Afterward, she tries the phone again before checking the fluid level in the makeshift IV bottle. Greycloud must be in a world of discomfort, so she asks if he wants something for the pain, but he refuses. Greycloud explains in a near whisper that he does not want to sleep too deeply until Keith or Jeremiah returns. However, they do agree to him telling her the moment it becomes intolerable. She gently places the palm of her right hand against the side of his face and smiles.

Just as she is about to stand, Greycloud takes her hand in his own to say, "Thank you. Little Bear has chosen well. I am happy for you both. Cherish him as he cherishes you, young lady."

"I promise you, Mr. Greycloud. I already do. Thank you. Now rest, it's going to be a long, rigorous day." She leans forward and kisses his warm cheek before walking out.

Sabrina sits on the couch to watch the sporadic morning news on some far away station before she finally dozes off. She is tired after checking on her patient every hour on the hour since charged with his care. After last night's disturbing dream, she found it difficult to rest. While moving quietly about the cabin, she realized that she had the raw materials needed for the IV bottle.

Now, with sleep calling to her, she allows her body and mind to succumb; figuring the worst is behind them.

When Sabina Martin is awakened by a noise outside, she gets up and hurries to the door. "Keith? Jeremiah? Did you forget...?"

She opens the door to George's black face with a gun in hand, ready to shoot any male that comes to the door. She screams before running through the den to the kitchen for the gun on the countertop, but Billy Fellows kicks in the kitchen door and knocks the weapon from her hands. When he attempts to grab her, she gives him a swift knee to the groin that sends him down. She is stumbling backward, trying to get away when George issues a quick clip to the base of her skull to knock her unconscious.

Bo Tuttle takes a position at the front door while Jim Morton enters the cabin.

Billy recovers from Sabrina's blow and instructs Jim Morton to check the front bedroom while he searches the rear. George secures Sabrina's hands with duct tape.

As he has seen on so many cop shows, Jim Morton kicks open the bedroom door where Greycloud lay. Upon seeing the man in the bed, he closes the gap quickly and points the gun at Greycloud's face. Morton is about to pull the trigger when he sees the staring eyes of the dead man. John Greycloud's mouth is agape and he is not breathing.

Jim Morton feels triumphant and somewhat vindicated when he looks over the bloody clothes, sheets, and towels. He smiles before walking out.

"That injun in there is deader than a doornail. I told you the Widow Maker got him." Billy directs Bo Tuttle's attention to the cellar door. He quickly kicks the door in and descends the steps, searching the dim for anyone hiding down there. Nothing.

George Fellows looks toward Greycloud's open bedroom door and barks, "Are you sure he's dead?"

Jim sticks out his proud chest. "Come and see for yourself. He ain't breathin', and there's blood everywhere. His eyes are wide open to the great blue yonder. He's dead alright. Probably went up to that big trading post in the sky. I'll bet my life on it."

George crosses the room after gagging Sabrina. He looks into the room briefly, seeing what Jim had seen and closes the door with a gloved hand.

Squeaky Smith comes to the door to report, "There's nobody in the barn. Checked out another cabin up the trail, but it is empty."

They all gather in the den where Billy says, "Okay, here's the plan. My brother and I will deliver the woman to her father. You three will deploy around the cabin where you will wait for the lawyer and the other old man to return. They must have gone to get help, but they can't get to the highway because the roads are blocked or should be. Even if they do, someone is waiting. And for the love of God, keep your gloves on until it's over with. Leave no evidence."

George says, "That must have been the vehicle we heard leaving. They will have to come back here eventually, so don't screw this up. Wear your fucking gloves at all times, got it? If they return with others, you have to kill them all. There can be no witnesses." He glares at them with disdain.

Billy nods. "Someone stays in the cabin. One of you will take the barn and the third person hits the bushes across from the stable. That way, if you stay out of sight and remain very quiet, you will catch them in a crossfire. If any of you feels the need to smoke, police your area and leave no trace of your being here. We can't stress the importance of this enough."

George looks them over with doubt. "Maybe one of us should stay behind, just in case."

Bo Tuttle and Jim Morton say, "We can handle it," at the same time. They are a bit defensive, still upset about last night's 'dumb hick in a crop-duster' comment. They do have something to prove.

Billy Fellows looks them over with a scowl. "There is one more thing, fellas. Leave this place intact and take nothing. Bo, you're in charge here. I'm trusting you to assure that our instructions are followed without deviation."

Bo looks at the others with serious eyes because he knows his life depends upon it. These men are not to be trifled with. "To the letter. Don't worry. I've got this."

With that, the Fellows brothers go to their horses. Sabrina's unconscious form is carried across George's shoulder like a sack of potatoes.

Jim elects to take the cabin. Squeaky doesn't want any part of sharing it with a dead man all by his lonesome, so he opts to take the bushes behind the smokehouse. Bo Tuttle wants the barn because he does not intend on anyone making it to the cabin. Whoever spots the men first is given strict orders to report, so they can spring the lethal trap together.

John Greycloud has been holding his breath while struggling, desperately, against the reflexive urge to blink or look at the man that shoved a gun in his face. Playing possum has brought him great agony. Just as he was forced to take a breath, the man walked away convinced that he was indeed dead. At that moment, he eased the stale air out of his burning lungs, wanting badly to gulp in more.

Greycloud managed to take in a few breaths before hearing the heavier footsteps of the much larger man approaching his bedroom door. That time, he only had to hold it for a moment because the second man did not come in all the way. If he had, he would have seen the telltale teardrop running down Greycloud's face. Dead men aren't usually given to tears. When the second intruder closed his door, Greycloud lay silent, listening to their plans for ambush.

John Greycloud knows that the person claiming to have pulled the trigger will be the one to stay inside of the cabin alone, so he has to wait quietly. Most of all, he has to stay awake in hopes that the radio they spoke of will be loud enough for him to hear.

He hopes to get some revenge, and the thought sustains against the sleep that threatens to overtake him. Along with every excruciating pang that accompanies each pulsing beat of his heart, it keeps him awake.

Jeremiah is snoozing when the two horses and three people careen down the slope, never to see them crossing the ridge into the south valley beneath him. Because he has endured much in the last twenty-four hours, a few hours of sleep is far from sufficient. It doesn't matter how much coffee he drinks, it is impossible to ignore the call of exhaustion.

Keith is less than two miles from the main highway. When he suddenly stands on the brakes, a cloud of dust engulfs the world just as he crashes into a tree!

When the truck comes to an abrupt stop, Keith's head hits the windshield, rendering him unconscious. The Hummer sits with its tailgate on the other side of a ditch while its rear tires spin slowly in midair.

From where the road to Big Bear meets Route 112, there still remains a winding twenty-eight mile trek to Mills' camp. The trip lessens considerably when traveling through the southern valley, which is only nine or ten rugged miles.

Billy and George are taking their prisoner to judgment, but there are no stipulations concerning Sabrina's condition when she is delivered to Jud Martin other than that she is still breathing. When she awakens in the company of strangers, there is fingernail hell to pay. She scratches and bucks wildly until Billy topples from the saddle in an attempt to escape.

Before the dust clears, Sabrina is running. As she tries to get away, she rips the tape from her mouth so she could breathe more freely. George flanks the woman, cornering her long enough for Billy to catch up.

Sabrina runs up a deer trail, breaking limbs and enduring thorns that tear at her blouse and arms. Because Sabrina does not notice that the trail veers right, she hits the brakes when she realizes that she is approaching the end of a stone precipice. Her feet skid on loose pebbles, taking her to the very brink where she freezes with her toes dangling over the edge. She fights to control her balance, looking down into a deep gully with terrified eyes. Because her hands are bound before her, she cannot use them as a counterbalance.

"Oh God!" she cries as she topples toward a crushing death. Billy Fellows snatches her by the hair and drags her back to the deer trail where they both can catch their breaths before her punishment.

A trickle of blood runs freely from her nose. She is still breathing hard when Billy brandishes a long knife, allowing the flawless metal to do a shimmering dance back and forth, just inches from her throat.

When Billy is sure that he has her full attention, he reaches out and grabs her left breast. Sabrina is revolted, but does not move.

Looking at her with those cold blue eyes, he snarls. "You know, that was quite a kick in the balls back at the cabin, but I blame myself for being careless. However, you've been getting on my fucking nerves ever since!" He smiles. "You have very nice tits, by the way." He rubs her breast hard, while looking down her shirt and licking his lips.

Sabrina Martin whimpers, "Please..."

While the woman cringes, he says, "Women really know how to hurt a man, don't they, baby? Well, you will see that I'm one of the truly enlightened because I know how to hurt women, too. You must understand that messing around with a man's sack is very serious business. Believe me, I know. However, a women has her own sacred ground. Tell me when it hurts. Come on, don't be shy."

Billy's heart is as dark as a sealed tunnel, the depths of which Sabrina could not fathom until he begins to squeeze her left nipple. With those incredibly strong fingers, he squeezes as if smashing a tick. Sabrina's squinting eyes water, but she cannot scream. Nor could she move, except for the horrible quivering of her weakened knees. When Billy Fellows turns her loose, he knows by the look in her eyes that she will yield rather than try his patience again.

☙❧

This place mimics a military base to her, only smaller. Having heard one of her captors mention her father, Sabrina is filled with questions. She wonders how such cruel men could know her dad.

Jud Martin, Willard St. John, Joe Mills, and the rest of the Orphan Squad are standing in the middle of the compound, awaiting the approaching horses. Sabrina does not recognize her father, unless he is the man wearing the white hood and robe. That could not be.

Governor Martin now adorns his ceremonial garb for this occasion. His eyes and face are red. His breathing is slow and deep, and he is enraged. She is rudely thrown to the ground at his feet. At this point, Sabrina wants to wake up. However, for her, the nightmare is merely beginning.

Martin stares at the terrified woman at his feet as she gets to her hands and knees. Her heart is pounding faster with each beat. Sweat pours from her body, as she looks from face to face, wondering about her fate. Nothing better than death rings through the sullen expressions and sneers that mark each countenance.

The younger boy stands farthest away, but he is not so distant that she cannot gauge him properly. At a glance, he seems even more terrified than she is. Even so, Sabrina does not know just how desperately he wishes to be somewhere else, anywhere far from this place. He must be the kid Jeremiah spoke of earlier.

Sabrina Martin has committed a cardinal sin. She is a nigger-lover, and the Klan scowls on such immoral sexual proclivities. Most of these men have no idea that Martin once considered her his daughter. Some think she is a traitor to the Klan. Others guess Sabrina to have been Martin's lover, who went astray in search of pleasures more perverse in nature.

The Glover brothers move in close with their rotten, grinning mouths stuffed full of chew. They are looking at Sabrina as if she is dinner.

When George removes her gag, she shouts, "Who the hell are you people? Why have you brought me here? Answer me, God damn it!"

The Glover brothers grin and chuckle at her frustration. She ignores them, turning her attention to the person beneath the hood. To Sabrina's horror, she recognizes the watch on his wrist and the eyes beneath the hood. Her mind reels because this is indeed her father dressed in the garb of the most maligned hate group in the western hemisphere. Crawling closer, she takes hold of his robe and asks, "Dad? Daddy, is that you? Please say something."

The Glover brothers stop snickering; their enlightened eyes darting to others of the group.

Martin is pricked deeply when the nigger-kissing bitch addresses him as "*daddy.*" He sees no daughter of his kneeling in the gravel before him. He sees only prey. He sees an unworthy whore among all women.

Jud Martin is consumed by thoughts of revenge and restitution for all the years and money vested in raising the whelp of an African American that he had foolishly called his own. She is going to repay him for every moment and every penny, with interest, before she dies.

He only regrets that Keith Williams is not down on the ground beside her. His death would have been nice and slow.

In the silence, anger displaces Sabrina's fear. She stands and screams, "Talk to me, damn it!" Without warning, she rips the hood from Martin's head only to back away from the face she uncovers.

Her father has aged a great deal since the last time she saw him, showing signs of grey. His eyes burn holes in her, and a contemptuous glower frames the evil in them. He almost looks insane, but he has to be, if he is a part of conspiracies to commit murder...kidnapping.

With desperation now growing in her voice, Sabrina sobs. "Dad? Daddy, please tell me you're not one of them. Please. You're not... you're not a Klansman, are you? Why are you doing this to me?"

Suddenly, Martin backhands Sabrina and quickly issues a second, even more punishing blow to her face. Her lips split open before she falls to the ground in a heap.

He steps up to the plate and says, "You're no child of mine, bitch. Don't you ever call me that, again!"

Sabrina looks up from where she lay. Her eyes plead for help from the indifferent men, who stand rigidly above. "Why, dad? Why are you doing this to me? Is it because I didn't tell you about me and Keith?"

This is a terrible mistake. Martin buries his shoe into her stomach, causing Sabrina to curl up in the fetal position as she gasps for air. She is choking and retching. Her eyes water as the world plays funny tricks on her vision.

Martin screeches, "I warned you, didn't I? I'm not your father. I never was so keep those nigger-loving lips shut. You're just like your nigger-kissing bitch of a mother, and you're going to die just like she did!" He raises his arms and declares, "All that you see is mine to control and much more. You will not bring about the downfall of all that we have endeavored to accomplish in accordance to God's will. You and your spook lawyer are dead. After you're gone, nothing will stand in the way of our cause. I will be President of the United States and the Supreme Imperial Wizard of the Ku Klux Klan. We will rid this country of half-breed abominations like you, and the shame that you bring on us all by tainting bloodlines that God never meant to be crossed!"

When her eyes refocus, Sabrina considers the man she loved and respected for so much of her lifetime with his outstretched arms and those enraged eyes. She sees the madness and the raw malfeasance of evil in him that was once only hinted; an ugliness she only glimpsed as a teen. She trembles with unprecedented fear, but she still has to know.

Sabrina drags herself to her feet. Through her sobs she asks, "Did you kill my mother? You told me that she left us because she didn't want children. You said that she did not love me. Now, you're saying that she's dead…that you…killed her. You couldn't have. Please say it's not true!"

The pleading grief etched upon her face and shattering in her voice seems to fill Jud Martin with some strange sense of satisfaction. He is positively drunk with it.

"I killed her like the nigger-kissing dog that she was."

Sabrina attacks, screaming and cursing him to all damnation. As she kicks him in the groin and tears at his eyes with her bound hands, she spits, "You son of a bitch. Bastard. I will kill you. I'll kill you!"

Billy and George step in to immobilize her. She fights them, kicking and scratching to no avail. When Martin recovers, he rubs the scratches high on his cheek, just below his left eye. He looks at the blood on his right palm and slaps her with the same. He continues to slap Sabrina while they hold her upright.

Martin spits in her face and growls, "Slut!" Through the fog and the haze, she hears him say, "So you like sleeping with Blacks, well I'm gonna teach you the lesson I should have taught a long time ago. By the time we're finished with you, you'll love your better half again. Only then will you die!"

Sabrina is dragged to the shack, the place of punishment, where she is thrown to the floor inside. There are no windows in this dark, extremely hot little building. Martin enters soon after.

He hisses, "Are you ready for lesson number one?" Without warning, he hits her again and rips her clothes away!

Governor Martin rapes his daughter, never to know that Ezra Krantz was wrong about her conception. Krantz only assumes that Sabrina's father was Black because Martin killed her mother after catching her in a somewhat compromising position; a position that his mind twisted in an insane instance that changed lives as well as eliminating them.

Krantz was convinced that Martin might not execute Sabrina for her involvement with Keith Williams, choosing to excommunicate her. That will never do, and there is no time for paternity tests and such, which might leak to the public. Knowing a little something of the ties that bind, Krantz is actually guilty of embellishing to add granulated salt to an extremely irritable wound that is still very deep and volatile. He interpreted all things, bitter or bittersweet, as God's work, for a supreme sacrifice has to be made of one who aspires so much.

Outside, Tommy stands paralyzed in the middle of the compound, feeling sick to his stomach. This is all wrong. If she looks White, then she is White. And White is always right, right? He has been taught all of his righteous life that the Black man is the enemy. Taught that the Black man steals, rapes, and plunders—not White folks—who are God's chosen people. God is a white being, sitting on a white throne, floating high up in the lily white clouds of heaven. Satan had been burned black by the flames of hell. His children, who are supposed to be no better than animals, are born Black that they are recognized as the servants of evil or the slaves of humankind.

Tommy hears that woman's screams. Even after he clasps his hands over ears that refuse to go deaf, he hears her. The kid closes his eyes tightly against the tears, which will eventually escape despite his effort to contain them. He is once again only five-years-old and crashing!

Sabrina is fifteen-years-old when her inebriated father walks into the bathroom where she has just taken a bath. She only recently moved back from her Aunt Janie's home, where she spent seven years following her mother's disgraceful disappearance, and during Jud Martin's political climb. Martin asks her if she had allowed the young boys to do nasty things to her during her stay with her aunt. She denies the insinuation, but he is not convinced.

Only wearing a towel over her well-developed young body, the frightened girl retreats until her back is pressed against the wall. God, she looks just like her mother. With the strangest look in his eyes, Jud Martin places his right hand under the towel and gropes her naked vagina.

She cries, "Daddy, please don't. I'm a good girl. Please don't!" She closes her eyes and turns her face away in shame.

He is forced to let go when he feels the hymen, which is still intact. Sabrina is still a virgin after all. Sabrina runs to her room and dresses quickly. She runs away, returning to her aunt's house where she stays until she can forgive him. She is a resilient young lady, so she finds the strength to bag the shame and bury it deep.

Even though he apologizes to no end, in that state of mind, there is no telling how far it might have gone if she were not untouched. Martin learns to regret his actions when his sister wades hip-deep into his shit regarding his method of determining Sabrina's virginity. Janie sees the intrusion as a question of her own moral teachings and the child's honesty.

That was a long time ago, and Jud Martin lived many days in regret of it, until the opportunity presents itself again.

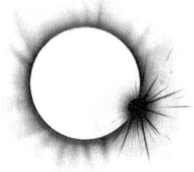

Chapter 27

AMBUSH!

Keith comes to with a painful jerk. For a moment, the attorney is disoriented, confused. He forces himself to backtrack the sequence of events until fully aware of the situation. As he wipes a trickle of blood from his forehead, it all hits him. The Klan must have blocked the road because those healthy trees certainly did not decide to lie down and commit suicide all by themselves.

The truck is sideways in the road, parallel to a tall pine. The door only opens a few inches before jamming, so he crawls out of the passenger's side. The engine is still running, welcomed proof that the truck has only suffered minor damage.

Keith tumbles out and lies in one of the long tire ruts made by the dragging brakes.

The rear wheels are suspended in the air and the truck rests on its chassis. Not good. He eases back inside and puts it in four-wheel drive. The front tires do not have enough surface on the road, not enough weight, so they only dig a bit before spinning freely. His situation is now more precarious as the truck teeter-totters a bit. He is forced to sit still, so the weight does not cause the vehicle to topple backwards into the treacherous terrain below.

Keith is frustrated, placing his aching head on the steering wheel to think. He remembers the winch and prays it remains undamaged. He carefully eases out of the truck to find that it is okay, so he puts the winch control in neutral and pulls the cable from the spool. He quickly drags the cable across the road, stumbling once before wrapping it around another tree. Thankfully, he is able to pull the Hummer back onto the road. After taking precious time to pour the extra gas into the tank, he roars back up the mountain road.

If the Klan is responsible for blocking the road, it means that they are coming for them. He has to get the others to safety no matter how critical Greycloud's condition. His chances will be better with the bumps in the road than with those god-fearing racists.

While barreling back up the road, Keith nearly flies into a ravine. There is no time for caution. He only hopes he is not too late.

ఴ

Jeremiah wakes up with a gaping yawn, and then his eyes pop open when he hears movement behind him. He turns quickly, bringing his gun about, but it is only Zeus.

Feeling a little silly, he relaxes and sweeps the valley floor with his powerful binoculars. He detects movement in the northwestern flow of the south valley, but it is gone. Keith's telescope would have served him better and he kicks himself for not thinking of it sooner.

336

When he stands, his knees sound their protest with a snap, crackle, and a bang. Jeremiah stretches, feeling much stronger, much better. Though dull aches plague his muscles and joints, it feels better than being dead.

The lukewarm coffee is good from the mouth of the thermos bottle. Fluids push fluids, so he takes a well-deserved leak. When finished, he digs into his pocket for a sweet granola cube for Zeus before mounting the horse to head home.

Jeremiah is anxious about Greycloud's condition, but he takes his time going down the trail. He glances at his watch and wonders if Keith is on his way back, praying that his grandson has not run into trouble. The sheriff is foremost in his mind.

Jeremiah never liked or trusted the sheriff of Caribou Lake. He is suspicious of how the sheriff always stares at him and Greycloud with his thumbs tucked in his gun belt. The man must have watched one cowboy movie too many.

Now he wonders about something that never crossed his mind. That wily grizzly could have been sneaking onto the homestead from this general direction. He and Greycloud always look for the exit trail when the animal raids, never for a point of entrance. Funny how the bear never came near when the ground was wet enough to leave its unmistakable imprints.

Zeus snorts and shakes his head up and down as if in agreement with the old man's thoughts. In reality, however, the horse notices the scent of unfamiliar people in the breeze. Having recently dealt with Dingahay, his sensitivity has become much more acute to new odors.

Bo Tuttle is in the barn, which faces the trail that leads to Totem Rock. The rear of the barn faces the track that Keith had used to get to his vehicle. Bo moves back and forth between the two sets of doors. This time, when he peers through the crack in the doors at the south end, he spots Jeremiah about sixty or seventy-yards away. He radios the others.

Squeaky Smith is sleeping, lying on his stomach beneath some shrubbery. He is dreaming about Cynthia, his perfectly imaginary Playboy playmate.

Jim Morton, on the other hand, has left the radio on the couch, seizing the opportunity to rifle through the drawers of the back bedroom for things to steal. He feels that it would be such a shame to burn anything of value when they leave, and the two old geezers seem to have collected some nice junk over the years. Without the key to the large gun safe, he settles for the hefty wad of cash from Jerimiah's top drawer.

Jim Morton has been inside long enough to thaw and cook a venison steak. A frosted glass of corn liquor is poised upon the table to wash the sandwich down. Only a morally bankrupt individual can make himself at home so easily.

In Jim Morton's infinite boredom, he pokes the shaft of an arrow through the screen at the extremely agitated rattlers, which strike repeatedly at the tempered glass of the tank. Less attention is paid to the arrow because they want the Neanderthal using it to taunt them. Because he is liquored up, his heat signature is strong.

Jim is a bit tipsy, giggling to himself as he harasses the snakes, but the novelty of it begins to wear off. It is time to check Greycloud's room. He has already collected a tidy pile of spoils, but there could be more.

The head orphan intends to ignore the last thing Billy Fellows said about them taking nothing. They have been ordered to leave the place intact, but Jim still intends to burn it all to the ground. Bo Tuttle will probably have to explain it all again. A raging fire on a mountain attracts attention. He tosses the arrow to the floor near the pile of plundered goods and starts for Greycloud's bedroom, but suddenly bolts across the room for the radio.

"Hello. That you, Bo? Squeaky? Come in." He turns the volume up and Bo Tuttle's angry voice screeches across the room, causing Jim to drop his tasty sandwich. No problem. He just picks it up, blows on it, and says, "God bless the germs."

Greycloud is listening and knows it is time to act.

Keith is a mile away, coming swiftly with a billowing plume of dust trailing his banged up vehicle. He makes sure that the clip is in the handgun and loads the shotgun with one hand, praying all the while.

War Paint is pacing back and forth in the corral. He whinnies, seemingly agitated for no reason. Jeremiah is about forty-yards away when Zeus stops of his own accord. The rider becomes alert, looking about. He pats the horse's neck and says, "What is it, boy, something wrong?" He sits there for a second, looking down the quiet trail. Seeing nothing amiss, he gently spurs Zeus with his heels and clicks his tongue against his front teeth. The horse hesitates before slowly continuing toward home.

Jim Morton grabs his M-16. As if it would have made any difference at all, he left the famed Widow Maker at the camp because it may have served as a reminder of ridicule.

Bo informs them that the old man is still about forty-yards out and he will soon ride his horse right past the camouflaged Squeaky, whom he warns to remain absolutely motionless.

Jim Morton is heading for the door when he hears a noise come from the dead man's bedroom. He dismisses it until he hears the scraping sound again, louder than before. He quickly moves to the bedroom door, not wanting to miss the action. Nevertheless, he has to check on the noise. The missing lawyer could have returned without their knowledge, and he could be up to something.

He kicks the door in and points the weapon at the window. Nothing. The dead man's feet are right where they should be and nothing seems to have changed. He walks in and glances at the window again, looking for anything that could be responsible for the scraping sound. When he surveys the bloody bed, he sees the crossbow. He did not notice it before because it lies hidden beneath a large, bloody towel.

Jim smiles. This is definitely his day. He will have two crossbows, already thinking that he will sell one of them and…

His foggy mind reminds him that he has business to take care of first. Just as Jim is about to turn away, it moves. He blinks and his mouth falls open, which is all his paralyzed mind can manage while he watches a miracle unfold before his very eyes.

The Indian is breathing and looking at Jim as he raises the crossbow! There is a click and a lightning fast zip as the shredder jettisons through the air, covering the short distance in less than a heartbeat. It slices a neat X in Jim's uniform, dead center of the insignia. The razor sharp arrowhead easily passes through his rib cage before shredding his heart to lodge into the wall.

Bending the shaft as he goes down, Jim Morton crumples to his knees, staring in utter disbelief at the man who just shot him. He looks down as the bloody shaft slowly disappearing into the gushing X and then looks at Greycloud. He tries to move, wishing to raise the gun, but it hurts too much.

340

He manages to say, "But…you're dead. I saw you…"

"Not as dead as you," Greycloud whispers back.

Blood spurts from Jim's twitching mouth as he tries to finish his last sentence. He falls face first to the floor. The second X exiting his back is not so neat, but it definitely marks the spot. The special-order arrow has done its job.

Greycloud pulls the needle from his arm and gets to his feet in immense agony, tearing open several of Sabrina's stitches. He limps as fast as he can to the bedroom door, picking up Jim's gun on the way. When he bends over to get it, the world goes fuzzy and threatens to desert him again. He shakes his head and struggles to hold onto consciousness because his friend's life is threatened.

The withering hero gets to the door. Upon opening it, he shouts, "Geronimo, take cover!"

Because Greycloud loses his balance, he accidentally stumbles outside. There, he leans against the cabin wall for support and begins to fire. He scrapes the ground in front of Squeaky to reveal his position, and then fires at the barn door.

Jeremiah is about fifteen yards from Squeaky when the ground seems to come to life. The assassin spins over on his back and fires his weapon blindly. Bullets fly over Jeremiah's head as he dodges and tries to get off the horse, which Squeaky shoots dead beneath him. When the horse crashes, Jeremiah struggles to get his feet out of both stirrups. He has to use the horse as a barrier, feeling every bullet that pelts the noble Zeus.

Bo Tuttle shoots back at Greycloud, who is slow to dodge the bullets. With a sickening crunch, his busted leg shatters again and he slides to the ground just outside the cabin door!

Keith Williams plows up the trail and slides to a stop just yards from the barn door. When he gets out, gunshots are ringing out. He runs to the barn where he hears shots, so he slips inside.

From the north end, Keith could see the stranger shooting through the barn doors at Jeremiah. He moves quickly with no need for stealth because the shots are covering his approach.

When Bo senses him and tries to turn around, Keith pulls the trigger on the shotgun. The buckshot hits Tuttle squarely in the chest, lifting him from his feet. The second and third volleys tatter Bo's body in midair, slamming him into and through the partially open barn doors. Before the buckshot deposits him on a mound, a red mist plumes. Bo Tuttle soon stops kicking on the wood chip pile near the corral. The two remaining horses are raising hell outside.

Jeremiah struggles to get his rifle out of its sheath, but it's pinned under the dead horse. His handgun is on the ground between Zeus and Squeaky!

Zeus is being picked apart. The bullets being fired at Jeremiah are eating away at the horse's belly. Soon, the bullets will be coming through to the saddle. Chunks of prime horseflesh fly through the air and the foul odor of bowel is thick.

Squeaky slams in a new magazine and rolls to his left for a better angle. Had he known the old man has no weapon available, he could have stood to take his shots. Squeaky's assault on Jeremiah Williams continues, completely unaware of the grandson's unanticipated presence. There is a window of opportunity because Squeaky thinks it is Bo approaching from the rear, so Keith Williams runs right up behind him with the shotgun and blows his right leg off at the knee!

Squeaky's gun and the fresh magazine fly out of his hands as he rolls, screaming and grabbing at the limb rudely severed from his person. His blood spurts to stain the ground.

Bloody from head to toe, Jeremiah scuttles to where Greycloud lays dying.

Keith kicks the gun further away from the agonized man, who attempts to cinch his wounded leg so he does not bleed out. Keith joins his grandfather and the badly wounded Greycloud. He sees all that blood on his grandfather and frantically pats him down, asking if he's been hit.

Jeremiah has superficial wounds, but his lifelong friend has been shot several times in the chest. His burning lungs are filling with blood, some of which already floods his mouth to run from his pale lips. Jeremiah cradles Greycloud in his arms, listening to his last words.

Greycloud is looking at the swaying grass of the meadow high up on a plateau as he speaks to his friends for the final time from this side of Totem Rock.

"Geronimo, do not grieve for me. It is a far better place I go to." He coughs up some blood and then says to Keith, "I am so sorry that I could not stop them from taking your woman."

Keith runs inside, shouting Sabrina's name. He soon comes back to the doorway in dismay.

"Before they left, one of them said they are taking her to her father. He may not harm her, unless his soul is truly evil. I'm so sorry." A tear cascades down his cheek, and his eyes roll back in their sockets. His raspy, labored breathing stops as the last bit of air in his lungs eases out to form a bloody bubble upon his lips. He goes forever limp in Jeremiah's arms.

343

Jeremiah Williams rocks him back and forth as he and Keith weep. Keith Williams strokes John Greycloud's bloody grey hair and says, "It's okay, Old Father. There was nothing you could do… nothing you could do."

After a moment more of abject sadness, Squeaky begs for help. Keith and Jeremiah's eyes meet with a total singularity of thought. After carefully laying Greycloud on the ground, they move on Squeaky. What Squeaky sees in their eyes causes him to crawl away.

They stand over the Klansman, seething. Keith is staring him squarely in the eyes when he slams the butt of the shotgun into the injured man's fresh stump. Squeaky wails as brilliant flares of fresh pain rip through his body, and then the old man is upon him. Jeremiah Williams sits the whimpering man upright and decks him several times, driving his fist into Squeaky's face.

Keith demands, "Where is she? Where did they take Sabrina? Talk, motherfucker, or I'll blow your damn head off next!" He points the gun at Squeaky's face.

Squeaky lays on his back, writhing in pain. He begs, "I'll tell you, mister. Just please don't let me die!"

Jeremiah grabs him by the collar and yanks him back to a sitting position.

"Okay, but you better talk fast!" His spit flies all over Squeaky's face, but the badly injured man doesn't seem to mind.

"They…they took her to our camp. Camp Righteous," Squeaky cries.

Keith takes over the interrogation. "Where damn it? Where is the camp, and why did they take her there?"

"It's at the end of the valley, south of here. They took her to her father. Mr. Martin is one of our leaders."

Jeremiah holds Squeaky up while his head lulls between his shoulder blades. Keith asks, "Does he plan to hurt her? Answer me. Is he going to harm her in any way?"

Even in his pain, Squeaky figures that the truth will not help him.

"Jesus no, mister. He just wants to get her away from you. That's all, I swear to God. I swear to God, mister. Oh God." Jeremiah shoves him to the ground and Squeaky says, "I told you, mister. You won't let me die like this, will you? Please, I need a doctor!"

Jeremiah stands, looking at Greycloud and then back at the writhing Klansman at his feet. He says, "No. I won't just let you die because you bastards tried to kill us both yesterday." He snatches the nine-millimeter from Keith's belt. "I'm going to help you to die. See a doctor in hell." Jeremiah unloads the clip into Squeaky's head!

As the echoes die and the breeze carries the smoke of expended gunpowder away from their burning eyes, they can assume that there isn't enough of the cranium left for a forensics team to match Squeaky's dental records. It is an ugly sight, this man, after Jeremiah pumped the fifteenth round into his head.

Keith did nothing to halt his grandfather's brutality. For this dead man at his feet, he feels nothing; except, that he deserved to die in the worst possible way.

Keith turns, charging for the trail without warning, and then he remembers the tree blocking the road. There is little doubt that it had been only one of several.

Jeremiah knows what he is thinking. He meets his grandson at the corral and stops him. Holding fast the hand whose sole mission is to open the corral, Jeremiah shouts, "No, Keith. You can't go alone, and you certainly can't go half-cocked!"

His saddened eyes plead, appealing to Keith's logic and sanity. This is a very nasty moment, a littered pool of conflicting emotions and suspicion. For one overwhelming instance, Keith truly questions his grandfather's motivation...or lack of it.

Jeremiah looks beyond Keith's shoulder at the body of his lifelong friend and says, "Besides, son, we don't know how many of them are down there. Once we go, we may never enjoy this place ever again. We have one last funeral to go to before we try to avoid attending our own in person. We have to give Greycloud a proper send off—a traditional burial—if we can. We may never make it back here, and he would be left for the scavengers. We must cremate his body according to tradition. We would want the same for ourselves, son." Tears fall from his eyes as they embrace. Keith thinks of the law's attitude toward destroying evidence, especially where a murder is involved. However, he will acquiesce.

Keith and Jeremiah hitch a trailer to Apollo's harness. After carefully wrapping Greycloud in his favorite, handwoven blanket, they stack lots of wood in the trailer and place him on top. Leading the horse with their heads hung low and their somber eyes to the ground, they carry Greycloud to Totem Rock.

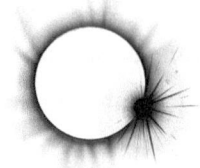

Chapter 28

THE DESTRUCTION
OF SABRINA MARTIN

This foul shadow is a stranger to neither. They discover to what degree it has lain dormant; morphing into something more horrid until it finally wins its profane prize by claiming both souls. It is not only her body Governor Martin takes twice, but also Sabrina's honor, her pride, and her mind. The rickety little bed and chair lay broken and askew after immense struggles. During the cruel assault, with the vile silt of a thousand polluted riverbeds washing over her mind, she can only pray for the end.

While her woefully misinformed biological father takes her, Sabrina Martin finds death a most irrational fellow, who chooses to abandon victims in their most miserable and willing of hours. She

347

can see it standing on the shore of her despair, just out of reach as she drowns in the lather of her father's sweat and foaming saliva. This grim reaper watches Sabrina's suffering, hungrily feeding on the fraying, splintering fragments of her soul.

Having sated something dark and unseemly, Jud Martin leaves Sabrina trembling on the floor of the shack in the throes of his savage wake. A monster has fully arisen in his soul, venting decades of inhuman refuse at her through those angry fists. After living such endless pain, such endless horror, such unrelenting misery, Sabrina Martin is lost within a black hole and she is sliding to its destructive core.

Like a tattered beast, his murky silhouetted form stands abeam the doorframe. A hulking mass of rage, still, he breathes heavily like a seething animal. His head slowly swivels to look back at her on the dusty floor.

Governor Jud Martin slams the door shut, walking into the cleansing light of day, ripping away the ragged remnants of his bloody white robe. He willfully strides across the compound. Etched upon his face and forearms are new scratches and bite marks, but they are negligible. Though laden with sweat, he feels not their sting.

When Mississippi's governor approaches Willard St. John on the steps of the headquarter building, the baton is passed with disturbingly casual care. Surprisingly, Willard is not as enthusiastic as expected.

The thought of the lawyer killed at someone else's hands forces him to consider relieving the burdens of his twisted frustration. However, who better to use for this purpose? After all, the vile intrusion has always been his intent for Keith's woman, whomever she might turn out to be. He crosses the yard with feigned confidence and prideful determination.

For a brief moment, Sabrina is the loneliest woman in the world. Yet, something intangibly born of evolution drives a thought deep into her splintered center. Its tiny voice steels her to survive. It only lasts for an instant more, struggling to embed itself deeper into her wounded psyche. Her broken thoughts unite for one defiant instance, beckoning her to endure. Then it is gone.

Eric and Derrick Glover are standing guard outside the shack, eagerly awaiting a chance to get at her. Until their time comes, listening is quite a turn on.

The rusting hinges yawn upon Willard's entry. When Sabrina Martin's beleaguered screams resume, Tommy Swinton shuts his eyes and clenches his hands against his ears. The youngster shudders until his side of the separated fuselage stops sliding across the earth. He prays until his mother's burning body ceases squirming.

∞

After Keith stacks the planks and firewood four-feet high, they soak it with kerosene. Greycloud is lain in the center of the pile.

Jeremiah takes his flask of moonshine and pours some of it on Greycloud's lips before handing it to his grandson. Keith takes a swig of the stuff he has always compared to tequila.

Now Jeremiah tips the flask to the grey one and struggles to say, "Here's to you, old friend. May the wind be with you on your homeward journey. I never thought we'd have our last drink this way, but there's no accounting for the actions of others. You take care of the Laughing Spring Chicken until I get there, you hear me?"

Keith wonders at his strange saying for a moment before placing his arms around those heaving shoulders.

The old man drinks from the flask and gently caresses Greycloud's face before laying it on his motionless chest. Jeremiah Williams weeps the most bitter tears of his life. Together, they throw the match that ignites the flames, then walk away to make plans.

Animals are mating and having offspring. Even the thoughtless flowers bloom in their efforts to bring forth new life. The mountains are alive, but in the midst of all this natural beauty, woeful men are as given to their obsession with destruction and death as a sculptor is to untouched marble.

Back at the cabin, Jeremiah spreads a map of the mountain range on a table, pinning its corners down with a knife and Jim Morton's unfinished glass of moonshine. They first discuss taking horses through the valley, but decide it will be too risky because snipers could be waiting in case the others failed to kill them.

Keith suggests they use chainsaws to cut their way to the highway, but Jeremiah explains the pitfalls of a frontal attack. In addition, whoever cut the trees may be standing guard at the bottom.

Keith points at the map and asks, "What's this?"

Jeremiah grunts and says, "I'll be damned. That could be it. That old mining road runs parallel to Route 112. Do you remember it from your childhood? I forbade you from ever going near those mines because they were dangerous. They used to mine silver down in the east valley. When the silver played out, they used it as a logging road until the economy got sluggish and people stopped building houses." As Jeremiah traces the old road with a finger, he says, "See here? It cuts across the ridge separating the eastern and southern valleys. It runs clean through the south valley where it crosses another ridge and goes all the way to Lake Koocanusa. That's where the old pulp mill used to be before going belly up."

"Well, that's our ticket." Keith feels a ray of hope, but his heart nearly sinks when Jeremiah begins his next sentence.

"But…son…that stretch hasn't been used in ages. It probably doesn't even resemble a road anymore."

Keith thinks for a moment and suggests, "We'll take the chainsaws. If the road has grown over with trees, we'll simply cut them down. That Hummer can drive through or over almost anything. If we have to cut the trees that are too big to mow over, we'll just bring the stumps down low enough so the chassis won't bind as we go. I think it'll work if we just give it a try."

"It will be slow going, Keith, but it's the safest way. If we start soon, we might be there by nightfall. I heard those boys' horses out there. We'll take them along in case we can't get through. You can unhook the trailer if it gets to be rough going, and I'll just ride them in. If we have any chance of pulling this thing off, we'll need those animals to be fresh. That's why I think it'll be best to tow the trailer as far as possible."

"That sounds like a plan to me," Keith says.

"Not quite. We have to figure out what to do when we get there and what to do afterwards. Especially, if we should be separated."

They share thoughts on how to attack the camp. Of course, their plans are subject to adjustments due to unknowable difficulties, but those bridges are not yet in sight. The plan calls for a rather costly diversion, which Jeremiah will execute while Keith finds a way inside to locate Sabrina.

They finally agree on the plan of action when Jeremiah says, "I think we might end up coming back through here, one way or another, so we should set traps. If things go sour and one of us—if not both of us—makes it back, we're gonna have to take the backside of this mountain to get out of here alive. That's if we can't make the main highway or if there's heat on our asses. So let's lead 'em through here and then Totem Rock. I think Greycloud would get a kick out of seeing one of them snake bit and sliding off the cliff in wingless flight."

Jeremiah glances at the fish tank. They laugh, uneasily. It is uneasy because they know that they are going to have to do evil this night. The most frightening aspect of all is that deep down inside, they both want to go out and kill some White men. This entire situation, which is in no way of their volition, appeals to the baser man in each of them. Sabrina Martin's life may hang in the balance, which makes it very scary indeed.

Keith and the old man quickly gather some rope and a ball of very strong twine. They collect duct tape, a bow and arrows, Greycloud's crossbow, and two of the M-16 rifles belonging to the dead men outside. They use the grappler to put the rattlers in a sack and head back to Totem Rock. They carefully lay their deadly traps, wicked things meant to maim and kill evil men.

As they collect the weaponry that they will need to rescue Sabrina Martin, Keith places his hand on the crossbow held by studs on the wall.

Jeremiah says, "No son, none of those will do. We are going after the most dangerous animals in the world this time. Those faithful old Browning Furies won't do on this hunt."

"What do you suggest?" Keith asks.

His grandfather proudly opens a large metal locker in the corner of the room. He reaches inside and says, "The crossbows we took to hunt that bear are trustworthy and powerful, but that was to be their retirement hunt. These are Excalibur Matrix Mega 405 recurve crossbows, son. In fact, I helped to develop the prototype and the smart scopes. These beasts are much faster than any of the other crossbows. They are lighter, but stronger, so don't let the weight fool you. They will propel a shredder tipped arrow at 405 feet-per-second with a 127-foot pound test pull. They are lethal, even beyond eighty-yards. I had them both specially modified the same as the others with magnetic splines near the end of the arrow. Turn on the scope...here. For low-light shooting, push this button all the way forward. Place a distant target in the crosshairs for three seconds, but don't squeeze until the digital scope self-adjusts. If a moving target is just walking left or right, paint it with the crosshairs and a blue line will appear on either side in the direction of movement. When the line stops, hold. Take a breath, and squeeze off when that blue line blinks and turns red. It does not matter where your target is positioned on the horizontal, as long as the pace of its movement is relatively steady. Just squeeze off. We can't afford any misses or mishaps so you should take a few practice shots to get familiar with this beast. If there is any infighting...you know what to do. Just point and shoot. Otherwise, remember to squeeze, don't pull or jerk."

"You actually helped to develop the prototype for this? Impressive."

He hands one to Keith, holding on until their eyes meet.

"Keith," Jeremiah says.

"Yes."

"These are men, Keith. Although they behave like rabid animals, this will be different from taking down a deer. You cannot afford to hesitate. If you do, or feel you cannot squeeze the trigger, you need only recall Greycloud's death and the love of your woman. The good Lord will supply the strength."

Keith averts his burning eyes for a second. "If killing is required of me...then a killer I will become, Geronimo."

"That's the spirit, Little Bear. That's the spirit. Let's take these evil fuckers to task, son."

No more words need to be spoken at this moment. It is ritualist, after a fashion, of a man handing his son a very powerful weapon for a potentially deadly hunt. Such has always been Jerimiah and Greycloud's way on Big Bear. He releases the weapon.

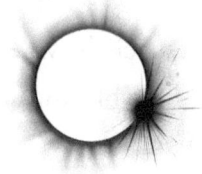

Chapter 29

RESCUE AND REVENGE

Jud Martin is standing alone on the back deck, listening to the mosquitoes buzzing the screen in search of a way inside. His sweat in the dim lighting draws them, just as his eyes are drawn skyward by a rising moon that illuminates the treetops. While leaning against a corner post, he lights the cigarette taken from Joe Mills' pack. When he hears heavy footsteps, he knows they are coming. Jud Martin sits with a loaded gun in his lap, finger on the trigger.

Billy and George Fellows walk onto the deck to join the governor in the corner. The brothers are a little uncomfortable because Willard is not present, but Billy has warned George to expect something like this.

Martin says, "I want to thank you for a job done well. You are efficient, loyal, and committed. I recognize and appreciate that."

"Thank you, sir," Billy says.

"This entire thing seems to be about hard choices and commitment. That is why I asked you to join me. Mills has filled me in on your history with Willard as well as the military. He told me why you retired and I understand. Being passed over because of reverse racial discrimination is a bitch; especially, when you've loyally served your country." They approach the table and sit his opposite. "Well, that's all over with now, if you want what you have coming to you."

George leans forward, meeting Martin's intense gaze head-on. He asks, "What is it you would have us do, Governor Martin?"

Martin eyes seem to grow darker when he smiles. "Security is important to a man in my position. This entire event has become a raging spectacle for too many eyes. These men are on our side, but they're not invulnerable. Regrettably, too many unforeseeable things have come into play that must scrub clean. When this is over, I want you to clean house for me."

The brothers look at each other. Billy asks, "To what degree?"

Martin says, "Total and complete, there can be no witnesses to this event. I'm afraid that other than you two, only Mills can be trusted to keep silent."

"And Willard," George asks. "what of him?"

Unflinchingly, Martin says, "Ezra believes that Willard—and I concur—has become a major liability to our organization's future. When we get word that the lawyer is dead, Willard dies alongside him with the smoking gun in his hands. As a token of my appreciation, you will equally share all that is his territory. Because I have complete confidence in you, the groundwork is already paved. Is this agreeable?"

George sits back in his chair. Both men are contemplating the offer they dare not refuse.

"You've been the backbone for that spineless man long enough. Now, the only people who can pass you over for someone less qualified are yourselves. You will give the orders instead of taking them. You will make the decisions instead of enforcing them for someone who only cares about himself. God has decreed this, men. Question is…will you answer the call?"

The brothers look at one another again with arched eyes that like what lies before them. They smile, simultaneously, nodding their heads in agreement.

Governor Martin places the gun on the table, depressing the hammer. The brothers realize the seriousness when they look at the weapon they did not know Martin had pointed at them in case they refused his advances.

"Then it's settled. Go about things as usual until the time comes." With a handshake and a sip of bourbon, a new alliance with lightning forms to seal fates.

Despite Willard St. John's best effort, he only gains minimal satisfaction from Sabrina's suffering. Something is missing from this exercise in power, something or someone. For the second or third time in his life, he is unable to reach a climax, so he ends his huffing and puffing by faking an ejaculation.

With a sigh of relief, he stands over Sabrina and zips his trousers. For the benefit of the two guardians, he leaves the small furnace with an insincere smile etched upon his face. By the time Willard tells the Fellows brothers that they are up at bat, he decides to see Ms. Diva Jones upon his return to Atlanta.

Because honor dictates that he not cheat on his wife, George Fellows respectfully declines the opportunity.

Billy Fellows, on the other hand, is feeling a bit randy because his girlfriend was on the rag and unwilling to bloody the sheets before all this started. Besides, he thinks Sabrina is pretty. He is, however, certain that she will be pretty messed up by the time he gets to her.

Those who participate in the rape of Sabrina Martin share a single commonality. Each wants to prove himself better than the Black man. Not only the one she has taken as a lover, but all Black men. It is most prevalent in their minds.

No Klansman ever stands around to measure the cocks of spooks they are about to castrate and kill. In fact, they don't really care to see this particular part of a Negro's anatomy.

Nevertheless, within the realm of their more perverse pleasures, one cannot lop off what one does not see or touch.

In many ways, they are haunted by their own obsession with the disgusting physical attraction some Caucasian females seem to have for males of the Negro race. The fact that many White women are enthralled by the myths surrounding the sexual prowess of African American men seems to eat at their resolve, turning mere myths into their own monsters. Therefore, in the mind of the truly racist, they consider the African American as seductive rapists of White women.

Some of their sisters are curious enough to cross that great Black-White barrier to find out for themselves. Moreover, many of those who brave these often-turbulent waters never return home. There is something to say about Jeremiah's viewpoints on why the Ku Klux Klan exists. If one actually allows oneself to think about it, the threat the White man feels to his money and his women almost makes perfect sense of a senseless way of life.

When Billy is finished with her, it is Derrick and Eric's turn. They do Sabrina together, like two panting dogs that have never seen a female in heat. Poor old Perdell Jakes is gone, and they will probably miss him more than most.

They are the worst of the lot by far. Even so, to Sabrina Martin, they have all become one. The brothers beat the already brutalized woman to the edge of oblivion and demand oral sex, while holding a knife to her throat. They will run nothing short of foul when she refuses their advances. Sabrina is forced to her hands and knees so Eric could have anal sex with her.

"Her pussy is all sloppy and used up," Eric says.

Derrick masturbates his unwashed penis in her swollen mouth while he holds the blade to her swollen-shut left eye. He threatens to cut it out if she even thinks about biting him.

After Derrick shoots his load, he manually moves Sabrina's puffy jaw up and down, demanding that she swallow it all. Otherwise, she will have to lick it from the dusty floor. She spits his bloody children into his face.

During a final moment of valiant desperation, Sabrina grabs the knife when Derrick is distracted and tries to drive it into her own heart. Derrick wrestles it from her weak, feeble hands.

"Please," she gasps. "Just kill me. God…just…kill me." Sabrina continues to beg for death while, from somewhere far away, Eric pounds into her with relentless abandon. She is only faintly aware of the excruciating pain he is causing her. By now, she is too far away to care.

Sabrina Martin sees the world float away on the frosted waves of a murky sea, where she hopes to find her end. She lays twitching on the dirty floor of the shack, bleeding from every orifice of her body;

yet, oblivious to all sensation. All she can think of is the child she will surely lose. She has always dreamt of girls, but secretly wishes for a strong, healthy son.

Derrick and Eric Glover emerge into the darkness of the new night, feeling refreshed and very manly. Each is swollen with the pride of having proven themselves the better men. Devoid of all feelings of guilt, they share a few racial jokes at any Black man's expense.

ତ୍ତ

Jeremiah and Keith find that the old logging road nearly leads right up to the camp's entrance. The truck is inside the forest about one-hundred yards from the front gate. They move closer on horse-back to survey the compound with binoculars before it gets too dark.

The two guards overlooking the entrance of the main gate have to be taken out quietly at the same time. Keith and Jeremiah see very few people. They mark what looks like a fuel dump, which Jeremiah intends to blow after taking the gate down. They are dressed in black. What better color in which to die?

After moving the Hummer into the closest position possible, they walk to the edge of the forest where they load the crossbows with the highly lethal shredder tips screwed on. After several deep breaths to calm their nerves, they aim at their respective targets. Jeremiah will take out the farther of the two because he is more experienced at using this weapon. On the count of three, the quiet night air tolerates the subtle zipping whir that ends with two distinctive thuds.

The furthest guard is struck in the back and falls from the tower. Meanwhile, the second man has no time to react before Keith's arrow crashes through the sternum and his spinal column. It exits, sticking into the wooden post he has been leaning against. Unable to cry out, he stares into space and convulses until death claims him.

The shaft of the arrow holds him upright so that he appears to be standing on his own.

Jeremiah allows the wasted air in his lungs to taste freedom. "You got him dead center," he says. "I knew I taught you well. It was a very good shot, Keith."

"Let's go." Keith is all business; he has no time for taking bows.

Jeremiah heads back to the truck while Keith rides his horse far enough into the forest to circle the camp, undetected. He waits anxiously for Jeremiah's show.

Derrick and Eric look across the compound at Tommy's lonely silhouette glued to one of the mess hall windows. Derrick snickers. "Go get him. He should have a little taste of her, too."

Eric trots to the building where the boy sits in a weird daze, which he quickly puts to an end. Eric drags Tommy to the shack where he is compelled to do it with the woman. They threaten to hurt him if he refuses because that is what punks, who don't want any free pussy, must like.

He fights them off and runs.

Governor Martin calls Mississippi to tell Krantz of the woman's capture, but the doctor tells him that Ezra is near the end and unable to speak. He places the phone to Ezra's ear, so Jud could tell him the news.

Krantz tries to talk, but he only manages to cough up some of the putrid brown phlegm that is slowly crawling to the top of his lungs. A sickly smile visits the old man's quivering lips as he lay in a pool of sweat, burning up from the inside out like a living ball of fire.

After telling him the news, Martin goes to his quarters and puts on a new robe. Ironically, this one is black, with red and green trim; the markings of a dragon.

Jeremiah is at the gate where he backs the Hummer close to the fencing. He threads two long chains through the meshing, and then he uses the hook end of a hammer to pull the cover of the rear light away. He yanks the guts out and pulls the wiring for the light from beneath the truck. After touching them together to be sure that they are not live, he tapes them to the side of the truck near the gas tank.

Derrick catches Tommy and drags him back to the shed, where they open the door just long enough to throw him and a flashlight to the floor inside. Sabrina, now conscious, immediately begins to scream while backing herself into a corner.

She begs, "Please don't hurt me anymore, daddy. Please don't. I've been a good girl. Please, daddy. Please!"

The flashlight rolls to a halt on the floor, settling its beam on Sabrina's badly mauled face. Her left eye is swollen shut and the other is halfway there. Her once pouting lips are ragged, torn, and bleeding. Through them, Tommy can see that she has lost a few teeth and he notices that blood also comes from her ears. He is sick to his stomach while she shies away from the light, naked and wretched beyond belief. The stench of vomit causes his eyes to water.

Outside, the brothers are banging on the walls of the shack and shouting, "Go get 'em, tiger. Better late than never. If you come out of there still a virgin, your corn hole won't be for long!"

Tommy looks back at the door and crawls toward Sabrina, but she screams louder still. He tries desperately to quiet her. "No. Please don't scream. I won't hurt you, honest I won't," he whispers. "Please be quiet."

The youngster removes his red and black flannel shirt, offering it to her. Sabrina takes it, finally, but she does not trust him. He picks up the flashlight so she can see his face and moves closer, but she still screams in her private terror. He persists until she finally allows him to help with the shirt.

The brothers are laughing hysterically. Derrick says, "Did you hear that last scream? He's got it in now and stroking for glory. Go, Tommy!"

Eric feels the drying blood and shit on his penis cracking as his erection threatens to return. There just might be time for another go at her.

Keith's blood runs cold when he hears Sabrina's cries. Deep down inside, he knows she is being tortured or, possibly, worse. His mind refuses to go any further.

He comes as close as he can to the fence, where he eases off the saddle and ties the horse he appeases to silence with a feed bag of oats. He readies the crossbow. Knowing that he must move fast, he leans the shotgun against the fence and locks onto his target with another shredder stuck in the ground in front of him. The shotgun is there in case he is not given a chance to reload and fire the second arrow to kill them both quietly.

Martin comes out of the door with St. John, Joe Mills, and the Fellows brothers. The rest of the Orphan Squad, and the hunters who followed them from Caribou Lake, riff-raff really, are summoned from the barracks to witness the execution of Sabrina Martin.

St. John is ragging on Joe Mills by saying, "Your trigger-happy rednecks have probably let the lawyer and that feeble old man kick their butts again. Deny it if you like, but where are they?" As they walk outside, wagering against Willard's last insult, the front gate and part of the fencing just fly away!

Jeremiah jams the Hummer into first gear and let her rip, yanking away the gate and fencing, which are connected to the guard towers.

The wooden fixtures topple and disintegrate on the ground with a gravel-shattering crunch.

Martin and his bunch run toward the front gate, fearing that those trigger-happy rednecks have failed the simple assignment on the mountain.

Jeremiah stops the truck, leaving it to idle in neutral as he exits the cab with the rifle. He pulls the wires free and shoves them into the open gas tank before running into the woods. He hustles along the fence without being seen, wanting to watch the fireworks, but he has another job to do.

Five full cans of gasoline and one of kerosene are in the back of the hummer where Jeremiah has dumped an entire bucket of roofing tacks and nails for shrapnel. The caps of the fuel cans are cracked open to allow the fumes to build up in the truck since it is the fumes that will ignite.

Inside the shack, Tommy sobs, "This just ain't right. They shouldn't have done you this way. It just ain't right. They say that Black people are the animals, but they did far worse. I didn't want to shoot that old-timer. Honest, I didn't."

Sabrina Martin sobs as she begs him to help her escape. To her surprise, he agrees, as long as he can go with. Now, they hear it.

When Keith squeezes the trigger, the arrow finds its mark with deadly accuracy. It bores through the upper thoracic vertebrae of Derrick's spine. Because of its upward trajectory, it stops just after the arrow's head shoots out of his Adam's apple. When Derrick's head droops, the four-pronged head punctures the floor of his mouth, slicing through his tongue like butter. He goes down with his mouth glued to his chest. All sensation is gone, as if his body is disconnected from his brain. As his startled brother watches him fall, Derrick rolls forward and eats his last supper; dirt, garnished with gravel sauce.

Eric Glover runs to his sibling, reaching for the shaft protruding from his back. He looks up just in time to see death coming as the arrow pierces his throat and explodes out the side of his neck. He feels a burning tug as the four prongs take a chunk of his jugular with it. Falling slowly to the ground with his blood gushing into the air, he clutches at his throat. The second arrow comes like lightning, perforating his liver and kidney. The arrowhead buries into a four by six inch post on the other side of the camp just as he wilts to his knees. His assassin watches as the life exits his convulsing body. Keith Williams quickly puts the wire cutters to use, making a doorway into Camp Hell.

Martin and the others reach the gate, spitting curses. Billy Fellows looks at his brother and says, "Diversion!"

George barks, "You men protect Governor Martin. We'll get him!" With weapons in hand, they run into the woods after spotting Jeremiah's tracks in the ditch on the right hand side of the road.

Joe Mills approaches cautiously, but no one's inside. He points his handgun into the window, hoping to find someone crouching on the floor. He curses the black son of a bitch's soul from here to eternity. Following his tirade, he orders someone to move the mess from the road.

Knowing Billy and George are after the saboteur, he turns away. He is merely a few yards from the truck when Ralph Oakley of the Orphan Squad jumps behind the wheel of the Hummer, hitting the brake pedal and igniting the fuel tank of the truck. There are seven men standing around the truck when it blows. From where Martin and St.

John stand, they witness a spectacular explosion that sends the vehicle flying into the air and them reeling in its percussive wake.

The open tanks of gas and kerosene go instantly, sending a hail of shrapnel and fire out in a pie shaped pattern, killing Mills and the other lackeys standing nearby. They are scorched and blinded. Ultimately, they all perish from having their bodies ripped to shreds by flying roofing tacks and sixteen-penny nails. Ralph Oakley simply ceases to exist, his reward for volunteering.

Martin and Willard do not escape injury. However, they are not too severely damaged, having been far enough away to survive the worst of the violent blast.

Keith yanks at the door of the shack and sees Tommy, whom he knocks to the floor. He draws his knife to kill him quietly. Tommy struggles, but Keith pins him down with his palm covering the kid's mouth to prevent him from crying out. Sabrina is terrified, but she manages to scream for him to stop once Keith no longer looks like a monster in her eyes.

Keith takes one look at her bruised, swollen face in the beam of light and raises his arm to drive the knife deep into the boy's chest. Tommy is paralyzed, quivering as the rabid man stares directly into his young eyes.

"No! No, Keith. He promised to help me escape. Please don't hurt him. It's…it's not his fault, Keith," she says with her voice trailing off.

Keith turns him loose and goes to her, only to discover that he does not know where he should touch her. His hands pause in midair, wanting desperately to hold her, but Sabrina looks as if she hurts all over.

A twisted mixture of relief and shame washes over her, so she breaks down and cries with her face turned away from the light. A deep need forces her to reach blindly for her lover, although a part of her wishes that he is not truly there.

Keith Williams remembers to move when her trembling touch meets his paralyzed hands. She turns to him with averted eyes, putting her arms around him ever so slowly. Keith returns the embrace, but he is crushed inside. He is caught in that unavoidable place where all men go when things of such horrific magnitude happen to the women in their lives. He feels that he has somehow caused the misery befallen the woman he so dearly loves. The dam breaks and he aches for her as they weep in one another's arms. Bright moonlight comes through the open doorway of the shack to illuminate their shared anguish as Keith gently strokes Sabrina's blood-caked hair.

Jeremiah has set fire to the fuel dump. He is beating it back through the woods when he falls, tripping over something that rises out of the darkness. Unluckily, he has crashed at the feet of Billy and George. One of them kicks him in the face with a booted foot. They pick him up and drag him to the front of the compound where Jud Martin is pulling tacks from his bleeding leg. St. John's left arm is riddled with them. It is the very arm he raised to protect his face when the explosion occurred. Bits of burning debris is scattered all around them.

Keith asks Tommy if he still wants to help, and if he can drive. The boy's answer is, "Yes, sir." Keith tells him to find a vehicle that will get them all out of here; a truck, preferably.

Tommy takes a second to survey the area for anyone, who may have heard Sabrina's plea for his life, before running to the garage for the big Chevy. A moment later, he pulls up alongside the shack, taking great care not to look at the two bodies on the ground nearby, lest he should freeze up, again.

Keith carries Sabrina outside and puts her in the backseat. He is about to get behind the wheel when the voice of Jud Martin comes to him from a bullhorn. To Sabrina, his voice is the sound of one-thousand fingernails raking along the surface of one-thousand chalkboards, and she reacts as if it is a physical touch.

Martin is still at the head of the compound with the bullhorn in one hand, aiming a gun at Jeremiah's head with the other. He says, "Hey, Mr. Lawyer, I know you're out there somewhere. You should know I've got the old man."

Keith flinches. "Shit, they have my grandfather." When he looks back at Sabrina, sadness fills his heart at the possibility of never seeing her ever again. He asks the boy if there is a back way out.

Tommy says, "Yes, sir. It loops around the southeast side of the camp through the woods before reconnecting with the main road about a quarter-mile from the camp's primary entrance."

"Good. Drive. Go quickly!" he says to Tommy.

Sabrina pleads with Keith not to stay, but he cannot abandon Jeremiah. He kisses her and holds her tight for too brief a moment. She clings to him, but Keith tells Tommy to take her to a hospital immediately.

While prying her arms away, he says, "You are my heart, Sabrina. I love you, baby, but I have to save my grandfather."

She is distressed beyond conveyance, looking down at her stomach. Touching herself there, she whimpers, "The baby, our baby. I'm going to lose our child, Keith. I can feel him dying inside of me. I'm sorry. I'm so sorry." She looks as if she is a child herself.

His mind does funny things to his eyes. "Our baby? Sabrina, you're pregnant?"

All she can do is hold herself and whimper, "I'm so sorry. I'm so sorry, I was a good girl. I was…good…"

Keith is silent, dumfounded by the news so untimely in its arrival. Tears begin to well I his eyes.

The fuel dump explodes, tossing barrels into the sky like giant bottle rockets. It takes the barracks, garage, supply shack, and most of the mess hall with it.

He snaps out of his daze and barks, "Go. Go now!"

Tommy turns the wheel hard to the right and floors it, raising a suffocating cloud of dust and gravel to shoot through the flames, racing for the back gate.

Sabrina holds herself as if she is rocking a cranky child to sleep. Then she looks back and waves to the man she loves, the man whom she is probably leaving to die in her stead. She continues to wave even when the camp is far behind them and Keith has long faded from view. She still sees him there, dressed in black with a shotgun and a crossbow in his hands.

She waves at his ghostly image until the cramp in her stomach rolls through her like a tidal surge. Sabrina cries out in utter pain.

The battered woman doubles over in the fetal position, bleeding badly when Tommy could finally bring himself to look. This young man is a cauldron of conflicting emotion, and guilt is the most prevalent of these. Somehow, he has been a part of the madness that now engulfs and slivers her soul in two.

Billy and George are binding Martin and Willard's wounds after plucking the rest of the tacks and nails from their bleeding limbs. No gauze is used, just duct tape.

The bullhorn that fell from one of the guard towers, rolled near Martin's feet during the blast. He now uses it to say, "If you don't show yourself, I'm going to kill him!"

Keith is at the far side of the shack where he reloads the crossbow and checks the shotgun. He peeks around the corner at the approaching men, wishing he had kept one of the M-16 rifles he placed in the front seat of the truck. He cannot chance the shotgun even though it is set on full choke. The pattern spread at this distance will most likely claim Jeremiah's life as well. He could see the gun at the old man's head and he curses himself for being shortsighted. Keith is stuck. He knows they will cut him down the moment he shows himself, and he hasn't stayed behind to die in vain.

The Fellows brothers want to fan out in search, but Willard's cowardice is showing. He forbids them to leave the group, citing the need to protect the next leader of the nation should Williams attack.

Governor Martin shouts, "Derrick, keep your eyes open." A moment later he says, "Do you hear me?"

When there is no report, Willard says, "Damn it, those piss-poor cowards ran off!"

"They're probably already dead," Billy whispers to his brother.

Martin is using Jeremiah as a shield when he says, "This is no trick, Williams. I really do have your grandfather here. Can't you see him? I suggest you show yourself, so we can discuss this rationally. If it's proof you want…" He shoves the bullhorn before Jeremiah's bleeding lips and says, "Say something."

Jeremiah refuses, directing his voice away from the microphone to say, "Why should I? You are just gonna kill us both, so fuck all you redneck crackers!" They stop inching forward and Martin rams the noisemaker into Jeremiah's kidney until he goes to his knees. He is hoisted from the gravel and Martin places the bullhorn back in position for Jeremiah to speak into it.

This time, he does. "I'm done for, Keith. Run, boy! They'll shoot you the minute you show yourself!" Martin snatches it away and shoots Jeremiah in the leg.

Jeremiah does not move when he falls to the ground, despite the burning. Keith thinks he is dead. When he raises the crossbow, the low battery indicator is blinking red. It dies just as he tries to sight in. Filled with rage, Keith yanks the trigger to send an arrow fleeting through the air. It hits one of the targets, lifting the unimportant man on Jud Martin's left from his feet.

Keith is holding back a scream just as his grandfather is doing. Jeremiah remains motionless on the ground. He is playing possum because he wants Keith to flee, which he will only do if there is no one to save in the face of these overwhelming odds.

Keith Williams is morose. For a faint moment, he wants to run into the open with his shotgun blazing while his opponents are confused and leery. However, he lines up a shot from his current position instead. He is aiming at Jud Martin, knowing that the spread pattern will claim others as well.

"We need to fan out and find him. We're too exposed, standing in the open like this," Billy recommends.

With the brightness of the moonlight and the fires blazing unchecked, George Fellows sees the sniper and yells as he fires at the corner of the shack. Again, Keith yanks the trigger instead of squeezing. His shot runs errant, but fatally wounds the two remaining orphans of Camp Righteous Kill.

They begin to fire their weapons at the plywood shack. With wood splintering all around, Keith hits the deck. He drags the shotgun and crossbow as he crawls to the rear of the building to slip through the fence. He fires a few rounds of suppression fire as he leaps the ditch and runs into the trees. The horse is still tied and anxious to be away from all those terribly loud human noises. Weapons' fire ricochets around Keith until he disappears.

He rides like the wind up the ravine toward Big Bear, hoping that they will follow him back to his own turf.

Keith Williams grieves the loss of his grandfather, who is dead to him. Possibly, because of him. Greycloud was murdered, and Sabrina brutally raped and beaten. And now, he's running away from the men who did these horrendous things. Leaving the disposition of Jeremiah's body in the hands of men who will probably throw him in a ditch rather than give him a proper burial does not sit well with Keith Williams. He hates himself for it, although he hates them much more.

He swears an oath of vengeance. If he cannot carry it out by the rules of his own two hands, then the law will be his weapon. And he means to see them all fry.

Keith pushes the frothing horse hard for the rock face under the shimmering moon. Inside, he roars. The exhausted horse suddenly falls out from under him! They both go sprawling as he reaches a mild slope on the rock face and slides a few yards before finding a foothold.

When Williams gets up and looks at the lame animal, he apologizes for riding it so hard. He removes its saddle and takes the bit from its mouth. He searches for the shotgun, which slid all the way to the bottom where it smashed to bits. That $850 piece of beautiful machinery will fire nevermore.

With only the nine-millimeter and the crossbow, he runs on, climbing the rest of the way on foot. Keith knows the Klan has to pursue him up this mountain.

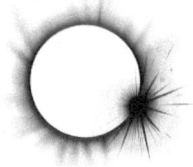

Chapter 30

ONWARD TO GLORY

Tommy was smart enough to disable the camp's other vehicles to prevent pursuit. He quickly ripped the distributor caps and plug wires out. The young man also saw to it that at least two tires of each vehicle were damaged, irreparably.

Governor Judson Martin is hopping mad when he realizes that both Sabrina and the lawyer have gotten away. After a body count, in retrospect, they realize that during the chaos set off by Jeremiah Williams, they heard a vehicle leaving the compound. However, Keith Williams stayed behind because of his grandfather. One of their own has betrayed them.

Martin contacts Sheriff Milt Percy about Sabrina's escape, suggesting that he check any doctors or hospitals in the area. She will undoubtedly seek medical attention. She is to be apprehended, and brought to him ASAP. Sheriff Percy is extremely willing to comply.

When Governor Martin walks out of HQ, which is just beginning to burn, he faces the six men that are left. He wants to know how something like this could happen, cursing Joe Mills for the incompetence of the men he boasted to have trained.

He approaches Jeremiah and kicks him in the groin and stomach several times. The poor old man lay on the ground, helpless under the vicious attack.

After venting a small portion of his wrath, Martin kneels and says to Jeremiah, "You and yours will suffer this night. For all the hell that you have caused me, you will pay ten times over. When we catch that high-classed nigger, and we will catch him, I am going to skin him alive. The only thing you will really have to worry about is whether or not you'll live long enough to see it. I know he probably went back to your cabin. Where else would he go?" Martin slaps Jeremiah, who is barely conscious. "Isn't that right, old-timer? That's where he went, didn't he?"

Jeremiah nods an affirmation. The whimpered words, "Keith, I'm so sorry, son. Forgive me. So sorry," brings a wry smile to Martin's face.

"Excellent, you're cooperating. Maybe you're not so stupid after all. If you keep up the good work, maybe I'll let you live, old man. After all, this was never really about anyone other than the woman. If you convince your grandson to tell us where she was taken, you can go on living out your lives as long as you promise to say nothing."

With the left side of his face in the dirt and gravel, Jeremiah says with a slight measure of defiance, "Yea. Yes, sir. Rapists and murderers are known for their instantaneous ability to change their ways by simply lying to themselves and everyone else until they actually believe it. The term false contrition never meant anything to me until now, you lying bastard."

Jud Martin says, calmly, "You will live to regret turning down my absolution, old man."

Jeremiah Williams smiles. "These here mountains have a cosmic way of meeting out its own justice, govna. I believe that because I live here with the God or nature. Before I die up yonder, I will be the one who gets the last few laughs."

Martin sneers at the stubborn man, but leaves Jeremiah on the ground. He limps back up the steps. Blame it on the moon or the impending eclipse, but there is madness in Jud Martin's eyes that he embraces fully.

Willard St. John recognizes that look from his own face-slapping sessions. Only this is far worse.

Standing on the top step of the smoldering building, with demonic gray smoke billowing from its eaves, Martin raises his hands to the heavens as if to summon the wind. There is an unusual mixture of smiling benevolence and passionate rage etched upon his face. Such visual contrast causes the next few moments to haunt and enthrall them all.

He decrees, "Tonight, oh Lord, we shall fulfill your command-ments. We shall wear the Holy cloth and commence your work, though it means spilling blood for blood!" He looks upon his army of six and says, "Tonight, in the finest of Klan tradition, we shall ride beneath the light of the moon with torches ablaze. Tonight, we will turn animal. Tonight…we hunt!"

From where he lays face down in the dust and gravel, Jeremiah peers up at this fanatic. He is disturbed by the power Martin's diatribe seems to have over the others. The onlookers are mesmerized as the moonlight transforms those arrogant eyes. They are hypnotized by Martin's venomous words, which passionately claim jurisdiction over life and death as if given by God himself. Evil seems to resonate within them all. Even George and Billy feel and display signs of awe. No longer in doubt, their total allegiance is his. Their very lives are his.

The earth's dark shadow will soon fall upon the face of the moon, charging ancient themes of evil. It carries them all into the sweeping throes of a bloodlust that will not be denied. Keith Williams is a dead man.

Seven Klansmen and a hostage now ride through the night. Martin wears black while the others adorn white as they push the last of the camp's horses north through the ravine. Their destiny is Big Bear and glory.

Lathered in sweat, froth running from their mouths, the horses stride onward. Beneath the light of the high full moon and torches, their coats are a deathly shimmer. This procession resembles the medieval witch-hunts of old, echoing like an avalanche through the valley. No animal dares sleep with the approach of such angry thunder.

Jeremiah, with all of his discomforts, rides willingly. He does not attempt to hinder their progress because he can hardly wait to see some of these men die before his time comes. Although he feels with a certainty that his time is nigh, he fears not.

For Jeremiah Williams, this is not nighttime deep within the heart of the valley of the shadow of death. It is the moment before a dawn, in which, he will hear the birds singing and see grass swaying in the warm breezes high up on some pristine plateau. He will see Greycloud, again, having made his peace with God.

 exo

The deputy has been dozing in his police cruiser at the foot of the road leading to Big Bear from Route 112. His sandwich bags and balled up scraps of tin foil lay next to empty packages of doughnuts on the passenger side. His stomach still growls for something more substantial. He is not usually the type of man who goes to sleep hungry, but weariness and boredom are factors.

He is here to make sure no one cuts through the barricade of trees to gain access to the highway, but he is dreaming about last Thanksgiving's dinner when the big Chevy blows by and rocks his car.

Milt Percy calls Farley Barton on the radio. When Farley finally wakes up, the sheriff orders him to get his ass in gear and beat it back to town. Forty-five minutes later, he will meet Sheriff Percy at the town doctor's office.

Dr. Phillip Crenshaw is seventy-two-years-old, with slouching posture. He has a chubby little belly. His thinning grey hair is swept over the top to cover the area of his head less endowed. He wears round spectacles and a kindly smile when most of his patients come for an appointment.

Crenshaw has been the only physician in Caribou Lake for nearly 30 years, and his eventual retirement will coincide with the opening of the new hospital. In all of this time, however, he's never seen or treated a case in his two-bed clinic that remotely resembles the condition of Sabrina Martin.

Upon their arrival, Tommy begs him not to call the sheriff. Tommy is so distraught about it that the doctor thinks it wise to comply because the frightened kid obviously has the inside track on things.

Doc Crenshaw is used to mending broken limbs or dealing with high blood pressure and arthritis. On occasion, he delivers a baby or two. He is not prepared for things like gang rape, forced sodomy, or even assault and battery of this magnitude, so he immediately calls for the Medivac chopper at Window Lake.

Sabrina is on the table in the examining room, retching in pain. While writhing, she begs, "Please—please—don't let my baby die. Please don't let my son die, doctor!"

"Ma'am, can you tell me who did this to you," Doc Crenshaw asks.

In a lucid moment, Sabrina Martin asks, "Please administer five milligrams of the synthetic Progetogen…Allylestrenol. Five milligrams, please."

Dumbfounded, Doctor Crenshaw looks away.

She screams as bitter agony raps her insides. Sabrina Martin is hemorrhaging profusely, and Doctor Crenshaw does not have the heart to tell her that she has probably already lost her child or she is in the process of doing so. He is very sad for this ravaged woman, but helpless to turn back the clock even if he possessed such drugs. The patient is in so much distress, he thinks it best to sedate her.

The doctor has just given Sabrina the shot when Milt Percy and Farley Barton slip in the door. Sabrina sees the look in their eyes and knows that her father sent them; she knows they are Klan. When they grab her, she struggles, but the Demerol is already taking hold and spiriting her away to a very quiet place.

When the good doctor protests, he is simply backhanded for his effort. After crashing to the floor, he offers no more interference. Doc Crenshaw is a good-natured old man, but he is not of the Klan. He cringes in a corner as they haul his unconscious patient out the back door to where they parked.

Farley Barton is opening the back door of the cruiser when Tommy's voice startles them from the shadows. The dog-tired kid has been snoozing restlessly amidst savage dreams in the front seat of the Chevy. He could no longer stand the sight of blood, and Sabrina's pleading only added to his helpless guilt. There is no denying that he has witnessed horrible things and his effort to help may have come too late, but not again.

When the surprised law enforcement officers spin around, the young man is pointing an M-16 rifle at them. They are somewhat relieved upon recognition, until Tommy says, "They can't have her no more."

Sheriff Percy glares at him and shouts, "What the hell do think you're doing, boy? You're one of us. You know we can't just let her go, so put the gun down."

Tommy watches them closely. Farley moves away from the sheriff while easing his hand toward his weapon. The deputy says, "You look here, kid. Be sensible and do as the sheriff says. You know he's right."

Sheriff Percy lets Sabrina slump to the ground and shouts, "Do it, or I'll be forced to cut you down. There's no need to die for this white trash bitch, so don't force my hand, son!" His voice contains a hint of pleading, but it carries a double-edged threat.

The kid's heart races away as he squints at his elders. An adrenaline-driven reality suddenly surges forth; this is no longer a bad dream. When the full force instinct of fight or flight kicks in, Tommy takes two steps back and says, "You can't have her, and I ain't one of you no more. I know how to use this thing, mister, so don't do it!"

Farley goes for his gun and Tommy shoots him dead. When the angry shots ring out, Farley is thrown backward into the very door he just opened to deposit Sabrina Martin's limp form.

Meanwhile, the sheriff doesn't exactly draw his weapon. He simply slides it out enough to slip his index finger over the trigger. His thumb depresses the hammer at the same time. He swivels the

Colt in its holster and shoots from the hip. The bullet goes right through the base of the holster!

Both the sheriff and Tommy are slammed backward. They shot one another, but the kid's rifle is set on fully automatic. Tommy hits the sheriff in the chest and face just as he is thrown to the ground. The echoes die quickly, and then there is silence.

After his fear subsides, Doc Crenshaw runs outside to do his duty. He checks for a pulse in Farley Barton. Finding none, he hurdles Sabrina to turn the sheriff over, but needs not have bothered. Half of the sheriff's face is gone. Crenshaw checks Sabrina by looking under the gown he and the boy managed to get on her when they first arrived. She is still such a mess that it is hard to tell if she has been hit by errant bullets. Sabrina is okay, as it were.

When Tommy groans from the dark lawn in the shadow of the building, the doctor hurries to him saying, "Oh dear Lord. Oh my God."

Doc Crenshaw feels such shame when he looks at the brave young man. He knows that the kid will probably lose his left arm. The sheriff's hollow point forty-five tore most of the left bicep away when it exploded through the muscular tissue to shatter the bone.

Though facing a few challenges, Crenshaw kicks himself in the rear because the boy will survive if he moves fast. He uses his belt as a tourniquet on Tommy, stemming the flow of blood. Though it takes some doing, the frail old man drags them both inside and goes to work. All the long while, he keeps an ear to the sky.

Tommy Swinton, a brave young man whose emancipation from the Ku Klux Klan comes at a very high price, is oblivious to the fact that he has just had his sixteenth birthday. Nor does he know his real last name. Sadly, that bit of information may have died with the sheriff and Joe Mills.

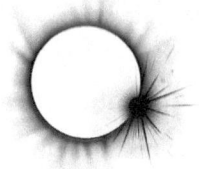

Chapter 31

ON TOTEM ROCK

As a whippoorwill calls to its mate, Dingahay smells blood and backs away. The drums are throbbing. Living flames blaze into the night sky. Down below, Keith sees eyes of black and gold. When he gazes upward, his heart races in the presence of a towering grizzly, whose iron teeth glisten in the brightness of the moon. The beast advances on him with a bellowing roar that shakes the earth and the air!

Keith Williams points the gun in the darkness, ready to kill anything that moves. He is soaked in sweat, listening to his own heart pounding over the echo of heavy breathing in the barn. The bad dream does not fade quickly.

He gets to his feet, climbs down from the hayloft and takes a cautious look outside to be sure the coast is clear before walking outside where the night air is cool.

Keith looks at War Paint and Apollo, which are saddled because he plans to ride down the mountain in search of Sabrina. One horse carries a bedroll. The other carries a pup tent because he may have to camp in the forest before reaching safety. He cannot expect help from unfamiliar people in this vast territory now that it is abundantly clear that anyone can be a member of the Ku Klux Klan.

He worries about Sabrina and the baby, but changed his mind about leaving for a couple of good reasons. He knows that he will never make it out of this country with those gun-carrying lunatics hot on his trail, and they are surely on the way. The most compelling reason for staying is the desire to hurt them. Consumed by an overwhelming need to lead them to the traps, he waits in the name of vengeance; the righteous kill.

He walks to the woods on the other side of the cabin where he looks down the eastern slope. They are coming. As the torches throughout the shadows mark their distance, the horses' hooves scrape and click on the stone below. Yes, they are finally coming!

Keith moves back into the shadows on the northeast end of the cabin, just below Greycloud's bedroom window. His heart thuds as he waits for them to get closer. When he can hear the labored breathing of their horses, he fires a few near misses. Martin's horse rears, throwing him to the ground.

Keith runs around the north end of the cabin to the front where he stops just long enough to tug on the strings, which pull the light switches downward. The locked cabin is now cast in total darkness.

Jeremiah reaches for the reins with his bound hands and yanks them free from the leading saddle in the confusion. When the old, cracked leather snaps midway, he grabs the horse by the mane and digs his heels into the mount's flanks, despite the painful leg wound.

Bending as far forward as he dares, he spurs the horse northward toward the dense brush.

Keith's only living relative makes a run for it, but his heart stammers when George Fellows suddenly yanks down on the horse's harness. Closer to the bit where the leather is still strong, he clamps down, digs his heels in, and steels his bulging muscles for the strain.

Jeremiah's horse takes an abrupt bow, tumbling head over heels. The old man is thrown clear, but his landing is not much better than the animal's. He tried when the opportunity presented itself, but his effort only gains him more pain. Before his head clears, he is dragged back to the others.

While Keith moves unseen, just as darkness touches the outer rim of the moon, the Klansmen take cover to return fire at the cabin. With Jeremiah Williams secure, Billy and George begin to move.

Billy shouts, "He's pinned himself down in the cabin. Let's move it."

Martin drags Jeremiah in the rear as they converge on his home. Billy Joe signals his brother by pointing to himself and then the kitchen door as he had done before. Once he is in position, he radios George and they go on the count of three, simultaneously kicking in the front and back doors.

The Winchester and the M-16 explode, bringing sudden bursts of light to the darkened doorways of the cabin. While the Winchester only fires one deadly round, the M-16 wails until its magazine is completely empty.

The 30 ought 6 Winchester's single report rips a small tear in Billy's abdomen and a gaping hole as it blast through the spine. He is riveted to the ground where he will slowly die, while calling his brother's name.

George, on the other hand, is riddled with bullets that force his legs to do a jig while he is driven backwards by each new dance partner. Nearly every bullet hits him, filling his dance card permanently. He is dead on his feet by the time he finally hits the ground. The Fellows brothers have officially stormed their last frontier.

Jeremiah's hands are tied behind his back to dissuade the temptation to grab at a weapon. The bullhorn hangs around his neck like a cowbell, but the joke of it is lost in this most distressing moment. Disgusted at this point, Jud Martin uses the old man as a human shield with a gun trained on his head.

Willard St. John, who is cringing beside a tree, curses at what he just witnessed. He shouts at George to get up. This should not have happened. They were imperviously durable and, seemingly, indestructible men. He has never known them to be careless enough to stroll into a rank amateur's trap.

Martin's eyes inadvertently reflect a sudden disquiet as he cries, "That son of a bitch booby trapped the fucking cabin!"

With the brothers gone, the odds suddenly improve for the quarry. When Jeremiah makes the mistake of giggling, he is severely punished.

Only Governor Jud Martin, Willard St. John, Rudy Wilson, Tom Jason, and a man named Mark Olsen are left. The latter three are residents of the Caribou Lake area, who wish they had not come along for this little coon hunt.

After the fear washes away, their anger returns. Two more of their comrades have been slain at the hands of that cagey, Black bastard, but he will soon be made to suffer untold for his blatant transgressions against the brotherhood.

With spittle flying from his politically polished lips, Martin shouts at the cabin, "You're going to pay for that shit, boy!" He looks sharply at Mark Olsen and says, "We'll burn him out."

Just as Olsen tosses two torches on the roof, Keith answers by firing a few rounds from the trail to Totem Rock, taking them all by surprise. Until now, they still believed him to be hiding somewhere inside the dark cabin.

After the Klan's dwindling war party finishes eating dirt, and the echoes finally play out, they can hear Keith running. They fire in his general direction.

Driven by rage and hate, Rudy Wilson and Tom Jason are the first to their feet. "Come on," Rudy Wilson shouts. "Let's get that coon!" They both charge up the path to glory.

Tom Jason had turned an ankle by hastily dismounting his frightened horse upon their arrival, so he is much slower. Rudy Wilson is in perfect health, however. His running stride is wide, so he misses the first tripwire when he hurdles a small rock.

Tom Jason is not so lucky, though. His hurt foot catches on the cord strung across the path. The crossbow, contrary to its design, slips to a downward angle. It shifts just as the trigger pulls, allowing it to fire its single projectile towards the ground. The crossbow is not supposed to move, but Tom Jason's luck is so bad that the arrow races toward his feet where it strikes the same rock that might have saved Rudy Wilson's life seconds before. There is a single spark, as metal strikes stone. The arrow deflects upward between his legs, piercing his scrotum and puncturing his bladder!

Tom Jason's harsh shriek penetrates the night when the cold steel hits him. When his feet tangle with the tripwire, it causes him to sit on the arrow, driving it upward through the groin into his intestines. It nicks his heart before jamming into his clavicle. In an utterly painful moment, his mouth stands agape while his tongue now prances a muted dance. Clutching at his groin, he rolls to the side where he quakes to the end.

Rudy Wilson is much further up the trail when he hears Tom's shrill cry. He stops and turns, calling out for a man who is no longer there.

"Tom? Tom, are you okay? Tom!" No one answers.

His eyes jerk about as he steps backward, thinking that he hears a noise to his left. His knees threatened to buckle when he looks up and sees Jim Morton's dead stare as he hangs from a nearby tree, twisting slightly with the breeze. When Rudy stumbles backward, the two crisscrossed M-16 rifles come alive! The recoil action causes both rifles to slightly pivot back and forth, almost cutting Rudy Wilson in half as Teflon, lead, flesh, blood, and bone, meet most violently. Flesh, blood, and bone explode from his chest and stomach in wads.

When only smoke comes from the barrels of the two weapons, Rudy's top half nearly separates from his bottom half. The only things they now have in common are a few strips of tightly stretched skin. Steam rises from his innards in the cool night air.

By the time Martin, St. John, and Mark Olsen stop at the second of the two bodies, fear has already crept into their hearts. They are no longer the sure hunters they set out to be, with the death of four in a matter of minutes. This is no longer just a challenging hunt. The unexpected has happened since reaching this plateau. Surely, this is no ordinary nigger. He is too damn smart.

All it took were too hefty rocks tied to double slip-knotted M-16 triggers on full auto. When the tripwire pulled the rocks from the bough of trees into the tow of gravity, the twine cinched high on the triggers while the rocks plummeted to a sudden stop.

As they stand over Rudy Wilson, looking at the deadly rig, Mark Olsen begins to blubber. He shows the first shameful signs of a panic attack, mumbling, "Too much. This is too much!" While backing away, threatening to run off, he turns and pukes his guts out.

When the puking is over, the 35-year-old man-hunter sobs, "They were my friends. We grew up together, and now they're both dead. Fuck this shit. I'm getting the hell out of here!"

Willard St. John grabs him and slaps him for being cowardly. However, this is no implication that Willard has suddenly become courageous. His reasons for trying to control Olsen's panic are simple enough to equate. Firstly, there is safety in numbers. They still outnumber Williams three to one. They need to stick together. Secondly, Willard has been only one twig from snapping since George and Billy went down. Deep within his cowardly soul, he fears himself sure to follow if Mark Olsen blows his stack.

Willard snatches Olsen by the collar again. "Are you shittin' me? You think you're just gonna run out on us, now? Those are your friends down there and you want to run like a whipped pussy. Try it. Just try it. I'll shoot you myself!"

Jud Martin cuts the rope, but he does not attempt to stop Jimmy Morton's body from hitting the ground with a thud. He will receive no ceremony or words of kindness to see him to the afterlife. He failed in his mission, and the demise of a miserable failure is rarely celebrated, even among goodly Christians.

"But he just ain't human. I'm telling you, he just ain't human." Olsen struggles to resist the sight of another body.

Jud Martin takes hold of his heaving shoulders and says, "Just slow down for a second and take a breath. Listen to me now. We almost have him, son. I promise you, we'll get that bastard, so don't fall apart on me. If you turn jellyfish in front of this old, Black fucker, you will never see the same man in the mirror, again. Do not give him the satisfaction. God is on our side, but we must pass his tests throughout our lives. I will not allow anything to happen to you. You believe me, don't you, son?" Martin's eyes sparkle as he casts Mark Olsen under his spell.

Olsen grows calmer, looking down at the blood on his boots. His friend's blood. "You're right, this is God's work and I have to avenge them. I'm sorry, Mr. Martin. I'll be okay." Olsen looks at Jeremiah and takes instant offense at the smirk on that black face. He asks, "What the fuck are you looking at?"

With unwise hostility and ridicule, Jeremiah Williams says, "A sorry ass piece of shit tops my list of main ingredients right about now."

All three of them attack, punching and kicking Jeremiah until he lay curled up on the ground, gasping for air. Jeremiah loses four teeth by the end of this beating. His nose is broken, and at least two ribs are fractured. Along with the bullet hole in his leg, he is in sorry shape.

Moments later, and out of breath, Martin says, "We have to track him slowly to avoid walking into any traps. I can't believe he did all this in so little time." He glares at Jeremiah. "Get him to his feet. If there are more nasty little surprises, he'll walk ahead to find them for us."

☙❧

Keith passes near the pile of smoldering ashes that was once Greycloud. In the moonlight, he can see Greycloud's skull and the shimmer of the melted flask in the warm dust. His grandfather told him that the burial custom of the Mymawgua requires that their bodies are cremated. The remaining bones are crushed, and ground into a powder. The remains are scattered at the cliff's edge with the coming of the next dawn.

Keith looks down the trail, detecting the silhouettes of four pursuers. Although they are now moving at a considerably slower, less reckless pace, they are still the most relentless bunch of religious fanatics he has ever run into. He says to Greycloud's remains, "Well, enjoy the show. Take care of Jeremiah for me, Greycloud."

He crosses the granite slate, leaping over the stream. Stopping to snap a long branch from a tree, Keith Williams slaps at both rattlers. "That's it, get real mad. Maybe you'll get to bite a few bad people. Come on, motherfuckers, get good and mad," he goads.

Keith wisely decides not to stick around. The game is getting too dangerous. He plans to travel the southwest slope for a few hundred yards before climbing to double back to the cabin. If their horses are still around, he will force them to flee, along with War Paint and Apollo. He has already altered his escape plan, intending to drive the Bronco to the old logging road that they had used to get to the Klan's camp earlier. There are several areas where the old road comes very close to Route 112 and his chances at getting out before going all the way back to the burning camp are quite good.

With the moon half-gone as the sun, the earth, and the moon approach alignment, the total eclipse is imminent. Keith fires his last two rounds down the trail to make them angry again before heading southwest. He will go far enough to turn around without them suspecting what he plans to do. He had hoped to injure at least one of them, but accuracy with a pistol is next to impossible at that distance.

One of the bullets ricochets off a tree, striking Jeremiah in the head! It only grazes him, but he falls to the ground stunned. The three remaining captors laugh at the wounded man.

Mark Olsen says, "See there, old fella, your grandson is a blood-thirsty mad dog. He's trying to kill you, too!"

Jeremiah is dizzy when they get him to his feet, but his mind is still calculating. He thinks he can possibly use the injury to his advantage, so he easily forgives his grandson as they force him toward that sacred place.

Jeremiah recovers from the stinging head wound by the time they reach the granite slab, but continues to walk as if he is drunk. When the time is right, the old man moans and pretends to lose his balance. He stumbles forward with enough momentum to slide across the water to dry ground on the other side.

Martin bends at the waist and pants for oxygen in the thin mountain air. Although he is lathered in sweat and suffering from multiple aches and cramps, he also feels exhilarated. From this bent position, he smiles a crooked smile and uses the bullhorn he has beaten Jeremiah with to taunt Keith Williams.

"You see what you've done? You just shot your own grandfather. Now is that any way to show appreciation for those who helped raise you?" His words sweep through the air to find the attorney's unbelieving ears.

Keith stops running. "No, it can't be. They killed him!" He looks over his shoulders.

Back at the rock, Martin says, "You thought he was dead, didn't you? Well, I only shot him in the leg to shut him up, but you just shot him, again. What rotten luck!"

Keith sits on the ground and catches his breath. There is no motivation to trust Jud Martin after all he and his evil minions have done. He mutters to himself, "It's a trick. It's got to be a stinking trick!"

Mark Olsen says to Jeremiah, "Get your lazy ass up, boy!" as he approaches the stream. When he steps into the water, the moss-like slime that thrives there causes his feet to skid!

Mark falls on his back, sliding toward the cliff's edge. His weapon flies out of sight as he cries for help. He is picking up momentum when he catches hold of the stump of the broken totem and jerks to a stop with his feet dangling over the edge.

He breathes a sigh of relief, but something moves through his water-blurred vision. As he begins to pull himself up. He definitely feels something move when he reaches for the top of the stump. Suddenly, fiery fangs are driven into his hand. They are sharp, hot like freshly sterilized needles.

Mark freezes. His eyes come into focus just before the rattler bites his forearm. He screams when he looks into those black eyes. The next strike is to Mark's cheek, just below the right eye. This time, the serpent does not release right away. Instead, the rattler latches on. It wiggles its head and contracts its muscles to inject all the venom it can. The snake withdraws and hits Mark in the face once more as he struggles to hold on. When it comes again, Mark sees the brilliant, blurring white flesh of its mouth as its curved, one-inch fangs puncture his left eyeball!

With all that poison in him, his face puffs-up almost instantly, as Martin and Willard look on in disbelief. His hands are swelling as well, but he manages to grab the snake. It continues to backlash until he catches it behind the head and wrings it off. At this point, he is hanging over the cliff at his waistline. The twine that has been tied and duct-taped to the snake's tail is stretched to its maximum, and it is slipping. Mark reaches one hand into the air, begging for help.

Martin and St. John are horrified, watching helplessly while the rattler punished Mark Olsen for all the injustices it has suffered in a day.

Willard's mind fragments, sensing the need to save Olsen as the key to saving himself.

Willard leaps to the other side of the deadly stream. He runs toward Olsen, who is slipping away. Willard's rabid mind is frenzied and unraveling, watching the doomed volunteer as he goes to sleep. Olsen lets go and falls silently to the rocky landing below.

Willard almost feels it when every bone in Olsen's body shatters and splinters like pellets of shrapnel through his skin. He can almost hear the surge of blood gushing from Olsen's ears and eyes as he slams into a jagged boulder that bends him unnaturally.

In his hurry to reach Olsen, Willard feels as if he has wrenched something in his back, but he ignores the burning pain. Frozen in horror, he simply stares down into the black abyss. Then he begins to stomp the ground, shouting, "Fuck, fuck! I can't believe this shit! You're dead. Do you hear me, nigga? You are fucking dead!"

The insanity of the moment, tempered by his hatred and contempt for Keith Williams, sends him over the top. Willard runs past Jeremiah, kicking him in the face before blindly roaring off to the south after Keith. He runs yelling and screaming. Strangely enough, it is very easy to follow the lawyer's trail in the fading moonlight because no one ever goes beyond Totem Rock in this direction.

Soon, Willard begins to slobber like a rabid animal, completely unaware that he was bitten by a snake himself as he attempted to grab

Olsen's swollen hand. Willard's backside is warm with the poison. His mind is feverish as he crashes through the forest shouting, shooting at everything and nothing at all.

The venom in Willard St. John is substantially less than the amount introduced into Mark Olsen's system. Nevertheless, he was hit near the right kidney, spreading venom through his bloodstream with every willful stride.

His feet tangle on a bed of vines, causing him to slide on a carpet of leaves and pine needles to the bottom of a small knoll. There he lies on his back, laughing at what is left of the moon.

Somewhere in the night, a wolf howls as if in pain. Other wolves soon join it. They begin to bay throughout the entire mountain range, continuing to do so until their temporary madness passes.

As St. John howls back, blood sputters from his lips and runs down his cheek. Although his vision is blurred, he clearly discerns the black-hearted devil himself when Keith's face suddenly appears above.

Keith looks deeply into Willard's crazed eyes, but his own are reflecting a measure of insanity.

He never expected this part of the bad dream. He is awestruck, wondering where and when Willard St. John crept into the picture. What could possibly be his connection to this nightmare?

Willard giggles in some strangely twisted euphoria. Though dying, he manages to threaten, "I'm gonna kill you and your ghost, nigga. But first, you're gonna watch your granddaddy die." He aborts an attempt to raise his heavy weapon. Vertigo rushes the Black man's sweaty face closer and closer to his own. Keith's face retreats over and again as Willard's queasy stomach rolls, threatening to heave. His final, labored words to Keith are filthy beyond imagination.

"Then I'm gonna make you watch me fuck your woman… again."

When the horrified attorney screams, "No!" his voice echoes to mock him. Willard giggles and Keith shoots the last arrow directly into his heart for the foul thing he insinuates. Willard's brain is frozen stiff, and his heart quits just before Keith Williams impales him.

Keith wants to scream as his grievous tears flow. He is confused as to Willard's place in this drama, and torn apart by the thought of such a vile man having defiled the woman he loves. The very thought causes his blood to run cold.

The maliciously distraught mother of the murdered teenager recently said to him, "Let's see how you feel when one of them turns on you and takes your child away. Would you care then…?"

The only thing that traverses this reeling tangle of emotions is the fact that his grandfather may still be alive, if Willard's words are to be trusted. Keith snatches Willard's M-16 and doubles back, making a wide loop in the direction of Totem Rock.

♡♡

When Jeremiah gets up laughing, Jud Martin slams him into the totem pole. The reflexive action of the old man's eyes warns the governor. He follows Jeremiah's gaze to the ground where he sees the second rattler coiling silently for a strike.

The silencer muffles the gunfire when he shoots the reptile as it launches its venomous fangs at one of them. Although dying, it rolls and wriggles to entangle itself with the twine that holds it captive.

Governor Martin thinks it clever of them to have removed the rattle, convinced Jeremiah had a hand in setting those lethal traps because he knew the snake was there. There is little doubt that he actually engineered Mark Olsen's terrible death moments ago.

Martin says, "You think this is funny, boy? Well, we're about to have us some big fun now, motherfucker!" He loosens and re-ties Jeremiah's hands behind his back, around the totem pole.

Jeremiah Williams looks at Jud Martin and chuckles before saying, "Do you hear that, Mr. Martin? Do you hear the deep quiet that surrounds you when you're all alone? Now you have no redneck army to protect you from the total eclipse of your miserable life. Can you see that fading moon up yonder? Seems so close you can just reach out and touch it with your bloody hands. When it casts its final rays of light on you tonight, all of hell shall be your new home, mister." He chuckles, again.

Martin rushes Jeremiah, striking him repeatedly before drawing his knife, which he holds to Jeremiah's crotch!

He says into the bullhorn, "Your grandfather is a dead man if you don't come out where I can see you, Williams. No more games. No more Mr. Nice Guy. Do you hear me, Williams? Do you hear me?"

Jeremiah taunts Martin by saying, "He's probably long gone by now, just like the boogeyman. But you never know. He might just jump out at you from the shadows and go…boo!" He raves when Martin flinches, inflaming the governor's wrath.

"Shut up. Shut the fuck up!"

Mercilessly, Martin rakes the knife upward into Jeremiah's scrotum, slicing through his black jeans to split his testicles and penis in two. Jeremiah lets loose a scream that echoes throughout the land, while Martin holds the bullhorn to his bleeding lips so Keith could hear his amplified anguish.

Jeremiah Williams quakes, bleeding from a ghastly wound. Jud Martin smiles, forcing Jeremiah's head back to look into his eyes to ask, "How does it feel to be a neutered dog? My daddy always used to say that's what we should do to all you lowlife so you can't breed. It hurts don't it, boy? Don't worry, you're never gonna need them ever again."

Martin laughs wildly, but his smile wipes clean away when Jeremiah joins him. The defiant old man says, "Fuck all you bitch-made crackers!" and spits in Governor Martin's face.

Martin wipes the bloody saliva from his face and rips Jeremiah's shirt away. "Laugh at this, dog!" He plunges the knife into Jeremiah's unprotected side!

Martin's eyes are those of a demon as he stares through Jeremiah's eyes to his agonizing core. With no mercy, he slices a deep wound across the old man's abdomen. While Jeremiah Williams gags, Martin watches his intestines fall and dangle to the ground. This time, much to Martin's dissatisfaction, Jeremiah does not scream. His head only slumps forward as he expels his final breath.

Jud Martin drops the blood-drenched knife at his feet. He wipes his hand on Jeremiah's face and grabs his M-16, trotting in the direction Willard St. John had taken.

Jeremiah hears Greycloud's voice over the soft, slow pulsing beat of drums that must be nearby. He hears songbirds as darkness slowly turns to light. He sees grass swaying in a honeysuckle breeze that gently sweeps across the plateau. Now, he hears a small child laughing.

When Greycloud appears at his side in the tree line, they shake hands and embrace one another. Greycloud speaks to Jeremiah in his slow, calming voice. "It must be our destiny to make this final journey in such good company, brother. I heard the thunderous voice of Shashana as he summoned our guide into the afterlife. Now, while we await him, would you like to meet your great-grandson? He says that you are a brave warrior, and he is most anxious to greet you. He only wishes that he might have been there to fight at your side. Come, Geronimo." He takes Jeremiah by the hand and leads him through the river of green into a land that knows no winters.

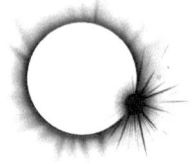

Chapter 32

THE HAND OF GOD

Winkling lips, intense eyes, laid-back ears, lowered head… emerging. The stalking grizzly moves within a yard of the man before bellowing. With neck-twisting aggression, its teeth glisten in the moonlight. It sniffs at the foul air and snarls, rising on its hind legs. The growling animal swipes at the air, but in the face of terror, Jeremiah does not move to protect himself. The dark Indian does not bow to the greater force, which now stands brazenly before him.

The animal returns to all fours for a closer inspection, sniffing and grunting before licking blood from the old man's leaking entrails. Strangely, it begins to prance up and down, as if it wants to be chased. The bear threatens to run, whipping its massive head to-and-fro, up and down with saliva-slinging force. It bellows a growl that quickly trails off.

When Jeremiah refuses to cooperate, it raises its right forepaw and then it sweeps dirt at the man's feet before turning to do the same with both hind paws. It looks over its shoulder, through the cloud of dust, and makes a sound of utter disappointment.

Dingahay sniffs at a broken branch and vacuums the air with his leathery lips curled away from his teeth. He quickly gallops out of sight.

ಐఠ

The doctor and nurse bear witness as Ezra Krantz's terror-consumed eyes fly open. They can almost hear his silent scream as his desperate hands search for purchase.

The white paint of the vaulted ceiling begins to crack and flake. Paint chips begin to fall away, fluttering to the floor and upon the bed, leaving the stained gray boards naked above him. The ceiling begins to cry out as if billions of termites are eating at the wood. When it fractures like aged bone beneath immense pressure, he can see a brilliant light just before purple maggots begin to rain down from the jagged rift.

He sees the gates of hell open up to swallow him! The black stone of the entrance, glows with the crimson hew of the inferno that waits to claim his soul for all eternity.

God is standing on a billowing mist of immaculate white. His face is indiscernible. The atmosphere below is marred with thick black smoke.

God holds the man aloft by one hand, allowing his feeble body to dangle. Sweltering air rushes upward, carrying the stench of burning sulfur and flesh. The hot, rushing wind balloons the gown of the sinner while blowing black soot and ash into his eyes and mouth. The gown suddenly ignites, flaming into nothingness to render him naked before his Almighty God. The whimpering old man pleads, but his cries are mute and essentially meaningless.

His only words to Ezra are, "Judge not, lest ye be judged." With great disgust, God flings him into the inferno to join the wailing masses of the tortured and the damned.

Ezra's silent scream ends in a sputtering stream of phlegm that splatters the oxygen mask. In this world—a world he has striven to change with hatred, bloodshed, and pain—the eyes of Ezra Theodore Krantz go forever dim. His final thought is of God's hands. God's hands are… brown?

The moon is three quarters into its total eclipse. Ezra's soul is cast into the pit where Satan, the great deceiver, greets his foolish child with grim laughter. As he falls, Ezra Theodore Krantz begins to shriek, "Dear God, forgive me. Have mercy!"

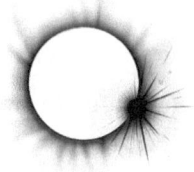

Chapter 33

THE ECLIPSE

With his head hung low and knees bent, he looks like an immortal's sculpture. As Keith Williams kneels at the bloody feet of his grandfather, he weeps with the eyes of the tormented. Seeing Jeremiah in death twice renders him empty inside. This time, it is real. Although the pain of watching what he thought to be Jeremiah's death at the camp had been tremendous, it cannot compare to the aching desolation that consumes Keith after experiencing the hope that his grandfather still lives. That hope is now dashed upon the harsh rocks of reality, for Keith is too late to save him.

He blames himself, placing all that blood upon his hands as if he wielded the weapons of destruction himself. Greycloud suffered greatly, before dark night claimed him. Sabrina Martin was kidnapped, severely beaten, and brutally raped. The child she carries—his child—has been ravaged by the evils of mankind before he or she ever sees a sunrise. His grandfather, who sacrificed much to assure that Keith and his brother had secure futures…gutted like a fish while tied to a totem.

All of these things bombard Keith Williams at once, sending his spirit crashing to the earth. As if these things are not a sufficient curse, the resurrected ghosts of Meridian, Mississippi dance across his heart, mind, and his grief-stricken soul.

Keith Williams feels cursed, beset upon by unending pestilences. Unlike the unflinching faith of Job of the Bible, he is flagging in the end. Suicidal depression looms like fog and smoke in an airless vacuum, and he is dangerously close to the suffocating pit.

Triumphantly, Governor Martin watches Sabrina's lover there upon his knees. The expression on the beaten man's face gives him more pleasure than all the sexual climaxes he has experienced in an entire lifetime. Jud Martin feels a powerful, invincible exaltation that he can only top by an opportunity to stare Keith in the eyes as the last vestige of life drains from his body. This is the moment of which Ezra spoke, standing on the pinnacle of greatness, standing at the precipice of total power.

The God of heaven has chosen him to usher in a new age, alone, and above all others. He has been put to tests that try men's souls, and will now reign victoriously because he is blessed. He envisions himself at the helm of Noah's ark, steadfastly repulsing the thrashing tide. Only, in this twisted vision, the tide surging against Martin's ark is blood red and littered with bodies, which are slamming mercilessly against the hull. Somewhere in the back of his mind, beneath his tingling scalp, Jud Martin feels he is too close to the moon.

As Governor Jud Martin smiles that menacing smile, his eyes twinkle in the final rays of light still escaping the rim of the moon. A look of madness is upon him when he steps from the bushes that concealed his approach and gloating revelry.

Keith hears him, knowing that the man is making no attempt at stealth. It is not the threat of danger that forces Keith Williams out of that emotional stupor. An intense hunger for vengeance injects him with adrenaline, rushing his reeling mind to the surface of self-pity.

Keith moves swiftly, rising and pivoting! He snatches at the trigger of the M-16 taken from Willard St. John! But cursed he is, as if all the denizens of heaven and hell have plotted only to render him a weapon that is empty and mute in his hands.

Wicked laughter roars forth from Martin's lips as the lawyer, pitted against him by God, glares down at the useless weapon. When Keith's eyes seek the sky, he almost curses God, but thinks better of it since it appears he will soon meet his maker. He tosses the useless weapon to the ground in utter disgust at another fatal oversight, for it would seem that crazy old Willard St. John has found a way to kill him after all.

While Martin stands about fifteen-feet away, holding his loaded gun on Keith, they stare into one another's eyes.

"So I'm finally face to face with the illustrious Keith Williams. I owe you, boy. I owe you, big." Martin's smile never graces his eyes.

Keith discerns madness in this man's face, can almost smell it wafting from his sweaty skin. He wonders how anyone would elect this man to run a pay toilet, much less an entire state. A vivid flash of Sabrina's face and her desperate plea streaks across his mind.

"How could you allow your own daughter to be beaten and raped that way? What kind of sick motherfucker are you?" Keith glances down at the knife used to ventilate Jeremiah. "Why, Mr. Martin. Is it all because of me? Because she was with a Black man, you would simply kill us all. She's your own flesh and blood, for Christ's sake!"

Martin sneers. His hands creak like old leather when his grip tightens on the weapon. "I don't intend to justify my actions to a worthless piece of crap like you. She simply has to go!"

Keith detects such great agitation in Martin that he knows the man is too close to the edge for reason. "But why?"

"God has chosen me to lead this nation into a new era. To get rid of you is my test. To be rid of you all—that is my calling. I don't expect you to grasp this, but there's a reason we're created differently. That filthy whore is a blemish upon my good name, and she has to be removed like a speck of dust once and for all."

Risking another question, Keith ventures, "Do you really think you can just kill us all for some so-called, God-given calling? If you would do this for something as filthy as political aspiration, you are insane!"

Looking at what is left of the moon, Martin's laughter returns. He raises his arms and raves, "We have all but taken this nation back from those who'd give our life's blood to utter heathens. We now control enough of both houses of the U.S. Congress to do as we wish. We have tolerated the token Blacks, the gays, and the female sympathizers in the government because it was to our advantage to do so. It has taken decades to put in place, biding our time in complete silence while this great nation went to hell and hooligans. Now, our time has come. Upon my return to Mississippi, I will officially announce my presidential intent and no one will bat an eye because no one will know what lies ahead."

"What?"

Martin's wicked eyes come to rest upon his disadvantaged adversary. "All that you see is mine and more, including such pathetic lives as your own." Without further ceremony, he levels the gun at Keith and shoots him in the right shoulder!

The force of the bullet whips Keith around, sending him crashing to his back in a cloud of dust at Jeremiah's feet. Keith groans in pain, his shoulder is on fire. As the laughing lunatic approaches, Keith rolls over, grabbing a fistful of dirt. He rises to his knees. Through gritting teeth, he asks, "What are you waiting for? Just get it over with!"

Yards away, smoldering embers reignite amongst the ashes.

Martin stands above him to proclaim, "Oh no, mister. You will die slow…just like old Kuunta." He looks at Jeremiah almost lovingly.

Keith throws the sand into Martin's face! He snatches the knife from the ground and drives it with his left hand, which was never as strong or accurate as his right. The knife connects with Martin's upper right thigh, but Keith was aiming for the gut. The steel blade bites into the muscular flesh of Martin's leg and jams into his femur. Keith's hand slides forward on the blade, slitting four of his fingers to the bone.

Martin howls in pain and anger. Ignoring his own agony, Keith throws a punch with his bloody fist, managing to drive Martin backward. However, the governor does not fall. A small window of opportunity blazes before the attorney's eyes. He charges, thinking to close ranks while his opponent is off balance. As he approaches, Martin nails him with a punishing upward stroke of the M-16.

Keith Williams crashes to the ground with a fractured jaw. The motion of the vicious swing causes Martin to stumble backward even further. As he grabs the knife to pull it out, he slips on the edge of the granite slate. The knife comes free and he quickly jams it into the dirt, not wanting to share the same fate as Mark Olsen. Both their pains are quite exquisite, like newborn stars exploding.

Keith tries to clear some of the cobwebs from his mind. He grabs the bullhorn and advances while Jud Martin tries to regain his feet. Martin sees Keith coming and fires! Once again, the attorney is thrown to the ground at his grandfather's feet. Hot lead has left a burning trail through his abdomen.

Behind him, Martin shouts, "You're a dead man. Get up. Get up, you mangy son of a bitch!"

Keith tries to rise, but falls back to the ground when the rope he has taken hold of gives way. He is sickened to realize that it is actually his grandfather's intestines. Now consigned to his fate, he forces himself to his feet to face death like a man, refusing to die on his knees as his father had done many years ago.

From where Martin stands, he can almost hear Keith's heartbeat fading, and this madman is afire. His whispering lips reverberate the words, "Yes, turn around. That's it, turn around."

Martin looks into Keith's fluttering eyes and levels the gun on him. The taste of blood is upon his lips, but to him it is the lawyer's blood. Darkness consumes the world, smothering the air where serenity is forever stained crimson. In this darkness, there is an all-encompassing silence.

As Martin's finger touches the trigger, a sudden growl obliterates the hush!

The moon disappears in total eclipse. When he turns, Jud Martin needs no light to see the nineteen-hundred pound grizzly towering above him. This brown death has huge claws and many sharp teeth in its threat.

Martin raises the gun and fires at pointblank range, but the animal seems undaunted. Dingahay roars at him, urging Martin's wet hair to fly away from his face. Then the angry grizzly slashes the wrist of his left hand. Flesh, tendons, and bone yield readily. Martin's hand goes limp with nothing but spasmodic muscular activity to make it twitch; like that snake, still moving long after it was killed.

The grizzly swipes at Martin again, ripping his left collarbone from his chest! The man screams as soaring agony sweeps through his body on bundles of torn nerves. The bear crashes into him with a gaping mouthful of razor blades. All flesh below Martin's right eye vanishes. He screams a funny scream because the sound of his voice is no longer coming through his lips, but from the side of his mouth.

When Dingahay and Martin hit the water, they shoot toward the edge of the cliff. The bear's claws scrape for footing on the slick surface, backpedaling in the thin slip of a current to no avail. Martin's back snaps when he is driven into the broken totem pole just before he takes wingless flight. He screams all the way to the bottom!

Dingahay manages to turn his bulk around as he continues to slide toward the edge. His hind legs hang in the air for a moment as he hooks his left paw on the base of the totem pole from which Jeremiah hangs crucified. His right paw barely grasps the broken stump. The night sky is quiet and as black as the devil's bowel.

Keith slumps to the ground, powerless, watching the bear hold on with one paw as the other slips and scrapes uselessly on the wet granite surface. He hears the hind claws scraping for grip on the face of the stone precipice. Then in the slowest of motion, Dingahay looks up at Jeremiah, and Keith swears that he sees a measure of sadness in the bone black eyes this beast soon trains on him. The brief moment of silence is broken when the wolves resume their howling at the missing light in the sky.

Then Dingahay looks to the eclipsed moon above, bellowing a final roar that echoes over the entire mountain range and the valleys below. The birds of night take restless flight and every animal stands and twitches nervously before cringing in the shadows where they will vividly dream of that sound.

Dingahay roars once more and releases his hold, plummeting to the valley below. The ground upon which Keith lay, seems to quake upon impact. The standing totem ignites as if some invisible hand has set a match to gasoline. The flames rush skyward.

A sudden gust of wind carries Greycloud's ashes over the cliff's edge as if a vacuum has been released, forcing the atmosphere to flee. Then Shashana, God of the Moon, opens his eye once again unto the worthy.

Keith Williams clutches his bleeding abdomen, reaching for the image of Sabrina Martin, the unblemished image that he wants to take to his grave. He is fading into dark oblivion, awaiting a slow death on the mountain of the moon—a place where some kind of God must have once resided.

Drawn by the burning cabin and the fire further up the mountain, a whirling banshee suddenly comes from the sky to cast a bright light on the wounded lawyer. It is the Medivac chopper from Window Lake. Sabrina has sent them and state authorities in search of him. They have seen the blazing cabin and headed directly for the burst of light where Keith Williams lies unconscious.

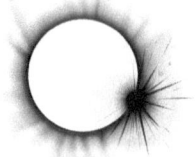

EPILOGUE

Keith Williams, Sabrina Martin, and young Tommy Swinton, are all transported to Yves Baptist Hospital in Great Falls, Montana.

Tommy is eventually fitted with a prosthetic arm. Following an investigation to determine his identity, he's reunited with his grandparents and older sister. His name is actually Thomas Rosenblum, and he is very Jewish.

When Keith awakens in a hospital bed, he thinks the nightmare is finally over. He will have to go home to find his only brother's body on a cold slab.

Within the soothing alchemy of passing time, the lovers of different races heal each in their own way, apart from one another. Only then could they truly heal together. It would be over a year before they make love again because they both have deeply profound wounds to mend.

Afterward, those ragged scars have to be tended almost daily. Somehow, however, their love conquers all. They eventually go on to marry, which produces fraternal twins. They have a boy and girl. A year later, they co-found an organization in Atlanta that deals with the problems of interracial couples and their families in the United States.

Although Keith Williams has never had political aspirations, their compelling story serves as an overwhelming springboard. It inspires perfect strangers to urge—pressure—him to answer the call of the people.

The tragic events that tore gaping holes in the fabrics of their lives brings about such a scandal that new, more intensive investigations are launched into the covert activities of the Ku Klux Klan and all hate groups. The FBI starts at the Governor's Mansion in Mississippi and at the home and offices of Willard St. John in Atlanta. Telephone records will lead them to the home of Ezra T. Krantz, where they discover Willard's shocking copy of a video recording that shows the murder of a gay man, who had left the ranks of the Ku Klux Klan. It also shows the castration of his African American lover.

Mississippi Senator Peter Black's premature announcement of his vice presidential intent to the national press, just days before these events trickle into light, renders him squarely between the investigative crosshairs.

Strangely enough, and to the Ku Klux Klan's disgrace, Willard St. John's video is not the only one of its kind. What is even stranger is where the others will be found. Because the death certificates of unscrupulous characters have been faked throughout history, Ezra T. Krantz's body is exhumed. Thirty-three tapes have been buried with this sainted man, each more hideous than the last.

With new revelations coming as a nearly constant flood, despite best efforts to limit them, there comes a ghost from the past in the aging form of a man both Ezra Theodore Krantz and Abraham Martin shot as he dove into the Mississippi River. Thought dead and washed away by the big river's strong, early spring current of the mid-1930s, a man named Malachi Morgens, who washed up miles away on the opposite shore steps from the shadows of fear to tell the world an amazing and horrifying story of surviving being kidnapped and hunted by the Klan like an animal. With his scarred chest and facial wounds as testament, he gives a true accounting of how the woman he married saved his life and nursed him back to health after being riddled with buckshot. Marisonya Morgens, and the children they raised together, shed tears as Malachi Morgens tells the story of how their family came to be...of how they were never to speak of it for fear of the visitation of death one moonless night. During his shocking expose, which led to an official deposition, Malachi pointed the sword of justice in the direction of public officials and other Klan members he kept in a scrapbook. His eldest daughter, an aspiring author, chronicled the tail of a loving father who had never learned to read or write. Mia recalled the many tears she shed as she sat by the firelight with pencil and paper to record her father's tail. As the years progressed, photographs and newspaper clippings surfaced to provide the faces of those Malachi knew and recognized from the hunt.

Because they are not hampered by starting from the bottom to work their way up, federal agents make disturbing connections during the investigations. Many faces are recognized as important political figures on the earlier tapes to validate Malachi Morgens' deposition. The FBI eventually destroys most of the Klan's organized hierarchy in American government, though quietly done in the name of national security.

Moreover, the sheer breadth of this scandal is kept to minimal public disclosures. It blackens the eyes of all America, threatening to ruin ongoing diplomatic standing across the globe. What the Ku Klux Klan has managed in the great wide-open, shames all Americans to a world full of skeptics. It disgraces a shining beacon where global hatred and mistrust for a system riddled with hypocrisy continues to grow because it has the audacity to claim to be *one nation under God, indivisible, with liberty and justice for all.*

Many members of the Ku Klux Klan will be imprisoned, convicted on charges ranging from murder to conspiracy to undermine the U.S. Government…treason. Most, but not all of them fall under the knife. Those who escaped retribution, go on to continue their *goodly work* behind the scenes.

Sadly, TJ Brown's mother is now locked in a padded room in Georgia's best mental institution. She claims to see a swamp witch in her nightmares. She is terrified of the dark, claiming to hear wicked sounds that resound at a frequency that only she hears. Every dismal day and every sweaty night, locked in her own private corner of hell, she screams, and screams…and she screams.

The witching woman of Thorny Bend advises from the living shadows, "Hatred destroys us all from within, child. Careful what you ask for. Careful what you ask."

THE END

Personal Notation: Because I believe that God Almighty requires that I do my part by attempting to write this world a better place, you must all…D.I.E.

Written by: Kelvin L. Singleton
First drafted in 1995. First published in 2016.
Right on time.

www.ingramcontent.com/pod-product-compliance
Lightning Source LLC
Chambersburg PA
CBHW051516250626
47156CB00001B/109